Readers love Dam

M000286795

Hot Head

A Romantic Times "Favorite Firefighters in romance" on 9/11/2012
A Band of Thebes Best LGBT Book of 2012

"Up front, this is one of the best M/M romances I have read lately … The story is simple but hot as hell … It had that level of romanticism that makes your heart ache good … I strongly recommend this novel to all romance lovers."

—Elisa's Reviews and Ramblings

"Magical and beautiful even when it gets down and dirty. Not only is there hot sex, but it is hot, emotional sex …The one thing this book has that no other does is Mr. Damon Suede and his unique and authentic voice … A raw, emotional, very hot, worth-every-penny read! Awarded the Golden Nib: for books that knock our socks off!"

—Miss Love Loves Books

"This is not your run-of-the-mill gay romance. All of the usual formulas apply: friends-to-lovers, gay-for-you, out-for-you, gay-for-money, all of this with the hottest, most steamy homoerotic sex scenes I've read, and yet… the story is about none of that and so much more than that … If you are ready to be scorched, read it!"

5 Star Romance Read
—Viv Santos, *Queer'd Magazine*

"Grip-you-by-the-gut angst … and Mr. Suede's unique, fascinating voice … Wildly entertaining and fresh … I just could not put this book down."

5 Gold Crowns and a Recommended Read
—Laurel, Readers' Roundtable

"Four out of four stars! HOT! HOT! HOT! Damon Suede has a surefire hit on his hands with *Hot Head*. This book is sexy, fun, hot, interesting and the best book of my summer … Man, I couldn't put it down … Talk about captivating! … I'm not going to tell you anything else except that you gotta buy it and read it!"

—Stephen Jackson, TLAGay.com

Red hot reviews for Damon Suede's

Hot Head

"A powerful, epic, bold romance. Very erotic. Very emotional. The unrequited love is so wrenching [and the] final union is so earned and worthwhile."

—Book Robot Reviews

"*Hot Head* is a book you will want to savour … gritty … raw … delicious … more than a romance … Entertaining, vibrant and original … kept me on the brink and will stay with me for a long time. Highly recommended."

5+ stars Desert Island Keeper

—Reviews by Jessewave

"I really loved this book. It has it all … firemen, passion, humor, and an amazing love story to tie it all together. … I loved the writing style of Damon Suede. This is the first book of his I have read, and I promise it will not be the last. He has a way to do more than just tell a great story, he takes you on a journey you never want to end."

5 Stars

—Guilty Pleasures Book Reviews

"If you are looking for an emotional, unique story filled with hunky firemen, scorching hot sex that will blow your mind and romance that is based in friendship, then grab *Hot Head*. I do recommend you make sure you have eaten dinner, done the dishes or other house chores before starting because once you start this book, and you won't want to put it down."

5 Hearts

—Love Romances and More Reviews

"Talk about steamy hot men and lots of emotion! You've got it and more in *Hot Head*. … If you want a heartwarming story, filled with lots of heat in all sorts of ways, grab a copy…"

—Whipped Cream Reviews

"Damon Suede has written *Hot Head* as a multi-layered novel that weaves multiple stories together. It is beautifully staggered and coiled so that the various tiers mesh and become one well-written narrative."

—BlackRaven's Reviews

BAD IDEA

DAMON SUEDE

Dreamspinner Press

Published by
Dreamspinner Press
5032 Capital Circle SW
Suite 2, PMB# 279
Tallahassee, FL 32305-7886
USA
http://www.dreamspinnerpress.com/

Cover Art
© 2013 Paul Richmond.
http://www.paulrichmondstudio.com
Illustration by Bill Walko
Cover content is for illustrative purposes only and any person depicted on the cover is a model.

ISBN: 978-1-62798-171-2
Digital ISBN: 978-1-62798-172-9

Printed in the United States of America
First Edition
October 2013

To everyone brave enough to let wrong turns
take them the right way.

FOR LELIA

MAY ALL YOUR WORST IDEAS
UNLEASH MIRACLES ON THE WORLD.

DREAM HARD!

1

THE zombies weren't scheduled to attack until three o'clock.

"Trip!" Rina shrieked, but he could only see white lace arms above the mob. Central Park buzzed around him: a couple of news vans idled alongside a huge arch-banner that read "OUTRUN: ORGAN TRAIL. Zombie Runners This Way!" Trip tried to pick a path toward his friend through the costumes and New Year's partiers starting early, but the insanity at the tents made navigation almost impossible.

His armpits slid with sweat. For December 31, the muggy air felt unseasonably warm. Afternoon sun spilled across the concrete, gilding the bare trees. Trip's nose ran and his eyes itched, looking at all that untamed Nature; a few of his allergies were already doing the tango.

Finally, a petite hand grabbed the waist of his sweats and yanked: Jillian.

"C'mon! They're calling people to the starting line." Jillian sported an iridescent pink dress with a ruched pouf skirt that reminded Trip of the prom in Westchester and blowing his lab partner. Jillian had pinned a scalloped rhinestone tiara aggressively atop her black bob. On her pale, pert figure, the getup made her look like Audrey Hepburn on crystal meth.

The OutRun volunteers had set up base camp by the reservoir. An old Armenian man sold bright T-shirts to the crowds that had turned up to watch these jogging idiots gather to flee the undead beneath an upholstered winter sky.

Jillian used her delicate elbows like meat hooks to clear a path through the boisterous, costumed mob to get to the changing tents. A squad of cheerleaders. A Spider-Man. Someone dressed as a slice of pizza. *A compost heap of borrowed imagination.*

"We have a cameraman!" Jillian pushed him through a flap and to the left but then abandoned him and veered right to rummage out of sight on the other side of the tent.

Rina lifted her pearl-studded veil and gave him the wet Brazilian doe eyes. At a stoop sale in Harlem, she'd bought a hoop-skirted horror of a wedding gown with fluttery lace panels that made her olive skin glow and hugged her bombshell figure. Sound logic: who didn't want to watch a busty blushing bride hunted and dismembered by a flesh-eating horde?

She rubbed his back in coaxing circles with her fingerless gloves. "You are my spirit animal, Trip! I swear."

"And I am her spirit litter box." Jillian returned to their corner, dragging a suspiciously heavy tote bag. She looked like a pixie walking a dead mastiff.

He consciously forced a hard sneeze back into his chest.

"We're gonna battle the living dead on video." With Rina, business always came first. She tucked another sprig of baby's breath into her brown tendrilly updo. "I got like two thousand people following my blog to watch."

"And I cannot run with a camera between my tits for three hours. The end." Jillian didn't even wheedle; her former life in musicals had worn her velvet away. "Where's your Unboyfriend? Staplegun."

"Staple*ton*. He's not a—" Trip scowled. "Stop calling him that. Cliff's my friend. And my editor. We're colleagues."

Holy crock of shit, Batman.

Jillian and Rina raised their eyebrows at each other. Caught between them, he almost felt their scorn frying him like a poodle in a microwave.

For four years, Trip had pined pointlessly over Cliff J. Stapleton. No secret. *Just buddies.* Cliff knew Trip was "like that," and Trip hoped Cliff might be "like that" one day. "I didn't drag my ass out here so you could talk shit about my—"

"Unboyfriend?" Rina covered her sarcastic smile with a lacy glove.

"Stop."

"Well, hun, Cliff ain't your boyfriend. Did you spend the night on his couch again?"

For a split second, Trip considered lying. He shrugged and held up his sneakers. "Yeah. We watched *X-Men: First Class* and I crashed."

True in its particulars. Actually, Trip threw a quilt over Cliff and resisted the urge to remove his boxer briefs, which had felt like a major moral victory.

Pathetic.

Rina wedged more baby's breath into her chignon, then varnished with hairspray until the wisps looked crispy. "You spend every fucking weekend with him and draw his comic instead of your own."

"All of the dickiness, none of the dick. Ergo: Unboyfriend." Jillian rummaged in the tote and extracted a pile of folded aqua cotton. "Costume."

"Costume?" Trip's eyes bulged. Maybe he should bail. He unfolded a set of surgical scrubs, size large and stiff with newness. Even worse, Jillian had bought them for her husband, and Ben had about thirty pounds on him, easy. *Great.* "I'm too skinny to wear these. And I'll freeze to death." Total lie: the humid air smeared him with sweat.

"No bitching." Jillian's pretty, angular features turned the demand into a children's game somehow: *Duck duck puke.* She flapped her hands at his clothes. "Strip!"

And then, somehow, he found himself standing in Central Park wearing a pair of striped lavender boxer briefs, clutching his munchables.

At least he'd worn underwear.

Trip glared at them. The good mood from waking up on Cliff's couch had evaporated, and he felt like a credulous tool. He stuffed his legs into the stiff unwashed scrub bottoms. Now he wanted to be gone.

Except Jillian and Rina had trained and planned for the zombie run for three months. They'd blogged and twatted all their preparations to the website fans. Then last Saturday, Jillian's husband cracked a crown at a bat mitzvah.

Exit coordinated cameraman. Enter spastic gay friend.

Please don't let me rupture something.

Trip sniffled. "So... the humans all run and fake zombies chase us? Or is it like an obstacle course where they pop out?"

"Both." Rina crouched in her huge gown and stapled the scrub-legs shorter so he could kill himself more easily. "Ghetto hem."

He shrugged into the chest harness.

"You don't have to wear the surgical mask if you don't want."

"I do want."

"Don't you dare!" Jillian smacked his shoulder and snatched the cotton mask away. Of his two closest friends, she worried the most about his personal life. "There's, like, a zillion hot fellas in the park." She hooked an arm through his. "A fucking tsunami of geek beef. You can't wear a bag over your face."

Funny thing: they wanted him to have a boyfriend way more than he did. Hell, they watched more gay porn than he did. As the gay friend in these situations, he always ended up in the corner holding someone's purse.

"Fine. No mask." *Fuck this.*

"Tons of comic buffs out here, too, y'know. Killer PR for you." Rina finished stapling and stood, then wiped leaf mold off her hands onto her bodice, blinding white against her coffee-and-cream cleavage. "Who knows what you'll catch?"

"Malaria." He scratched his arms.

Jillian piped up, "A real boyfriend."

Trip examined the tent flap. He couldn't walk out, but maybe he could miss the starting line. "I don't want a real boyfriend."

"Which is why you have a fake one." Jillian bent and snapped the digital camera in front of his sternum. "'Cause jerking off over your straight boss and waiting for him to green-light your comic is so fulfilling."

"Cliff is my editor, not my boss." Trip scowled at the top of her head. "We collaborate." He sniffed hard. By the end of the day, the pollen and mold would probably kill him. "Ugh. Nature." *I can't cope.* Would the girls forgive him if he just left?

Rina wrapped a belt with Velcro flags around his waist. *Ka-klamp, klamp.*

He peered down at the camera strapped to his chest like an electric barnacle. "Take the camera. Bladder break. I need a waz."

"Pain to reattach. Just turn it off."

Damn. Maybe he could "get separated" during the run and ditch.

Jillian jabbed at the camera till it bleeped and tapped her watch mock-sternly. "Tickety-tock, biological clock."

Rina nodded, all business. "You got fifteen, and then we gotta get down to the start. New York One is shooting live."

He stepped into the mosh pit outside the tent and struggled upstream through the crowd. His throat burned. He should've taken a nuclear antihistamine before setting foot in the park.

At the porta-pissers, the lines stood fifteen deep. He imagined a sprint through the crisp air with a gallon of coffee sloshing around in him.

Fuck it.

Trip veered toward a wide clump of forsythia. A ruptured bladder trumps a public indecency ticket any day. He prayed the muggers had slept in.

"Should be in bed." Trip grumbled. He couldn't flee with their only camera. He'd double back and shuck the camera before the gun went off.

He fished his dick over the waistband of his scrubs and did his thing against a scraggly oak that probably wished it had sprouted a hundred miles north. He muffled his sneeze. A twig snap reminded him his privacy was imaginary, even if he was hidden under the crest of bare branches.

He would fake an asthma attack. *That's it.* He'd go back, have trouble breathing, hand over the camera, and meet them at the finish line.

The underbrush rustled. *Hmmm.* For all he knew, it was pigeons humping or a rat taking a stroll. Maybe another hyperallergic wuss trying to escape.

He tucked his tool away and managed a casual glance over his shoulder.

The bubble of silence seemed exaggerated. He heard the milling crowd and the faraway rumble of Central Park West. But where he stood, the cotton-ball quiet raised the hairs on the back of his neck. Was someone watching him?

Jesus Christ, he'd end up mugged with no ID and borrowed hospital scrubs in broad daylight during a publicity stunt for his bestest fruit flies.

Thhwwwwwip.

Something ripped the seat of his pants. Trip spun to see a mangled, grayish hand holding one of his flags in its dead fingers. A beefy zombie knelt in front of him, grinning like a demented jack-o'-lantern.

Oh yeah. The run.

"Has it started?" Trip shook his head, confused.

The zombie looked gigantic down there, shoulders like a prizefighter. He shook the flag and winked. He must have taken a shortcut, seen Trip, and crept in to attack. Graveyard humor. *Har de har.*

Gray and olive shaded the undead face dramatically, really subtle even this close. One jagged foam latex cut stretched across his skull and up into his hairline. Bright hazel eyes. A square-square chin. *Jinkies.* His thick hands appeared tattered and gnawed open, but his meaty forearms glimmered a smooth silvery green that showed off the striations of muscle.

I'm cruising a corpse. Again a sneeze tried to squirm out of Trip and he choked it back.

Trip held up his hands in surrender, and the ghoul rose to his feet. Five ten and thickset under the tattered sport coat... like the Incredible Hulk in shades of grave. He had calico-colored hair, a springy dark-blond that probably went brindle in summer.

The hot zombie fanned his gory fingers. His eyes were set just a little too far apart and slightly slanted under the arched brows, which made his smile look like a rakish invitation.

The long forsythia stems screened the rest of the runners, hiding the two of them in their little bubble under the oak in the cold, bright air: fake doctor and fake zombie, ready to hit the Organ Trail.

Mr. Monster scuffed closer and offered him the flag. A reminder to be vigilant during the run? His filthy split shirt exposed a rugged torso and some unbelievably realistic ribs with guts glistening behind.

"Amazing." Without thinking, Trip reached out and touched the painted wounds. "So beautiful." He traced the *trompe l'oeil* heart with his fingers. The zombie flinched. Ticklish, apparently.

"Oh!" Trip yanked his hand back and shook it as if he'd scorched his skin.

"Thanks. Sorry." Deep hoarse twang. *Saw-ry.* The zombie grimaced. His nipples had risen hard and small under the paint.

Trip had almost forgotten he was touching a person. "I—that was rude. Airbrush?"

The zombie smiled then and wagged his head. "We're not supposed to speak. But I'm bad at rules."

Was he flirting? Trip squinted in confusion and struggled not to sneeze all over the most attractive man he'd spoken to in a year. Trip prayed his itchy eyes hadn't gone bloodshot just yet. "Not airbrush? Are you sure?"

"No, it is. I painted it. I was just… I saw you sneak off."

Trip twisted back toward the tents where Jillian and Rina counted on him to return. He felt like he'd forgotten his lines. *What was the plan again?*

"Shortcut to the holding area." The zombie jerked his dimpled chin toward the white tents but didn't leave. That raspy drawl made every word sound like mischief.

"My name's Silas." He offered his hand.

"Hey." Trip shook it, afraid to look up until he did. *If I'm bailing, I need to do it now.* He tried and failed to stop ogling the brawn under the wounds. "Texture's beautiful. Even this close, I can't tell it's fake."

A big proud smile, teeth blinding white against the painted skin, made the undead face eerily handsome under the latex. "I'm part of the makeup crew today, but one of the star creepers didn't show up."

"I'm here by accident too." Trip thanked all the gods Jillian's husband was beefier than him; the scrubs were roomy enough that no embarrassing bulges would advertise his interest. He was supposed to escape, wasn't he?

Silas leaned in as if confessing a terrible secret. "The zombie actors tend to be pretty flaky." A drowsy blink followed, and the deep dimple of his grin punctuated his scrutiny of Trip's body.

Without warning, Trip's breath caught and his eyes widened, widened, as a massive sneeze battled its way out of him.

Silas widened his eyes, too, and seemed confused, as if he expected Trip to burst into song or vomit.

"*Agh-ka-chooo!*" At the last minute, Trip twisted away. "Ugh."

"Bless *you!*" Silas whistled. "Wow."

"Sorry. Allergies." Trip wiped his nose with a tissue from his breast pocket and ignored the heat of his blush and his sinuses. "I should get back to my friends." *Why did I say that?* "I'm filming for their site."

Silas's painted face shone with questions. "You make movies!"

"No. Oh no." Trip wanted to stay here talking all day, costume or no costume.

"I do gore on a cop show out at Silvercup. In Queens?" A phone buzzed somewhere, and Silas wrinkled his nose.

That got a smile out of Trip. Once a fanboy, always a fanboy. "Monster gore?"

"TV thing. Gunshot wounds and scars mostly." He mock-snored and stuck out his very pink tongue.

Trip dried his palms on the scrubs. Heaven knows what the hell kind of pollen he'd aspirated out here. He didn't know how to offer his number or ask for one. *That dimple.* Where was he going again?

"Well, sir, I'll be your zombie this afternoon." A chuckle. "I look forward to hunting you down and eating your brain later."

Trip laughed finally. *Hot, talented, and funny.* "Trip. I'm Trip."

"Figures." That dimple took no prisoners. "I bet plenty of people fall for you."

Full-frontal deep-fried zombie attack. That was on purpose.

Their eyes met.

"Not really." First response Trip thought of that didn't sound like a slutty come-on. His brain had short-circuited.

An air-raid siren cranked into a protracted wail. At first he thought he was imagining it until Silas sighed and grinned. *Oh. Yeah. The OutRun.*

Silas regarded Trip's flag in his hand, then reattached it to the strap on Trip's waist, his knuckles firm against the hipbone. He smelled like vanilla and magic markers.

Trip stood frozen under the big digits, really boned now and curious what came next.

A breath. Another breath as they stood a little closer than necessary.

"C'mon. Anybody who had a pulse...." Silas swallowed, as if he was about to confess something and then thought better of it. "I mean, I'm not *really* a zombie...."

"Well, I'm not really brainy, so that's okay." He shook his foggy head.

The dimple made another appearance in the undead cheek, and again Trip had the weird sensation of double vision, the ghoulish veil over the healthy male. Silas licked his lips and opened them to say something, maybe something wonderful.

Suddenly, running through Nature wearing a camera barnacle sounded like the perfect plan.

The forsythia branches shook and rustled. A small sandy-haired woman poked in to hiss, "Si-*las.*" She saw Trip and nearly recoiled. "Oh! Oh jeez, doc. You scared me!"

Silas started and stepped away, guilt written all over him. He scowled at the intruder.

"Kurt's asking for you." She dissected Trip with her eyes, whittling him down to a sickly nub. "Quit humping the civilians."

Who's Kurt? Boyfriend, probably.

Trip turned away. He probably looked like liverwurst. With his luck he had poison ivy on his eyelids. Rina and Jillian were counting on him, and obviously Silas hadn't offered a number.

Trip opened his mouth to make an innocent excuse or to say something brilliant and irresistible to Silas, but instead held up both hands with his fingers spread— *Nothing up my sleeves*—and stepped away, right back into the tangled hedge behind him.

The slight woman closed her lips in a knowing smirk as if she'd discovered a dildo in a dishwasher.

Great.

"This is—" Silas turned to him.

"I gotta—" Trip unsmiled and spun to plow right into the forsythia, ignoring the bare branches that whipped his swollen face.

Air horns and applause revved up about fifty feet away.

He backtracked to the tents in a daze and found Rina wringing her hands, her veil thrown back. "We thought you...." Jillian's tiara sparkled at him.

Shell-shocked, he shrugged. Central Park loomed around them.

Up ahead, three white news vans with mounted satellite dishes had parked diagonally across the sidewalk where camera crews paced and prepped. The winter-bundled crowd jostled and elbowed at a police barrier erected around the risers and the podium.

Trip checked his watch. Five minutes past eight. Silas could be anywhere by now. No number, no last name. Unfair somehow. He sighed hard. "We should get to the starting line."

Jillian jogged his elbow. "You feel okay?"

How did he feel? He didn't want to tell them about Silas but didn't want to miss his chance, either. Trip studied the scrubby plants lining the path. He snorted. "I feel insane." But anticipation simmered under his anxiety. He thought of a million things he should have said. He swabbed the smile off his face.

Rina hugged him, smooshing him against her bosom. She smelled like cucumber perfume. "Sorry, *papa*. We shouldn't say that stuff about Cliff."

Jillian lifted a wicked eyebrow and adjusted her tiara. "Yeah-we-should, but not now." She tilted her head, and they walked between the ropes herding the army of runners into a holding tent clouded by fake fog that had a fruity chemical tang. Volunteers confirmed their numbers and flags. Finally another siren split the air and the tent flaps opened. Trip heard guttural moans and hisses as he stepped into the murk.

For three hours, they ran for their lives.

In the end, Jillian and Rina reached the finish line in *spite* of Trip. He almost got his friends "killed" several times when he slowed down to eyeball hunky zombies while the girls harangued him to keep up, but Silas never grabbed him. At the end, Trip had a single flag left and no idea how to find his zombie.

Idiot.

Twenty yards away, they got their invites to the OutRun bash that night, a fundraiser and thank-you to the survivors, courtesy of Unbored Games. Like he needed more humiliating disappointments to crown his year.

Stiff with dried mud and fake blood in his baggy, borrowed scrub suit, Trip snuck away in search of the makeup tents to leave the generic "Big Dog Comics" business card he took to conventions. *Nope.* Zombies milled and joked around him. Silas hadn't returned. Trip scribbled his name and cell number on the back and left it with a frazzled volunteer. Maybe Silas would remember. At least now he'd know how to find Trip.

Rina and Jillian were eager to get rolling by the time he returned. The battered trio caught a cab, and Trip stared at the trees as they pulled into traffic. "I don't know about this party thing." He gestured at the muddy scrubs and sore legs. He looked like hell in a nightie and felt pretty certain he stank even more.

"We ran the race, now we got free booze," Rina crowed, flush with victory. Her veil was a tattered wreck and bloody handprints decorated the skirt of her gown. Her baby's breath updo was starting to look a little *oh-no-she-didn't*, mainly because she was planning to make an "I survived" splash at the party.

"What was with you today? I thought we were goners." Jillian eyed him skeptically from under her crooked tiara. "Maybe jogging should be your New Year's resolution."

He stared out the window at the Lincoln Center as it rolled past and wondered where Silas had ended up. *Away.* "I hate resolutions. I never keep them and they never change anything."

"Yeah: no resolution is still a resolution," Jillian teased. "Maybe your resolution is to stagnate in a swamp of loneliness, despair, and anxiety."

"Fuck you, Jilly-bean." But he smiled back. She was right. No one could tread water in a river. "So what is my resolution?"

"Makeover!" Rina offered as she applied glossy eggplant lipstick.

"No. Not a makeover. The last time you did a makeover on me it took two months for my eyebrows to return to normal."

Jillian fluffed the skirt of her beslimed prom dress and rested her delicate hands on her lap like a little lady. "Therapy."

"Fuck off, Miss Stone." Trip sniffled and laughed. He read the invite again: "Trip Spector + 1" written in ballpoint. Silas *had* been working and maybe he expected Trip to celebrate like a normal person.

West End Avenue seemed oddly quiet for New Year's Eve. The cab swung east on Thirty-Third, well below the tourists mobbing the ball drop.

How bad could the party be? He swayed into Jilly as they hit Columbus Circle. "Okay. Gotham Hall. One drink." Trip hugged his chest under the scrubs. After all, Silas might be there, right?

"Fucking up!" Jillian gasped and slapped his arm sharp enough to sting. "You have to do one awful thing a day." She narrowed her eyes and pointed a slender finger at him. "Some batshit idea."

Rina dug in her big scary purse and extracted some kind of data cable. "Mmmh. I like that. Misbehaving. Rogues and randiness." She could turn anything into a bodice ripper.

Trip thought of Silas under the makeup, his sly hazel eyes and his Bruce Wayne chin. "Well...." He peered at the girls before he took the plunge. "I sorta met someone. I think."

Rina's dark eyes went wide. "No sir!"

Somehow, confessing to them made finding Silas more possible. "A zombie. Well, he did the makeup, but today he's a zombie."

Jillian squealed. "Mr. Right of the Living Dead! Did you get his number?"

"What? No." Trip goggled and chewed his lip. "He may not even be interested."

"Then we'll get his number and ask him. I say we go zombie hunting for New Year's." Jillian nodded slowly, as if she were Mother Superior of a convent for closeted gay singles. *The hiiiiills are alive....*

Rina removed the chest camera from its harness and plugged it into her iPad. "I wanna check the footage."

"I need a Kleenex." Trip wiped his nose. Silas must have hidden, for them to miss each other, but he'd probably go to the party. Trip had a chance. He felt a sweet twinge at the thought. *Ready or not.* "C'mon. I'm not gonna stalk some stranger. He was just a nice guy."

Jillian stroked an imaginary beard on her sharp chin. "He's one of the official monsters. He's gonna unwind. New Year's kiss, my friend." Her tone brooked no argument.

"Superheroes stalk people all the time." Rina looked at Jillian with meaningful intensity.

"They rescue. Different deal." Trip wiped his damp hands on his bloody scrubs. He didn't need a napkin because his entire body *was* a napkin. "Hell, I only know that his name is Silas. He might be a total dick."

"So? Everything you want cannot fit in one person or one job or one drawing. Yeah?" Rina fiddled with her iPad. "All these good-idea, backpedally, unrocked boats have kept you single in a cubicle drawing caped dildos and watching Netflix for the past four years." She had stopped teasing. "Perfection sucks. It's a trap, *papa*." She dropped her sequined veil back over her face.

Jillian swapped her running shoes for matching pink kitten heels. "This party's gonna be like a robotic sushi bar and he's the maki roll. We find a comfy bar, and you can grab him as he swings past."

The cab slammed on its brakes and they lurched forward. Their driver cursed at three drunk kids staggering against the light.

"Oh my God." Rina straightened with her mouth agape. "We taped him. The zombie!"

"Silas?" Trip peered down at the little evil nodule.

She stifled a giggle. "Jillian didn't turn it off."

His face heated quickly. "Wait a sec. You spied on me peeing!" He gawped at them, vulnerable in the thin scrubs. "Ugh."

"By accident." Jillian scoffed. "And it won't show your baloney. Though it does have audio." She peered at the iPad. "What's that big red thing?"

"His heart." Held up an annoyed hand. "Eww. Not like that. Latex. His chest was in front of—" Trip blew air out of his nostrils. "You're both horrible. I hate you."

"No…. You love us!" Rina high-fived Jillian. "We can track him down. Your… Silas."

Trip blinked. *Could they? Should they?* Silas had no idea who he was and vice versa. He might be better off as a sweet anecdote. Trip ditto.

The cab glided to a stop, and Jillian swiped a card to pay for it before she climbed carefully onto the sidewalk and offered Rina a steady hand. Blinding magenta spotlights lit up the side of Gotham Hall, and a giddy crowd had gathered to watch the red carpet.

He began to sweat in earnest, willing his feet to step out of the taxi. He rummaged for his inhaler and huffed a puff.

Rina hauled herself out onto the concrete curb and studied the velvet-roped lines of paparazzi. A couple flashes turned their way. Trip emerged last, his creased invite and the crumbled grocery bag with his clothes in his clammy hands. More flashes. *Just get inside.*

"Tits?" Rina adjusted the bodice of her dress and shifted for confirmation. She favored him with a happy, anxious blink of mascara. He clicked his tongue in the affirmative and gave the okay sign. "Let's go get 'em." She plowed into the lights.

Jillian hung back a moment. "We just don't want you to be lonesome on New Year's Eve."

"I'm not lonesome."

Lie. He thought it, and from the doubt in her eyes, she knew it. She wouldn't look away, so he couldn't either. Why couldn't Silas have attacked him during the run?

What would he say if he did find his zombie? *No clue.*

Trip hated dating for exactly this reason: the idea of everyone coping till they simply gave up. No way could he or Silas live up to any expectations they had about each other. *Only strangers can be perfect.*

Up ahead, Rina tipped her head in confusion and then beckoned to them. She fidgeted in her grisly bridal finery, but excited too. *What are we waiting for?*

"He's in there." Jillian fanned her pale face with the invitation, but she didn't turn. "Might be worth a shot."

Trip shrugged. "Maybe." Hell, for all he knew Silas might appear any minute with a date on his brawny arm. If so, Trip wanted to be long gone.

Jillian picked up Rina's backpack and cradled it like a cat. "It's only a party, booger." She eyeballed the costumes drifting along the velvet rope and the searchlights. "You could even wear a mask, go in a different disguise. We'll be with you."

Trip shivered in the chilly air for the first time that day. He shook his head. "I can't, Jilly."

Rina abandoned the bank of cameras and flounced back to them, frowning. "You're bailing?" She harrumphed and reclaimed her backpack.

"You swear to call him?" Jillian crossed her heart. "Or I'll go full psycho stalker and track him down."

He hugged her. "Maybe."

"There's video. We're stud hunters, y'know," Rina chided and raised her veil to kiss his cheek.

"Gross." Trip smiled, sadly, while he literally ran away from the possibility. "You're both evil and must be stopped. I hate you." He laughed and wiped his eyes.

No argument from Rina. Obviously she knew a lost cause when she saw one. She tossed a breezy farewell over her shoulder like salt. "G'night, Romeo." And with that, she picked up her foofy white skirt and marched off down the aisle for the cameras.

Trip dredged his raglan shirt out of the grocery bag and tugged it over the grubby scrubs. He coughed. "I'd rather fuck this up alone."

"Listen." Jillian crossed her arms a moment. The cameras flashed behind her, and her rhinestones threw fake fire back at him. "If this Silas could be something, if you're attracted and he's smart and interested and willing to take you on, meet you in the middle, then you need to make room for him in your life. Don't expect a hundred percent; if he's even *half* a hero, you need to be willing to adapt." She glanced at Rina up ahead and then back.

"Well, shit." Trip swallowed as she stepped closer to hug him good-bye. Her muddy prom dress rustled between them on the cold curb. "No pressure."

"No." She nodded, dead serious. "Pressure."

2

FOR New Year's Eve, Gotham Hall looked as Batman-tastic as the name suggested.

Silas wished he felt more like the Dark Knight and less like the Thing, but with no other shot at finding Trip, he'd kick himself if he didn't at least try. He'd spent three hours in Central Park trying to spot Trip in all the runners, but no dice.

Wrapped in neoclassical columns, the former bank loomed over the triangle of Broadway, Sixth Avenue, and Thirty-Sixth Street. For Kurt's party, the granite façade glowed a deep magenta visible from twenty blocks away, even without the searchlights on the red carpet and the sixty-foot vertical OUTRUN: ORGAN TRAIL banner over the entrance. Subtle, Kurt was not.

Silas arrived elevenish. Time had gotten away from him as he tried to find the energy and a jacket that fit him properly. Outside the brass doors, the sidewalk throbbed underfoot. A scatter of paparazzi and a few curious tourists stood across the street and stole snaps as the line of limos upchucked masked partygoers.

He'd forgotten to wear a mask. *Fuck it.* Silas wanted to get found.

He flashed his unopened invitation to a human refrigerator in a cheap suit who waved him into the lobby toward the pounding music and babble of a thousand people dancing on the grave of the old year.

Projections of the Unbored Games logo skated over the grooving crowd in the center of the rotunda to echoing dubstep. Five forty-foot banners advertising past OutRuns hung from the gilded ceiling at regular intervals around the room's perimeter. At the base of each poster, Kurt had installed a raised platform about eight feet square, roped off for VIPs. On the far side of the room on a mezzanine, Silas saw Kurt's stylish profile against a wide gory banner for *Chopping Mall 4*.

Unbored built cool video games. OutRun gave cool fund-raisers.

Silas checked his watch. 10:51. He might manage to reach Kurt by eleven thirty if his luck held… later if he managed to bump into Trip trapped somewhere. Most of the guests had worn masks, which complicated matters.

He veered left and began the agonizing, sweaty process of plowing in even rows through the crowd, ping-ponging back and forth between the curved teller walls from the days when this joint had been a bank.

This party is a dog, and I am a flea comb.

At one of the bars, Silas found Tiffany under three framed posters for the Miss game trilogy that had gotten so much feminist ink: *Miss Taken, Miss Demeanor, Miss Fortune.* Silas complimented her spangly beaded dress with a thumbs-up and a dishy nod. She'd piled her sandy hair on her head in a saucy tangle and wore dollar-sign contacts.

"Oh God. Silas!" She gasped with frog-eyed guilt and covered her mouth. "I had a number. That guy came by this afternoon. Later, with a number for you."

"What number?" Silas's insides surged with anticipation. *That simple?*

She grimaced and confessed, "Dark buzz cut. Cute. Whaddayacallem? Scrubs! Came by the tent during strike and left a card."

He smiled wide. "Trip? Was his name Trip?" Maybe he could blow this gig and just call.

"Maybe. I dunno. That's the thing." Tiffany pouted. "I couldn't find it when I got home. I lost it in my supplies."

Disappointment and irritation whipped through him, though he kept his voice steady. "Oh."

"He came by at the end. You were hanging with the Unbored VIPs. And the park service rushed us. I'm so sorry."

Bummer. He didn't yell at her. Not her fault. He should have gotten the number himself.

"It was so nuts after the run. The card had a dog on it, maybe. Or a wolf? No, I think it was a big… dog."

Dog? Trip did something with dogs? Didn't fit. He spoke like a painter and his fingers were ink-stained, but he'd worn a twelve hundred dollar watch. Silas ran through their brief conversation, but already the edges had gone fuzzy. He remembered being horny and rattle-brained and not much else. Trip's grin had knocked him sideways.

Tiffany half smiled and bit her lip. "He acted like you knew him, so I figured he was a friend."

"Sorta." Silas counted to five and pretended to smile. "No big."

Even though he knew better, he wanted to strangle her. He wanted to drag her home right now and pull her kit apart till they found Trip's digits. Instead he hugged her, lied that he'd see her later, and continued his search of Gotham Hall's rotunda with a mounting sense of desperation. *Crappy New Year!*

Silas's phone buzzed: a confirmation text from the hip-hop producer saying he'd scheduled the girl group for the second. Two days from now: alien bikinis. Good, he needed that paycheck. If only he could find his blood-spattered doctor boy.

Silas promised himself not to discuss Trip at all tonight.

"Goolsby! Silas Goolsby...." That was Barney, a stocky actor in his late thirties. He stood outside the bathroom like a tow-headed bouncer in a Dutch music video, all watery eyes and chapped lips. "I thought that was you." He played one of the recurring pimps on *Undercover Lovers*.

Barney only dated men extremely short-term, as in ten minutes max, mostly in public bathroom stalls while his faux-girlfriend claimed his jacket at the coat check.

God save me from closet cases.

"Barn." Silas waved noncommittally. "I gotta find Kurt before his ball drops." He pretended not to hear the reply and went back to searching for the scrub suit.

Almost an hour later, Silas had needle-in-a-haystacked his way through every square foot of the inlaid marble floor and navigated his way to Kurt's little riser sitting about nine feet off the floor. Good thing. The stuffy air had started to make him feel trapped. The mezzanine would, at least, give him a place to breathe, and the velvet ropes would protect him from the press of flesh.

Kurt Bogusz sat enthroned like a pinstriped Caligula, exhausted and defiant. Since it was New Year's Eve, he had worn a vintage one-button Dior tux, gray silk with a stripe, over today's OutRun T-shirt. Salt and pepper hair, chopped into expensive bedhead, with a trim beard to match. Even to Silas, Kurt claimed to be twenty-nine, but knowing the stories, he'd probably crept up on thirty-three. For gay Manhattan, anything past thirty was the Twilight Zone, and Kurt had no intention of going gently. They'd known each other since NYU, before Kurt had dropped out to start a video game company.

He founded OutRun about three years ago and it had quickly quadrupled in size. He had a lot of celebrity chums and a talent for whipping bullshit into meringue. The charity focused on getting press for "LGBT Issues That Refuse to Die": HIV, domestic violence, suicide prevention, elder care. For each run, he hired Silas to design a themed monster for the poster and the run itself: a gay-basher zombie, a hepatitis zombie, a teen runaway zombie... and then dressed a hundred young actors up as the problem so it got plenty of mass-media coverage and moolah—the whole point, after all, of spending six figures on a big tacky hootenanny.

Up on Kurt's mezzanine, a chiseled waiter in an extra-small "OutRun: Organ Trail" T-shirt stood with a tray. He'd torn his sleeves off to flaunt the glossy roll of his shoulders, and the cotton stretched so tightly across his torso it had ridden up to expose his sweet swirl of a navel and extra-large basket.

Silas paused at the bottom of the stairs. He fired a finger-gun at a kinky lawyer couple he'd tussled with one weekend in the Pines. *Great.* Then he climbed up a single tread to scan the party. Trip's dark shorn head was nowhere in sight.

Kurt's flirting flatlined with the waiter. Maybe the guy was straight. Maybe he wasn't interested. Maybe he didn't know Kurt was their host. *Impossible.* Not with him holding court up here in a tux that cost more than a used pickup.

"—because I make too much scratch to live in anybody's closet." Kurt's bluish eyes browsed the waiter's bod like he was a salad bar.

Silas climbed the last few steps to rescue the poor kid.

"Goolsby, you came!" Kurt jumped up to squeeze Silas hard and pat his back. "And you wore a jacket!"

"Diet Coke." Silas looked the waiter straight in the eye, trying to apologize telepathically for Kurt's sleaziness.

The athletic waiter bobbed his head and trotted down the stairs.

"That *ass.*" Kurt cocked his head at the golden ceiling as if balancing a mental checkbook. "I'm gonna say: high school wrestler. Two 'roid cycles, but he's weaning himself. Trying to be a fitness model."

"Stop it."

"Bitter jizz 'cause he smokes." Kurt bit his tongue with his gleaming caps and smiled. "Whimpers and pops when you go really deep."

Silas turned to his friend in irritation. "Kurt, not everyone's a whore." He scanned the dance floor and bars for Trip again. Nothing.

"Everyone but you." Kurt raised a shoulder. "Whatever. 'Cause you're a helpless slut at the mercy of your dangly unmentionables."

Silas kept his yap shut. Sure, he had a couple exes here. And he'd seen a couple tricks on his way to Kurt's VIP mezzanine. More than a couple. This is why Silas avoided bars and A-gay fund-raisers now. *Every ocean becomes a puddle.* If you stayed underwater long enough, you eventually swam into monsters you'd rather forget.

Kurt fingered Silas's lapels and clucked. "Sharp threads."

"I'm making an effort."

Silas had unearthed an old Hugo Boss blazer that hung right on his broad shoulders. The invite said "black tie/masquerade," i.e. Kurt being a pretentious asshole. Still, if Silas did manage to track Trip down, he at least wanted to pretend he had a steady paycheck.

"I been watching you cruise the room." Kurt sized up his blazer again. "Who's the lucky twinky-dink?" He leered.

"Who? No one." Silas frowned back. "I did not have sex in the park dressed as a zombie."

"Sh'yeah. 'Cause you're such an angel, Goolsby."

One thing had preserved their friendship: Kurt didn't date anyone, because he only paid for sex. He rented his men and discarded them when they got boring. More times than Silas could count, he got stuck doing the boyfriend shit for Kurt, like picking up the birthday tab and fending off trolls. They fucked other people but took care of each other.

Kurt's pocket buzzed, and he fished out his phone. Hot light stained Kurt's grayish hair magenta for a moment. "Don't worry. I ordered Italian for us. With a side of Greek."

"Dinner?"

"Dates. Duh." Escorts, he meant; a literal catalog was probably involved. "And there's plenty on the hoof besides…." Kurt leaned forward, holding the edge of his seat with his manicured fingers. "If he doesn't show, there are, like, a thousand people here. Gotta be at least five or six you haven't taken for a test drive."

"Fuck off. This guy was cool. Something else." Frown. "Trip."

"He *seemed* cool, you mean. As in: you projected imaginary coolness onto this Drip because of his bone structure and bod and the way it coincided with your porn collection." Kurt surveyed the crowd, jewel-toned under the swirling Lekos.

"I don't have a porn collection." *True.* Silas got laid plenty.

"Wait: he's hot." Kurt pointed down and to the right, Silas didn't bother to check. "Oh wait, I think you 'dated' him too. Jim? Jay? Never mind."

Silas sat down on a vinyl Barcelona chair. He'd started to sweat under his blazer, and he felt dumb for coming and wasting the past hour combing through the throng for a stranger.

Mentally Silas swapped the scrubs for something formal, obviously. He designed an imaginary Trip who might be searching for him this second. He could see the etched planes of Trip's face perfectly: big haunted eyes, pale pink skin, the aggressive chin, the black hair buzzed down close to the scalp. His knobby wrists and the expressive fingers.

Where are you?

"Score!" Kurt pushed away from the railing and took the chair beside him. "Timberlake's name was on the invite, so we got a thousand groupies outside ripe for the rumping." He nodded knowingly and pumping his arm. "Achievement unlocked."

Silas stared at the other mezzanine platforms that ringed the rotunda. Most of the roped-off platforms were empty. On one, shirtless men crouched, blowing lines. Across the way, a stick-thin girl with massive implants texted furiously.

He consoled himself with the number Tiffany had lost. If Trip had left his info, then he might come here on his own mission.

Except… he hadn't seen Trip on the way in. He hadn't seen Trip while crossing the dance floor. Even standing at the rail with a view of the entire three thousand square feet of rented party space, he hadn't seen Trip anywhere.

Smiling privately, Silas peered through the walls, trying to remember the planes of the boyish face, lean build, the close-cropped dark hair, the soft sparkle of—

Holy fuck!

At that exact moment, he realized what Trip would expect to find: ratty suit, exposed organs, gray skin, ruptured face.

"Oh shit!" Silas lifted a hand to his face. "I was a zombie."

"Yeah, zombie *run*?" Kurt looked over dubiously. "Verily, the dead have arisen." He signaled to someone over Silas's shoulder.

"Even if he wanted to find me, he couldn't." Silas kept his voice steady. His sense of humor on the subject was zilch.

"Your turbo-twink is probably blowing one of my bankers in the john." Kurt plucked something off his sleeve. "Maybe he's a hustler." That wasn't an insult. Kurt loved hustlers in general and was frank about their no-nonsense appeal.

"No." Silas sniffed. "He's just a nice guy."

"Hustlers are just guys. Some are nice, even."

Silas forced a distracted smile, mainly because nonreaction drove Kurt batshit and that was the best way to keep him from further sharpening his tongue on Trip.

Kurt squinted at him, then perused the dance floor. "He'll call." He stirred his glass with his finger and sucked it clean. "When they like you, they call."

A thirty-foot projection of a clock shone cobalt on the white wall, brighter even than the strobing lights. The big hand pointed at twelve and the little hand snuggled a little closer. Only a few minutes more and the year could get on with being new.

If he got lucky, Trip might be his midnight kiss. *Fat chance.* Silas pushed himself to his feet and drifted to the edge.

Down below, the music was *wumpa-thumping* the crowd into a sweaty frenzy under the enormous Unbored Games banners. The oldsters had split, and tipsy grinding had caught fire in several parts of the room.

No way was Trip a whore, no matter what Kurt said. Trip had dug him. He had come by with his number. Tiffany had lost it, but at least he'd followed through. They'd both made an effort, and no one in Manhattan wasted energy unless they had a real good reason.

"Hey, Goolsby. Remind me, again...." Kurt squeezed his leg and thumped it. The teal light chased over his gray-flecked hair, making him look like a Lost Boy waiting too long for Captain Hook. "Why aren't we a couple?"

Silas walked partway down the treads. "Because I'm too fat."

"You're not fat."

"Then I'm too polite and you're too selfish."

"Oh. Right." Kurt laughed and flattened his smile into a sideways parentheses. "Tricks and dicks. Good point." He shook his head.

Silas skimmed the crowd again as ugly hope flopped and withered inside him. What did it matter? Kurt was right. Trip was probably another twink out to get what he could.

The gigantic clock winked even closer to twelve, its big eye watching the corporate *fun-fun-fun*. Tray held high on bulging triceps, Kurt's studly waiter had paused to talk to a ponytailed guy on crutches. That one wore a tux too. The waiter twisted, and then the ponytail man turned a noble, solemn face their way and pointed a crutch at Kurt.

Unsmiling, Kurt inclined his head in reply; he'd stopped talking at least, though his mouth worked like a couple words wanted out as he stared at the disabled stranger. He shook his ashen face and smiled, then—*click*—inhaled as if to say something funny to Silas.

Before that could happen, Silas swatted him and waved his arm at the crowd below. "I'm gonna do another lap in your lackeys."

"Hey." Kurt blinked again at the man on crutches before he wheeled to watch the crowd parting for the hunky waiter's trek to the bar. "What about your drink? Your date—"

"You have mine. Have both." Silas hugged his friend good-bye and clumped down the stairs into the jolly coked-out mob. The music got quieter and the DJ grunted something indistinct into the mike. On the wall, a second hand blinked into existence and swept the face of the colossal clock that loomed over them, staining everyone blue.

No Trip.

Silas closed his eyes for a moment so he could stand in the bright, cold park again, hopeful and happy. He opened them with regret.

"Ten!" The crowd squealed and bobbed.

"Nine!" A thousand maniacs underwater bellowed the countdown over the relentless thrum of remixed Scissor Sisters.

Silas strode toward the doors that opened onto Broadway. He thrust his hands into his pockets, kept his face aimed at the floor so none of his exes and tricks—his dates and mistakes—would catch his eye and keep him trapped here in the glittering tar pit.

"Eiiiight!" A middle-aged woman in a plastic top hat waved her arms and screamed blissfully at the gold-tiled honeycomb ceiling. Against the wall, two guys making out; he'd dated both, screwed both, dumped both.

"*Se*ven! Six!" High fives.

Silas passed the bar where Kurt's sad, hunky waiter stared blankly up at the clock along with all the other underwater faces. Trip would never know his number had been lost, not tossed. *Life, baby.*

"Five!" Flash bulbs. Group hugs. The celebration felt like mockery. "Four!"

The room jumped up and down as Silas picked up speed. He pulled the tattered OutRun invite out of his pocket and tossed it at the trashcan. He hated mementos. Coming tonight had been a waste. He had a shoot to prep, sculpts to do. *Fake blood, fake pain.*

He wanted to be gone. He wanted to be home. He wanted this past year over and the world on the other side of a door he could lock. He wanted a real kiss at midnight from a future who didn't feel like his past. *Fucking fool.*

"Three!"

He pushed outside into the crisp air, nodded curtly at the oversized bouncers in baggy off-the-rack suits as he slipped through a gap in the velvet ropes. He secretly prayed the big door would swing shut behind him before he had to hear it. He stepped out into the street and raised his arm for a cab. Even in his jacket, he was freezing. The searchlights pointed straight into the sky, illuminating nothing.

"Two!"

Trip would fade into a memory, another missed opportunity that led nowhere. Anyways, what did some stranger matter?

Then far away, the muffled roar pounded through the bronze doors and the concrete walls while Silas shivered in an empty street and spoke the word with everyone else in the city. They shouted; he whispered:

"*One.*"

3

SOMETIMES an artistic career felt like climbing a glass mountain wearing nothing but bacon fat.

Trip had waited for Cliff's decision on his new comic pitch for three months. After four-plus years of *Hero High*, he'd worked up a whole "College" concept that built on the company's brand with grittier topics and grown-up issues. Nothing explicit, because Big Dog had to stay family-friendly, but *Campus Champions* would at least let him get the characters beyond second base with impunity... and save his sanity besides.

The "Super Graduation Day!" tweet from his editor had forced him into the office. Cliff had finally decided, and Trip was eager to get to work. He could hand off the Mighty Mites to one of the foreign pencillers, like Dee or Francú, and go work up a whole new cast of capes. The past year and a half had almost broken his spirit, but his patience had paid off. Trip also had an ulterior motive for schlepping uptown on January 10 in the freezing cold. He'd finally figured out what he wanted to say to Silas and worked up the nerve to do it—if he could track him down.

After Trip ditched the Gotham bash, he'd done his web digging in just under twenty minutes. Silvercup kept its general schedule posted online. Only one cop show shot in Queens: *Undercover Lovers*. And the producer had offices in Tribeca, which meant some intern doing television triage in a cubicle below Canal Street had Silas on speed dial. *Easy-squeezy.*

Trip's best shot at getting a real response from a TV crew was to make it sound like money was involved. Comic books commanded a special reverence from media suits, so his idiotic plan was to have the Big Dog receptionist place a call on his behalf, claim it involved makeup work related to *Hero High*, and leave his number. The ball would land on Silas, who would either call or blow him off. Even if it was a stupid waste of time, no one could say Trip hadn't taken a shot.

As long as I take the shot.

He'd try, it would fail, and life could go on as previously scheduled. Maybe he'd have a new comic to draw and Cliff would be so dazzled that he'd finally take the hint and ask Trip out.

Trip popped a Benadryl and took the C train uptown to Big Dog's cramped midtown offices on West Forty-Seventh Street, just off Ninth Avenue. They had three rooms that faced the back of a dingy pre-war apartment building in Hell's Kitchen filled with computer repair services, electronic wholesalers, and passport expediters. The mildew in this place would fuck up the Toxic Avenger. To prepare himself, Trip took another pill on the stoop and fought the urge to scratch his arms raw inside the chilly foyer.

The elevator literally squeaked as it huffed and puffed its way to the fifth floor. The tiny hallway T-boned toward a children's talent agency only open on random afternoons or back in the direction of Big Dog's bright red door.

Trip pressed the bell and got buzzed in pronto.

Kimmie, the latest Big Dog receptionist/intern, was on the phone, so he waved hello and sat in one of the battered office chairs. She smiled as she held up one elaborately manicured finger to indicate she'd wrap up the call.

Trip didn't see Cliff, but his door at the back was shut, so maybe he had a meeting. Trip picked up the latest candy-colored issue of *Hero High* from the coffee table. This one had sold several thousand copies, up from the fall definitely, but the series kept sucking. A perfect moment to move on.

"He is in a mood today." She craned her head to check Cliff's closed, silent door. Her hair was a loose manga mane exactly the color of mulberry sauce. "Diamond called to give him hell about some interview he owes them, and then they started talking numbers...." She thrust her chin at her monitor. "Didja have a meeting scheduled?"

"I can wait." Trip's mouth went dry instantly. *Where does spit go?* Sitting felt ridiculous with the carbonated anticipation fizzing in his veins, so he stood again. "I need a favor."

Kimmie closed her drawer and spun to face him.

"Listen, this isn't work-related at all. So you can say no." Trip crossed his arms.

Her instant conspiratorial smile made him feel sleazier than he did already. "No problem, Mr. Spector."

"Trip. It's just a phone call. I need to get hold of somebody and I don't—"

"Gotcha." Kimmie picked up a pen. "We got 'em on file?"

Begging her to stalk a total stranger left him feeling like a total scumbag. "I'm trying to reach somebody who works on *Undercover Lovers*. That is, he'd be in *their* file."

"I love that show." She sounded sincere. Maybe she was.

"Yeah. Uh... they have a makeup artist named Silas." He dropped his eyes. "I figured if you called from Big Dog and left my name and cell number...." He fell silent.

"Silas at Silvercup? Surname?"

"Dunno." His abject humiliation was now complete. He muffle-sneezed behind his hand and glanced down the hall, wondering if he could just ambush Cliff.

A tiny smile bent the edge of her lip. She looked right into his eyes and whispered, "No sweat, Trip. I'm in the intern mafia." She winked. "I got this."

"Thanks, Kimmie," he muttered, and she nodded, still smiling faintly. "Don't say anything to…."

Shit. She knew the deal. Everyone who worked at Big Dog knew the deal with him and Cliff. So they got great art at a shit rate, and Trip compared every guy he dated to someone he'd never even kissed.

"Triple-threat! 'S'up, my man?" Cliff stood in his open door, wavy brown hair and a slash of perfect teeth with all kinds of charming in between. His wide shoulders and tan forearms bulged with muscle. He had a loose-limbed college athlete's physique, more Silver Surfer than Batman.

Trip hated himself for being turned on, but a sliver of doubt stayed lodged. Maybe Cliff really questioned his orientation. Maybe Cliff liked him enough to cross over to the dark side. Maybe Cliff's nerves and confusion tied him into dumb homoerotic pretzels. Maybe working on this new book together would give Cliff a chance to face the connection between them. Hell, if Trip's life was a rom-com, all these innuendos and misunderstandings would end in a big dance-off and a gay wedding in Fag Harbor.

Cliff spoke with what Trip called his closing-the-deal voice, the plummy tenor of a cabinet salesman. "Come on back, bro. I'm just giving Diamond what for."

Well… maybe Trip would start on *Campus Champions* and Cliff would come to his homo senses. Drinking in his fratboy grin, Trip almost told Kimmie to forget the call, but before he could, Cliff was in motion.

Trip patted Kimmie's desk and walked back past the light boards and filing cabinets in the middle office toward the editor and CEO of Big Dog, his boss, no matter what he told the girls. The only window faced a brick wall.

Cliff pulled him into a firm embrace, hand pressed firmly at his lower back. He smelled damp and a little bitter, like a locker room after a circle jerk. Before he let go, he pulled his head back to read Trip's face from six inches away. "You look guilty as hell. Ya cheating on me already?" He stepped back and pressed a hand to his heart.

"I gotta take commissions, man." Trip let himself linger near Cliff. Totally unhealthy, but tell that to his gonads. "Just to keep my brain working. Give me something to sink my teeth into and I'll bite."

"Someone's cranky."

Cliff invaded his space. The gym-damp arm and sturdy length of his thigh rattled Trip's saddle. Cliff's loose workout clothes hung easily on the kind of blocky hairless sinew that spawned boy bands and gave Trip goose bumps. Cliff sat on the edge of his desk, his cock and balls wadded front and center under ripstop nylon. No underwear.

Does that feel good? Nobody has to know. We both need it.

None of the other proposals submitted could have come close to *Campus Champions*: full character workups, a script and a twelve-issue treatment, cameos for the Mighty Mites. "Why aren't you locked in your garret finishing the pages for Issue 51?"

"I…" *wanted to stalk Silas.* Perving over Cliff at the same time made him feel queasy and schizophrenic. "…had an appointment with my allergist." Trip dropped his gaze to the parti-colored comic in his lap. He still got a charge out of seeing his name there, even though he hated the perky blandness welded over his pencils and inks.

Hero High was pretty much a C-string title that had seen a surge since Cliff had taken it over and gotten it into Walmart and other big-box retailers. The whole series stayed squeaky clean: no sex appeal, no blood. The chipper, ethnically diverse adolescents solved problems like superacne and peer pressure in unthrilling compromise-a-thons, like demented anti-comics. Their average reader was a homeschooled ten-year-old whose parents watched professional wrestling without irony or lube.

In Cliff's mind, the Mighty Mites and *Hero High* occupied an alternate lobotomized universe where teenagers chained in the dungeons of puberty picked nice manners over hormonal insanity. Trip rolled his eyes and cashed the checks, secretly certain *Swamp Thing* and *Deadpool* were somehow more real.

Could one imaginary world be more imaginary than another? *How do you measure reality?*

Trip skimmed the pages of his comic and pretended to see the back-patting dreck he'd drawn. He wished he could leave before his boss confused him even more. He wondered if Kimmie had reached Silvercup or Silas.

Trip sighed. "So…. Graduation Day?"

"And how!" Cliff's hand was hooked in his waistband so that his fingertips brushed the head of his cock through the nylon. A lifetime of looking like a winner and getting what he wanted had corroded his modesty. He didn't even realize.

Originally, Trip's infatuation had brought him to Big Dog a couple of times a week to hover nearby. *Pathetic.* He'd draw for hours in the workroom and chat with Cliff every moment he could. For a month and a half he'd convinced himself Cliff just needed to work up the nerve. For six weeks, he'd jerked off in the bathroom and had elaborate kinky dreams about how he'd plunder Cliff and teach him how to want a man.

Cliff never bit.

Oh… he flirted and he preened. He praised Trip's work and treated him like a movie star when they went to conventions and signings. They shared hotel rooms and bar tabs. He learned Trip's private jokes and knew his history. He craved Trip's adoration and the chance to scheme with a willing cohort.

Trip ignored the pumped triceps and the hard flank under Cliff's gym pants and leaned forward for approval. "You liked it. My proposal."

"Y'nuts! This college thing hooks a whole new market." Perched on the desk, Cliff cracked his neck like a deodorant commercial jock. "It's fucking genius, what you put together."

Cliff's grunt reminded Trip to turn another page: kooky cafeteria squabbles, a sidekick in a trashcan, a cheerleader with sauce in her hair.

"Wait'll you see those pinks," Cliff crowed like a proud papa.

Trip thumbed to the first splash page. Pink, it definitely was: an alien ship about as menacing as a throat lozenge landing on the baseball diamond of Hero High.

For whatever reason, Cliff Stapleton wasn't built for human contact. He loved to flirt and work a crowd, but he couldn't focus on anyone long enough to relate to them. By default, Trip had become Cliff's best friend. And all that terrible attraction got funneled into Cliff's pet comic: the Mighty Mites of *Hero High*.

Everything began and ended with his work at Big Dog. Since Cliff had hired Trip four years ago, Cliff had never had a relationship: a boyfriend or a girlfriend. No romance at all. The fantasy lingered, but Trip had grown pragmatic about his chances. He went on a date or two. He whacked off a whole bunch. Every once in a while, Cliff actually seemed to want him for more than adoring approval and standout pages.

Maybe he didn't want Trip Spector. Or maybe he didn't want a man. Or maybe he didn't want anybody. Who knew for sure?

Trip glanced down the hall toward Kimmie as she hopefully made the call to Silvercup. Maybe Silas would swoop in and save him.

Cliff didn't need to know about Silas. *Eesh.* Trip would never admit it out loud, but for a few minutes in the park on New Year's, Silas radiated the same addictive charm that left Trip boneless and weightless in the Big Dog offices. *Empty calories.*

"So?" Cliff gripped the desk and flexed his oversized forearms as he leaned forward.

"Really sharp." Trip rubbed his face in frustration. Still, he'd ostensibly come by for the comic. "The, uh, pinks are bonkers. Beautiful. Did Dolores color this?"

"She costs a couple cents more, but she just did some trading cards for Marvel. Can't hurt us in the big leagues." Cliff wanted to sell up as soon as he could swing it. If DC or Marvel bought Big Dog, he'd end up with some real power in the industry.

Trip nodded. Was it safe to change the subject? Cliff'd had the proposal for months.

"These South Americans keep making the Mighty Mites too old. These kids aren't horny. They're nice." Cliff leafed through pictures: a happy scatter of nubile teenagers in crayon-bright spandex. "I wish they'd stop sexing it up."

"Well, dude...." Trip laid the sarcasm on with a knife. "Teenagers get horny, I hear."

"You know what I mean. When you draw them, they're nice. I mean, they're sexy, but they don't read like prosti-tots."

"Sharp modeling, though." Trip flipped more pages. "And no way could I pencil that fast." He gripped the chair arms and took the plunge. "So what about *Campus*?"

"Sold!" Cliff chewed on a hangnail. A pleat appeared between his brows. "Six months."

Trip stood, revved with anticipation. "Six months what?"

"We'll announce in six months." He held up a hand before any excitement could froth over. "Bad news, bro: Dee's gonna draw it."

"What?" Trip's brain skidded to a halt. "Cliff, that's my pitch!"

"And it's awesome. We pay you for the concept, but she's a better fit."

"I'm not a good fit for the genius pitch you just bought... from *me*!" A cold fist gathered Trip's guts into a sailor's coil.

"Your guys have gotten a little too sexy. Your ladies are a little too... I dunno." Cliff ambled around the stool, leaned directly against Trip's right side, and looped an elbow over his neck as if they were best buds in seventh grade, as if all guys hung on each other like marmosets, as if he didn't know Trip was a big fagoo who pulled his putz more often than he ate solid food. "You're just a little too... alternative for something like this."

"What the fuck does 'alternative' mean?" Trip's hands shook. He squirmed free, even though it felt good to be maneuvered into that kind of humid proximity. "Because I'm a cocksucker. Are you fucking her?"

"That's not what I said." Cliff stroked the bristly air between them. "C'mon... I don't care about all those labels."

Trapped in Hero High. Trip's insides went shaky and loose. Any second, he might just shit his lungs onto the floor. His nose tickled, but he was too furious to sneeze. He stared at the office, at the brick wall visible through the frosted window. *Stop thinking with your dick.* He couldn't afford to lose this job. Cliff paid him a fortune to draw crap.

"By the end of the summer, I'm gonna sell Big Dog's titles and set us up somewhere we can do the kinda shit we want." Cliff leered.

Trip's phone jangled; he glanced at the screen but didn't recognize the number.

"Go ahead and take it." Cliff circled the desk and sat down.

What if it was Silas? Trip shook his head. "Nah. I'm gonna split." He should go out with his hot zombie and forget anything he'd ever thought about this schmuck. *Fuck Cliff and fuck Hero High.*

Cliff looked at him strangely, so he waved and went before he gave anything away. Trip's poker face sucked. And maybe, too, he didn't want Cliff to have any more leverage... if such a thing were possible.

Trip turned his back on Cliff's dim-witted curiosity and started down the hall. He nodded thanks to Kimmie but kept walking, past the posters and out to the elevator. In the last second before the phone flipped to voice mail, he pressed the green Accept icon on the screen. "Hello?"

And then Silas's hoarse voice was in his ear, exactly the way he remembered it. "Well, hell yeah."

"Uhh." Trip wanted to swallow but his mouth had gone dry. *Shit.* Again, he didn't know what to say. All his banter evaporated. *No script.* He should have practiced some before he answered. *Hurray for hormones.* Mindless lechery to the rescue.

"Trip? You there?"

"Yes. Ugh. Yeah. Sorry. Signal sucks in this building. This is short notice, but would you wanna, maybe...." *Fuck? Make out? Help me hide a dead editor?*

Silas chuckled. "I sure would." Only the sure sounded like *shore* and the torn-silk raspiness of his drawl melted Trip's insides.

Trip chuckled too. "Jeez. Gimme a chance. I haven't made you an offer yet." He stepped out of the pokey elevator and walked toward the sunlight outside. "What are you doing later?"

Silas rumbled. "Mmm. Something special, I bet."

Fuck Big Dog. Fuck the Unboyfriend. Fuck his phobias and mine.

"Sorry. I was so psyched to track you down, I forgot to make a plan." Trip sighed. "You got any good ideas?"

Silas laughed, low and lusty. "One or two."

SILAS almost screened the call he'd stopped hoping for.

This particular Thursday morning had started off normal. He'd booked another three weeks on *Undercover Lovers*, so he'd taken the E train out to Silvercup to assist the beauty crew, mostly second-unit bullshit. The midseason episode was titled "Sex Bomb." Based on the female extras on the call sheet (twelve) and the location in the script ("Int. Strip Joint—Night"), the showrunners had dialed up the tits and gore for Showtime.

All his setups today had been pretty tame: scorching, a couple of black eyes, and the elaborate tattoo 'n' trackmarks workup on the show's new bad boy. Make some scratch, and then the weekend beckoned like cheap jewelry.

Starting tomorrow, the cast was gonna shoot the insane bomb scene that had gotten Silas the job in the first place. He'd sculpted for a month, and he had over seventy-five latex and silicone appliances prepped: burns, lacerations, even some grisly bits and blobs for the scenic artists. Friday to Monday he'd be in his glory:

collecting overtime for night shoots, showing off for the Showtime brass with his own FX designs.

A week after the zombie run, he hadn't exactly forgotten about Trip, but he'd shelved the possibility. Since he had no way of contacting him beyond posting a blind item in the personals, Silas gave up. And then... when he was covered wrist to elbow in alginate, his taped-together phone rang on the workroom table. He wiped his hands and picked it up. The screen read BIG DOG COM.

The "Dog" should've reminded him, but it didn't. He knew comics, so he assumed they wanted him for a fabrication gig for a comic convention. "Yello?" He held the phone with his cheek and scrubbed his forearms with a grubby towel.

"Kimmie calling from Big Dog Comics; your production office gave me this number." A lady's voice, crisp as pine shavings. "I'm trying to reach a Silas Goolsby."

"You found'm. I am a Goolsby named Silas." He could sure use the money from a con, and some publishers paid—

"For Trip Spector. Trip—"

Plonk. Silas sat down on his work stool. In truth, his ass sat down for him and air whooshed out of his lungs like someone had socked him in the gut.

"—asked that I call and leave his contact info."

Laughter churned out of him for a few seconds before he got hold of it. "You gotta be shitting me."

"Uh. No. He just asked that I call and leave you his number and e-mail and all. He said you—"

"That's perfect, darlin'. Let me grab a pen." No pen in sight, he grabbed a fabric marker and wrote the details right on his forearm. "You said Spector? Trip Spector."

Ten minutes later, he and Trip had a date. And now, two hours later, Silas stood on East Twelfth Street in his peacoat hoping this guy could live up to the anticipation.

Silas loved the East Village. The brownstoned streets and scraggly trees felt homier; the bars and bistros never really stopped bubbling. Right now, when the NYU students had come back after Christmas, the streets bustled with funky youngsters.

S'MAC looked jammed with mac-n-cheese addicts eager to escape January. Its yellow and orange plastic furniture hollered cheery and nonthreatening. As he crossed Twelfth, the line for a table spilled out into the bitter cold. Inside, the air shimmered with butterfat.

He'd wanted to make a reservation, but in this place you turned up early and waited. As soon as a two-top opened, he swung into action so they'd have a little spot to themselves: a high table with swiveling barstools. He draped his coat over one and sat in the other. *Come into my parlor....*

"Silas?"

He spun, and Trip stood there, nervous and gorgeous as before. "Perfect timing."

Trip stared for a few seconds, his pale arms held out as if he was trying to balance in the doorway. Taller than Silas remembered, maybe six feet or six one and that long neck like a ballet prince.

"Oh...." Trip still hadn't come closer. The glass door swung shut behind him with a January gust that blew him forward.

Silas held out a hand to shake. "Everything okay?"

"Nothing. I mean, yeah." Methodically, Trip scrutinized his hair, mouth, eyes, ears, nose, torso. "Wow." He gulped. "You're really handsome." The line between his eyebrows vanished. "Is that okay to say?"

"Buddy, you will hear no complaints from me."

"You don't look as dead. As you did."

"Right. Of course. You never seen the real me, have you?" Silas shifted nervously and spread his arms for inspection. "Still interested?"

Trip nodded and examined the floor with a stricken expression. His hands shook.

Silas stepped closer. "Hey... hey."

"I got some rotten news today." Trip closed his eyes and rubbed them. "Horrible. Sorry. My editor."

"You shoulda said something." Silas wished he'd chosen someplace less public. Stupid move. After all, what did they know about each other?

"I wasn't sure you'd show." Trip checked his titanium watch, showing fragile wrists and elegant fingers that talked for him.

"Uhh. I called *you*, goofball." Silas gave him the full grin-wattage and tamped down his confusion.

"Right." Trip responded with a tentative smile. "Yeah. I know. But people forget things sometimes."

"No chance." Silas bumped against him. "Tiffany lost the card. I 'bout died when she told me. So I can't believe you tracked me down. I been trying to find you since the park."

"Me too." Trip grimaced and his wet glance veered off Silas like a slap. "That sounds retarded. Obviously, because I called you, so you know that. I mean, I had someone call you. I mean...." He shut his mouth and gave a little strained exhale. "Agh."

"Take a breath. I ain't gonna bite." Silas took a step closer and steered Trip unsubtly toward the table he'd claimed, pulling a tall stool out for him to sit. That felt better. What the hell had happened to the geeky charmer he'd met in the park?

Trip looked around at the emphatic orange and yellow interior, the plastic chairs, and the exposed kitchen. "What is this place?"

"S'MAC. All they do is macaroni and cheese... but imagine a Baskin-Robbins of mac and cheese: prosciutto and curry and figs and pretty much anything you would ever want. I'm a Southern boy... religious about this place. Can I get you a drink? Beer, juice, soda?"

"Water is fine."

Silas walked to the counter to ask for a bottled water and a Heineken. He couldn't find his footing at all. *Take your time.* He returned with the bottles.

"I needed something to look forward to, after this morning." Trip opened his water. "I mean, he has no fucking shame."

With a tickle of alarm, Silas held up his hands. "You lost me again."

"Going to the office, I mean. Big Dog. I've kinda been wandering around trying to get my head on straight." Trip opened his mouth wide, and a laughing sound stalled there. "I'm a mess."

Understatement. Trip looked like he was fixing to rattle apart like an old tractor.

"I'm not really this crazy most of the time."

"Don't sweat it." Silas put his hand on the table between them, as if to steady the entire room around them. "Wasn't sure I'd ever see you again. I went to the after-party on New Year's. Hunting you down."

"Yeah?"

"To find you at Gotham Hall. Seemed important somehow."

"I flaked out at the last second." Trip shrugged. "I'm not big on crowds."

Silas crossed his arms to make his pecs bulge. "I felt like there was a conversation we hadn't had. Y'know?"

"That was my New Year's resolution. Risks."

Silas sat and offered him a napkin from the basket. "I'm big on 'em."

Trip relaxed a little. "At first I felt like a stalker. This is okay?"

"And how." Silas relaxed a bit too. *Better.* For the first time tonight, he felt some of the strange chemistry that flowed between them a couple of weeks ago. "I'm so hungry I could eat the asshole out of a bobcat."

Trip acted shocked and then burst out laughing. "You what?"

"Sorry." He flushed. "Figure of speech."

"Some figure." Trip grinned and his shoulders settled.

Silas knocked their bottles together. "Our first real date."

Trip set his hands on the table. "So this *is* a date?"

"Well, I'm not interviewing for a job." Silas winked and prayed he wasn't coming on too hard. He raked a hand through his mussed hair and tried to imagine what he looked like to Trip, with his scarred fingers and his burly thighs under the corduroy.

Trip took a shallow breath before speaking. "I have a confession: I have a couple allergies. Nothing crazy, but I gotta be careful."

"I ordered the sampler: eight flavors. You can sample a bunch, and then you'll know what to order when we come back." Silas winced at his own presumption.

Neither of them acknowledged *that* little faux pas... so they both must have noticed it.

"Pretty crowded. That's a good sign." Trip blinked. "I smell butter."

"This is the temple of butter." Silas tipped his pelvis forward. "Bless me, butter, for I have sinned."

Trip pinked and laughed. "I kinda live on junk food."

"And I bet you don't even work out. No justice!" Silas groaned and slid a fork his way. "Confession: I googled you. You're a pretty big deal."

"Nah." A grateful smile slipped across Trip's face. "I just draw and script. Total crap but Big Dog pays out the wazoo."

Silas covered a twinge of envy. "I bet you deserve it."

Trip shrugged. "Most of my friends don't get it. The art thing."

"Likewise. Everybody I ever dated thinks I just sit around playing Xbox and blowing Viggo Mortensen while they sit in a cubicle." Silas let the full force of his smile slam into Trip, wielding it like a big, happy club.

Trip snorted and covered his mouth. "Don't you?"

Smile for smile, they gazed at each other. Nothing was going according to plan, but maybe that was okay.

A paunchy man set a skillet between them, divided into eight pie slices of mac and cheese, sizzling ivory and orange. "Hot." He slapped a little flavor map down.

"Thanks."

Trip eyed it dubiously. "Only thing I can't eat on this is figs. Which is...?"

"That one. Fig and Gruyere." Silas tapped the wedge in question with his fork. "Twist my arm." He scooped a big mouthful to give Trip permission to do the same.

"I've got all kinds of stupid allergies: cats, pollen, mold, feathers, berries, grass." Trip pulled an inhaler out of his pocket. "Pretty much anything alive."

"Not everything, though." Silas waved a fork at him.

"It just seems so junior high. And asthma? All I need is headgear and acne for the trifecta."

"Hey. Hey. It's okay." A sleepy tenderness softened the words.

Trip's cheeks pinked, and he devoured the mac and cheese like a starved greyhound. "I needed to eat, I think." He flushed a deeper rose. "I'm being a pig."

At least that spark still sizzled between them. "Not at all. I love that you have an appetite. You're so lean." He waggled his eyebrows.

"I forget to eat."

"I wish!" Silas coughed. "I was huge growing up." He patted his belly.

"You're big now. In a good way! I've always been a stick insect."

"No." Silas tried to keep the frown down. "I mean, I was *porky*. Like fat-camp fat. Didn't get into shape till I was in college."

"Bullshit."

"My dad was the same before he died. Heart attack. Butter and beer." Why had he shared that?

"Sorry." Trip dropped his soft gaze. "I'm sorry."

"Naw. He died right."

Trip's wary brown eyes melted a little.

Silas rubbed his stomach self-consciously. "But I gotta work to keep it off. Even now I couldn't have a six pack if I drew it with a sharpie. And I say that as someone who has drawn abs on people. Mainly I got a rep for really good wounds."

Trip snorted. "Nice."

"That sounded creepy. I was a sculptor. Or I thought I was gonna be. Anatomy came easy, I guess. Comes easy to me." He flexed his hands and spread his fingers. "That sounded even creepier."

Trip's gaze drifted over them, as if the hands were Silas's portfolio and four years of FX were visible in the lines and calluses. "Right. Zombies. I knew that." Trip scowled at his lap. "Sorry. I bet you've had some crazy adventures."

A flurry of movement outside caught Trip's attention. For a moment, Silas saw nothing but a freckled hand waving.

"Silas?" The plaintive word came from outside, hushed by the sheet glass between.

Oh please no.

Silas swiveled toward the frosty street and discovered one of his exes: a freckled face, auburn hair—*Jesus Christ*—Paddy Wilton stood outside on the sidewalk waving at him through the front window and shouting. A lanky Tom Sawyer with pierced ears and a tattooed collar. *Not now.* A couple of other patrons turned to ogle the boyish face.

Trip twisted. "A friend?"

"A loony-toon model with a pill problem." Aka five ridiculous weeks of sex and overdoses. *Walk away. Walk away!* Silas kept the bland smile nailed over his nerves and waved back with warning in his eyes.

Crestfallen in his puffy jacket, Paddy looked between them and offered something between a smile and a prayer.

Trip turned back with a strange expression. "Should you say hi?"

"This is plenty." With a frown, Silas waved and tilted his head toward Trip, his eyes wide. *Date.*

Paddy moved to open the door, and Silas pinned him with a cold glower. *Don't you fucking dare.* Paddy shook his head and gave a gloved salute before he left.

Awkward silence.

Silas broke it. "Long story. We went out for about ten seconds."

Trip scraped stubbornly at the iron skillet with his fork. "I shoulda figured you did movies, looking like you do. You ever act?"

"Nope. Cosmetics and prosthetics." Silas glanced at the sidewalk. *No Paddy.* He sat back and licked his teeth. "Bad guys are what I'm best at, by far. I mean, that's what I love: creature modeling. Hitchcock said, 'The greater the evil, the greater the film.'"

"What?" Trip glanced up with a sudden, dazzling smile. His dark eyes flashed like a nocturnal animal's. "That's— Wow."

"I didn't say it. Hitchcock did. I *wish* I had." Silas demurred with his hands. "But the darkness in a story. The pain. That's where you squeeze for the juice. 'S'my favorite thing. Magneto. Lex Luthor. Green Goblin. Villains."

"Wait a sec...." Trip leaned forward as if a lamp had flicked on inside him. "You read comics?"

"Hell, yeah." Silas rubbed his hard tummy in mock satisfaction. "Talk nerdy to me."

Trip gaped. "Bull. Shit."

"Yeah, buddy. I'm a comic dork from way back." Silas rocked in his chair a little.

"What d'ya collect?"

"Mostly vintage these days. Silver Age are my favorite: goofy bad guys. Dumb puns. Antiauthority and snarky as hell."

"Marvel or DC?" Trip seemed to be testing him.

Silas sucked a buttery fingertip, getting into the geek groove. "Marvel mostly. *Spider-Man. X-Men.* Well, Nightcrawler really. The first time I jerked off, it was to a *Nightcrawler* poster."

Trip did laugh then, right out loud. The soft sound bounced off the brick wall and made Silas laugh too. "He's so creepy." Trip's eyes traced Silas and his edges.

Silas grinned back. "When I was thirteen, my dick didn't think so. Sexy devil."

They cracked up as if sharing a private joke.

Silas leaned over the table. "I like 'em long and lean." Wink. "Dark prince." Silas's gaze roamed over Trip's trim body. "Sarcastic and acrobatic."

Trip blushed—the pink started at his collarbone and swept up the pale column of his throat and over his cheekbones.

A-dork-able.

"Make me do bad things. Wake me in the middle of the night." Silas didn't quite touch Trip's hand. *How much is too much?*

"Oh."

"Sorry. That sounded cheeseball."

"It didn't." Trip shredded a matchbook with those long fingers. "Nobody says things like that."

Silas tried to see past the glitter at the shyness swimming there. Maybe Trip imagined he'd had some kind of Norman Rockwell boyhood climbing trees and scaring cats in Alabama. *Fuckleberry Finn*, his daddy called that crap. Yankees always expected rednecks to be a little simple.

"You?" Silas brushed Trip's forearm a moment before he pulled his hand back into his lap. "What were your favorites?"

Trip quirked his mouth. "The first comic I ever read was *Vampirella*. Then *Hellblazer. Dr. Strange*, if I got desperate. I loved *Promethea*."

Silas rested his gaze on Trip. "Sexy comics, then."

"Not—no! Hardly." Trip creased his forehead, his mouth a rosy O till he closed it. He stared through the walls at something. "More the gothic adventure stuff. Totally passé now. Just my luck I ended up at Big Dog drawing tweens in spandex for too much money. Bills to pay."

"Same. Not a lot of money in makeup, but compromise. Totally." Silas dug a forkful out of the skillet and promised himself an extra half hour on the elliptical to make up for indulging his worst impulses.

"My friends think I'm a hermit."

"So how the hell did you wind up in scrubs for the zombie run?"

Trip bounced in his seat. "Drafted. Rina shot this whole crazy video at OutRun and then edited it together to recreate a whacko wedding from one of her novels. With a veil and a big dress. The link's posted."

Silas snorted and barked with laughter. "C'mon...."

"For real. She writes romance. Erotic fantasy stuff." He flapped a hand like a big moth and dropped it. "Boys and ghouls. She had this idea that the zombie run would be a great promo spot for her new series."

"Wait a minute! I saw her. Big foofy dress and updo. The photogs went batshit. Smart lady." He tried to sculpt her outfit and coif in the air. "Puerto Rican?"

"Brazilian and Dutch." Trip's shoulders relaxed a little as he talked about her. "She has a series about a vampire archaeologist. Another with gargoyles. Pretty awesome, actually, and I can't stand romance."

"Well, that's a shame." Silas let a little Alabama leak out and lowered his voice to a wet rumble. "I love romance." He let the word come out of his mouth like *rohh-*

manse. Up north, a Southern accent could be a powerful weapon. Yankees assumed you were dumber, but at the right moments, it sounded nostalgic and seductive.

Trip studied his mouth for a moment, then blinked.

Bull's-eye.

Silas speared another bite of cheesy goodness. "Now I gotta buy her books and make sure everyone I know does the same." He dipped his head decisively. "Otherwise we'd never have met, huh?"

"I needed this. That sounds weird, I guess. You seemed so nice." Trip regarded him, whip-thin and whip-smart. "Thanks for coming on such short notice. I mean it."

Silas took a risk. "The thing you were upset about before. That guy. From this morning. Is he an ex?"

"Cliff?" Trip snorted. "Hardly. He's my editor at Big Dog… swiped something I pitched." Trip swallowed a bite as if it were soot.

"And then you spent most of the day wandering around thinking of shit you should have said."

"Exactly! The wisdom of the staircase."

Silas crumpled his napkin and dropped it on the skillet. "What's that?"

"Y'know when you leave a party and you're standing on the landing before you finally think of all the stuff you should have said on the spot? The French call it 'wisdom of the staircase.' 'S'like my worst habit." Trip sighed. "That's what writers do. They can write conversations the way they oughtta happen."

"Staircase wisdom. I like that."

"And *that* is why art is better than life." Trip folded his napkin into a neat square.

"Know something?" Silas waited for Trip to look up. "Keanu Reeves has bad skin. For real. And most starlets get weaves because their hair's too thin. Only cartoons have perfect hair. And don't get me started on the Botox. Actors gotta be as 2-D friendly as possible because cameras flatten everything."

"C'mon." A laugh.

"I do makeup for those people. It's all a front. Nobody is James Bond on their own. Studios pay armies of queens like me to put Humpty Dumpty together for the camera. Right?"

Trip frowned. "You're not a queen."

"Well, I know a bunch who'd argue." Silas burst out laughing. "I wish Kurt could hear you say that. My friend. He gives me shit about being a Beauty School Dropout."

Trip's forehead stitched close.

Obviously he'd said something that made Trip uncomfortable. But what?

Trip considered the macaroni again. "I'm pretty, I dunno, *crappy* at being gay. I never really wrapped my head around what I was supposed to be doing. Like everyone else got a memo I didn't."

"It isn't a secret handshake. I mean, there aren't rules, no matter what people pretend." Still, Trip's twitchiness left Silas off balance.

"We should get going." Trip rose and stuck an arm into his jacket.

The restaurant had gotten crowded, and predatory diners circled like puffy vultures. Or was Trip just trying to flee?

Are we finished? By the time Silas retrieved his coat, another party had crowded in to claim the table, so Trip had stepped out onto Twelfth Street by the time Silas got free.

Strangest date ever. Not bad, just *impossible.*

Silas shifted his weight. "You okay?"

"I did this all wrong." Trip stared toward Second Avenue, as if lost and far from home.

"Whaddayamean?" The Paddy sighting had sucked, but they'd had a great time, right? Silas reached out and took Trip's gloved hand. "I dig you, huh? Maybe you think I'm okay too."

Trip nodded and blinked his lemur eyes.

"Look: I'm awful at bushes and beating around 'em." He put a quick kiss on Trip's cheek.

Trip's face froze, and his gaze skated side to side.

"Was that bad?"

"Uh, no. Surprised me. It was great." Trip touched the invisible lip print. "I was so terrified this was just a hookup."

"Buster, I couldn't wait that long to get you shucked and greased."

Trip looked baffled. "Okay...."

"No." Silas took a breath. "For a hookup, I'd have had your pants around your ankles in Central Park ten days ago. I got no kinda patience." Silas didn't share the fact that he'd happily have done all of the above and still come to dinner tonight, but Trip was a nice guy. He probably didn't treat men like meat.

Like I do.

"You're so—" Trip indicated Silas head to toe. "Sexy. And I didn't know. But no way could I have kept it together. So thank you for... I dunno. Talking to me like a person. Calming me down."

Silas relaxed. "I try to do something terrifying every day. Keeps my heart on its toes."

Trip chuckled. "Your heart has toes?"

"Maybe. It runs around enough." Silas touched Trip's shoulder blade casually, brushing away imaginary dust.

Trip shrugged. "I'm way better company than this, I promise. I don't even know you, and I've been acting like a total dick."

"You made time to see me. If this is you acting like a total dick, then I definitely want to go out again."

A hopeful smile. "Seriously?"

"I'm being serious. Speaking from vast dick experience, that's a pretty manageable dickiness as dicks go." Silas raised his arm to hail a taxi up the block.

Trip opened his mouth to say something, closed it, and opened it again. "So... still counts as a date."

"I sure thought so."

"Truth?" Trip shivered. "This is gonna come out wrong... but you're like every gorgeous jock meathead I ever wanted in school." A glance at the street. "I know you're not a meathead. You're just a lot to take in. Funny and sweet and smart—"

Silas kissed him. He couldn't think of what else to do to stop the strange spiral of anxiety, so he just stepped forward and planted a chaste peck directly on Trip's lips.

Trip froze and then softened.

Silas stepped back. "Sorry. You left me no choice."

"*I'm* sorry." Trip still looked anxious.

"What you are—" Grin. "—is charming." Silas kept his hands to himself, just barely. "I gotta take sips of you. What may seem like me being standoffish is me trying not to throw you over my shoulder and haul you back to my greasy Batcave."

Trip gulped but said nothing. The taxi slowed to a halt.

"I think you had a shit day. And I'm honored that you trust me enough to come here and spend time. I wanna see you again. And not as some kind of *Superfriends* social work. That sound okay?"

Trip didn't—or couldn't—answer.

"Unless you don't. But just so we're clear, I think you're fucking adorable, and I would like to see you again and find out what happens next. Okay?" Silas, full gentleman-mode, opened the cab door. "No pressure."

Trip laughed at that. It had to be some kind of private joke. He laughed long enough that Silas laughed too. All the fight-or-flight seemed to drain out of Trip's body, until Silas could make out the real person.

"Okay?"

Trip seemed to weigh the matter and scratched his forearm hard enough to raise pinks lines. "Okay."

Silas resisted the urge to steal another kiss from the lush mouth, because this spark deserved patience. His watch showed nearly ten, and he planned to be a good boy with Mr. Spector. Plus, he needed to finish his sculpts for tomorrow's strip club shoot. "Okay you will or okay you'll remember?"

"Both." Trip smiled and slid into the cab. "I think."

Silas smiled and closed the door gently. He patted the cold glass and watched Trip watch him as the yellow car pulled away and headed toward a moon as bright as a flipped nickel.

4

THE next day, Rina helped him come up with an outrageous artistic revenge for the Unboyfriend's betrayal, assault-and-batteries not included.

He'd buzzed her in, poured her a Fresca, and dropped his bomb. He expected scorn, rage, pity even.

"Congratulations, honey." She gave a serene Madonna smile. Vatican, not "Vogue."

"I know—" His mouth stayed open, startled. "What?"

"Trip, you taught him to do this. You give Cliff a face that says welcome, and he wiped his feet again." She sipped her pale soda.

"No-no-no. You're not hearing me. Cliff stole my pitch. Well, he paid for it and then gave my professional parachute out of this pastel spandex gulag to some chick born after cell phones were invented."

"Imagine! An Unboyfriend who's uncertain and unsupportive." Rina faked a sad face.

He had always felt guilty hearing the nickname, but Jillian and Rina were right. Cliff sucked.

That morning, he'd finally gathered up the entire *Campus Champions* proposal, all seventy-one pages, and stuffed it into an old briefcase under his bed so he wouldn't keep poring over it, trying to work out what he could've done better or *straighter*. At least Silas had offered to give him another shot. He hadn't called, but then again, maybe he was working.

"This is exactly what you wanted."

"It most certainly is not." Trip's voice rose.

Finally, her anger flared. "Then it's a fucking radioactive Bat-Signal." She put her Fresca on the coffee table.

He fought the impulse to put a coaster under the glass.

"Staplegun fucks you over 'cause you gave him permission." Rina flapped a hand at him. "Listen to me. What did you say when I fired my first agent? Peed my pants at Balthazar. Stopped eating."

She'd lost fifteen pounds in a month and almost ended up in the hospital in kidney failure. "He was a schnorrer."

"Best thing coulda happened. He hated paranormal. He wasn't a bridge to anywhere: he was a fucking wall between me and my future. I woulda ended up as one of those bitter hacks who look like pimento loaf stretched over a knee bone. He only seemed like a bridge because I wasn't crossing it and I never could."

Trip groaned in irritation. "Rina, it took three days to feel like I was walking around the city and not some kind of hellish despair-scape. I went on a date, which I almost ruined, but then Silas was so cool that he actually pulled me out of it...."

"Silas?" Rina put a hand on his arm. "Tsk! You gambled." A nod. She seemed pleased, for some inscrutable reason.

"Rina, I unleashed *Fagnarok*." He grimaced. "That poor guy. I mean, we had fun when I wasn't acting like a complete maniac." He closed his eyes to keep the shame and pain inside his head.

"Duh." Rina sat back. "You'd just gotten hosed by Captain Cocktease."

"Silas spent the whole time flirting like Cliff, which means he thought I was a head case."

"These are not problems; they are invitations."

He pulled a pillow over his face. "With all due respect, fuck off." He tossed it away.

"Okay. Well, okay." She nodded, then wiped her mouth on a paper napkin, which left a taupe smear of lipstick behind.

Rina twisted to scan the big framed Justice League poster over the couch, "D'you know? Wonder Woman is the reason I write." She tapped the Amazon placed front and center by Alex Ross.

Trip would never confess it to Rina, but he didn't like *Wonder Woman* comics. He had gone through a brief period of Wonder Woman infatuation as a teenager; he loved the mythic backstory, and all those butch guys getting roped and rescued didn't hurt either. Even now they flirted with a campy bondage-y quality. Truth was, he owned all of the old Lynda Carter series on DVD because Lyle Waggoner was so fucking shaggy-seventies sexy. But because she was female, the academics and the suits always self-consciously screwed her up to match trends: in the sixties she was a vampy vixen, in the nineties she'd been a kickass *grrl*-power fem-bot... so she felt more *fake* to him than other superheroes.

Déjà vu. When had he thought that before?

"She sort of taught me how to be a lady. Because my family couldn't." Rina pored over the Alex Ross painting, which made the Amazon princess look butch and cold. "She isn't the most famous... the most loved. She isn't the hippest or the smartest, but she is my heroine and I'm addicted. It's the comic book I'd write if I ever wrote comics."

Trip held up a hand as if weighing the idea. "There are comics that I've loved that way."

"Not one, though." Rina stood and paced in a spiral, which she did whenever she had something brewing that hadn't formed fully. When she worked, she stirred and stirred the room like a giant cauldron until magic came out of it. "You might like individual storylines, and you like parts of the different characters. But they aren't *your* hero."

"Huh." He'd never thought of it that way.

"With Wonder Woman, I literally stop and think to myself... what would she do here? How would she react? What's the Wonder Woman solution to this problem?" Rina pressed a hand to her heart. "Not 'cause I'm crazy, but 'cause she resonates inside me like a bell. We're tuned in the same key."

When had he last felt like that with a character he drew?

"What I mean is: when I write a book, I'm in the book. Every page. It isn't memoir, but my Rina-ness needs to live in the words, or why the hell am I putting my name on it? Your sleazy Unboyfriend pays you to grind out that white-bread goop you despise. That's why you complain so much and live in this stuffy box. I mean, some other artist loves *Hero High*, but you don't. That's why you itch and sneeze. You're allergic to phoniness."

"Tell that to my asthma."

"Your monkey brain pops out to right wrongs." She jabbed him with a finger. "I swear: a real project and a good night's sleep skin to skin against the right person, all that itching and scratching would go away."

"Abracadabra," he scoffed.

Rina sank to her knees with a kind of self-conscious melodrama, like a doomed pulp virgin summoning a big nasty from beyond.

"It's always pretty gross down there."

"You gotta be shitting me." Rina did a double take at him. "This place is cleaner than my dishes." Without warning, she lay back on the floor and stared at the ceiling.

Trip lived in a second-floor studio apartment above the dive bar that owned the building. The ample paychecks from *Hero High* let him afford a Village address as long as he wasn't picky. The holes in the floor meant he basically heard drunks hooking up downstairs unless he wore earphones to bed, but the swiss-cheesy hardwood also lowered the rent to a thousand bucks a month... about a third of the going rate in Manhattan. Sure, he had to step over frozen vomit on his stoop in the winter and crying co-eds in the summer, but he had a big open alcove studio with lots of light: a must for a working artist.

The housekeeper had been in the day before. Dust and pollen got unholy this close to the street. His eyes watered in sympathy. "Dusty, then. Mold. The radiator leaks." Seeing her down there quickened Trip's nerves.

"I don't have your allergies, *pa*. Frankly, neither do you. My cat is onto you."

"She's a supervillain." Rina had a psychic tortoiseshell cat named Abigail who served as Trip's bullshit excuse for never visiting or house-sitting for her. The cat predicted Amazon rankings, gobbled any kind of living plant, and apparently did life-coaching on the side. *Terrific.*

"Just riff with me. If you had all the time in the world and no bills to pay? Pretend you're not just some doodlebug in the crap-factory." She reached the edge of his kitchenette and then reversed and coiled back toward him.

"I dunno." Trip didn't feel like playing.

Rina rocked her head back and forth on the hardwood planks. She excelled at this kinda stuff, spinning gold out of cobwebs. "Okay, I'll start. Day or night."

Trip spoke without thinking. "Night."

"Duh. You like spooky stuff. Okay, good." She chewed on her hair absently. "But not violent."

"Spooky? What, like *Scooby-Doo*?" Truthfully, Trip had a soft spot for Fred.

Rina squinted at the rays of light sneaking through his blinds. "No. Well, yeah, but no. I mean shadows. Maybe some occult woo-woo. Not like *Buffy* or *Harry Potter*. More like.... Hammer Films: pentagrams and candles. Blood and skin. A little dry ice. Titties but not silicone."

She had him cold.

"God...." Trip winced. "I feel so cheap."

"*Bellaco*." Rina giggled and patted his arm. "You gotta stop thinking that what you love is some kinda race you can win."

No harm in talking. "I'd wanna to do a real hero. No capes. No radiation." He sensed the hazy outline of a real idea: a pale, muscular chest, a peaked eyebrow, horns in moonlight.

Horns?

Rina tapped her mouth with a mauve fingernail. "Warlocks? Vampires?"

"Ugh. No. Not dead people. There has to be intimacy in this. Skin and spit. Some humanity. Subtlety. It's for grown-ups." The character floated just beyond sight in deep water... the murky ocean of notions he'd avoided for so long.

Tap-a-tap. His chewed pencil had left a little spatter of dots on the paper. He erased them without looking down.

"You'd want a character that fans can dream about. *Hmmph.* I like the seduction scenario. A sexy beast who won't take no." Trip shut his mouth. *Embarrassing.*

"Uh-huh." She crowed. "Male. Obviously."

"Fuck you." Trip shot her a look. "I draw great women."

"Did I say you didn't?"

"And most of my favorite books are about chicks. *Vampirella. Promethea.*"

"Yeah, because you grew up in the '90s and male action heroes aren't allowed to be vulnerable or sexy unless they're suffering." She had a point. "What do editors pay you for? What do you doodle? What do you dream about and whack off to? Macho men in peril."

"I'm not that gay."

"Trip, you're gay. Okay? I'm just saying you dig the menfolk, and you make 'em beautiful when you chill the fuck—"

"Hot guys. Okay. Fine. Yes. Great." Trip rubbed his eyes. "This is humiliating. Why don't we just drag out all my porn and childhood diaries while we're at it?" But it felt good to fish for an idea, even if he had no bait. "I cannot draw a triple-X comic."

"Is this a triple-X comic?" She said the word without judgment. She could have asked, *Marvel or DC?*

"No. I guess not. But no Lycra suits." A big sleek idea with teeth swam around down below him, like a shark on a moonless night. "Lotsa skin…. Fetishy style. But not necessarily *bowchickabowmow* hornification."

"It could be. We like hornification." Rina had zero hang-ups about sex. "What's the spookiest, dirtiest, funniest, silliest, sweetest story you can imagine telling?" She glared at him and beckoned. "Will you come down here?" Trip knelt awkwardly and squeezed his chest.

"Okay… now close your eyes."

He closed them, even though he felt stupid. He smelled her sugary cucumber perfume.

"Just pretend a sec." Rina's voice got quieter. "You had a crappy day at work. You're going into Midtown Comics on Wednesday. You climb the stairs, pass the counter to the big wall. All the new covers like ripe fruit. And then—*pow*—something fabulous catches your eye…."

"Huh." For a split second, a picture flashed across the inside of Trip's eyelids, too fast to catch clearly. "That's weird."

"Yeah? Whatchagot?"

His knees creaked on the floor. He imagined the dust, though he saw none; he preemptively tensed against the impulse to sneeze. "Mystery. It's a mystery."

"Cool. Like murders or spies or what? Mr. Scarlet with the wrench in the john."

"No. Mysteri-*ous*, I guess. Puzzle-ish." *That* he knew, at least. "A dark city, more Gotham than Metropolis, y'know?" Actually she didn't know, but he did. "But not crime-fighting shtick. More soapy. A little kinky. Schemes and secrets and rescues." His pencil rat-a-tapped more quickly on the floor between them. *Telegraph from the Muse.*

"That's not a mystery?"

He fought the impulse to sketch blind. "No, more... haunting. But not autopsies and courtrooms. Gothic." He tried to see it in his head. The slinky comics he'd loved as a kid where laws didn't protect people. "Sexiness. Tragedy. Obsession. Happy endings that scare the bejeebus out of you."

"A romance."

"And again I'll say fuck *off,* Sabrina." But she was right; he hated to admit it.

"Babe, that's my turf. You say gothic, I say romance."

The word "romance" bled into the ocean of his imagination, and a few hungry concepts circled it with razor-packed mouths. Images floated up to him: a church filled with owls... a crescent moon over flames... a garden of swords... a naked man with hooves, face craned to whisper at the sky. Trip's hands twitched and itched to draw: not stories yet, but the shimmering trail. He stood blinking and lurched toward the table and his sketchbook.

Then he knew. "A demon."

As soon as he said the word out loud, he could feel the big idea turn and swim toward him in the dark. As he bent his brainwave into words, he spoke quietly, afraid to scare it back into the shadows. "Not brimstone and nuns. No pitchforks or preachers. And not Lovecraftian fthooloo-marula bibbity-bobbity monster mash." He recalled his date last night. "Something seductive."

"Mmmh." Rina rocked up on her knees. "Yeah. A broody devil who humps the hell outta people. Whaddayacallem? Succu—"

"Incubus." He said the word like a sleepwalker and took a breath. The word threw sparks across the vault of his dark imagination. "If he's male, then he's an incubus." And somehow his hero *was.* The pencil he hadn't realized he still held *swish-skiffed* across the sketchbook he hadn't noticed tugging open on the drafting table without bothering to sit.

Trip could just make out a studly silhouette as it coalesced between them. "Like... they ravish people and claim their souls. He's a seducer. Not good or bad." He rubbed his bristly scalp against the nap. "Y'know how Catwoman is a thief, but sometimes she's a heroine. Anti-hero."

Rina stayed silent.

Already Trip saw the broad shoulders, the burnished skin, the tiny horns, the cocked brow, a jaw like an anvil, thick lashes.

"Can he have hazel eyes?"

"Not hazel." Did he sound defensive?

Definitely not hazel. He'd make his hero's eyes wolf-silver. No connection to any recent events.

In a few seconds, the exact slant of Silas's gaze stared back from the paper; Trip's incubus come-hithered him with borrowed eyes again. No one would ever notice.

Silas did have a rakish vibe and that easy laughter which gave all kinds of permission. "This guy holds people in thrall. Men and women both." Not that he'd use Silas as a model, but maybe the upper face, the torso, and hands. *Getting warmer.*

Just to balance, Trip gave him Cliff's widow's peak and high forehead... better for the horn buds anyway, short and blunt, like a baby goat's. "I don't think I wanna call it a comic. This is gonna be a"—quotey fingers—"graphic novel. Okay? Smart. Dark. Mature. For adults."

"Okay... not porn, but an erotic comic, so call it a *very* graphic novel."

Laughter sloshed out of him. "Awesome. A very graphic novel."

Rina joined him. She leaned her head almost to her shoulder as the figure took shape on the page.

"So wait." He tapped the drafting table with the pencil. *Tap-tap-tap.* "What's the story arc? Incubus fucks strangers, rinse, repeat." Eye roll.

"*Papa*, if it was me, you'd say—"

He sagged in defeat. "Yeah.... What's he need? What's missing?" He stopped treading water and concentrated on baiting the idea-shark. As though on its own, his pencil crept over the paper, carved solid shoulders and a brooding profile out of the white space. *The greater the evil....*

Trip leaned against the windowsill. Down in the street, a brownish mutt nosed in a pile of restaurant garbage in front of the Korean place he ordered from sometimes. His stomach rumbled. He'd forgotten to eat again, and he'd whittled his pantry down to a lone box of questionable Devil Dogs. He'd have to run down to the deli.

"Well, what does a sex demon dream about?" Rina asked.

"No fucking idea. Penicillin? Truth, Justice, and Gummy Dildos for all?" Trip stared out at the dog and pretended not to see the sleek idea sliding closer. *Come bite me, motherfucker.* "Touch?"

She plucked at the edge of the paper. "Like... maybe he has to touch people."

"Yeah: skin contact feeds him. He doesn't kill them, but he drains their mojo. An assassin. Or a spy. Archaeologist." His pencil laid down blocks of shadow on the page. "Something haunty."

"Like, he fucks the truth out of them."

"No. Jeez." He sighed in frustration. "With his ninja-humping skills." He traced the swell of a round haunch and exaggerated pectorals. "Fiddling sinners, for Satan, forever. What do I call him?"

"I dunno." She snapped her fingers and pointed. "Horny Bastard!"

Trip snorted silently. "Sure. Placeholder."

"Uh-huh." Rina wiped the edge of her dark lashes. "I wonder where that idea came from. Not."

"Silas is not a superhero. Or a sex demon." He erased the impish smirk to convince himself. *Stop that.*

Silas would dig this kind of book. The risky rightness of the "sex demon" concept felt like bones in his drawing arm, like a tank full of gas in a brand new car. *Why haven't I ever done this before?* Trip might not be cool enough to date Silas, but this "very graphic novel" would make him cooler by association.

"What's the downside?" She patted her thigh. "What's his whatchamacallit— kryptonite?" Rina stayed very still, as if afraid to scare the idea away. "Sexy devil, live forever, no bills, glam digs, six-pack and good hair days, hot meat all the hell over. Hard life."

Tchoo. The sneeze burst out of him. "Sorry." Trip remembered that strange sustained languor of Silas taking his time in front of S'MAC, wanting Silas to step closer... the other Silas hidden under the sexy shimmer, the secret geek who got Trip's jokes. *I gotta take sips of you.* "Actually, being an incubus must suck."

Rina eyes shone. "But he's a total rock star."

"And everyone knows how happy rock stars are." He sniffed. "I think he's lonesome."

Chomp! He froze as the glossy idea-shark sank its beautiful pearly whites into him. He almost arched with the pleasure, the answer so sharp and true it practically drew blood.

"Is he?" A small smile played at the edge of her rusty lips.

"Yeah." *Yeah.* Relief and certainty gushed through him in bright red ribbons. The character took shape, fleshy and solid. "He has the whole tortured immortal thing, like a vampire. But no gore; he feeds on connection and can't find it." Irrationally happy, Trip smudged the lines on the sketchbook page with a shaking hand.

Rina tilted her head to get a better view. "Wait, are you talking about Horny Bastard or you or one of your gentlemen?"

"How 'bout 'E) All of the Above'? The male animal." Trip barely controlled the huge wet idea bleeding out of his hand. "He needs the connection. To be touched. Maybe if he goes without intimacy for a period of time, he's weakened."

She leaned toward him, loomed over him. "Pretty goddamned romantic when you think about it."

"Romance sucks." Trip paced while the sleek idea slid through his nerves and slammed against the insides of his fingertips, wanting out. "In a comic book?"

"Don't say comic. It isn't." She frowned in distaste. "It's kinda serious, actually. You were right."

"Rina, who's gonna publish a 'very graphic novel' starring a lonely monster with a kickstand cock?"

"Bitch, anyone will publish anything that makes money."

Trip ignored her. Horny Bastard took shape under the pencil as his hand cut light and shadow into rotations, profile, the leg… the knotty foreskin, a straining hand, a corded throat, the skull tipped back to shout at the stars.

Trip was not his own master. He felt like a horse being ridden by a warrior.

Rina counted the specifics on her short plum nails. "Nude dude? Check. Spooky occult woo-woo? Check. Movie and merchandising appeal? Big check, with lotsa zeroes. Tortured erotic romance I could fap to? And you're Jewish, yo. Add some Kabbalah and Madonna might blurb you." She leered conspiratorially. "Slashtastic-*Sandman* with low-hangers. H'*yeah*. I'm a straight girl getting worked up just imagining that shit."

Even as he slammed his own idea, Trip saw the hypocrisy. He might be ashamed to put his name on it or take credit, but he'd order a copy in a heartbeat and read it to rags. Horny Bastard distilled every comic he'd ever wanted to read, like a smutty liqueur. "'S'kinda deranged. Depressing."

"Demons." Rina's eyes flashed melodramatically. "Deceit?" She extended her arm like a sorceress and intoned the last word. "Debauchery!" She tittered.

"He can only screw strangers, and they have to stay strangers 'cause they die and poor Horny Bastard lives forever. He can only touch *them*."

"Until someone touches him back," Rina answered quietly.

Chowmp-chomp. A deeper, truer bite as the idea closed its jagged teeth inside him and tore a chunk out of his doubts. Trip's stomach fizzed and his balls literally drew up as if the idea was about to squirt out of him onto the pine floor; his voice was a reverent whisper.

"I'm not writing about myself."

"You write it, you're in there. That's the deal." She rubbed his bristly noggin affectionately. "You taught me that."

"Bullshitski. You think I'm afraid of getting serious with… Silas… or Cliff or whoever."

"Didn't say that." Her lilting tone said plenty. "And I hate to break it to you, hun bun, but dating won't kill you or damn you to Helsinki or any other crap you've cooked up to justify holing up here instead of living in the world. Cliff blows you off, and that nice Silas isn't trying to ruin you or save your soul for valuable cash prizes."

Trip traced the incubus smoldering on the drafting table and wrestled with the urge to see Silas, to study him up close and personal. "Horny Bastard is not Silas."

"No shit, *cabron*. You don't know the poor guy well enough. After one date and a wet dream or two?" She scrunched up her face in cartoon confusion.

"Well, he can't be Cliff, either."

"Nobody said he was. This fucker's way too cool and tortured to be anyone's Unboyfriend. And if he wanted someone, he'd just *possess* 'em."

"No. People lose control with him. They make stupid choices."

"Yeahhh?" Her Cheshire cat smile got wider. Ten more seconds and she'd vanish, leaving nothing but perfect teeth and cucumber perfume.

"Who, then?" Trip chuffed his confusion.

"Lonely. Sexy. Obsessive."

Oh. He waved the notion away as if wiping a dry erase board.

She stood and examined her nails, offhand. "Feeds on attention while he stays hidden."

"Wait… you can't possibly think—"

"Hair-trigger libido but allergic to anything alive." She shimmied into her coat by the door and buttoned up. "I don't need to think. I know."

"Where are you going? I thought we'd have Lebanese."

"Pfft." She glanced at the semisketch, then at him. "A big Horny Bastard's banging on your gate." She yanked open the swollen front door and stepped into the hall. "Sounds to me like you got hell to raise."

Thunk. His door closed. Rina's descent got quieter until he couldn't hear her above the hum of the Greenwich traffic. He picked up the phone, put it down, and picked it up again. What could it hurt to feed his imagination a little raw meat?

Trip stared at the demon staring back at him. "You are not Silas." But he found himself dialing the number anyway.

5

NEVER underestimate the irresistible allure of a big-budget flop. From the ashes of fiasco grows many a homo romance…and for date 2.0 with Mr. Goolsby, Trip agreed to revisit one of the worst movies in history.

Situated on the corner of Eighth and Twenty-third, the Chelsea Clearview was a frequent destination for gay Manhattan. The gayborhood theater showed plenty of cheeseball blockbusters but also did specialty screenings of camp classics: *Rocky Horror*, *Showgirls*, *The Covenant*. On any given night, the audience would be two-thirds LGBT or more. So what if the mold and dust tortured his sinuses? Even Trip with all his PDA anxiety had made out once or twice on dates inside these walls.

Trip peeled off his seriously uncool jacket and glanced at his watch. Ten minutes early. He'd worn a tighter-than-comfortable Casper the Friendly Ghost T-shirt, and now he'd spent the entire walk uptown worried his triceps weren't big enough.

Silas had texted that he'd bought tickets, so Trip just pushed through the door and paused outside the cavernous lobby area. He stepped in out of the cold to get his bearings.

He shifted his weight nervously. Next to the usher tearing stubs, a poster on an easel read "Nerd Herd" with a kind of pink triangle shieldy-thing and trumpeted Unbored Games as their sponsor. *Right*. Silas knew the owner, Kurt-something. On paper at least, Chelsea Classics made sense for fanboys on a date.

Thwump. A red-lycra Daredevil bumped into him and didn't apologize, too busy talking to a Loki date, horns and all.

Oh shit: costumes. Like actual for real head-to-toe Halloween ensembles.

A tall mocha-skinned Green Lantern leaned against the wall between movie posters next to a stocky lesbian wearing a foam rubber Thing suit that turned her body into orange rubble. Catwomen in abundance, naturally, both male and female: six in the Julie Newmar disco suit, a handful in the classic purple unitard, and at least three working Michelle Pfeiffer-y bondage goddess getups. Why had he worn a T-shirt? These people took the Nerd Herd thing seriously: a couple of folks wore prosthetic makeup. *Why?*

Did Silas think Trip an incurable dweeb, or was this costume thing because they'd talked about comics? Trip's eyes watered, his nose tickled, and he squinted to hold back the sneeze. He wiped his damp palms on his upper thighs. The Nerd Herd clustered at the base of the stairs and the up escalator where a teenage usher scanned tickets.

As Silas had promised in his text, the Nerd Herd planned to screen *Catwoman*, God help them.

In the annals of superhero blockbusters, this flop remained one of the all-time worst comic book adaptations in history. DC had botched the project on an epic scale and created an instant camp classic that offered everything a gay geek could want: slutty cosmetic tycoons, whips and nips, a lame hip-hop score, sleazy catfights, and "pussy" puns galore.

Someone had scrounged up the infamous poster of poor Halle Berry wearing leather ears, fresh off her Best Actress Oscar, squatting like a kitten on the edge of a litter box. Trip frowned at her picture in sympathy.

Krash! Pow. Me-ow!

A couple of people examined him strangely. He obviously didn't fit in. *I'm not gay enough for this.* The other patrons in street clothes stared openly at the Nerd Herders, and Trip spent a moment wondering if he should flee while he had the chance. Then he worried he might have already seen Silas and not recognized him behind his disguise.

Silas might already have seen his freaky entrance. *Shit.* Just in case, Trip moved to a central point with a clear view of the whole lobby and vice versa.

Another clump of guests came through the doors, this one led by a trim man with his face painted blue and a long tail wired into a curve behind him: Gleek, the Wonder Twins' annoying monkey sidekick from Saturday morning cartoons. He held the arm of a steroidal Captain America with a dimpled chin and led a clump of Teen Titans just to round out the insanity.

Dork-tastic.

Just as the little gaggle of faggles reached Trip's vantage point, a sneeze escaped his face. He covered his nose too late to do much good and sprayed all of them with his bacteria and saliva. "Gross. God." He grimaced in apology.

"Ugh!" Gleek goggled at him with a wheeze and a sneer. A gangly Starfire pretended to wipe her tits dry in hyperbolic nausea. Captain America judged him with a scowl.

"Sorry. Oh man. I'm sorry." Trip flushed in horror.

Gleek shuddered and said nothing. The group continued toward the quagmire of costumes at the base of the stairs.

Please let Silas have missed that stupidity.

Again, that small irrational part of Trip thought of bolting. Maybe he could text Silas with a fake last-minute emergency that would let him off the hook. But then he heard Jillian in his head: *This is your little freaky-deaky tribe.* He belonged here if he belonged anywhere, just by virtue of the fact he could name every single character in the masked mob.

"You made it!" Silas's warm Alabama baritone came from midair. "Trip!"

He-Man. A golden grinning Masters of the Universe barbarian waved a brawny arm and strode down the stairs. He gleamed in his fur diaper and fur boots, and his pectorals bounced at each tread. *Holy jock itch, Batman!* A dull metallic harness crisscrossed his torso so that his heavy shoulders seemed a yard wide. His hair was a thick thatch. Several would-be rivals in and out of costume rubbernecked with obvious appetite. As he crossed the lobby, the shining slice of teeth widened.

"I was keeping a lookout." Silas hooked a thumb back toward the staircase he'd just descended.

"Hi." Trip's greeting came out in a choked whisper. He cleared his throat. "Uh, hello." He took his hands out of his pockets.

Silas opened his arms and embraced Trip firmly. "I'm so glad you came."

Trip hesitated a moment and then squeezed back, keenly aware of his bony hips and lean chest under his stupid T-shirt. Again, he savored that sweet marker scent. *Vanilla and sharpies.* The hug lasted a heartbeat longer than necessary, until he forced himself to step back. "You really are a He-Man."

"Is it okay?" For one heartbeat, Silas looked nervous.

Trip tried not to stare at Silas's tiny nipples and ended up stuck on the long stretch of thigh that led into the packed furry briefs. His skin wasn't tan so much as tawny under the dark blond hair. *Gulp.*

"It's awesome. You look awesome." Trip licked his lower lip.

Standing with Silas with all that charm aimed at him gave him a funny buzzing pleasure that made his limbs heavy and knocked him sideways. He'd felt this way before but couldn't remember when. *In control.* Weird enough to feel that way alone at his desk with a pencil in his hand, but with a handsome man, it stole his breath.

The sensation wasn't exactly superiority or lust, but the details hypnotized him. He regarded Silas with an intimate attention that gave him a chub in his shorts and dropped his eyelids to half-mast. He felt like he'd eaten a hash brownie that was giving him a prostate massage.

"By the power of Greyskull?" Trip looked askance, even though he liked the sound of it.

"*Gay*-skull." Silas laughed.

Trip pretended to smile. Hearing the word out loud squeezed his stomach into knots, pretty idiotic standing ten feet from a Filipino transvestite in a wheelchair dressed up as Oracle.

Silas's abs tensed when he peeked over his shoulder. "The Herd is really into cosplay, and we have a sorta unofficial competition to see who can out-fanboy the others." He peered upward. "I even tried to blond up, but it's only metallic gel."

"I didn't get that you meant *costume*-costume." Trip wavered a little, joking-not-joking.

"Anytime I can take my shirt off in public, I try to." Silas slapped his hard stomach. "Forces me to haul my fat ass to the gym."

Trip cringed inwardly. He never took his shirt off in public—ever.

Silas shifted the straps of his harness. The pearly paint on his torso made it glimmer. "It's your first time. So I wanted to dress up for you." His dimple was so deep that his sly smile seemed like a perpetual state. "I didn't do the sword or the hair, but I figured He-Man would give me a chance to strong-arm you."

"I wish I'd known."

Silas shook his head. "Oh man! Oh, jeez. I'm sorry. Doesn't matter. We're just gonna watch a shit-tacular movie and have some drinks with the gang." He bumped shoulders with Trip. "No pressure."

No. Trip flashed back on Jillian's warning. *Pressure.*

Silas leaned closer, sloe-eyed. "'Sides, you don't need to dress up; you're like a celebrity. Everybody knows Big Dog comics. A bunch of these loonies collect the Mighty Mites."

Not hardly. "Wait…. How did they know?"

"Everyone googled you. Fair warning: Randy and Mary are gonna corner you at some point and demand that you sign his foreskin in Sharpie."

Blink-blink. "Gah. Yah. *Umm.* You know 'em? They're okay?"

Silas jerked his head toward the costumed flock. "Fans. They're wigging about meeting Trip Spector. I swear: Randy *came* as Alphalad tonight. Boots and all."

Trip bowed at the waist. "Autographs it is."

"Fuck that. I'm not gonna share you with these goons. Anybody trying to cop a feel has to get past me." He flexed his shimmering pecs and grinned, as if he knew Trip was stealing glances.

"I should—" Trip tightened his jaw. His face burned. "Crowds. People. Wig me out sometimes." A shrug.

"No prob. I'm big enough to be your human shield. Cross my heart." Silas dragged his scarred finger across the He-Man harness, which had crossed his heart already. He licked the glittery finger.

They stared at each other in happy conspiracy.

"Okay." Trip liked him even more than he had at dinner or in the park. *Where has he been hiding all this time?*

Silas wiggled his eyebrows. "Sodomy powers, activate." His warm eyes shone.

And then Trip's smile got off the leash and he couldn't stop it. At this rate he'd have a dimple too. Hell, if he got nervous, he'd just rest his eyes on the gilded muscle Silas showed under his harness, at least until the lights went down. He wasn't shredded and shaved like a real Chelsea juicehead; his body had a slight fleshiness that reminded Trip of construction workers and words like "ripe" and "lush." Trip's cock thickened in agreement, like a fat exclamation point.

"This has gotta prove my comic fan bona fides." Silas waved at a Harley Quinn, who cruised Trip from head to toe.

"You realize, I've only seen you in, y'know, clothes, once."

Silas snorted and nearly split himself laughing.

"Oh! Not like that. I mean, I didn't—" Trip covered his mouth. "That's not what I meant. Eesh. Sorry."

"'S'the fucking truth. What gay boy doesn't love dressing up?"

Me. But Trip fake-grinned... as if the idea of standing near-naked in a crowded movie theater didn't feel like an anxiety dream with rabies.

"I mean, alla time in a gym? The creativity gene? Any gathering, y'got an 80 percent chance of costumes with possible public indecency showers."

A Human Torch in low-rise jeans trotted over, all of five two in his sneakers, and stroked Silas's chest casually. "*Sigh-*las." He said the name as two breathless words.

Trip's cold irritation swept over him. *Instant loathing.* This prick resembled a nelly golf caddy disguised as a bright orange buffalo wing.

"Keith." Silas removed the roaming hand from his pec and turned to Trip. "I brought Trip for his first-ever Herd."

"Of course you did." Keith slid his eyes over to Trip but didn't turn. "And what are you supposed to be?" He appraised the T-shirt and jeans.

"Pfffft! C'mon!" Silas squawked like it was a no-brainer. "He's Peter Parker." He wrapped a paw around Trip's shoulder and squeezed. "The real costume is underneath." A possessive grin.

Trip tensed under the affection but didn't step away.

The bitchy Gleek Trip had sneezed on earlier skittered over to join the fun-fun-fun and draped a blue paw over Keith's orange shoulder pads.

Silas raised a friendly hand at Gleek. *Great.* Everyone knew everyone.

"Sigh-las," Keith scolded and flicked his gaze to Trip for a moment, then back. "You're supposed to share your toys." The little putz reached out and pinched Silas's nipple, then tugged at it.

"I don't need toys." To his credit, Silas ran his arm around Trip's beltline and drew him closer. "If I got the real thing."

Keith rolled Silas's tit gently. This was Chelsea, so no one even blinked.

"Yeah, uhh. See you inside." Silas leaned back to pull free. He put his face close to Trip's ear. "C'mon."

Trip gave a forced wave to the hostile blue monkey and the flirty Dorito gnome. "Flame on." As Silas headed for the concession stand, Trip left space between them and his hands became fists.

"Sorry about Keith. Bad mistake from a couple years back."

"Cool." It wasn't cool, but Trip felt queasy and determined. Silas hadn't run for the exit or punched him in the face. *So far so good.*

Silas blinked at the display. "You want any crap?" He said the word with respect.

"Yeah." The word popped out of Trip's mouth with a "Duh!" sarcasm he immediately regretted: junk food wasn't exactly sexy. They were on a date, in Chelsea, and Silas obviously worked out. "Uh. Yes, please. If that's okay."

"Well...." Silas faltered for a beat. "That's why I asked, mister. I try to eat healthy, but He-Man knows no flab," he rumbled in a radio-announcer voice that sounded like some kind of private joke. "Brace yourself while corporate America tries to sell us its wretched things."

Trip laughed even though he didn't get the reference.

Silas steered them into the line and nodded hello to a very tall She-Hulk as she passed.

Trip's gaze roamed the room: men, women... mostly twenties and thirties, looked like. "Is the Nerd Herd just gay people?"

"Aw *hell* no. I mean, the movie nights are mostly because of the neighborhood, but the Herd is a wide-open welcome wagon for every fandom. Comics. Sci-fi. Horror. Slash fanatics. But I'm all about superheroes myself. Gimme a hot guy in tights any day." Silas winked. "And a mask? Fuck *me.*"

Without thinking, Trip winked back, glad he had.

The line bumped up.

Silas spread his arms to the crowd and declaimed. "Give us your freaks, your geeks—"

"Your order?" A happy Middle Eastern high school—*boy? Girl? Who could say?*—person asked from under lots of eye makeup and the brim of a Clearview Cinemas cap.

"Large Diet Coke, popcorn, and uh...." Silas turned to Trip.

"A small Diet Coke."

The concession androgyne reappeared.

"You're welcome to share my urn." Silas's He-Man arm bulged as he accepted a bucket of soda the size of a birdbath.

"Oh!"

"If that doesn't gross you out or whatever. Y'know. I'm fully cootie-free." His crooked smile showed one perfect canine. "You can have your own straw."

"Right. Sure. No. Great." *Stop with the word-burps, idiot.*

"Besides, if you don't help me drink some of this, I might rupture something and you'll have to rush me to the hospital."

"I wasn't thinking." Trip dug for his wallet, but Silas held up a hand: no. "I always feel crazy drinking diet soda with a heap of gummies, but I like to pretend they cancel each other out."

"Gummies?"

"Oh, I didn't mean…. Popcorn is great." More grown-up than candy, and Trip didn't need to breathe corn syrup on the poor guy.

But Silas had already flagged the cheerful employee behind the counter, and a jumbo bag of *Avengers*-branded gummies smacked down hard enough to make Trip flinch. He could not refuse the unholy siren song of carbs and dye. *FD&C number 69.* Silas tucked it into the waistband of his furry loincloth diaper thing. "I gotcha."

Trip flashed a smile in assent. The waves of Silas's easy charm overwhelmed him, and for the hundredth time, he felt like a pitiful fraud standing here in a T-shirt next to someone whose superhero costume was literally his glowing caramel skin.

A terrible nose-tickle built and built until he sneezed, loudly and wetly. He held his face in abject humiliation.

"Bless *you!*" Silas offered a napkin. "Cold?"

"Sorry." Trip took it and wiped his nose. *Sexy.* "Allergies. I took a Zyrtec so they'd let up."

A chattering line of Nerd Herders formed along the wall, snaking toward their theater.

"We should wade in or you're gonna have to sit in my lap." Silas seemed to contemplate the Fig Newtons. "Cookies?"

Trip opened his mouth to answer.

Please God don't let him eat a hundred processed fig bars and then try to kiss me so that I choke on his tongue and die in a movie theater with Halle Berry and Gleek watching me and snickering—

"Sorry." Silas snapped his fingers and pointed at him. "You're allergic to figs."

What if I die on a date because I'm too embarrassed to say no to third base?

Trip made a puke face. "Really allergic. Like anaphylactic shock, EpiPen allergic."

Silas seemed embarrassed. "I shoulda remembered." He pivoted to the concession counter. "Never mind."

Trip exhaled. Crisis averted. Reason number three million why he never dated anymore. He hugged himself like a lonely porcupine, isolated in public, hoping Silas didn't notice. *Say something. Be interested.* Trip opened his mouth and words came out. "You're in the movie business."

"Sorta. The way a hose fights fires. I just spray where they aim me. Mosta what they shoot won't even make the DVD extras." Silas sounded glum but smiled brightly.

"Comics are the Wild West for that shit. You can make a killing, but you can't always make a living."

"Yeah, but you get to start with a blank page and decide what's gonna happen and how things look."

Trip laughed. "It sounds glamorous when you describe it. But I have to navigate all this slop."

Silas jogged his elbow and nudged him toward the crazy line. "Your friend writes vampires. Straight borrow of Euro superstition by way of Bram Stoker, who also stole it. But who's written all the big vampires in the past hundred years? Americans. You got hundreds of millions of people obsessing over vampires written by us. We're good at stories."

"Rina nags me to create my own book. From the ground up, right? Just turn it loose." Trip thought of the Horny Bastard portfolio and shrugged.

"I figured all comic book artists had a trunk full of dream projects they sketch in their spare time."

"I'm always racing the clock. If I wanna get paid, then I draw for Big Dog. I hate all that Atomic Age bullshit. Aliens and radiation. I dig the supernatural stuff, but I don't have time to draw for fun." Trip resisted the urge to crow about his new demon.

"I don't mean for fun. For art. I mean, like to let the ideas out on the paper. I'm always doodling and futzing."

Trip fished in his pockets. "I'm *lucky*. A thousand people want my job. A lotta books use artists in South America, Italy, the Eastern Bloc. They cost so much less than we do. Cliff uses them to fill in."

"Huh-yeah. That's kinda my point." Silas double-checked the ticket stubs. "American movies. Music. Games. Fan fiction. We have the gift of bullshit."

"At selling it."

"Pop culture. Nobody does bullshit better than us. Right? China took over manufacturing. And the Middle East has us on fossil fuels. That's just geography and politics. We're a nation of whacko immigrants. Scavengers and con men. We crossed the ocean on faith, stole some land, and then stone-cold made up a whole country out of nothing but balls and bullshit. Superhero comics got invented by crazy genius Jews who showed up and revamped the refugee experience into a Man of Steel sent from Krypton with a secret identity."

Trip nodded. "*Chutzpah.*"

"What?"

Trip tilted his head. "What you're talking about. It sorta means 'balls plus bullshit' in Yiddish: *chutzpah*."

"I always thought you said it with a 'chuh,' like cheese." Silas grinned, then produced a sound like clearing his throat. "*Hhcc*hutzpah."

"Nice." Trip grinned.

Silas peered at him sideways. "Ninety-nine percent of the monsters I'm asked to build are rehashes of something some twenty-three-year-old director saw in a comic or in a game. My job is to make the monster fresh so the project doesn't feel like a regurgitated TV dinner. But it's someone else's story. You get your own because you're in New York. That's huge."

Way up at the head of the line, a middle-aged Alphalad whooped and hollered, and the Herd echoed. The chatty crowd began to shuffle past the ushers.

"Lemme grab my shit." Silas rescued a short peacoat from one of the chairs under a sconce.

Trip rolled that thought around. Silas was right. Funny thing: *Hero High* was just as borrowed as any folklore. No high school existed with that kind of plasticine perfection. Cliff had swiped it from sitcoms.

Silas held the door and Trip stepped through. Inside the crowded theater, they searched for a pair of seats in the rowdy rows. For half a second, Trip's nose tickled, but he blinked and battled the sneeze silently.

With shame, Trip realized his *Campus Champions* idea had been another regurgitation: just the same old bland shit crammed into push-up bras and dorm rooms.

But not Horny Bastard. He owned his big incubus, balls to bones. A panicked fizzy hope sprouted in his heart and the sneeze faded.

Silas apparently didn't notice. "All our monsters come from somewhere else. Our whole country was dreamed up. Natural selection. Bullshitters took over a couple cities where stories can fuck like rabbits."

"What?" Trip snickered and snuck another glimpse.

"Why duke it out in New York or LA? Why pull up your roots? I mean, Bulgaria has stories, right? But those artists fight a tidal wave of ideas if they want to get anywhere, without the same—" He waved his hand at Trip.

"*Chutzpah.*" Watching someone get so juiced about his work bowled him over.

"That *chutzpah*... you do. Their economies and opportunities suck in ways we can't imagine because we're spoiled. I starved a lot to move to the city." Silas nodded toward two likely seats near the back, which they claimed without difficulty. Piling their coats, Silas plunked down, bare thighs wide.

Trip said nothing as they sat down. His easy, buzzy connection with Silas made him feel stoned. He relished the chance to talk with someone who actually thought about all this crap as much as he did. Why had he never dated an artist before?

Because comics were still weirdly closeted. No: *because of Cliff.* He shrugged. "I guess…. Art is important, but importance is not."

In the first few rows, the flirty Human Torch sat with the irritated Gleek, their heads tipped close like bitchy pigeons. Trip smiled, pleased that they'd sat far away. Gleek glanced back at them before he faced the screen. Trip could tell he wanted Silas to notice them and wave, but Silas didn't seem to see either one.

Silas chuckled. "You have a gift. Not just your talent, or smarts, or luck, or—" He paused and closed his mouth, as if trying to slow his breathing. He poked Trip's chest. "Looks. You, Mr. Spector, have the cultural DNA and magical zip code to weave beautiful bullshit, and you're a fool to waste it."

Jillian and Rina are gonna flip when they meet him. As soon as he had the thought, Trip wanted Silas to meet his friends. *A real, live superhero.*

"All I mean is that you shouldn't postpone joy. It's a trap." Silas squeezed Trip's knee. "Always be working on at least one thing you'd be jealous of. My dad always said he'd rather lose big than win small. You gotta gamble."

Trip wanted to argue, but he enjoyed the sight of impassioned Silas arguing business while dressed as a barbarian too much to form a coherent thought. He relaxed in the seat and sighed.

Silas bumped his bare leg against Trip's jeans. "Sorry."

In his rush to explain, Trip stuttered and coughed. "N—don't apologize! I never get to talk about this stuff, and I…. Well, just don't apologize." What a strange, terrific time.

"For real?" Silas grinned wide. "Good." He sat back with a proud smile. "Most people think I'm a nutbag."

Maybe this date would turn out better than the last. What did Silas expect? What would he want to do after? If only there were thought-bubbles he could read. Trip's anxiety returned. Without thinking, he glanced down at the splayed thighs and saw the delicate tracery of one bluish vein that forked near the fur loincloth where Silas wasn't as tan… pumping barbarian blood into his He-Man pelvis.

Jinkies.

The impossible fragility of the flesh and the pale tenderness of the inner thigh made Trip's palms and scalp sweat. The seam had bunched up to reveal a lighter slice of Silas's groin… not his balls, but the edge of the swell.

As Trip stared at that unlikely vein and the bulging slope, Silas spread his legs wider and hunched his pelvis forward on the seat. "Am I flashing my bedoobies?" His fingers grabbed at the edge of the fake fur.

Busted.

"Sorry!"

No irritation on Silas's face in the least. He leaned over and confessed into Trip's ear. "I wore a Speedo underneath so my Sword of Power didn't flop out."

"Good thinking." Trip's heart galloped in his chest. "It's an awesome costume."

"Yeah?" Again, his voice sounded oddly hesitant and dubious.

Trip snorted. "Duh."

Silas didn't laugh. He nudged closer to mutter under his breath. "I needed to get your attention."

Would they go out to the bars with Silas all barbarianed? The thought of a room full of sleazy schmucks groping that solid body furrowed Trip's forehead and set his pulse thumping in his throat.

Trip opened his mouth, but before he spoke, a high tenor squawked through the speakers.

"What's up, squirrel-friends!" Down front, a willowy drag queen in owl-eyed horn-rims stood in front of the screen. "I'm Deanna Mince, superhosting for our Nerd Herd Pussy-tack-ular this evening."

Hoots and howls.

Trip cackled, because everyone else had, but he'd never gotten the appeal of drag. Another thing that proved he was a bad queer. He loved the superhero in-jokes, but genderbending made him feel slow and excluded. Still, the crowd's enthusiasm compelled him to join in with fake *ha-has* so Silas didn't peg him as a freak.

Peering over her glasses, the drag queen shushed the crowd like a crazed librarian. "Hedda Lettuce is kryptonite green that she can't be with us tonight, but she's having a cat flap installed in her Fortress of Attitude." She pressed her glossy talons into her pelvis bone and offered a sour puss. "Ho? No!" The crowd roared the word along with her, as if they knew their cue.

As casually as he could, Trip drew his inhaler from his pocket and took a quick huff. He swallowed bitter saliva as the theater dimmed to merciful blackness. The lights down front only left their seats in deeper shadow. Trip exhaled in relief.

The 1970s *Wonder Woman* TV theme music blared. While they roared at her, Deanna did some kind of mod cat ballet they seemed to love. Every so often she paused and the audience roared, "Ho? No!"

Without turning or asking permission, Silas reached and claimed Trip's fingers, lacing them with his. When Trip looked over, he was just staring down front, smiling. "That uncomfortable?"

"No, sir." Trip considered the dark auditorium. No one could see. He didn't check, but Silas *whuffed* with pleasure and squeezed. *So this is what a good date feels like.*

In front of the screen, the cat ballet ended along with the tinny disco-era music. Deanna Mince spun rapidly in one spot as she gradually picked up speed. The audience hooted and stamped as she paddled herself around-around-around on one crimson high-heeled go-go boot.

Applause and catcalls.

While she spun, she ripped off her glasses, shook her big wig loose, and whipped the secretarial suit free to unveil a fringed, bedazzled bathing suit exactly nothing like Wonder Woman's costume. She spun to a stop and planted her fists on her hips, sweaty and proud.

The audience went bonkers, whistling and clapping. And since Silas clapped, Trip did too, although he hated to give up Silas's grip.

Thankfully Silas reclaimed it in the dark as the lanky Wonder Woman bellowed, "And now… with further doo-doo…."

Drumroll from the speakers. She shimmied, and her stars-'n'-stripes kept on shimmying after she stopped.

In the murky light, only Trip could see and touch Silas's exposed skin. *Movie's not such a terrible idea after all.*

"Starring Miss Doo-Lally-Berry and Sharon Stone-Cold-Bee-yatch… if you're nasty!" *Nasteh* is how it sounded, and she held the word in a deranged hiss with her eyes bulging like spangled kabuki Lynda Carter. "*Catwoman!*"

The Nerd Herd went berserk as the lights faded to black and Trip held his polite barbarian's rough hand.

6

"YOU gotta kidnap me, quick."

Surprised, Trip nodded and rose, letting go of Silas's hand. Up front, a sixty-foot Halle Berry had just scampered away and the screen gone black, from shame, probably.

They'd laughed so hard Trip's ribs ached and his throat was raw. *Catwoman* sucked… supersonic sucked, as only a hundred million dollars crashing together to burn Oscar-winning careers to the ground can suck.

While the credits rolled, they scuttled speechless up the dark aisle ahead of the rest of the Nerd Herd. Silas held the door like a prom date. *Why would he ditch his friends?* Maybe he didn't care about going to some bar after all. *Oh.* Trip blinked at the sudden glare and fought to keep the dopey smile off his face.

In the lobby proper, Silas slid into his wool peacoat, turning up the collar, the top half of him a sailor, the lower half still a gleaming hooligan in fur boots.

As Silas had promised, Randy ambushed them in the lobby to say hi. He was a shy craggy man in his forties with piercing blue eyes. He and his wife, Mary, shared molasses twangs and raunchy cackles. Randy asked for Trip's autograph, but *not* on his foreskin. Shameless, Mary pulled her husband's tight Alphalad shirt up to bare his hard pecs and asked Trip to sign in paint pen so that one of her husband's pierced nipples could dot Trip's I. They weren't even gay, just enthusiastic and frisky. Charmed by their sweetness, Trip promised he'd come back to the Nerd Herd.

He meant it.

Then Trip held open the door to Twenty-Third Street for his date. He prayed Silas wouldn't try to take his hand out here, and somehow he knew not to. Trip wasn't sure what happened next. He didn't know how to ask, so he let the current drag him and trusted Silas would steer them in the right direction.

They strolled downtown in easy silence. Eighth Avenue was busy for a January Thursday, and guys stared at Silas's naked skin. Hard for the lonesome barflies to miss a hot barbarian at moonrise. Silas didn't pay any attention. When they hooked a right onto West Seventeenth, he bumped their shoulders together a little.

Pleased to sneak off together, Trip smiled, more than willing to skip the rest of the Nerd Herd's night out. He hadn't liked that snippy guy dressed as Gleek. And he wanted to keep the Human Torch's paws far away from Silas. One thing he'd learned, Silas had dated a lot of men in this city. One had sat behind them with his new Punisher boyfriend, who'd looked about as delighted as Trip at the idea. At least three other exes floated around the Herd's margin.

Whether two-year exes or two-hour exes, he didn't know and didn't want to. Silas had invited *him* tonight, leaving those losers stuck as a decorative, envious background.

"Here's me." Silas stopped in front of a poky building on West Seventeenth and climbed one step so that *he* stood a couple of inches taller, then shifted his weight foot to foot. He almost shone with contentment, the face of a farmer at an Impressionist picnic.

The streetlamp spilled sallow light over them; the glitter on Silas had rubbed off on Trip's arm and jeans and left hand: borrowed sparkle. At the top of the four stairs, a dim front vestibule almost hid the door where the lamplight didn't reach.

Trip had calmed down, away from the crowd and all the flirty fanboys. He'd stopped itching as well. He hadn't realized the walk was so short. He snuck a peek at his watch. Was the date over at 10:20? He stepped closer. "You must be freezing."

Silas nodded but didn't climb up or down. He waited as if he'd asked Trip a casual question.

"I had a way better time than I expected." Trip's eyes went wide. "No! Wait…. Not with you, but with *Catwoman*. I get it, I think. The Nerd Herd deal."

"Cool." Silas glanced at the street, where a cab had slowed down. He looked oddly nervous. "So…?"

Trip had never struggled so much trying to read someone… but somehow had gotten addicted to the warm discombobulation. *Fuck it.* He backtracked to the steps. "Wait, I suck at being cool." *Take a risk.* "I mean, we could just make a plan right this second."

Silas laughed, but he didn't come back. "Sure. Name the place."

Trip stepped nearer, his stomach knotting. He scrabbled through the credible options. Gallery? Dancing? Fancy dinner? Bowling? Orgy? He had no idea what Silas expected, so he had no idea how to meet the expectations. How the hell was he supposed to come up with a killer date when he could barely *survive* one?

"Unless you don't want. I mean, you don't have to decide right now." Silas shuffled on the steps. He didn't seem impatient, more confused.

Trip swayed. Manhattan offered anything at all. Hell, he lived here; he could have anything delivered to his damn door. But with a cleft-chinned hero smiling at him like a gun at his head, he couldn't muster any suggestion that didn't sound dumb or tacky. "I do."

A car drove by slowly, searching for a parking space. They watched until the cone of headlights reached the end of the snow-dusted block.

"Well...." Silas inhaled raggedly. "I want—"

Trip turned first, admiring Silas's profile. "You want...?"

"You." Silas swung the hazel gaze back, almost green in the amber light, and considered Trip's waist, shoulder, chin, eyes. "I *want* you to come upstairs right now."

"I don't think that's such a good idea." Trip took a breath of that vanilla-and-ink smell he'd come to associate with Silas. "Right away."

"Sorry." Silas shook his head and crossed his arms. "Do-over." He wiped his hands on his coat. "You make me so fucking nervous."

"I do?" Maybe they weren't so different.

"Everything." Silas looked up at the cloudy night sky, then back. "Y'see? All I want is for you to come upstairs right this minute and help me take all this crap off so I can make you dessert and we can get into my bed." Head shake. "Eventually. Eventually, y'understand? I want the next thing. But then, of course, I don't want any of that because I don't want *just* that. You, I mean. That is, all that would probably be a horrible mistake because it's what I would do, not what I should do."

Not a question. *No script.* Did Silas want an answer? He seemed happy and smelled delicious, but the cold had started Trip shivering—and he was wearing pants!

"You make me nervous too."

"Sorry." Silas frowned. "I don't mean to."

"Not in a bad way. I guess—" Trip took a step back. "Thank you for, I dunno, a super evening." His bones buzzed with that strange calm.

"Super date."

Trip grinned. "Date, yeah. I'm gonna... catch a...."

"Cab." Now Silas mirrored his Joker's grin. "Right."

Before Trip questioned the impulse, before he stopped his feet or his hands, he closed the three yards between them, brought their mouths together, and... kept going, actually, so that instantly his arms were full of peacoat and barbarian.

"Tha—" Trip swallowed whatever Silas almost said when their mouths came together again. His coat gaped to let Trip take hold of him.

Trip's momentum pushed Silas against the front door, so they kissed in a pocket of shadow created by the overhang. The harness pressed against Trip through his T-shirt.

"*Gnnngh.*" Silas wrapped those corded arms around Trip and rolled over him, shielding them from the street with his broad back, and pressed Trip's spine against the cool metal door. The surface warmed quickly. They struggled to get at each other, tugging at clothes.

Silas crushed Trip under his brawn and scrubbed his shirt between them. He sucked and bit at Trip's mouth, chin, and throat with a hunger that tore Trip open with spikes of heaven and involuntary shudders. Trapped against his inner thigh, his bulge strained against the denim.

Trip chuckled and bit back. Silas didn't complain. *Not so terrible after all.*

Silas's rough, clever fingers plucked at Trip's nipples, and then he squirmed closer. Those huge arms enfolded Trip without permission or patience.

Silas gritted his teeth and groaned. "Mistake. I didn't. I don't." Headshake. "I gotta—" His rigid cock held the fur waistband a little open. "Wait-wait. Slow down." He took his own advice. Shoulder to elbow, he stroked Trip gently, reverently, but the crazed grappling stopped.

Trip stayed put, not wanting to break the spell. He counted his breaths.

Silas held Trip's head lightly with one hand, pulled their faces together, and planted a kiss on him. No tongues, no slobbering. Just a firm, openmouthed kiss that blew out the back of Trip's head. *Ker-pow!*

Abandoning his better judgment, Trip couldn't help but kiss back, tilting his head to get closer and wrapping his wiry arm around all that brawn to pull it closer. His erection rubbed Silas's bare abs through two layers of cotton. An answering ramrod tented the hairy He-Man briefs.

Silas retreated, dazed and lazy. "Wow. Okay." He exhaled in a near laugh. "I'm trying to be a gentleman here."

Trip gulped and nodded, but his tongue was too stunned to speak. He couldn't get a handle on anything. Worse, he didn't care. He had no map and he didn't want one. If this was fucking up, he was all for it. He blinked. "Was that bad?"

Silas pulled away with deliberate slowness. "I promised—I'm gonna say good night."

"Sorry… I suck at dating. Obviously."

"Who told you that? You're making me stupid." He held Trip's shoulders gently but definitely. "I gotta get inside before I get dumber." He still blocked them from any prying passers-by. "Jesus, Trip."

Trip wedged himself against the door, completely in darkness, not wanting to leave, knowing he should. He couldn't figure out what he was supposed to do or want or have.

Glitter streaks covered them. *Thud-thud-thud.* Heartbeats in the dark. They inhaled and exhaled raggedly.

The amber lamplight backlit Silas, shadowing his rugged face; the barbarian chest rose and fell, rose and fell, framed in the open navy coat. His hands chased Trip's shivers tentatively, over his clothes; the calluses caught the cotton. "Better now." He kissed Trip softly. "Sorry. I got carried away."

"I jumped you, remember?" *No script again.*

"True." Silas petted him with nitroglycerine patience: arms, ribs, ass, chest. "Fuck. Like a Cellini."

Trip exhaled and tried to get ahold of his body. As always, Silas's nearness drugged him and slowed time to a syrupy crawl. Trip's eyes closed and his hands twitched involuntarily as the drowsy surrender stole over him.

Relentless and patient, Silas found his way back to Trip's nipples, tugging gently but firmly on them with his scarred fingers and rucked the shirt over his pecs. "That hurt?"

Trip grunted and arched. "Nuh. Uh-uh. Feels—" He flinched when Silas pinched a little harder. "*Ahhk!*"

Silas whispered, "So sensitive."

"I never noticed 'em before. When people pinched them, I mean." What was happening to him? Trip felt terrified and triumphant at the same time. "Not sensitive, I guess." He trembled.

"I think we'll have to agree to disagree." Silas licked one thumb and then the other and put them back to work. The wet scrape against his nipples sent a scatter of shocks through Trip's nervous system.

"I.... Uhh."

"What?" Silas pushed his arms around Trip, the hot skin of their abdomens pressed together, and rubbed himself against the crisp trail that led into Trip's trousers. Silas lapped at Trip's tongue and only pulled back to breathe heavily. His eyes stayed half-lidded and happy. He whispered. "Y'okay there?"

"Nehhh." Trip shook his head side to side slowly, but the slippery words wouldn't congeal in his mind. The winter air should have chilled him, but it didn't. His eyes should have itched from the wool coat or the glitter, but nothing. Everything smelled like vanilla bourbon, like Silas, and the world moved around them in trickle-time. He choked. "Oh-muh...." His shaft jerked out of control, a squeeze or two from squirting.

Apparently, he'd never kissed anyone. Or else he'd only practiced with amateurs.

Silas hunched and pushed against his erection, opened his mouth against the column of Trip's throat and gently bit into the muscle. He didn't slobber or gnaw, just nursed at the flesh with an unhurried hunger. He worked one paw down the seat of Trip's jeans, tracing his crack and cupping the cheek.

Hypnotized by the buzz in his veins, Trip rolled his head to expose his throat to the demanding mouth, letting Silas's soft stubble tickle and scrape him, and he thought he knew:

Silas wants to fuck me.

Trip's handfuls of thick navy lapels held him steady even though his knees had given way. He imagined the kind of pleasure he'd feel, smothered under all this tender strength. The thought unnerved him, but some dark corner of his desire wanted to submit entirely. The weakness in his legs made kneeling and serving seem completely natural. Was that a rotten idea or a perfect one?

Is there a difference?

Trip usually felt too claustrophobic on the bottom of butt sex, squashed under oafs who called him things like "boy" and "bitch." In general he'd kept his ass off-limits. Even with his big honker, once a date held a hundred and fifty pounds in their arms, the boners tended to head in one direction... and Trip'd ended up eating a pillow. Then he'd spend the rest of the week feeling like an alligator had crawled out of his butthole. *Skip-a-doodle.*

Silas panted through his spit-slick mouth as his rib cage expanded and contracted. A spatter of sweat shone on his chest, smearing the glitter into arcs. He still held himself back, bracing his weight against the doorframe as if afraid he'd flatten Trip.

"I won't—" Trip kissed the side of his head. "—break."

"I don't wanna—"

"But I'll bend." Trip spread his thighs and dropped so that their faces were the same level, giving Silas nowhere else to go. "C'mon, Mr. Goolsby."

"—smush you."

"You won't. I know you won't." Trip let himself feel passive, overpowered even under all that manly bulk, but for the first time in his life, he almost didn't mind.

Only one way to find out.

Finally Silas dropped forward to press full-length and crush the breath right out of him in one happy sobbing exhale. "*Unghh*-ah."

Trip squirmed against the delicious weight, loving all that heat wrapped around him against the cold door. He could take whatever Silas dished out. And actually... the big frame on top of him made him stronger somehow, not weaker. He rocked his pelvis in open invitation.

Change of plans. He'd—what had his friends said?—gamble a little. They'd told him one awful thing a day, right?

"We could go inside." Trip scanned the block. How many passers-by had seen them already? *Gack.* He had no clue, but they were hidden back here. Besides, if they moved, the spell might be broken. Why was he so afraid?

"Nuh." Silas wasn't going anywhere, apparently. The contrast between their bodies seemed to fascinate him. He kneaded Trip's arms and shoulders, driving shivery bolts of pleasure through Trip, so sharp they raised gooseflesh across his limbs. He hadn't touched Trip's outsized dick directly yet... which was strange.

Bottoming always left Trip anxious, but Silas's sweet hunger and fierce attention eased him. He'd make the fucking good, even if Trip preferred other things. He preferred *Silas*, and that was the most important thing. What should have been a stupid mistake suddenly seemed like a wise move. He was fed up with letting his habits bury him alive. Trip let his knees fall wider, making room for Silas to press closer.

Fuck scruples. "Or stay right here."

Instead, Silas swayed back. *Whuh?*

"Something wrong?"

Silas's forehead clouded. "Whaddayamean?" His jacket hung wide, exposing the little eddy of fuzz around his navel. The loincloth had skidded lower to reveal the top of his pubes. "Slow down...." A sneaky smile.

Trip chewed his lip. "Every time I think you're going one way, you go the other."

Silas's eyes twinkled. "And that's bad?"

"No! No. I just don't know what you like and I'm trying to read you...."

Silas tilted his head to one side and shook it. "You don't need to read me, mister. I'm right here. In the flesh. Yeah?" He fell forward again. Trip flinched and held up his hands defensively, but Silas caught himself on his hands at the last minute. "Your heart's knocking something fierce." He even spoke slowly. "You in a hurry?"

Trip didn't fully trust himself. "Well, yeah, but I guess not."

"'S'okay." Silas arched. "I'm not going anywhere, Mr. Spector."

Trip smiled wide. He felt stupid with testosterone and blue balls. "Then we'd better stop." He worked to catch his breath. "Or I don't know what I'm gonna do."

"Naw. I like taking you in easy doses. You're pretty strong medicine for a weak man." There was so much of Silas: a ripe wall of bourbon-scented muscle, springy calico hair, sly smiling eyes that wouldn't look away.

"Are you sure?"

"No sir." Silas kissed him again. "I'm not good at being sure of anything."

Trip surrendered to the tickling, itching insanity he associated with hay fever and spring. The fizzy energy gathered in his hands until he growled, spun Silas sideways against the wall, and pressed chest-to-thigh against him. He couldn't curb the sweet tumble of his heart in there somewhere.

They grappled against the door. Mouths and legs tangled with aching slowness. Who was in control here?

"*Mmrhh.*" Instead of resisting, Silas sighed and sagged against the cold metal. He clutched at Trip's T-shirt and yanked him closer.

Again he worried that if they moved from this dark nook, the moment would vanish. *Abracadabra.* Trip ran a possessive hand over the swell of Silas's chest and shoulder to pin him down playfully, firmly. He expected Silas to wrestle with him for control, but everything against him was hungry permission. Had he misread the situation? He pushed farther, braced his forearm on Silas's sternum, not high enough to choke, but hard enough to dominate.

Silas struggled but kept himself restrained by Trip's wiry arm. Against all odds, Silas didn't push back. His arms hung impotent and his loincloth tented comically over a trapped erection with a wide knob. No words, but the silky glint of his eyes held Trip's, asked something painful, shameful. Silas dropped his gaze and couldn't seem to raise it again.

Trip reached around Silas with both hands and took two handfuls of that jutting ass, grinding their rods together painfully. Emboldened, he knocked Silas's legs wider with his knees and held him firmly against the bricks. Breathing hard through clenched teeth, he ran his hands over the exaggerated chest, his manners and patience lost as he went. He pinched Silas's nipples harder than Keith could have, claiming them.

When Trip gripped a square pec roughly, Silas shivered and gave a little rustling laugh of approval. For all the manly bulk, a boyish vulnerability had stolen over him.

Another change of plans?

"Big stud." Trip sucked on his own lip and shook his head with wonder. "Huh?"

Silas didn't answer. His downcast eyes stared, unguarded, at Trip's insistent erection, angled toward the waistband like an axe handle jammed into his pants. The narrowness of Trip's torso and hips made it even more obscene.

Silas's tongue snaked out to wet his upper lip, and his fingers twitched. He appeared hypnotized. His stillness and Bruce Wayne chin left Trip feeling like the Boy Wonder, only he didn't wonder at all.

He's a bottom.

Trip fumbled for restraint and gave it up for lost. Nothing mattered. The sight of all that gilded muscle needing to surrender just *withered* his boyhood fantasies of brute control like shrink-wrap in a furnace. The hidden, wicked part of Trip that had tied up his action figures as a boy whited out with satisfaction.

No plans. Fuck plans.

The discovery felt like stealing something from the straight and narrow, breaking some Boy Scout code, even though no one was watching and he knew better. For a moment, he was at summer camp out on the lake with one of his secret jock-y crushes, the wholesome boneheads he jerked off to every night under the covers who had that same lazy charm Cliff swung around so casually.

Stop! Trip refused to think about that smug bastard. He refused to dwell on the bullshit betrayal and the dead book. He had all the permission he needed. He was here with Silas. *In the flesh.*

The Neanderthal inside him, the primal force Trip shared with every man, grunted in the amoral satisfaction at conquering another so completely.

Wolverine on all fours. Superman with his legs in the air. Batman choking on his pole.

"I wanna—" Trip swallowed, because his mouth was so wet. "—*do* things to you, Mr. Goolsby." He couldn't think any further than this slow, sliding moment.

"Yeah?" Silas smiled slightly as if expecting a punch line. Trip pressed forward again, to give them both a feel of the hot iron bar against his belly, the crest swollen fat as a plum. "If you'll let me."

Silas moaned and peered at him, so close he seemed blurry.

What now? What next?

Wild and witless, Trip shifted his hips side to side, hidden in the dark vestibule. "I wanna open you up. Put my tongue, my fingers, my cock in you." He skimmed the back of his shaking hand over the stubble on Silas's face. "If I can."

Silas swallowed. He didn't blink.

Trip leaned close to his ear and took a deep breath of sweet glue and sweat. "You make me crazy." He couldn't seem to stop telling the truth. "Maybe I can return the favor."

Silas didn't respond at first. He admired Trip's face greedily, and a crooked grin carved his dimple deep again. Finally he relaxed a little and crooned in that soft rasp, "Hell yeah."

I can't stop. I don't want to. Trip's own total abandon terrified and thrilled him.

He licked his hand and reached under Silas's balls. Without taking his eyes off Silas or asking out loud for consent, he felt for the edge of the loincloth, then the stretchy Speedo beneath, pushed roughly against the musky, warm skin with his wet fingertips.

At the top of Silas's throat, the pulse jerked.

Trip petted the broad ridge behind his balls and farther beneath until he found the tiny dry opening. The skin scorched his spit-slick fingers. He pressed upward with the pad rather than the tip so he wouldn't penetrate right away.

Silas gulped, misunderstanding.

"Not inside. I'm just there. You feel me there?" Trip's cockhead had surged above his belt loops, but somehow, with his back to the street and his hand against Silas, he didn't care. He tapped the hole lightly, then waited for Silas to drop his shoulders.

Silas whistled slowly—*phewwww*. "'Kay."

Trip kissed him, licking the upper lip. "Beautiful." He brought the hand back up to their faces and put his knuckles in Silas's mouth. Silas sucked his index and middle fingers, licking between them until his saliva ran to Trip's palm.

Good.

"Thank you." Improvising, Trip snaked his hand back under the Speedo, and this time the wetness let him slide right back. This time the tips pushed inside a little.

Silas blinked then and shuddered.

"Hurt?"

He shook his head and gasped. "Go." His wet mouth hung open, and he breathed hard.

Trip whispered and pushed closer. "That where you need scratching?"

Silas nodded and blinked again.

"Or is it deeper?" Trip pushed inside just past the first knuckles, panicked by his lust and recklessness.

Silas yelped and groaned roughly. "Augh. Ugh." His mouth fell open, and his head smacked against the metal door with a *doonk*. He bent his legs and bore down, sucked air in sharply through his teeth as he used Trip to get at what he needed.

"Yeah?" Trip pushed farther. "Almost there. I don't wanna miss the spot." He pushed to the second knuckle and bent his wrist for leverage.

Over his shoulder, Trip heard some vehicle pass by in the street without pausing, but now the risk excited him, the madness of claiming his horny barbarian on a stoop, taking Silas apart with his bare hands to get at the sticky gold inside.

"Go. *Hngh*." Silas grunted and pushed as far down as he could. "Go on. *Gahhd*."

Trip lurched forward and covered that open mouth with his own, tasting butter from the movie popcorn. He drove his tongue back and flexed his digits inside Silas. He only moved them a few millimeters, up and back, to pet the inside carefully.

"Oh, that." Silas hissed and pushed back. He turned his face to the opposite angle and kissed in kind, reached behind Trip's head to pull their lips together. He bent his knees more and whined at the back of this throat.

Trip crouched and twisted his arm a bit to keep the fingers where they needed to be. Again he flexed them and wrung a hoarse bark out of Silas. He flexed his wrist and pressed directly into Silas's fundament while he massaged the little nut from the inside, fucking his barbarian with two hooked digits.

"*Whoa*-ohh." Silas dropped his head to the side to gasp for breath and cry out. He braced his legs and pushed down harder to ride the hand. "Ohh! Wait! Naw!" His eyes went white and wide in shock. "Making me—"

Trip reclaimed his lower lip, sucked at it, tasting his tongue. "Nnnph."

"Trip? It's too—" Silas battled for breath like a gladiator strung for whipping. His thighs quaked and his fists lost hold of the edges of Trip's coat and twitched in the air, clawing at Trip's T-shirt to expose the skin underneath. "You."

Trip twisted the hand and drove straight upward into the spot, skewering Silas implacably and staring directly into his eyes. Silas's quads quivered and his joint stabbed the air between them. Trip pressed as close as he could, as close as he dared. He could feel Silas's heart galloping.

Silas howled low against his chest. The wet rumble echoed in the dim entryway. His hands shook and his eyes shut and he rose all the way up on his barbarian-booted tiptoes and braced his arms on each of the vestibule walls. "Gah! *Eesh*.... No-no—"

And for one perfect defenseless instant, he owned Silas and Silas owned him and they both knew-knew-knew it for the first fierce time like light flashing in a dark cave to render them weak and invincible.

Thwit-thitit-thwit. Silas spasmed around his fingers, and pleasure boiled out of him onto them both.

Molten wetness lashed Trip's arm and soaked into his T-shirt until the stickiness striped his belly. Semen dripped to the threshold around their feet like hot vanilla butter.

"No. No." Silas shuddered against the door, choking and moaning in animal satisfaction. "Ho.... *Man*." He sagged and smiled. "Oh, Trip." He couldn't seem to lift his head. "You made... me."

Gingerly, mindful of the abraded skin, Trip eased his fingers free and stole another smooth kiss. "Don't know what that was."

"Made me." Settling gradually, Silas regarded him with total boneless surrender. He opened his mouth and shut it. "No idea." He breathed hard and smooth, as if he'd run a race.

"Good?"

Silas chuckled silently and got his legs under him. He scooped the load from his leg and wiped it on his solid, fuzzy chest. He tasted the slick fingers. "That wasn't supposed to happen that way. Tonight."

Trip stopped fidgeting. "Meaning you didn't want to." He fought the awkward urge to flee or faint.

"Trip.... No." Silas took a deep breath and released it. "Meaning, it's all I've thought about since the zombie run. I been trying to act a gentleman and not jump your bones."

"I jumped you." Trip'd been caught completely off guard. *The hell was I thinking?* Silas left him stunned and stupid.

Silas clasped his forearms. "Sure did. *Juh*." He slid down the door until he knelt on the little stone stoop. He leaned forward and lapped the streaks of cum off Trip's arm with his flat tongue. Then he did the same with Trip's shirt and the skin of his belly, sucking it nearly dry and clean.

"Whoa!" As he watched Silas's patient sleepy submission, Trip worried he might bust without anything touching his cock. He held his jittery hands open, his eyes wide, almost terrified by the sensation.

When Silas stood and craned up to kiss him, Trip tasted briny nectar, their mouths loose and soft together. Silas had short-circuited him again.

"Can't... think." Silas fumbled at Trip's basket. "You taste so good."

"Oh-kay." Trip blushed, defenseless. He pulled back to reclaim control. Their surroundings swam back into view along with his anxiety. His boner hurt now, and it wouldn't go down. His balls had drawn so high up, he was racking himself. "It's okay."

"You kidding? Now you got me crazy for it. You. All my grown-up control shot to shit." Silas ran a broad palm over the ridge of flesh behind Trip's zipper. "Please. Please let me." He licked Trip's jaw.

Trip hissed in pain. "Blue balls."

"Oh!" Silas stilled and straightened. "Oh man, that's my fault. Please lemme. I had to jerk off twice before I met you so I didn't—"

"Molest me in the street?" Trip quirked his mouth. "Same! Three times since this morning, and a lotta good it did me."

Silas licked his plump lip. "I can handle that beast for ya."

"No doubt." Trip laughed as he resisted the urge to lose control again so soon. "But I should get home. I'm trying to do this right." He took one wobbly step back. "Gonna turn me into a sex demon."

Silas sighed hard and adjusted his costume so he was semidecent. "Me too. God." His sticky chest rose and fell, rose and fell. "Don't you wanna come up? I'll be a gentleman." The air between them smelled briny. He pressed a hand over Trip's heart. "Or at least I'll try real hard." His puckish eyes made it sound so reasonable.

I can trust him.

"Mr. Goolsby." Trip cleared his throat and spoke the words almost formally. "I would like to see you again, if that would be acceptable."

"Aw, man. I wanna see you right now." Silas blinked, and he squeezed himself. "Hi."

"Hi." Trip grinned at his eagerness. "Okay. Yeah. But after shaking the bottle, I think coming upstairs and trying to keep the cap on might not be the most grown-up idea."

"Debatable." Silas looked disappointed and anxious. "That was the best… date I ever had, Mr. Spector. In my whole dumb life."

"So let's have another."

"Yes, please."

Trip straightened his clothes, secretly proud of the spooge on his jacket. "I'm not vanishing. I wanna get to know you, is all. Like a person." That sounded weird. "You know what I mean."

"'Kay." Silas's twang sounded thick as honey now, whether from exhaustion or horniness. *Interesting.* He didn't seem aware of how Alabama he sounded, and Trip loved the lazy rhythm too much to point it out. "Feel like a new man."

"I liked the old one." Trip descended one step, hating to walk away but knowing it was the right decision. The evening had discombobulated him, and he couldn't trust himself. "When can I see you?"

Silas's answer was instant. "Any time."

"Really?"

"Yes." Silas sounded adamant. "If I have anything, I'll cancel it."

Trip grinned as he went down another two steps against his will, ashamed and exulted by what he'd just done. Just to be safe, he'd wait a few days to call. "Thank you, sir."

"You are absolutely welcome, sir," Silas called after him and laughed. "Don't postpone joy!"

Trip backed away, slowly. His balls felt like they were being crushed in a wine press. His dick had rubbed itself raw.

Silas scuffed his boots in the dark doorway. "Can I get one more, Mr. Spector?"

"More than one." Trip stopped, still shell-shocked. "But one now to tide me over." He beckoned with his head, and Silas came right to him and wrapped himself around Trip so that he felt the delicious stickiness and the He-Man harness pressed between them.

Silas cupped the aching bulge in Trip's pants and put his mouth to Trip's ear. "You think you can save yourself?"

Heart... beat.

"Nah." Trip met his gaze. "But I bet you can."

7

SILAS had a gift for monsters. Scaring people, getting under their skin, gave him *joy*.

The morning after *Catwoman* and Trip and that crazy good-night kiss, Silas wanted to sleep in, maybe sculpt all day. Instead he caught the 6:00 a.m. production shuttle from Rockefeller Center out to Silvercup.

The production designer knew Silas because the same agent repped them. To the delight of everyone's bills and budgets, Showtime had ordered a twelve-episode season three that cost a little over a million-per to produce. *Undercover Lovers* was about two detectives having an extramarital affair while busting up warring crime families. Sleazy as a bus station toilet, but it paid on time.

Silas leafed through the call sheet in the crisp air.

This outfit was a small production company used to working on the cheap, a step up from *Baywatch* but not exactly *Boardwalk Empire*. Still, it was TV, and a recent show on his résumé gave him street cred.

Silas just wanted to work. FX makeup had nowhere near the homo population glamor did. Beauty artists attracted a whole different clan, way gayer with an alien lexicon and skill set. He knew how faces worked, bones and muscles and shadows. He could make any model generically pretty, but fashion was beyond him and interested him not at all. On the other hand, he could crank out realistic pincers or an articulated eyestalk in nine hours.

At security, he waved to one of the showrunners. Francesca, her name was—scrappy, beautiful, Italian, and no-fucking-nonsense. She had a knack for upgrading the B-unit footage and a habit of covering for late actors, which guaranteed her popularity in the ranks. She'd end up an executive producer in a couple of years.

"They're waiting on Benita Luiz." She flicked through papers on her clipboard without raising her eyes as they walked and spoke. "*You* lit out of here yesterday...." She let the subject dangle.

"Friend." He prayed she'd let it drop.

As he watched, she tried on a few smiles to see which fit before she looked up at him patiently.

"Okay, kind of a date. No, it was a date." Silas had turned into a seventh grader at recess.

They reached the makeup trailer and stopped.

"Good?" Francesca's question sounded sincere, respectful.

Silas let a slow grin flare on his face. "So good."

She winked, but her face stayed serious.

Speaking of.... Silas dug in his pocket to check his phone. The screen was a spider web of cracks because he constantly dropped it and slammed it into things, but it kept on ticking despite the licking.

Trip still hadn't called.

Only the accidental orgasm worried Silas. He'd tried to be a gentleman. He was so used to hooking up immediately that this dating thing was *terra incognita*. At the same time, if they were gonna date like grown-ups, dressing up as He-Man and then getting finger-fucked on his stoop might not have been the classiest option.

How did adults date anyway? Tricking he could do. He had random booty calls and fuckbuddies out the hoo-hah. But exchanging names, meeting for dinner, having adult conversations that didn't involve inches or kinks... and he'd sailed off the edge of the map. *Here be dragons.*

"'Sup, *pa*." A lean gaffer smoking near the video village monitors nodded hello. Mexican, maybe, in his early twenties with a shredded eight-pack and a dinged Leatherman clipped on his belt. He rotated his head to exhale smoke in a rush.

Silas clocked him, bandana to boots. He'd slept with plenty of bi-curious techies. The gaffer sized up Silas casually and lipped the cigarette again. A wad of tackle pressed against his left pant leg.

Great secret of every movie set: techies were the best lays, hands down. Hot as hell, most of them, and way more gritty-interesting-fun than actors. They didn't scramble to get in front of every camera, and they tended to be pretty buff and clever. And since Silas spoke fluent geek, gay didn't factor much. He'd take sweaty tattoos and a goatee over caps and a chemical tan any day.

Normally, Silas would have ambled over, eyed the chunk of meat hanging loose under the gaffer's ripped jeans, and planted the small-talk seeds of a *chorizo* lunch break. He knew a bi-for-now offer when he saw one. Instead, Silas dropped his gaze and kept walking, his head full of Trip and that good-night kiss with benefits. *What are you doing?*

He unlocked the door to the trailer and climbed inside its warmth. The big five-station units were bigger than the cramped location trailers. Because the show had a small crew, the extra stations became holding pens for actors in the assembly line, giving them a place to park it while their magical gloop dried, set, and gelled.

Silas ignored the closed door and decided the Mexican gaffer wasn't that cute. Besides, today was gonna be a busy day. *Yeah.*

"Paul." Silas bowed his head at a stocky guy with a scraggly mustache and a backward baseball cap bending over a big hardware box.

Paul was one of the show's longtime artists—fast and economical with his applications, not to mention very respectful with young ladies. He added Silas for prosthetics whenever he could. His wife, Tiffany, had worked the New Year's OutRun.

"We were worried you mighta eloped." Paul took off the cap and settled it back on his hair. "You cleared out of here like shit through a Shriner."

"Yesterday? Yeah." So everyone on set knew Silas had had a date. *Great.* "I had to get to a screening." He did not say it had been *Catwoman.*

Heading farther into the trailer to avoid further questions, Silas started loading up his airbrushes immediately at two different stations. Filming an accident this scale, reds and purples were gonna go fast. Ditto silicone, so he prepped the PlatSil compounds in two buckets so he could mix quickly when the background talent started pushing through. When doing this many burned extras, the important point was to convey a general impression of charred mayhem without getting bogged down in details.

Fair or not, most of the "background talent" would end up in the dark edges of every shot like scorched human throw pillows. Odds were this would be a high point in their careers and "Charred waitress" would be their biggest credit on IMDb.

TV folks always bent over backward to find ways to blow up buildings and get everyone's tits out... but on a shoestring budget and in a family-friendly way. Like Lawrence Welk for sadistic juvies.

Suit-itis. Studio executives lived in mortal terror of new ideas, but they could only get ahead by taking horrible risks.

Narrow shoulders. Narrow bias. Narrow view.

Silas rummaged in the cabinet for the drums of TraumaSkin FX, both the pre-burnt and pre-blood, to skip the need for a base coat. Running thirty extras in this little time, he needed all the help he could get. Mixing additional pigment and flocking into the silicone cut his painting time to a third.

Paul spoke firmly. "Nothing too grim. And no exposed bone." Finger wag. "A little blood is okay. Some contusions. But these ladies are strictly background."

Silas left the buckets stewing and went back to his stations.

His pocket buzzed and Silas checked his phone. *Not Trip.* Kurt couldn't meet later because he had a "Z meeting," whatever that meant. So not only had Silas blown their date, he couldn't get drunk and obsess about it with his best friend the way he wanted.

"Boys!" A busty starlet in a black robe waved hello, and Silas waved back as she stepped up into the trailer in satin mules. He had a major soft spot for Leigh Ann because she resembled a hot Sunday school teacher but flirted like a gangster's moll.

Paul patted his chair and got her settled. She had long purple pieces sewn into her silky brown mane and a fake dragon tattoo across one creamy breast and around her throat. Silas assisted with the silicone piece for her left eye. Applying the PlatSil directly, he built up charring across her jawline onto her neck and the swell of her cleavage but mainly stayed out of Paul's way.

Makeup occupied a funny gray area on a film set because it was a visual medium. They were below-the-line crew but literally in the actors' faces and privy to every private moment, more than the director or costars, even. Makeup artists existed somewhere between therapist and terrorist, surgeon and janitor. A great makeup team kept the cast balanced and on time, sent them out looking fabulous and ready to catch lightning in a can.

"Here she is." Paul beckoned. "Ms. Luiz."

A slim girl wearing an orange kimono leaned into the trailer. Benita was gorgeous, light brown skin and sly doe eyes, but looked all of sixteen.

Leigh Ann waved and they puckered a hello kiss at each other.

Silas scanned the call sheet again and the words "Sex Bomb" at the top. *Please tell me I'm not supposed to make this sweet kid into a mangled hooker.* He kept his smile level.

"No worries. I'm the goody-two-shoes red herring caught in the crossfire." Benita shook her head.

Silas relaxed.

"Everyone gets to wear spangles and thongs but me. And I'm a trained ballroom dancer. So dumb." Benita's face crumpled in irritation.

Francesca poked her head in from the cold and tossed a brown paper bag at Benita. "Bagel, butter!"

Silas leaned back just in time.

"Fran!" Benita caught the bag. "Saving me, girl."

"By the way, it's official: your boyfriend died in the shootout." Francesca mimed cutting her throat and grimaced.

Silas whirled, horror-struck.

"Character, not life." Francesca shrugged.

"Fitness model." Leigh Ann twisted to comment. "He asked for a raise."

"Idiot. I warned him." Benita held her eyes toward the ceiling as Silas brushed adhesive onto her lower lid. Already the silicone was starting to set up, so Silas sculpted a little scabbing and thinned the edges.

All three women nodded sagely. Television was no country for weaklings or whiners.

Benita turned to him. "Can I wash my hands?" She stood and put the unwrapped bagel on her seat.

A couple of the walk-ons had hunkered down with their iPods and crosswords on the cramped breakroom couch in case they could get through makeup early. Poor closeted Barney rustled his newspaper in greeting; they hadn't run into each other since New Year's, but obviously he'd kept the candle burning.

As Silas tested the airbrush trigger, his phone *may* have buzzed again in his pocket, but he didn't check it. *Be cool.* If Trip called, he didn't need to reply instantly. And his agents knew where he was if it was a gig.

"Hi, Sigh."

Fuck. A skinny blond boy stood at his station and dissected Silas with his gray-green gaze.

When they'd dated, Lance Tibby had been a day player on a soap: icicle thin with a serrated tongue. Because of his androgyny, leads were out of his grasp, but he earned a steady paycheck in cable and indies playing pervs, flakes, and weasels. Nothing permanent, but enough to keep him in Botox and Emporio Armani.

Lance perused himself in the mirror for a long moment. "I saw your name on the sheet." His mouth smiled, but his eyes didn't. "Been ages."

"Couple years at least." They'd dated summer into fall on a sitcom shoot in Vancouver, back when Silas hadn't known better than to believe what lanky bastards from South Dakota said when they were seven inches deep. "Look great, man."

"You know me. Thirty-two and can't keep weight on." He studied the mirror again.

Silas frowned. What the fuck-a-*duck* had he been thinking? Easy to get sucked into casual hookups on set. Sometimes the makeup trailer was the only climate-controlled space for fifty miles and any shoot was 90 percent waiting around.

"Sigh...?" Lance scrutinized him dismissively. "If you need a gym, I could sign you into my hotel. It's a shithole, but they have an elliptical trainer."

Fuck you. "I live in Manhattan."

Lance rubbed his taut belly, raising his shirt. "Crafty is hell on a six-pack." He stared pointedly at Silas's beefy midsection.

Craft services provided all the snacky crap on a set and consequently most of the calories on any shoot: anything from Dr Pepper and muffins to fresh-squeezed papaya and olive tapenade, depending on the budget. Cost a fortune, but the cushier the crafty, the happier the shoot. Smart actors steered clear because they had to mind their inches, but the rest of crew grazed nonstop like starving elk.

"You griping about our eats again, Tibia?" Stepping out of the bathroom, Benita raised her voice just loud enough that the whole trailer heard it. Her top-of-show billing put her about four rungs above Lance's glorified walk-on as a dealer.

Which was exactly why Silas loved working actresses. Survivors, every fucking one of them, and protective of their posse.

"Nope. The food's delish, Benita."

She puckered her lips at Silas. "Who wants to fuck a coat hanger? Am I right?"

Lance wiped his hands and backed away, making for the door. "Gotta scoot."

The ladies cackled in their chairs.

"Thirty-two! We sang medleys on cruise ships seven years ago, and Tibby was thirty-two *then*, giving the closet cases crabs." To their credit, nobody looked toward Barney, hidden behind his newsprint. Benita side-eyed Silas while he scorched her temples with a sponge. "Please."

"We gotcha back," Leigh Ann chirped and pointed to Benita. "Love her!"

Silas grinned and bowed a little to Benita. He felt better already. "I thank you, ma'am."

"—Oiselle!" She beamed. "You made me so pretty, I hadta get brave."

Paul beckoned. "Benita, right here." He waved her over and helped Leigh Ann to her feet.

"I gotta get outta this goody-two-shoes gulag." As Benita stood, she chewed a mouthful of bagel and swallowed. "My manager told me that if they don't let you use handcuffs or a stripper pole, you end up in SyFy original movies." She huffed and crossed her arms.

Leigh Ann exhaled grimly and sat down. She now wore three sets of fake eyelashes. "Or worse. Reality television. Gag." She peeped at Silas in the mirror to include him in the thought. "Which are justa fancy name for fucking game shows with models and train wrecks." Silas snorted in agreement. "Gotta be gorgeous, trashy, or both. You think Cate Blanchett ever worked on *Price is Right*? Bullshit."

"I never thought of it that way." Actually, he had, often, but actresses had the most hideous, degrading jobs on any set, so he did any fucking thing he could to validate them.

Leigh Ann smiled like Christmas. "Hey, at least I gotta shot playing an exploding lap dancer for two episodes. I'm on camera shaking my ya-yas. I'ma look smoking hot and tragic in flashbacks. Season finale, I'm even on the slab inna morgue." She squenched her girlish face in distaste. "But the day I book a game show?" Her willow-green eyes brimmed with scorn. "Hell, stick a fork in me, I'm done."

Silas used his fingers to smooth the flat line toward her temples, contouring her cheekbones for the neon and exaggerating the beautiful slope of her eyelids so that she looked like a Hungarian princess.

Leigh Ann sounded almost asleep. "You here next week too, babe?"

"Naw." Silas raised his brow fretfully. "I gotta run to Florida for a drug commercial and two weeks later some Western miniseries out in Phoenix."

His cell phone sat on the counter, silent as a cinderblock. Unable to stop himself, he glanced. He had imagined the call. *First time I want a guy to call me back and he's not gonna.*

For a long stretch, the trailer fell silent except for the hiss of his airbrushes and Paul humming as he daubed.

Silas heard a sound. Barney sat staring at him. He'd forgotten the closeted actor had parked there behind his paper wall, beating time to death. Maybe he hoped Silas was horny enough to bite.

Thank you, God, for not letting me be a closet case.

Trip hadn't called, and this asshole wouldn't give up. Silas sighed. He frowned at his phone. Maybe Trip was trying to play it cool.

Leigh Ann murmured, face immobile as a ventriloquist. "He hassling you?"

For one unsettling moment, Silas thought she meant Trip, but she blinked at Barney's hangdog face in the mirror. "Barney? Hush." Silas chided her. "He's a married man."

With an anxious air, Barney watched them watching him, but he stayed safely tucked into the sofa behind his upside-down paper.

Leigh Ann pursed her slick damson pout and considered his unsecret admirer. "Hun, you probably said something in passing, let Pinocchio feel human for the first time in his life." She peeked over the other shoulder. "Now he just sniffs around like you can make him into a real live boy toy."

Silas wiped his hands on the towel over his shoulder. "Funny thing is, I don't flirt with him. I don't take the bait, ever. He never gives up."

"He should know better." Leigh Ann lowered her voice conspiratorially. "You can only fuck your way to the middle. Pamela Anderson is never gonna win an Oscar in a tearaway dress."

He leaned close. "I love her. She's like the *happiest* ho-bag."

"Yeah, sure." She clucked in approval. "But dig, Angelina Jolie gets just as naked and trashy, but she didn't try to climb the ladder on her damn back." She sighed. "And Mama's at the Oscars every year on Brad's arm in vintage Valentino."

"Truth." Silas used a sable brush to float translucent powder over her face. "Just taking the shine down a little."

"I'm just saying...." She stole another glance at Barney, who stole his own glances. "You can do better than Teletubby over there."

"Thanks. I have. I mean, I'm seeing somebody. A couple times, now." *Fingers crossed.*

She softened. "Yeah?" Her girlish voice teetered on the edge of *Is he dreamy?*

"He's an artist. Comic books."

"Aww. Congrats." She scanned herself in the mirror, tipping her head as his hands moved. "My guy is a scientist. Engineering. And now he's in media research. Smart as hell, and he can write the Japanese kanji with his tongue." She winked and the triple lashes made it look like spiders fucking. "Always bet on the nerd."

He choked on a laugh.

"—walking in as we speak." Francesca pulled open the door. She pressed her headset close to her ear. She nodded an unspoken question at Paul; he bowed a little and whipped the smock off Benita.

The actress stood and curtsied to Silas before she joined Francesca.

Leigh Ann pointed at her and grinned in approval.

"We're on our way now." Francesca covered the mic and then whispered at Paul and Silas, "Im-fucking-possible. Ten minutes? That is some rock-star shit, boys." A big smile as she held the door for Benita to step down. Brisk air swirled into the trailer. Paul followed so he could help his wife with touch-ups under the lights. "Unreal."

Once the coast was clear, Silas crouched beside Leigh Ann and murmured, "Tell you what, doll. I seen the call sheet. If they're starting Benita's setups, you and me can swipe a little extra time. Pump the body paint and place one big, beautiful cut so you still look extra-heartbreaking. Every minute on camera is more for your reel, right?" He scoffed and tested the trigger of the airbrush. *Phht-pssst.* "Neutron bombshell."

"Silas, you are the fucking best." Leigh Ann lowered her chin and batted her eyelashes at him. Her expression might have come off sultry except for the split lip he'd painted and the dramatic swelling he'd glued around her socket. *Battered Aphrodite.*

Secret of all showbiz success: back-scratching. He made actors gorgeous and they remembered him as a good egg, which paid off the next time they worked together, maybe. Like his dad used to say, "Plant ten seeds and the twelfth comes up." A couple would sprout, most would fail, but any one of them might be the unicorn-jizz jackpot for his career.

As his teachers at Savini had said: *If you don't like it, go work in a fucking cubicle.*

Silas angled Leigh Ann back in the chair and laid on the kind of detail he loved best. Rich teal and crimsons. Heliotrope to pick up the streaks in her hair. After twenty or thirty minutes, he stopped to take a swig of water and dig out his phone. No text. No call. Maybe he had completely misread Trip's reaction on the stoop.

Then he noticed that Leigh Ann was peering at him, a drowsy smile on her face.

"It's not the paint. Y'know?" She raised one sloping lid. "You make us all feel brave."

"Bullshit." But the praise made him proud.

"I walk out on that set, and I can fucking leap tall buildings in a single lap dance." Leigh Ann rocked to her feet and preened in the mirror. "Voodoo." The long lines of color turned her taller and tragic.

Silas stared at the dark, cracked screen of his phone.

"You waiting for a call?"

He shrugged, sheepishly.

"He will. You watch."

Silas chuckled. "How do you figure that?"

"I bet you made him brave too." She spun for his inspection, then extended her hand. "You think they're ready for me?"

"Lady." He gave her a fist bump. "They won't know what hit 'em."

AFTER *Catwoman* and the astonishing kiss on the stoop, Trip spent all Friday doing the comic book equivalent of doodling hearts and flowers in his binder: snacking and napping, jerking off, and drawing his demon.

Silas leaked into all his Horny Bastard sketches, and the two blurred and simmered together. Trip spent all day killing time until he got to gossip about his date with Jillian and the rest of her brood.

The Stones didn't keep kosher, didn't go to services, didn't bother sending Max to Hebrew school... but after they'd started their family, Ben and Jillian had kept up the tradition of open-invite Shabbos dinner every Friday night as a way of staying in touch with their friends.

Ben and Jillian had pronounced Trip an unofficial "uncle" before Max was born, and Trip ate takeout at their house most Friday nights.

They always said having a kid was "like immigrating to Canada." All new parents were sorta nearby, spoke English still, and they dressed the same, but you never saw them and they seemed to have this secret understanding of their new countrymen. Shabbos guaranteed that any friends who wanted to stay in touch with the Stones could invite themselves over, no questions asked.

Tonight, they'd finished eating around eight, and laughter floated down the hall. Ben and Max still dried dishes with the *Rocky and Bullwinkle* tea towels Trip had given the family as an ironic christening gift. Father and son gave instructions to each other in pig latin and gargling.

Jillian and Trip sat on the sofa nursing cocktails in the yellowish glow of the family room where the Stones spent most of their time. The room was a Salvation Army mishmosh of ratty chairs and kitschy ornaments found at flea markets: a fake Tiffany mushroom lamp, a basket of beaded vegetables, a bust of George Bernard Shaw.

He wanted to spill the entire date and pick it apart with Jillian, but the telling would hurt Ben if he didn't hear and Max had no interest in his stunted love life.

In the meantime, Trip confessed his new comic idea. Horny Bastard still felt vague, but with the nine-year-old safely scrubbing plates in the other room, Trip fished out his sketchbook and showed her his rough studies.

"Bullshit! You filthy pig." Jillian squealed and wiggled her fingers like an amateur magician as she grilled him breathlessly. "A sex demon? How many issues? You think Big Dog will publish it?"

Ahem.

"Not exactly." Trip took a burning gulp of scotch he'd regret later. "Funny thing… Cliff bought *Campus Champions* and gave the project away. So now I have time for this big fella." He patted the Horny Bastard page.

"He *what*?" Jillian's rage drained the blood from her face.

"'S'fine." In truth, so much had happened since New Year's that Trip had forgotten he'd never told her about Cliff hijacking his idea. He'd been too embarrassed when it happened and then too caught up in Silas and his sexy new project. "I'm over it now. We don't have to talk about it."

Jillian opened and shut her mouth. She'd always had a bias against Cliff. She wasn't a gay guy, so she just didn't understand the enticing closet-case tension or Trip's willingness to hold out hope. Hell, Cliff bragged about bagging a fellow fratboy or two after a couple of gins. From her perspective, the *Campus Champions* fuck-over probably appeared inevitable: evil frosting on a five-tiered cock-teasing villainy cake. "Do you need me to be a nag hag right now?"

"No. I'm punishing myself plenty. Rina forced me to come up with a kind of career plan." He indicated the sketchbook.

"Oh, kiddo. Thank fuck you came for Shabbos." Jillian pressed her hand to her forehead and stared at him balefully, but thankfully did not push further. "Forget Staplegun." She crossed her legs on the seat. "It wouldn't hurt for you to, y'know, go out with someone nice."

"Funny you mention it…. In other news—" Trip smiled. "—my date was awesome." He glanced at the kitchen knowing Ben would want to hear this.

"F'real!" She applauded and scooted closer. "The zombie?"

"Well, last night he was a barbarian." Trip leaned sideways and pretended to confess a dirty secret. "He dressed up as He-Man for the movies. It was with this crazy fan group." How to explain the Nerd Herd and *Catwoman* to straight people? "A comic book thing."

"He's a dork!" Jillian shouted it, the way a soap opera nurse might cry "It's a boy!"

"Apparently."

She squeezed his hand. *Marco.* He squeezed back. *Polo.*

Silas felt more impossible with each day that passed. Still, the memory of that slow-motion warmness kept Trip from freaking out too much. "He's sexy and he does creature makeup. We saw *Catwoman.*"

"Interesting. A filmed entertainment of trashy genius." Jillian stroked her imaginary supervillain beard with slow fingers. "Is he a *sheygitz*?"

Non-Jewish guy, she meant. The word could mean any gentile who had the sturdy blond outsider-ness Jews found endlessly fascinating, seductive, and a little insulting.

"I don't care about that shit." Frankly, Trip never thought of himself as Jewish. "Hell, you're only Jewish by marriage." Consequently, Jillian had a soft spot for Jews losing their hearts to gorgeous outsiders.

"Amaze-balls." She lowered her lashes suggestively. "He's some big strapping buck who can bench-press a car and goes shark fishing in a thong. Good. You need someone who isn't a neurotic Jew."

Ben and Trip had been a dynamic Jew duo since middle school: Trip the skinny queer with inkblot knuckles and Ben the swarthy jock who always went to the right parties and took the smart shortcuts. After college they'd gotten a lot closer when they'd moved into Manhattan as roomies with no money between them.

Trip had stood as best man at the wedding, and Jillian became one of his closest gal-pals after he airbrushed reptile scales onto her for a high school reunion that ended with them drinking Midori out of the bottle in the women's powder room and dressing Max up as a miniature Hellboy for his first Halloween.

The floorboards creaked as someone came down the hall from the kitchen and into the cluttered living room. Ben leaned against the doorframe and wiped his hands on his jeans.

Jillian tapped her nose and pointed at Trip emphatically. "Zombie date." She poured a few more fingers of amber perfection into Trip's tumbler. "We'll discuss after bedtime."

Max came down the hall, spattered with dishwater but jolly.

Jillian raised her hand as her boy wonder passed by. "What's shakin', bacon?"

Max gave her five. "Not much, eggs." He walked the loop of the living room, then headed for the hall again.

Trip smiled at his godson. Hard to believe he'd ever been small enough to hold in one hand. "Where y'going?"

"Room." Max shrugged. "I gotta do homework. And sleep."

"If you say so." Ben regarded his son with proud detachment.

Jillian frowned and went to Max. "What homework? You're in fourth grade!"

Ben countered calmly, "He has a project. Extra credit."

"But Trip is here and he'd like to see you." One perfect eyebrow floated up. Jillian could maim bystanders with her eyebrows.

Max pivoted to Trip and bugged his eyes out, and Trip bugged back. "There! He saw me. And I saw him. And we saw each other seeing each other. May I be excused?"

"No problem." Trip high-fived him. He tried to remember being that small and believing your parents knew everything. *When did I grow up?* As a little boy, he'd wanted to escape his father's boring suburban friends so he could run upstairs to read *Sandman* or *Vampirella*.

"Homework?" Jillian sulked. "Don't you wanna watch *Hellraiser?*"

"No, Mom. I need to get to bed early."

"Let'm go, Jilly. 'S'totally normal. We're grown-ups and he's bored." Ben nodded with his son as if this was something they'd debated at length.

Jillian crossed her arms and *hmmphed*. "Okay. I'm just trying to be your mom." She crouched so she and her little boy were face to face. "Honey, don't you want a tattoo?" She seemed serious.

"Gross. No." Max glanced at his dad. "I wanna be a doctor." He held up some book with a bright photo of a tree frog on its cover. "A doctor has t'know science."

Seemed logical to Trip, but he wasn't a parent or Jillian.

"That's so unfun. I want you to have fun." Her forehead wrinkled and she touched his hair.

"Science is fun." Max looked at his dad again. "To me, science is fun." Ben blinked at him in Dad-code; apparently there had been some kind of pep talkage before Trip arrived. Max snuck a look-see at Trip, and Trip smiled supportively although he'd rather have a back-alley colostomy in Siberia than study a periodic table.

"Just remember. You cannot go to medical school until you have been arrested at least twice." Jillian kept hoping Max would cave in and become a rock star or join a circus, but nothing doing. His diligence unsettled her. Her panic mounted as he won spelling bees and turned in his straight-A assignments on time… early even.

When Trip brought home his first comic to show his parents, his mother had twisted her Kleenex into yarn while he flipped the pages. His father had sighed and asked when he was going to find a real job. "Something steady, like advertising." He would've given anything to have folks who wanted him to take risks, while Max would probably love Trip's fussy parental robots.

No grass is greener.

Max stacked a pile of books on the coffee table into a careful pyramid that reached his chest. "You're supposed to tell me I can do anything if I'm gonna end up… normal."

"You'll end up dead under some doughnut truck." Jillian favored her son with a pitying smile. "Or in a cubicle."

Max scowled. "I will not. Parents are s'posedta support my dreams." As soon as he said the word, he blushed and shut his mouth, blinking rapidly.

"Ugh! *Dreams*?" Jillian froze, and her face drained. Her eyes blazed like a horror heroine. "Gross. Says who?"

Trip glanced at Ben.

Ben shook his head and started at the ceiling. "Jilly——"

She braced herself against the sofa and wall in revulsion. "Max Stone, have you been watching *television* again?" Her disdain made the word a synonym for "vomit cupcakes."

Max looked miserable. "Dr. Phil." He stared at the floor.

"Who isn't even a real doctor." Jillian scowled and pointed a short maroon nail at him. "And where are you watching shyster talk shows, anyways? I'm gonna have to call Arnel's dad. Besides, Dr. Phil's never been arrested, and would you want to marry him?" She shuddered. "Pleat-front khakis. Lima beans."

"No, Mom." Max leaned against his dad's knee. "You watch. I'm gonna go to prison, and then I'm gonna be a...." He took a little boy breath. "Lawyer."

Jillian's eyes twitched.

Ben whispered to his giggling son, who slid the knife in.... "A *tax* one."

"Auggh!" Jillian clutched her heart, and her eyes protruded as she pretended to die a rattling death as she pitched forward over the arm of the sofa. "*Urrrrgggkk....*" Her arms flapped and her face contorted.

Max bragged about his mother's stage deaths even more than her singing, which was saying something. She slid to the carpet to moan and thrash on the rug. She fell completely still.

"Mom. Mom?"

She flinched and drooled.

Max rolled his eyes. "Fine. Prison first, but with cable."

Jillian's eyelids popped open on the floor. "*Max*imum security." She paused for the groan. "Or just do something really crazy."

Max sighed. "Yeah. No."

Jillian sat up. "It's for your own good, mister. You gotta color outside the lines."

Trip tried to broker a truce. "Or draw them."

She wasn't having it. "It's important you learn how to improvise... well, think on your feet and make stuff up. Your dad agrees with me on this."

Ben glanced at Trip but kept his yap shut, wisely.

Max straightened his ziggurat of books. "I know what 'improvise' is."

Ben shrugged at his son. "Them's the rules, kiddo. Maybe you can become a televangelist."

Jillian pinched her husband. "That's not what I meant and you know it. How is he gonna be alive if he grows up on a couch and doesn't take risks?"

"You're awful." Max smiled and kissed his mother.

She kissed him back. "Well, lucky for me you're not."

"Nuts." Max sighed and gave Trip a fist bump. "G'night, Trip. Night, Dad." Max submitted to a squeeze from Ben and a kiss from his mom before clomping upstairs.

Trip watched him go. "Boy, did you two luck out."

Ben had already dragged the sketchbook closer and started flipping silently and slowly through the incubus sketches.

Jillian leaned over and whispered in her keeping-a-secret voice, "Having a kid is like having your heart walking around outside your body for the rest of your life."

Lonely thought. Trip would never have a kid, even if he managed to find a partner. With his neuroses, he could never take responsibility for another human's well-being. He couldn't even handle a pet. Or a plant, for that matter. Of course, if he said that out loud, Jillian would squawk things about surrogates and adoptions and all kinds of complicated shit, but the bottom line was: no one he'd ever love would have the equipment to make a baby without the involvement of other folks. Somehow, not being able to confess his inadequacy to his best friend left him even lonelier, as if his kidlessness and his careful silence on the subject amplified each other.

When Trip looked up, both Stones stared at him as if reading his eyes and his thoughts written there. He tried to smile. Ben slowly pawed through the Horny Bastard studies.

Before Trip could make any excuses or explanations, the phone rang and Jillian went to the kitchen to answer.

"Trip. These are…." Ben gawped at Trip as if staggered. "Genius."

"The character's still really rough."

Ben nodded sagely. "Big mojo, my man."

Trip shrugged. "Dirty, mainly."

"Nope. Wrong. And mongo dong."

"And insane."

"Gate of Horn, I'm telling you." Ben was a fanatic mythology buff in college. In the *Odyssey*, Homer described a gate built of ivory, where all the fake dreams came from, and then another gate, one built of horn, that let out true visions, like prophecies and inspiration. He ranked everything as ivory or horn.

"I'm still fiddling." Trip paged through the pencils and charcoals slowly.

"Horn." Ben wrinkled his nose rapidly in a convincing impression of a wine-tasting rabbit. "Big shiny horn, man. I can smell it."

"Eww." Trip fake-retched. "Can we not be so Freudian?"

"Totally a Gate of Horn idea. Can't you feel it?" Ben didn't have a creative bone in his body, but he loved being around artists. So whenever Trip had an authentic idea of his own, Ben was quick to give it the stamp of mythological approval and ladle encouragement over it. *Hero High* had never been anything but ivory, and they all knew it.

Jillian came back from the kitchen, and Ben pulled her into his lap. She fluttered her fingers around her husband's smiling face and spoke with a thick Slavic accent. "Listen to the Benjamin. The Stone knows."

Ben prodded his wife. "Young Master Spector has concocted a demon without trousers or undergarments."

"Indeed? I surmised as much."

Trip loved seeing them happy together but looked at the floor. "We'll see."

"And his dates were successful." Jillian held up her index finger. "With extra barbarian flavoring."

Ben scratched his head. "This is the...."

"Zombie." Ben, Trip, and Jillian intoned the word together, as a question, statement, and accusation respectively.

Trip pulled his legs up to his chest. "He's not a zombie."

"Barbarian." Ben flipped another incubus page.

"He-Man, not Conan." Jillian patted her husband's thigh. "Sorry."

"He was... I can't explain. Funny. Weird. Smart. Relaxing." Trip took a sip of scotch. "He said that what we're good at is *chutzpah*. Americans."

Jillian spun and goggled. "He said *chutzpah*?"

"No, but he meant it. I thought he was gonna be a buff bohunk with a bubble butt, but then he opens up and out pops this whole theory about pop culture and cultural imperialism."

"Say what?" Ben looked aghast.

Jillian looked aghaster.

"But not in a wacky, tacky way. He's hilarious and he listens. Really easy to talk to. He's—" Trip scrubbed his teeth with his lips trying to find the right word for everything the date had been. "Unforgettable. We got into this bizarre discussion about capes and comparative folklore. He's way brainier than I thought."

Jillian's eyes bulged like a sci-fi virgin tied to a doomsday device. "Your movie-magic muscle-Mary said this? During a—" She glanced at the ceiling where they heard her son creaking around. "—sex date?"

"No. We weren't…. Nothing like that."

"The *huh*?" She glared at him as though Trip had activated said doomsday device.

"Con-ver-sation…." Ben stroked *his* imaginary beard and peered at Jillian again, telegraphing something.

Trip shut his eyes and sighed. "There has been no full-on hankying *or* pankying. We saw a movie and I walked him home, that's all." Which was true-ish.

Ben gave him two thumbs up. "Ballsy play. I smell a winner." In classic hetero "it's perfect, you're both gay" logic, he always thought any guy who was polite to Trip would become the love of his life.

Jillian rubbed Ben's leg affectionately. "Ben was like a gold-medal dater. I'm telling you: I gave up showbiz because of his ninja dating skills."

Ben put on his paternal voice. "Is he a *mensch*?" As in, an all-around nice guy who does the right thing. When it came to type, mensches tended toward more noble "salt of the earth" than "spank me, yank me."

"I have no idea." Trip shrugged. *Lie.* Silas was a total mensch.

"Trip Spector." Jillian nudged him with her sockfoot. "I keep saying you need a nice mensch-y boyfriend instead of some cocksink. And if he's hot and a mensch, don't waste any time. A sexy mensch is a rare beast. Like a purple unicorn." Jillian swatted his arm. "And you said yes."

"Gross. I don't want to talk about my sex life with you."

Ben grinned. "Why not?"

"Not that." She glowered at him. "I mean when he asked you out again. Did you say yes?"

Trip frowned. "How do you know he asked me out again?"

She looked at Ben and then back. "Bitch, any man who discusses superhero sociology and talks you off a ledge on a sex date has intentions. Like, Jane *Austen* intentions."

Trip chewed on that. Did Silas have intentions? Well, they'd… waited, after all. Well, sort of. He'd screwed that up with the doorway-jism deal. At least it hadn't been a no-names hookup.

Ben patted his stomach, less firm and formed than the high school edition, but Jillian didn't seem to mind. Yet again Trip thought about how much easier it was to be a straight guy. "Full." Ben poured himself a short glass of seltzer and shook the last drops out of the bottle. "So you like him."

"Well, yeah. Sure. I guess." Trip thought of Silas's cocky grin, his scarred hands, and the golden stubble on his jaw. "I mean, it's like we're both wondering if it's friendly or serious."

"That's dating." Ben considered him quizzically. "If anybody wants to shack up before they know shit about you, *run*."

Jillian grumbled. "Spoken like a man."

"Spoken like a grown-up, Jilly-bean." Ben grinned.

She poked Trip. "This guy's in showbiz. You should take him to a black-tie thing."

"I don't need to wear a tux with Silas."

Ben pointed upstairs. "You could wear mine."

"No! What is it with that goddamn tux?" Trip smacked him. "He's dating other people too."

"He told you that?" Ben seemed surprised.

Trip rubbed his itchy eyes. "No. Not flat out told-told. Standard gay date rules. Silas is too handsome to not be dating people. He has a lotta exes."

Ben pulled an apologetic face. "Schmucko, people date. I mean, other people date, and that means they have romantic histories."

"But not romantic meat lockers. We keep running into them."

"So… he's auditioning for Mr. Right." Ben squeezed his shoulder.

Jillian scoffed, "You might have more exes if you'd actually, y'know, dated."

"That's not fair."

"Ohhh-kay." She favored Trip with a faint smile, as if humoring a supervillain dressed in lunchmeat. *Captain Baloney!* "The Unboyfriend has blocked your view. That's all. He's a shitty coping mechanism."

"Dad." Max stood at the foot of the stairs. "I'm ready to read to you." Every night Max read to Ben before bed. Family tradition.

Ben cocked his fingers and shot Trip with an imaginary bullet. "Back shortly. I wanna hear." He rose and pecked his wife, then followed his little boy upstairs.

When Trip looked back, he discovered Jillian staring at him.

"Cliff will always fuck you." She pulled a cushion into her lap. "But he is never gonna *fuck* you, y'know?"

"I don't know what you're talking about," he lied.

"Hey, guys fuck. And straight guys are never as straight as they pretend. Duh." The naughty smile on her face made him self-conscious. "I spent too many years in musical theater not to know what's what."

"Sure." He hugged himself, rested his glass on his bloated and rumbly stomach.

"No, listen. I'm not saying Ben would screw a dude, but I'm sure he's had his homo moments. Fucking is complicated. We aren't bugs."

"A few of us aren't."

"Touché." Another sip. "But some part of you believes that one day, Cliff's going to look up and see you and want you and love you and carry you away to his Tower of Power where he will—" She craned toward the stairs to make sure Max wasn't spying and lowered her voice to a whisper. "—hork your dork and watch *Smallville* reruns with you for the rest of time."

"Untrue." Trip popped another Benadryl, his second in as many hours, which was bad with the booze, but his itchy skin had begun to actually make him scratch.

"You do hope."

Trip scowled. "Fuck hope. Hope is a four-letter word. Cliff just signs my checks. He shot me down on the graphic novel." He waved a hand at her. "But *Hero High* pays for me to live my filthy, degenerate, homo-tastic life." Trip snorted and choked on the alcohol. "Cliff's just confused, I guess. Maybe he has issues. I have issues."

"Okay, you have an issue or two, but he's a fucking *magazine*. You ever think you might be misreading things?"

"Nah." He took another nip and savored the warmth that trickled into his gut. "One of these days the partnership could be more."

"I say this with love: nobody is a superhero. Okay?" She proceeded as if clipping wires on a bomb. "Listen. The night I met Ben, I was about to go on this tour. I mean, I met him at a Halloween party. We were all dressed as Japanese movie monsters." She tapped her own chest. "Mothra, *obv*iously. We made out for all of fifteen minutes, and then pow! I'm in motels all over the Midwest." Jillian had sung in musicals back then.

"I didn't know that." He knew they'd met as monsters, but not about her tour.

"I ignored everybody. Friends. My family. Professors. My own gut. Because I could be in a real show with a live audience that might make it to Broadway someday. *Could. Might.*" Again she tasted the words like rancid oysters.

"Pursuing your dream."

"Thanks, Dr. Phil. What a crock! I *knew* I should marry him. That first night I knew. I was so into Ben and vice versa, but I was twenty and I needed a gig and it was the lead. I had the chance to star as Dorothy in a nonunion musical version of *The Wizard of Oz*. Bus and truck tour of the flyover states."

He patted her knees in belated congratulations. "You never told me."

"I didn't." She took a swig of booze. "Because it was a fucking *shanda*: a complete shameful fraud. *Non*union, right? I mean, they paid me and it was a real tour, with buses and costumes, and I had curtain calls, but it wasn't based on the MGM movie at all because the sleazebag producers did it on the cheap. Whole cast was washups and nimrods who didn't know better with terminal egomania. Like yours truly." Jillian plopped into the brown velvet armchair she preferred.

"How did they get around lawsuits or whatever?" Trip squirmed into the sofa cushions, happily warm, buzzed, and with his best friend, hearing a humiliating anecdote. *Schadenfreude for the win!*

"By fudging the songs and the script. Original novel is public domain. They hired some lazy shnook to slop together a bunch of half-ass numbers to remind you of Judy Garland without landing them in court. They built the sets with duct tape and actual cardboard. I wore my own shoes onstage."

"I don't get it. He...." What did *The Wizard of Oz* have to do with Cliff being straight? "You were getting paid. You got to sing 'Over the Rainbow' right out of school, right?"

"That's my point. That's the deal right there!" She snorted. "The lyrics to my starring-role, no-budget, nonunion big ballad number went...." Her face lit up with vinyl perkiness. "*Some-where...*"—her crisp soprano fizzed out of her throat, Julie Andrews in steel-toed boots—"*...there's a land of lollipops and rainbows....*"

"Lollipops and rainbows?"

"Like you would *not* fucking believe." She took a thirsty swig of hooch.

"Eesh."

"Just enough words to remind you. Just enough overlap that the audience got the gist. Just enough that we couldn't get sued and the cast felt like assholes every time. Standing in my own fucking shoes." She drained the glass and shook her head, frowning and blinking her wet eyes. "Ben snuck out to Cleveland to see me anyways, because I was the lead and he couldn't stay away. But I couldn't even invite my parents."

"Sorry." He squeezed her hand. *Marco!* She squeezed back. *Polo!*

"So one night, this little girl comes backstage and asks if I'd forgotten the words. Six years old, maybe, but she loves the movie. I shake my head no and she starts singing 'Somewhere Over the Rainbow' in her perfect little voice, and I almost died of shame." She gave a chuff of nonlaughter and fake-shuddered. "I gave notice the next day. And Ben and I got married seven months later."

They sat silently for a few seconds and listened to the creak of Max's and Ben's footsteps overhead. The clock on the wall and the TiVo showed different times.

Trip broke the silence. "I don't get it. Cliff isn't a made-up person."

"Honey." She put a hand on his forearm and kept it there. "Cliff Stapleton the Third is the imitation of the real deal, and you know it. You've drawn yourself into a corner. Between your allergies and your art, you live in an airtight box."

A cold tickle of doubt wormed its way under Trip's ribs. Maybe he'd overreacted about the new book. Maybe they should trust each other because they were partners. Cliff was just focused. His dumb sex comic hadn't changed anything yet. Nothing was ruined. Every comic book needed a hero, a villain, and a secret identity.

Just don't make me a sidekick.

"You pray you're wrong and I'm wrong, but you know we're not." Jillian patted him firmly, like a horse. "Some corners you can't cut. Some days come once." She pointed at him. "And some night a six-year-old is gonna come in and remind you that anything that can be faked isn't worth faking."

Trip didn't say anything. He kept waiting for her to break or crack a joke. *Nothing doing.*

"I say this as your happy married friend. I am terrible at being alone. And for all the practice you have had, you are even worse at being alone." Quick shrug. "We both know plenty of people who will spend the next twenty years fucking around and making a wreck of their lives, but you are not built to hack that."

Was he? "Okay." Trip squeezed her hand.

Crick-crickkk-crick. Ben entered in his socks carrying a bottle of seltzer and tried to sit on Jillian's lap.

"Hey!" She shoved him onto the empty end of the couch and then pulled his socked feet onto her thighs.

"What'd I miss?" Ben leaned back into the cushions.

"Casual." Jillian jerked her head at Trip's disbelieving face. Again some kind of uncanny marital telegraph flickered between husband and wife, much to Trip's annoyance and awe.

"Yeah?" Ben stretched. "Huh."

Trip groaned. "Will you both stop the X-Men telepathy routine?"

Ben looked between them. The seltzer cap gave a slow hiss as he eased it open. "What lies are you telling him?"

"That I've sold out to a selfish prick tease." Trip scooted back to let him pass.

"Staplegun?" Ben crossed his arms. "Duh!"

"See?" Although Trip didn't know what he was asking them to look at.

Ben turned to Jillian, a smile roaming his face. "Anything good?"

She paused for effect and used her tongue to unfurl the word like a poisonous scarf. "Lollipops..." She spoke the word as a blessing. She closed her eyes and nodded like a Buddha. "And *rain*bows."

"*Gahhh.*" Ben gurgled in apparent terror. He wrenched his lips into a fish mouth and his eyes bulged. "Agh! Oh man, you can't imagine. That was—I still have nightmares 'bout that shit twelve years later." He shuddered.

"Benjy, I wasn't that bad." Jillian shoved him with her foot.

"You? Pfft." He shook his head firmly. "You were the hottest bitch in a pinafore ever came outta Kansas." He raised a hand to let it help tell the story. "No, I mean that song. It was so...." He swiveled to Trip. "Weird! Freaky, like I cannot explain.

Cardboard Oz. All these farting church ladies in the dark. And Jilly-bean would start singing about lollipops, and then little by little they'd start rustling and shuffling and they'd know they were suckers. Y'know?"

"I died every fucking time." Jillian pretended to hurl. "And they'd sit out there and applaud like their hands were made of wet Saltines. Like that phony-ass song was my fault." She closed her eyes and shook herself again.

Ben nudged his wife fondly. "And then she came home and rescued me from a whirlpool of J-Dating and ESPN." Big grin. He leaned close to her neck and smelled her skin. "For a life of *Friday the 13th* marathons, Volvo financing, and Hebrew Pokémon." He kissed her smile and sighed. "Heaven."

"Well," Jillian piped up, "better than lollipops and rainbows."

Trip chuckled. "High praise."

"And that is because Ben Stone—" She kissed his face. "—is my fucking spirit animal."

Her husband's eyelids were closed and peaceful. "A sloth." He sighed.

"Trip, you'll find your Mothra. And invite him over here." Jillian laced her fingers through his. "Better late than never." She smiled at their hands.

Ben inclined his head. "Hey, late is fine. Later is greater." He scratched at the back of the couch, almost but not quite touching Trip.

Since the coming-out speech in eleventh grade and Trip confessing his awful crush, Ben had always been a little funny about physical affection with him. Not mean or cold, but definitely drawing a clear line between their friendship and anything else. He could even flirt at times, as a joke, but he wasn't a cheater or even a little queer. At first Trip had resented it, but over time he'd learned to appreciate Ben's honesty and strength. He understood the hips-held-back, *thap-thap* straight-boy hugs. A lotta guys would have simply disappeared from his life, but Ben had included him completely and guarded their friendship from sexual tension. And Jillian kept dragging Trip out of his cave into the light of day.

Before the feeling slipped away, Trip smiled. "I love you guys."

Ben swung an imaginary tennis racket and mouthed a *smott* sound for the imaginary ball. "Back atcha, boy wonder."

Jillian punched his shoulder. "Who else is gonna gimme advice on how to massage my husband's butt-nut?" In a flash, she scooted away from Trip, giggling. Ben cracked up.

"Gross!" Trip gasped. "Bull!" He swatted at her with a pillow. "That is bullshit."

"So that's where…. Sweet!" Ben held a stubby hand up for a high five. "Thanks, man."

Trip threw a cushion at Ben, gagged, and grimaced. "Gah! *Eggh!*"

Jillian crowed. "Prostate cancer is no laughing matter."

"Hitting the headboard with your spratz is no laughing matter." Ben tried to look serious.

Trip shouted. "Augh!"

"Can you people please keep it down?" Max stood on the lowest step, exasperated and exhausted. Eye roll.

Jillian got ahold of herself first. "Sorry, booger."

"We're sorry. You're right, kiddo." Ben fought his smile into submission. Trip held up a hand by way of apology.

Max scowled at the grown-ups and stomped upstairs. From faraway they heard his nine-year-old voice mutter, "Not a booger," just before a door closed.

They busted into stifled snickers.

Trip sighed. His knotted stomach had eased a bit and his eyes had stopped itching. The Benadryl and whiskey had helped him calm the fuck down. He had his job. Cliff could still come through. He had a date with Silas next week. He had his crazy demon book to play with. Better that he fuck up than fuck off completely.

Jillian jostled him. "Just keep making all the wrong moves and you'll be fine."

8

TRIP was stuck at the staple.

He'd stalled out in the middle of his story where the staples held the comic book together.

Comics were often stapled right at climactic midpoints… and woe betide the writer who can't conquer that little piece of metal. He'd started pencilling the first twelve pages, at which point the story…stopped. In desperation, he went out to the fenced-in Fourth Street basketball court to sketch the guys in the Cage.

After some flirty texting back and forth, Silas was back in town. They'd planned a dinner date. With Trip's apartment only a couple of minutes' walk away, he'd told Silas to meet him at the court and then hunkered down to watch the last game of pickup before the park shut down for the night.

Even in January, the air was warm enough that the teams were Shirts versus Skins. Silas should have arrived a half hour ago, but he'd texted an on-his-way, so Trip had pulled out his book and doodled.

Sometimes on Saturdays Trip braved the streets and came down here to draw because the games got so acrobatic, and even if they were ripped, the players weren't models by any stretch. The court was smaller than regulation and the chain-link surrounding it meant the games often got bloody. The acrobatic showmanship and exaggerated expressions made for wild comic-ready images.

A couple of players were nodding acquaintances, but they ignored the skinny fag with the big pad. Rubberneckers tended to crowd the Cage and howl at the men. Trip's favorite bench was tucked around the side and gave no great view of the games, but a superb view of the players. Sitting there offered some of the best athletic modeling in Manhattan, and it didn't cost a dime.

At the moment, the bodies under the streetlamps added up to something else on the page under his scudding pencil. Trip had drawn a lanky character he hadn't named yet. The demon's love interest, once lust and panic burnt away his humanity. After he'd succumbed—

"Mr. Spector." A husky voice crooned from the dim subway steps. "You're a sports fan?"

When Trip twisted in his seat, he didn't see Silas, but an anticipatory spark lit him up inside. Their *Catwoman* date had been nine days ago.

There. Wholesome, hard-limbed Goolsby goodness jogging his way.

"Sorry!" Silas came up the sidewalk flushed and rushed. "Normally, I take the train, but Leigh Ann convinced me to share the actor shuttle to Times Square." He dropped his eyes. "It's late."

Is he embarrassed?

"Hi."

"Commuting sucks." Silas dropped his backpack and a grocery bag. His stubble had flecks of red and gold in it. He'd gotten a lot of sun somewhere. "Hate missing time with you."

"Don't sweat it." The words sounded right. Trip meant them. "I knew you wouldn't stand me up." *True.* He didn't even mind sitting this close, if no one paid attention.

"I forgot to shave." Silas seemed guilty and ran a hand over the scruff on his jaw. "I meant to, I mean. I wanted to look nice for you."

"Well, you don't look *mean*. No worries." The light emphasized how thick Silas's whiskers were. His whole face had scruffed out with several days' growth at least; not quite a beard yet, but about two days past five-o'clock shadow. It appeared soft to the touch—but he didn't. "Very handsome."

"My dad was Finnish, so I gotta shave twice a day."

"That's why you stay so tan. Gold, I mean. You keep your color. I'm always like an overexposed photo." Trip rubbed his arms.

"C'mon. You're not that pale." Silas held out his thick forearm next to Trip's bony one. "Well, you're lighter than me, but I was in Miami for a week."

"Vacation?"

"Shoot. 'S'crazy! The partying down there."

Trip gulped and waited for a punch line, any punch line. "Not really my scene."

Silas shook his head. "No. Me neither. I just meant that's what they all do down there. All that salty sunlight and everybody's in the discos till daybreak."

"*Vato!*" On the street ball court, a stocky Cuban kid in blue shorts scored a point. The crowd hanging on the chain-link roared approval and dismay.

"I'm really sorry. I shoulda taken a cab." Silas sighed, and finally he grinned. "Hey, sailor."

"We're good." Trip grinned. "I hid over here to sketch like a lazy bum." He leaned and whispered, "Free models."

"How izzat lazy?" Silas plopped down beside him on the bench. He put his hand next to Trip's, obviously wanting to take it.

Trip moved his fingers away, faux-casually, and battled the impulse to slam the sketchbook closed. He hated anyone watching him work up close. Even at comic cons, he took commissions but wouldn't put marker to page till the fans cleared out of artist alley.

"Not *work*-work. Not the Mighty Mites." Trip lowered his head and finished the jawline on the page. "I took your advice."

"Don't do that. I give the worst advice!" Silas snickered and leaned over to look.

Again, Trip's chest tightened as he restrained himself. *He gets it.*

Oddly enough, Silas only glanced at the page before he rummaged in his backpack. "My ideas usually don't turn out that good."

"About drawing my own book." Trip crosshatched rough shading around the margins. "I think you said, 'Something I wish I could buy.' So I'm drawing it."

Big grin from Silas. "F'real?"

Trip peered down at the drawing again. He'd slowed his hand, but he hadn't stopped. "Yup. Making up a book from scratch."

"That's...." Silas beamed before he finished the thought. "Amazing. I knew at least one of my ideas hadda be good."

Trip shrugged. "Your fault." He narrowed his eyes and tested the idea gently with a single word. "Incubus."

"No way!" Silas clapped and his face lit up.

"A lonely, horny demon who rejects the world he's addicted to."

"Asmodeus, Lord of Asslicking?"

"Not porno, though." Trip glanced around them to make sure Silas hadn't offended anyone. They were in the Village, surrounded by NYU students and gym rats. Some of these hipsters probably licked ass on public access channels.

"So... not cumshots. More erotica." Silas almost tasted the word.

"My friend Rina says it's erotic *romance*. Love stories for geeks and zombies." Trip snickered. "If you can't join 'em, eat 'em."

"From the creator of *Hero High*?" Silas nodded appreciatively. "You, sir, are a mad genius." He plucked at his crotch for a minute and saw Trip seeing it.

For a second he seemed about to lean forward and kiss Trip, but Trip stiffened and returned to his page. He'd only half finished the drawing, but he'd use lots of detail later. "Crazy is what it is."

Silas rubbed his nose. "Or badass. Anything graphic can be revolutionary. I mean, there's *Barb Wire* and then there's *Belle de Jour*. It isn't just pimping."

Trip raised a shoulder in assent. He didn't know movies, but he got the gist. "We can go."

Silas moved with easy grace, all the time in the world. "But you don't look finished."

"I can be." He closed his pad.

Silas studied Trip's face instead of the page. "Naw. Go 'head."

"I'm stuck. Same diff."

"C'mon, man." Silas spoke softly. "I been cooped up all day. Feels good to sit outside. You thirsty?"

"Please."

"Two secs. Watch my bag?"

And then Silas left to jog across Sixth Avenue on his fuzzy muscular legs, past the playground, and toward the fluorescent glare of a bodega. Trip smiled at the way Silas threw himself into everything with so much appetite.

Silas understands. The bubble of happiness in Trip's gut swelled and wobbled. So, this was what it felt like to date a grown-up.

He opened the sketchbook again and drew. Maybe he'd finish out the drawing before the game finished. The tall figure under his hand didn't feel like any kind of nemesis. The long stretch of his muscles seemed potent and painful.

Trip needed a big battle, but he still hadn't cooked up any kind of real villain. It drove him nuts. Years of working on *Hero High* had atrophied his story muscles. Cliff handed him pages and he drew them. Easy to bitch about something you hadn't made. He'd gotten lazy and sloppy.

Without an adversary, Trip had no book, and he knew it. *Fucking staple.*

The fact that Trip had filled half a book with Silas reimagined as a barbaric sex demon only rubbed salt into the situation. The interiors he'd drawn were ecstatic and uncanny. Something felt so strange about his furtive obsession with Silas and him wondering who his villains might be. It felt like stealing. Trip considered showing Silas the entire sketchbook and asking, *What would you come back from hell to fight for?*

Still, he'd opened with his incubus tortured and imprisoned. Most of the pieces had popped into place: occult mystery, spooky sex club, the nosy mortal sidekick who rushed in to free a horny demon... he just didn't know whodunit. *Yet.*

Trip needed a big baddie to carry him past the staple.

"Whatsamatter?"

Silas stood over him and held out a bottle of water.

"Nothing." Trip sighed heavily.

"You muttered something."

"Bad habit. I'm a little stumped." Trip took the bottle from the square hand.

Silas sat down and crossed his legs. "Wanna talk about it?"

"My own fault." Trip shrugged. "I've gotten so flabby at Big Dog. Four years I been griping about creative freedom, but comes down to it, and I wish Cliff would just hand me a script and tell me what to do."

"'S'fucking scary. Fuck up and there's nobody to blame."

Trip's pencil traced the lines roughly. The man on his page looked injured; his face stretched into pain. "Exactly. Now I'm off doing my own thing, totally lost."

"But that also means that when this thing takes off, you get the credit. Art, my man. That's the deal."

"I don't have a bad guy. I don't have a plot. I don't even have a name for my main character. What have I got? A horny devil. A clumsy sidekick."

The crowd hanging on the chain-link applauded and catcalled. Inside the Cage, the game had ended. The players thumped each other and walked toward the gate. From the smiles, he'd say the Skins had won.

Silas twisted to check, and the bronze chevron of his hairline gleamed above his collar. Trip fought the urge to lick his neck like a dog.

They hadn't yet spent a whole night together. Hell, Cliff was the only guy who'd slept over in years. Trip got weird about people being in his personal space, and once Silas spent time there, who knew what he'd think? And Silas appeared relaxed, not at all rushed. The attraction obviously existed, their unspoken agreement to delay the inevitable felt simultaneously sexy and maddening.

Big mojo, my man. Ben's honest gate of horn popped into his head. "You wanna…." Trip blinked. "Maybe come back—"

Silas popped to his feet, his jaw rigid. "Yes."

"Well, okay, then." He wheezed nervously.

"I mean, yes, please, Mr. Spector." Silas grinned.

Trip was pretty sure a whole lot of fucking would happen, and fucking in his bed would feel intense because he couldn't pretend it happened to someone else or that he'd imagined it. Come to think of it, he hadn't taken anyone home in a long time. He could hear Jillian's scolding voice in his head. *Besides the Unboyfriend.* Had he done laundry or made his bed this week?

"May I please come back to your house and slip into something more comfortable?" Silas hefted the overfilled grocery bag: "I picked up some groceries, so I could make dinner. Wherever we ended up."

Whole Foods bag. Trip could see a lot of adamantly fresh produce, red and green. Zero cans or snacks. Food which obviously required some kind of expert preparation. *Nutrition. Eek.* "Or we could order—"

"Trust me."

What did folks say about the devil you know? Trip realized Silas was holding out a hand to him. "I wasn't sure if—"

"No." Silas closed his eyes for a beat. "We're taking it slow, but I'd like to hang out somewhere that we won't get arrested for making out."

Trip remembered how Silas had surrendered and squirted on him after the movie. Now he did have a branch in his briefs.

Silas noticed. *Great.*

"Tell you what. How about we both pretend to be grown-ups for as long as we can?" The knot in Trip's stomach warred with the great musky truncheon trapped against his leg.

Silas brandished a defiant fist. "You wanna live forever?"

Trip stared at him a moment.

Silas tossed his empty water bottle into a trash can, then slung Trip's backpack over his thick shoulder and scooped up the groceries with that arm. "What?"

"That's what Jillian and Ben say alla time." Trip stood up, closer than he'd intended. "College friends."

"Any fan of *Conan* is a friend of mine." Silas scanned the dark clouds and then looked back at Trip. His eyes softened at something he saw.

As they headed uptown, the Fourth Street Station belched commuters onto the sidewalk. The lights changed, but the cars sat parked in traffic while people jaywalked toward the smoke shops, tattoo parlors, and porn emporiums.

"I never would've survived that first year without Ben. No money. My folks dead against it. Couch surfing. And he and Jilly just let me have the basement for four months while I got my feet under me. Ben's been my best friend since high school."

"Did you two ever...?" Silas kept his eyes on Trip.

"No!" Trip sniffed. "No. Nothing like—I mean, I had the worst crush on him junior year, but he was so straight that he didn't even get offended. Hell, he used to try and fix me up with curious guys on the wrestling team." Trip snorted quietly. "Ben's so *real*. And Jillian."

They navigated the roving packs of students and tourists, and somehow Silas knew not to take his hand. He proved surprisingly nimble for a big lug: when they had to get through a passel of bodies, he'd step a little forward and sort of clear the way for Trip with his free arm. Very old school.

"'S'important to have old friends." Silas wagged a finger. "They remember who you were before you made yourself up. That's what my dad used to say." He dropped his voice to a sorghum drawl. "They keep ya honest and call your shit."

"You miss him." Not a question.

Silas took a second to reply. "Every fucking day." His jaw tightened and he shook his head, just once. "My daddy was my biggest fan. Took no guff. Gave no quarter. He always knew the right thing." He shook his head again and closed his eyes. "Say. Do."

"Sorry."

"What for?" The smile was minnow-quick, but his eyes shone. "Parents die. Kids live. He raised me so good that I felt bad for the other kids I knew. Hell, he mostly raised them too."

As the moon rose over the Jefferson Market tower, they walked up Greenwich, where the foot traffic was lighter. Cold as it was, a clump of secretaries stood jammed into a Red Mango, eating frozen glop out of cups.

One short block from his front door, Trip stopped walking. "Wait.... You hungry?"

Silas shrugged. "I love cooking."

"Except I don't really have any real food. From nature."

Silas clasped the bags of suspiciously wholesome ingredients. "Taken care of."

"I just...." Trip pulled a panicked face. "I don't think I straightened up."

"You can get as messy as you fucking want." Silas adjusted his crotch.

I bet he's not wearing underwear. Trip dislodged his own bone with the hand in his pocket.

"We're a caution." Silas giggled and rubbed his cleft chin roughly. "Let's get inside before we end up on YouTube."

Their arms bumped together as they walked, and Trip reached his door feeling like a sticky ticking jism-bomb.

"This is us." On the first landing, Trip reached into his pocket for his keys. He had to shove his erection out of the way before he dug them free.

He unlocked the street door and led the way to the second floor, trying not to think about Silas watching his backside as he climbed. He flicked the lights on to reveal the open room. *Not horrible.* No laundry and only a couple of glasses in the sink. He glanced across at the alcove by the windows. He hadn't made the bed.

"Home sweet hovel."

Instead of stepping past him, Silas stopped close. "Big."

Trip gestured at his cluttered shelves and the framed posters. "Nicer apartment than most New Yorkers can afford, but *Hero High* pays well."

"Cool." Silas stayed put. He didn't touch but stood near enough that he warmed Trip's back. "Am I making you nervous?"

Trip didn't turn. "Yeah. No. I mean, yeah, you do, but in a good way."

"Likewise." Silas put one rough hand against Trip's head.

Did he want dinner? Had they only come upstairs to fuck? Trip wasn't sure what script to use. His heart stuttered somewhere inside him.

With Silas, sex apparently didn't follow any of the normal routines. When on the prowl, Trip went out and gradually climbed the ladder from flirt to fondle to fuck, like an erotic Lego set that required permissions and patterns if you wanted to build anything.

Silas didn't play by any of the rules. His frank horniness rattled Trip and unleashed him… exhilarating, but scary at the same time. All bets were off. Maybe that was his appeal. Silas seemed just as likely to fuck on the stoop and then snuggle watching the *Justice League* as the reverse.

Silas brushed a gentle hand across Trip's cheek. "Whatcha grinning about?"

Trip let out a puff of awkward air. "That you're bad for the rules."

Silas shrugged. "You show me some rules and I'll consider 'em. But nobody ever gave me a manual worth shit. You?" His calluses whispered over Trip's throat and collar as he pulled their faces close.

They didn't kiss.

Trip breathed as easily as he could and waited for a signal. Their cheeks sandpapered together.

"We don't have to rush, Mr. Spector."

Maybe anticipation was a good thing.

Silas tugged his shirt loose and took a couple of steps onto the rug of Trip's living room area. "Down Alabama, we like taking our time." He toed off his shoes comfortably. "Just getting situated."

"Sorry about alla junk." Trip adjusted his clothes. Maybe they were both nervous.

Silas crossed to cast an eye over the bookshelves, the rows of bound comic archives and figurines, pop culture clutter. "This is a great pad. I don't wanna know what you pay."

Trip tapped the floor with his foot. "Well, the bar downstairs gets loud as hell, and the heat is for shit, but you can't beat the location. Light's good."

"But you have so much space." Silas held a white Guy Fawkes mask over his face. "*V for Vendetta!*"

"Mostly freebies and swag. From cons." Trip felt thin and washed out next to all that bronze muscle. He wiped his damp hands on his thighs. "You're like a stealth dork."

Silas peered out the windows. "That's Greenwich? All the boys floating by."

"And I can get to Big Dog in twelve minutes on the A." Trip's erection hadn't shrunk. He closed his eyes for a long beat and inhaled. "You're killing me."

"Uh-huh."

By the time he opened them again, Silas had unbuttoned his jeans to reveal unexpected briefs. *Shows what I know.*

Silas peeled out of his pants and step-step-stepped free of them. "Didja get good sketches at the game?" He flopped onto the couch with an easy grin.

Trip moved to join him, his crank seriously tenting his pants at an obscene angle. "See what you did?" He shifted it inside his underwear, which didn't help matters.

Silas reached and squeezed the oversized roll of meat, his eyes fixed. "Spector, that thing is something else."

"Sorry."

"Boy howdy." Silas swallowed, breathing audibly.

"In high school I felt like an ugly unicorn." Trip grabbed his buckle firmly. "Big fucking shank hanging off me."

Silas fell back on the couch. "Hey, I like unicorns. Unicorns are just weaponized ponies."

Trip frowned, but for once he didn't try to cover his face with his hands or arms, or bury it in the cushions.

Silas rolled onto his belly. "And you're awful cute for an ugly guy."

Trip knelt beside Silas and the couch and ran a reverent hand over the fleshy jut of his haunch, the dimples at his lower back, and the hillock of muscle under his red cotton briefs.

"Spent my whole life wishing I weighed a hundred and fifty pounds. You don't know. My teammates called me dumpling."

Trip tried not to grin but failed. "Well…."

"Don't say it!" But Silas smiled.

"Okay." Trip bent to press his face to the firm sweep of Silas's lower back. He craned closer to kiss one cheek. "But I'm gonna think it a lot."

"But you probably expected me to be like this burly power top and then I pull a switcheroo and—"

"And I guess you can stop talking now." Trip teased the elastic with his fingertips and squeezed a handful of the firm glute. "Aren't dumplings always better with gravy?"

Silas blinked.

"Stop telling me what you think I want. Okay? I bet we'll figure it out." Trip crawled up onto the sofa to lie full-length on top of Silas, his fat joint tucked between the globes in question through the thin briefs. "Ungh! I *love* that."

"Feels fantastic."

Sure enough, the thunder of Silas's heartbeat and the slow drag of air energized Trip as he relaxed onto the broad torso and pressed his belly against the hot slope of Silas's back. "You really love being on bottom. Why didn't you say something?"

"Why didn't you?"

"Touché."

They lay together for a few minutes, just breathing, each in his own thoughts. Trip broke the silence first. "Don't get me wrong. I haven't been—"

"Fucked."

"Yeah. In a while. Like a long while. College, maybe." Trip growled and kneaded the heavy shoulders. "I spent my whole life wishing I looked like Superman so I could have what I wanted: Captain America in a sling. Tarzan greased and spread-eagled. Robin jackhammering Batman."

Silas grinned. "You're playin' my song." His buttery accent came through thick, dragging two syllables out of one. "I love it when you take over like that." The big man squirmed. "Make me take it."

"You make me make you." Trip chuckled low in his chest. "Fucking powerless to resist. This"—he squeezed it lightly—"is the most beautiful ass I've seen in twenty-six years of nude models and porn addiction."

"Alabama hams. They grow 'em big."

Trip ran a tentative hand over the ripeness of Silas's flank. "Not just that." He nuzzled the back of Silas's neck and then his ear. "You are something super special, Mr. Goolsby."

Silas stiffened.

"Sorry?" Trip stopped hunching. "Am I crushing you?"

"Naw. You kidding?" Silas turned his grinning face. "I could go to sleep like this. A hung blanket." He pushed up on his elbows and shifted away.

Did I say something bad? Trip scooted back to lean against the opposite arm of the sofa. Silas seemed serious.

"We got time." Silas sat up and gave a wary smile. "Let's take it." He grabbed at the distended pouch of his red briefs as he stood up. "No hurry. I should start supper."

Trip wavered, trying to get his bearings.

"'S'my fault. I keep trying to push." Silas pressed the heels of his hands against his eye sockets. He drifted to the drafting table in front of the bricked-up fireplace. He put his hand on the big sketches of Horny Bastard. "You mind?"

Agh! Trip sprang to his feet. Last thing he needed was Silas finding a bunch of naked demons who had his face and body.

Trip reached for his sketchbook and flipped back a couple of pages as he tried to find a drawing of Horny Bastard that didn't resemble Silas. He found one and held it up to the mirror on the brick wall beside his chair, then examined it. *Not great.* Using all Cliff's notes for this version of the face made the character too… flat, or hollow. There was no fire, no color or movement. He stayed a sketch, but at least he wasn't Silas.

"Oh."

"He's still pretty rough." Horny Bastard never felt right without the cheeky stare and those wicked eyes. Funny how a character decides how he's going to look.

Trip regarded Silas's confusion in the mirror. This Staplegun version of the hero had come out creepier than he should've, more vulpine. More horror than erotic.

"Okay. Huh." Silas sounded hesitant. "He's so intense. Dirty."

"Erotic comic." Trip flipped forward to the later, more impressive images when he'd softened the lines and let Silas's goofiness and flirty appeal seep back into the character. "He's a full-on sex demon."

Silas laughed. "F'real? I didn't expect that." He pondered the infernal Cliff. "He *is* sexy."

Trip waited for Silas to notice his own features. Then again, maybe he'd given himself too much credit.

"So goddamn talented." Silas perused the incubus drawings. He clucked and nodded at whatever he saw.

The wonky foreshortening drove Trip crazy. "Hold on a sec. I need to fix something." Trip held the drawing up to the mirror, reflecting the entire page back at him. Staring into the glass, Trip erased the bicep and lengthened its roundness.

Silas watched him with a bemused smile on his face. "Is that like a two-way mirror? Are you showing it to the cops?"

"No!" Trip grinned and turned back to his revisions on the reversed pad in the mirror. "Your eye gets trained to read left to right, and so your hand will build flaws into a drawing. That mirror is there so I remember to check the balance as I go. I've gotten in the habit of drawing in the mirror pretty regularly. Makes for more dynamic posing, everything."

"Gonna be something special when you're done. You watch." Silas ran his hand over the drawing and turned the pages thoughtfully. Finally he looked up. "Art. This is art. I mean, more than capes and scrapes. This sumbitch is gonna rattle a lotta cages when he gets loose. Change shit even." He smiled up at Trip with a sloe-eyed stare. "Sometimes you do it to teach them a lesson."

"If I can finish the script." Trip scowled. "I don't even know his goddamned name." He thumped the pencil in irritation. "There's no story. I can't find a bad guy."

Silas bumped his bulge against Trip's forearm. "Practice, practice, practice."

Trip sighed. "I mean the big bad, for his story. First issue is him chained up and breaking free. To do what, I have no idea."

Silas scratched his scalp. "You've just gotta find his villain. What's he fighting for?"

"No idea."

"C'mon. You have some idea. I mean, look at him. Not fighting for tax reform."

Trip snickered. "Point taken."

"You're not seeing what's there." Silas wiped his wide mouth and smiled. "I bet you'll find your foe and your name, and once you do they'll both seem obvious."

"I don't know. If he did fall for someone, he'd have to defy his masters, and he'd put his boyfriend in danger."

"Ah! The demon has a boyfriend."

Trip peered at the floor. "Maybe."

"So this is a *gay* erotic adventure you're whipping up." Silas bent close and kissed the nape of Trip's neck.

Trip squirmed and jerked as the soft stubble scraped him just enough. "If I can figure him out."

Silas straightened. "Y'got so much to go on. Picasso said 'No artist is a bastard.'"

Trip snorted. "Obviously he didn't get out much."

"Ha!" Silas laughed at that, a rumbly bark. "Naw. It just means that there's no such thing as a blank slate when we make something. Art starts somewhere." He sighed happily. "We do."

Silas paused at an angle to the apartment windows; his shadow became a long black tongue that licked the floor. Chased by moonlight, he seemed more imaginary than his demonic doppelgänger in the open sketchbook.

Trip grumbled, wished his clumsy hands understood what his eyes saw. If only he could capture that open, sweet heat. He'd draw that window, that moon, that ripe muscle... with no guilt and no guard. Silas had given him permission to dream, and no matter where he stood, he looked like a hellish hero.

"I mean...." Silas swung his chin to glance over his shoulder, half his face in shadow. "Nobody starts from scratch." He shrugged. "There's no such thing as *scratch*."

Trip nearly stumbled, stopped. "Who?"

"Not who, *what*." Silas chuffed. "Scratch."

"Wait...." For a second he thought he'd misheard. "What did you say?"

"Scratch doesn't exist." Silas's brows drew together in confusion. "What?"

"Oh. My. God." A wide, stupid grin bloomed on Trip's face.

"What'd I say?" He widened his eyes. "Trip?"

"Perfect." Trip gaped at him as a pile of invisible cinder blocks floated off his shoulders on invisible wings.

Silas smiled. "You sure are, bubba." His lazy gaze roamed over Trip.

"No, I mean—" Trip shook his head. "You said *Scratch*. I thought you meant it like a nickname for him." He waved a hand at the scattered drawings.

"So?"

"Scratch. You see?" Blink. He felt like a hot, shaken soda all set to spray. "You don't see." Trip held his hands open and waited for Silas to make the leap with him.

"Go with me…. Old Scratch is a name for Satan. And touch and money. Claw marks. And you can start from scratch."

Silas gathered Trip into strong arms, "'S'pretty badass, Mr. Spector."

"Sh'yeah." Trip managed to shut his mouth. *What just happened?* He contemplated the drawings of Horny Bastard.

No: Scratch.

"I like it." But Silas didn't seem to hear. "A lot."

The light outside had gone deep indigo. The bulge in Silas's briefs firmed up, and Trip's followed along.

Trip took another lungful of sharp vanilla, and a quicksilver certainty flickered through him: the name Scratch spun inside his hero's moving parts like a key, tumbling the lock.

The future crooked its finger.

How exhilarating and odd to talk about his crazy incubus project while their cocks jousted somewhere below. He'd never imagined a world where his art and his heart mingled and smeared together, the possibilities explosive and infinite.

"I cannot believe… I been trying to find his name for two damn weeks. How d'you do that?" He stared at Silas.

"Hey. That's how art works. Happy accidents." Silas swung his head and bent to butt Trip's chest, like a dog wanting to be petted.

Trip nudged his sketchbook. "Thank you. For understanding." He stroked the two-dimensional Scratch, and Silas kissed the base of his throat with Scratch's mouth. "For the name."

"Uh-huh." The sound a puff against Trip's collarbone. All Silas's earlier hesitation had melted. "You came up with it."

"Well, I thought you did…."

"By accident." Silas kissed him. "Scratch." Another kiss, slower this time, more open. "You're a genius."

"Not really. More like: *we're* a genius." Trip kissed back then, fiercely and gently devoured that sinful smile, crushed Silas close in that way that made the big man go boneless against him.

And still, and still, Silas stood there sturdy as an oak to offer more than he realized. He pushed up Trip's shirt and kissed the line of hair on his belly while he popped the button on Trip's jeans and fumbled to get them lower.

Trip looked down at the urgent ridges bumping below.

Silas sighed against him, too close to see clearly. "Please," he whispered. A request or an objection?

Trip spread his hand behind that perfect skull, the bronze neck, and whispered into his skin, "Anything."

Gingerly, Silas hoisted the elastic over Trip's knob and revealed the shaft to the air. "There's no hurry." Silas traced spirals on his back.

"There isn't?" Trip laughed. "Tell that to my boner."

And *wham*, Silas grabbed his cock directly for the first time and wrapped his thick paw around its bare skin to speak into the head like a microphone. "There is no hurry." Silas chuckled, and sucked the head, just once. "Over."

H'okay!

Trip gasped and held his breath. His heartbeat thumped in the erection—*a-one, a-two, a-three*—encircled by Silas's coarse fist, where it seemed to fit.

Silas let go, and his hard-on *thwumped* back against Trip's pale stomach just to the side of the springy treasure trail. A little stripe of precum drizzled across its firm skin.

Trip let out the breath. "Fuck. Warn me next time."

"That'd be dumb." The wolfish smile lifted one side of Silas's mouth and made his eyes flash. "If I warn you, how am I gonna surprise you?"

Silas slid to his knees and sucked Trip's shivery stomach. "You know me. Can't help feeding the lions. No matter—" He rocked up and kissed Trip's sternum. "How many—" He licked Trip's navel. "Times they—" He pressed his stubbled cheek against Trip's erection. "Warn me."

"I don't think that's a warning." Trip stroked the mussed calico hair. "Exactly."

"That's what you think." Silas opened his mouth and pushed his face to the root.

Whoa.

Trip opened his mouth, a shocked O that choked on oxygen as Silas somehow didn't gag on his fat cap. *How can he breathe?* Another superpower, apparently.

Silas gulped around the stiffness and the inside of his throat did crazy things to Trip's nervous system till his legs twitched and buckled. Silas slid back an inch to breathe roughly through his nose and then drilled down again, skewered himself while his throat spasmed gently around Trip's hardness.

Trip always thought of blowjobs as something rushed and rough. Masturbation with a mouth at one end. Most of his experience involved guys who licked around and then whacked his honker to a sticky finish. Having a big one could create some very awkward moments in oral sex. In the sexual cafeteria of New York dating, talk was cheap and eyes tended to be bigger than stomachs.

Not so, Silas. He worshiped the fat slab, lavishing patient, slobbery affection over every millimeter of veiny stiffness.

"Hold up. Wait." Trip pulled his hips back and slid out of the slippery bliss. "I don't want to come."

Silas pulled free and wiped the spit off his chin. "You don't have to."

"You're gonna make me."

"Nuh-huh." Silas strained forward and licked the crown with the very tip of his tongue. "You'll *wish* you could come. Southern fellas know how to take their time."

Trip trembled, hypnotized by Silas's frank hunger.

"You could work on your sketches, and I'll just blow you quietly for a spell. Slowly, y'know. Like pulling a thread… gently churn the cream out of you."

"Stop." Trip breathed harder.

Silas sat back, a long strand of drool hanging from his lip. It stretched until it broke and hit the floor. He didn't seem to notice and just stared at Trip. Silas pushed his briefs down to his knees. The tight T-shirt still stretched over Silas's chest, but otherwise his body was exposed to Trip's view. "I can keep you cantering right at the edge for a long-ass time." A rumbling exhale. "Hours, even."

"Please."

"*Mmh.* Mr. Spector. You say 'please' to me, and there's not much I won't do. Good manners will get you just about anything." Silas wiped absently at his cheek, exposing the pink flesh of his mouth for a moment. His hard-on bobbed to the right and his balls hugged its root. *Lust and musk.* His eyelids fell to half-mast and he swallowed lazily. "But bad manners will get you even more."

Trip reached down and hoisted the thick body up against his. He tucked his hand between the globes. "Fuck, Silas."

"If you insist."

9

CAUTION? Meet wind.

Silas wrapped his hand around that thick piston and milked its length. "I can't think straight with you like that."

"We going somewhere?" Trip followed with a grin on his face.

"Bed." Silas headed toward the long windows. He'd seen an alcove tucked there, the navy blue corner of unmade sheets and a chair that had three T-shirts draped over it. He squeezed Trip's big boner and let go as he reached the mattress.

Trip jogged back to the front door and flicked a switch. Only the streetlights outside lit the apartment. "Don't wanna give the neighbors a show." He dropped the blinds a ways.

"Speak for yourself." Silas sat and shrugged, admiring the lazy wave of Trip's monster. There was something so satisfying about the bob and swing of it as he moved confidently around his space. "Jesus."

"I know. I'm white. I'm not really a beach—"

"You're beautiful."

Trip snorted.

"Why do you do that?" Silas scooted back. "C'mere. I'll show you."

Trip reached back over his head and skinned out of his shirt to reveal his pale torso and the arrow of dark silky hair aimed at his navel. "Wow," he spoke under his breath.

Silas turned over his shoulder and caught Trip staring at his backside. "Such an ass man." Not a question. He ran a lazy hand over the light down dusting his crack.

Trip bent forward, held the cheeks apart, and swiped the skin with his wide, warm tongue. His face fit perfectly in the trench, and his mouth covered the hole completely. *Choonk.* Silas almost saw the sound effect as if on a lettered panel. Trip gripped Silas's ankles and pushed them farther apart so he could wedge even closer.

Silas groaned. On the off chance he could stop himself from jumping Trip or acting like a total slut in public, he'd jerked out a load in the shower at the gym and stuck a finger or two in himself to speed things along. "Yeah."

Trip exposed the little muscle and dove in hungrily as Silas reached back to hold his mouth where he needed it most. Trip bit the musky skin and rubbed his stubbled face and buzz cut against the sensitive crease. "Good?"

Silas jumped at the sensation and arched his back hard. "Like you wouldn't believe."

Trip squeezed the plump muscle while his fingertips grazed the hotter, damper skin close to the hole. "Who needs vegetables? This is like breakfast, lunch, and dinner right here. And a midnight snack." He curled and pushed closer, rubbed his entire head against the hole.

Silas whimpered and tried to relax the little iris, to give Trip full permission. He went boneless and stupid, focused on the slither of his golden forearms and face where they pressed against the lustrous cotton.

"'At's it." Trip bent the semierect cock back and pushed the head against the hole as he licked both with wide flat strokes of his tongue.

Silas slid his tense arms forward as if praying. He spread his knees another few inches apart. His ass clamped shut and his knob swelled and drizzled a slow crystal strand. "Do it."

Trip pulled away, and Silas heard the crackle of plastic and the squelch of lube. "Fuck." The mattress shook as Trip stretched the rubber over his girth.

Silas opened one eye and tried to twist around, then gave up. He could feel plenty, so didn't need to see anything.

Trip didn't give him any fingers to help. He'd licked and bitten the skin till it hummed. The spit ran down Silas's inner thigh and felt cool in the air. The glossy bulb scorched his opening but went no farther.

Silas growled in frustration. He'd played with his butthole all fucking day and finally had what he wanted ringing his buzzer.

"Take what you want." Trip sounded breathless. He gently rested greasy hands on Silas's hips. He didn't thrust or pull the pelvis closer, just let the fat crown kiss the entrance to Silas's body.

Eyes closed, Silas nodded and strained back. He bore down as best he could.

Ow.

Trip patted his flank.

Silas arched and muttered, "Gimme a sec." He wiggled his hips and took a deep breath. "I'm gonna—holy fuck!" His ass opened sharply, painfully, and caught the head just under the ridge. "One sec. One sec." The cock flexed but stayed put.

"Shhh. 'S'okay, man." Trip traced the soft crack and ran a hand up Silas's back. "Go easy. You take what you need."

With excruciating slowness, Silas pushed himself up on his elbows and arched harder to drill himself back on that club, inch by scalding inch. Even hard, Trip's dick felt like it had a spongy layer over it.

"There ya go." Trip petted him in long strokes and squeezed his cheeks together. "Look at that."

Silas rumbled and purred, drugged by the fullness. Trip's dick mashed his prostrate into butter. Precum leaked from his helmet onto the mattress.

"Doing okay?" Trip pulled out a bit and froze when Silas pushed back to reclaim the inch. "You got all of me."

"Nuh." Silas hung his head as Trip drove the breath out of his open mouth. "*You* do." He panted. "Again." He canted forward and let the fat length slip free and then pushed onto it again.

Trip held his hips close and moved gently at first, as he carefully tested Silas with fierce patience, as if he could see with his shaft and was looking for a diamond.

Silas spread his arms on the bed; his head was turned sideways and smashed into the mattress. "I knew—"

"Yeah?" Trip gasped and lunged forward. "What'd you know?" As Silas relaxed, Trip's aggression rose. He gripped Silas harder, demanded submission that came easily and eagerly when called. Silas groaned and chuckled. *Nerd sex.* He'd have to thank Leigh Ann for the advice.

"C'mon. C'mon, man." He stared back at Trip with gritted teeth. "Make me. Make me take it."

He saw Trip clearly for the first time. Folks always wondered why his exes stayed friendly. That was the reason. Even as a half-assed boyfriend, he got the best sex out of his partners. Like cosmetics really... he paid attention. You worked with who and what you had. "I can feel all of you, man. Make me—"

Trip fell forward, his cool belly against Silas's warm back. He wrapped his arms around Silas and drove his length in short rapid punches that made it hard to breathe.

Trip unleashed himself in the sack. Silas had subjected himself to a lot of clumsy camera-ready but butthole-brutal sawing back and forth. Most guys learned to fuck from porn and, without knowing it, screwed anus as if they were on a set in the San Fernando Valley, working for creeps with clammy hands. Truth was, unless someone aimed a camera at your ying-yang, the pleasure came from paying careful attention to each other. Trip screwed like he drew, building up a mosaic of details that gradually overwhelmed them both. *Too much.*

Silas gasped. "Thank you." He pushed back as best he could to amp the give-take and let Trip own him utterly. "*Augh!* Thank you."

Trip buried his nose in the nape of his neck, and the hot breath snuffled there. He gave small grumbling moans as his irregular strokes shortened and got rougher. The yielding layer over his dick had stiffened into punishing thickness.

Silas caught his breath. The friction hovered right on the edge of pain while Trip plucked at his tits. His own hard-on jabbed the slippery cotton beneath him as he jerked it. *So close.*

"Show me." Silas glanced back at Trip. "Make me feel it."

"Fuck. Fuck." Trip gasped and choked. His hips shook, and he nailed Silas to the mattress with a club that felt like it reached his lungs.

Silas's pleasure crested, and iridescent juice spilled over his hand. His hole squeezed and jerked, wringing a yelp out of Trip.

"Oh!" He tried to thrust but couldn't.

Silas melted forward into his own hot spooge. He couldn't catch his breath and stopped trying. His stretched ass relaxed enough for Trip to slam against him once, twice, again, then—

Silas collapsed and Trip sank with him, kissing and biting the slippery skin of his back. Spunk still drizzled from Silas's knob onto the sheets, and his head hung over the side of the bed. *I can't stop cumming.* He roared and bared his teeth while his spit ran onto the floor.

"Silas. God. Si—I'm gonna—" Trip wheezed at his neck and licked the skin. His fingers gripped Silas's ass and kneaded the cheeks as he hammered between them, howling, "I'm there!"

Silas surrendered to the honeyed hum in his bones as his softening cock ground seed into the bed. He flexed his back, pushing up so he actually lifted Trip for a moment.

They shouted together. The winter air cooled between them. By degrees, Trip unstiffened. Silas slid his hips forward gingerly to let the blunt pole slide free. His breath caught at the cold sting. He flipped over onto his starchy puddle and watched Trip settle back. "Thank you, man. Thank you and thank you."

Trip rolled Silas onto his lean chest and petted him. He leaned down to kiss the top of his head. "You like it rough?"

Silas licked his teeth. "Jam's out of that jar."

Trip clambered over him to lean against the headboard.

"I love giving up. Being forced. Not like whips, but being taken like that. *Jmpnh.*" Silas rolled his eyes back in his head. "You dunno."

Trip swallowed, and when he found his voice, it came out raw and weak as a hatched chick. "When I was a little boy, I would take these muscular plastic men and tie them up. Bondage, I guess, with string. But sometimes, just posing them. That always seemed so sexy. All that straining against knots and each other."

"Like bondage?" Normally, Silas would've loaded the word with flirty innuendo, but Trip's confession made him feel protective, something more primitive than playing Black Party dress up: one thing to wear a harness to a club, another thing entirely to be in fifth grade and stumble onto kink in the sandbox. "Comics get racy."

"Well, yeah. I guess. Without the sex part. I was a kid, but looking back, sure. Fantasy. Fan fiction with my toys."

"'Cause they were strong. And you had power over them."

"Yeah, but I don't wanna mess with rope and safewords. The props don't get me going at all. I don't even think it was the tying up; it was those big heroes doing what I told them."

"Control." Silas nodded.

"Heady shit for a skinny shut-in. Some boys flip out over professional wrestling. Some little girls go gaga for horses. Muscle. Power. Dreams. Tales. *Lust* before you have a name for it." Trip exhaled loudly. "And after all, superheroes live to serve. Suffering and sacrifice."

Silas smiled slowly. "That's how you started drawing."

"Yeah. Yeah! How did you know that?" Trip blinked. "You're too smart for me."

"Strong men in tight spots. And you cooked up all those images that needed to come out."

"Aquaman never looked right standing again. Kneeling, always. First time I jerked off was to He-Man wrestling a guard in a Saturday morning cartoon. I popped and it scared the shit out of me."

Silas licked his lower lip. "So the night I...."

"Yeah." Trip exhaled audibly. "God, yeah."

"I didn't know."

"Nahh. You did, though. I mean, you didn't *know* that you knew, but you must have seen whatever itch I had." Trip shifted his head. "You coaxed it out of me. That's what you do, Mr. Goolsby." He smiled as he said the words and ran an affectionate hand over Silas's scalp and back. "You're a terrible influence." He sighed. "Oh, I'm onto you now."

Chuckling as he slipped off the mattress, Silas padded to the kitchen for a glass of water. He drained it twice, taking hard chilly gulps that tasted delicious.

Best not to think about flying to Arizona on Monday. The shoot in the desert would last for over a week. A lot could happen in that time. Maybe he'd hook up with someone. Trip might do the same. They were both grown-ups. But some flimsy part of Silas wished he didn't have to be.

If not for the OutRun zombie event, they'd never have met. For the thousandth time, Silas thanked God he'd gotten off his lazy ass and gone to help Kurt that cold New Year's Eve. If he hadn't stepped in for the missing zombie... if he hadn't turned and seen the handsome anxious stranger in scrubs....

He opened the fridge: marshmallow fluff, Mountain Dew, frozen Hot Pockets, and a host of hydrogenated horrors. "Jee-zus. Junk food much?"

Trip winced. "I warned you."

Silas clocked the Pringles and gallon tub of Gummi Worms on the counter. "You must have the metabolism of a cheetah." He closed the door quickly, as if the snacks might escape. "How do you stay in shape?"

Trip appraised him. "If I was in shape the way you are, I'd be naked all the time."

"You're so full of it." Silas ambled back to the bed as if he'd slept in it a thousand times. He ran his hand over the swell of Trip's calves and the racehorse ankles.

"Hush." Shoulder bump. "I'm not saying you're just a piece of beef, but I fully appreciate the appeal of a high-protein diet." He bit Silas on the bicep.

"I played football from the time I was little. Center 'cause I was so big."

Trip quirked his mouth. "I can't imagine you heavy."

"I was super chunky in junior high. Right up until I grew, actually. Sophomore year, I stood five foot four and weighed two-sixty and had a fifty-one-inch waist. And then over the summer, I, like, exploded. Six inches in six months, it felt like. My knees hurt all the time. Horrible but then great."

"So you weren't fat, you were just building fuel reserves for liftoff." Trip ran a pale hand over Silas's firm stomach.

Silas barked with laughter. "I guess. When you grow up tubby, you never quite shake the feeling someone's gonna pull your shirt up and make your belly button gargle. Paddle your tits."

"Sorry." He watched Silas crawl onto the sheets with him.

"Or trip you and flick jizz on you in the shower."

"No way." Trip's mouth fell open.

"No. *That* was a secret sticky wish that never came true." Silas blushed. "You kidding? I woulda busted. Ugh!" He hid his face in wadded pillows. "I can't believe I just admitted that to another human being."

"Football, huh?"

"Junior high. High school. In Alabama? That's religion. You play so you don't get hassled." Silas ran a lazy hand over Trip's flat abdomen and plucked at the little stripe of dark brown hair.

Trip licked his upper lip. "I bet you looked good. Football farm boy."

"Not exactly."

"Near enough. If I'd gone to school with you, I'd have made a fool of myself." Trip peeped out the window, then back. "Crazy."

"Mr. Spector, are you having inappropriate thoughts about junior varsity athletics in these United States?"

"No. About your beautiful ass in those pants." Trip swallowed.

Silas shrugged. "That much, I cannot deny. I blew plenty of loads in 'em." He cupped his junk protectively. "All junior year, I jerked off thinking about Eric Klune touching my crack during the games. I practiced." He held up three fingers. "Hey, a hole has needs."

Trip tilted him sideways and squeezed a beefy cheek roughly. The tips of his fingers just grazed the smooth inner flesh near the hole. "I bet the team jerked off over your big glutes. How you didn't get pillaged in the locker room, I'll never know."

"That was the plan."

"Butch slut." Trip milked his pale, soft dick, making the head bulge. His hungry gaze skidded over Silas. "You coming out of the shower with a little wet towel. Slick and sore. Your quads bunching."

"Stop." But Silas didn't mean it. His heart rolled inside his ribs like a bear cub.

"They were probably afraid of you 'cause you were such a bruiser. They gave you hell and went home to spank it out." Trip shifted over on top of him. "I would've." He tipped his pelvis so his blunt head knocked against Silas's loose balls.

Silas laughed and inched closer. "Masturbation saved my life. Got wood doing crunches after football practice. I flipped over and humped the bed and *Eureka!* I thought I'd invented orgasms. For years I thought that was the only way to cum."

"And crunch your six-pack." Trip patted his abdominals.

Silas scootched up on the pillows. "Then when I started dating guys, being a little in shape made it easier to take my clothes off."

Trip stroked his backside. "Mmm-mmh. Soft." He whispered in his ear. "Dumpling." He fake-spanked the high haunch. *Swack.*

Silas frowned. "You're awful." He rubbed the heated handprint.

Trip gave him a wet kiss on the ear and got even quieter. "*Dumpling.*"

"Schmuck." But he knew they were both smiling.

Trip humped the air once. "That's what they call it."

Silas flexed his rear end once. "*Schmuck* means penis?"

"Mmh." With their skin too dry to allow much slide, lying trapped against each other felt delicious.

Silas exhaled. It felt funny to speak frankly, naked in bed. Usually he spent bed-time sucking in his gut and trying not to smother anyone by accident. "We fit pretty good."

Maybe he was getting old. Maybe Trip was different.

When Silas blinked, he discovered Trip regarding at him with a tender expression.

"Thanks." Trip gave him a quick smile and glanced up.

"For what?"

"This. You. *Scratch.* I dunno. Coming over. Being amazing. Nothing. Anything." Trip scowled at something and his fingers twitched. "I'm shutting up now. I don't know what I meant."

Yes, you do. Silas leaned forward and waited for Trip to look up again. "Me too."

Trip crawled off Silas. "I think I get bored. I mean... pretending alla time. I mean, I've bottomed. I like it fine, but what I really love is breaking a big guy open with my joint."

"Yeah...." A languid smile leaked over Silas's face.

"Finding out what makes him tick, what makes him grunt, what makes him shout."

Silas coughed. His prick rolled and unfurled toward his hip.

Trip raised an eyebrow and lowered his voice. "Oh, really?" As he watched, the shaft thickened in a heartbeat jerk.

"Sorry." Silas winced.

"Why sorry?" Trip reached under his leg. "Don't apologize for satisfying all my hang-ups and fantasies." He pretended to shudder. "Egad! The horror. Forced to sodomize He-Man into submission!"

How long could this last? Silas didn't hold out much hope. In his experience, New Yorkers got bored. Gay men in New York were like ADD hummingbirds. "Over-the-shoulder syndrome," he called it. No matter how happy city boys got, they were always checking over your shoulder to see any replacements who might be coming through the door: bigger job, bigger dick, bigger apartment, bigger wallet, bigger brain, bigger name. The pitfall of all those tantalizing options: settling in Gotham was next to impossible and upgrades were addictive.

"I dunno. You're so...." Trip watched the shaft in Silas's lap bob awake. "I don't get embarrassed."

"I'm afraid that's gonna keep happening. You watching me like that? Fuck." Fully aroused and he made no move to cover it. Trip's intense eyes raked over him, making him feel itchy and gorgeous at the same time. "You keep looking at me like that and I'm yours." He shut his mouth. That had slipped out.

Trip didn't seem to notice. "'F'you say so."

The tops of Silas's ears burned. *He noticed.* "Anybody ever point out you are hung like a moose?"

"I guess." Trip blinked at his crotch as if a fierce animal had built its lair in his pants. "They called me 'Triple-wiggle' in high school because it hung so low it—"

"Kids are monsters." Silas kissed him. "Grown-ups too, mostly. Why I work so fucking much. Monsters sell tickets." He petted Trip's lean chest.

"After I started, y'know, figuring out what was what and goin' with guys, I found out an oversized dork wasn't bad. But it still gets freaky reactions."

"This." Silas squeezed Trip's firm meat. "Is nice. But it's the least of your charms." Funny thing, he'd said it to come off as a gentleman, but he'd actually told the truth. He covered his embarrassment with a kiss. "Mr. Spector."

"I never cared."

"That's 'cause you have a whopper." Silas grinned.

"You're still bigger than a lot of guys." Trip flopped onto his belly; the ruddy crown poked out under his hip.

"Hey…." Silas gave him an impish grin. "There's a million pin-dicks out there playing the deuce they been dealt." How freaky and fun to talk like this on a date, *with* a date.

"I guess." Trip shrugged and shifted onto his side. "I just wish it didn't matter so much."

"With great power comes great responsibility." Silas took hold of the fat cannon.

"I know it takes getting used to." Trip's length flexed shiny in the rough fist. "One thing to tug on it, but some guys—"

"Some guys want something else." Silas licked his teeth.

"You." Trip squeezed the base and the crest bulged, dark and rosy. "Are a log hog. Admit it." He shook his erection as if it were a hungry, disobedient pet.

"Sure. But that's only part. And it isn't even a little ugly." Silas smiled. "Look, I ain't stuffing a black rubber baguette up my ass every night, but I sure don't mind a struggle." His chest rumbled in pleasure. "Let's say that early research indicates a dynamic duo at work: your beast cock and my supersonic butthole."

Trip cackled. "That's so wrong!"

"You *laughed*. If you laugh, then you think it's true."

"Who said that?"

"Everyone." He huffed. "People laugh at the truth because if they didn't laugh, they'd… I dunno. Cry or vomit."

Trip laughed loud and long at that.

Silas ran his palm over Trip's cheek and scalp. "I love the way that feels."

"My lazy-ass stubble? Cheapest haircut on earth."

"So clean and sharp. You're like an etching. Clean lines." Silas nudged Trip's ribs with his nose. He dragged the back of his hand across Trip's throat.

Their eyes caught.

They breathed a few seconds, regarding each other, as if communicating with amazing mutant telepathic powers.

Silas wondered if Trip realized they would spend the night together. They hadn't planned it, but he had no intention of leaving. For whatever reason, he wanted to know when they'd meet again before they'd even parted.

"Hi," Trip whispered and smiled.

"You are gonna"—Silas dropped his gaze and muttered—"mess me up."

"I am?"

"Or take me down. You watch. I got no defenses now."

Trip stared at the drafting table. Two spots of high color rose in his cheeks, and his eyes glittered in the dark when he tightened the blinds.

Silas pushed back against the pillows and dropped one leg to the floor. "Whatsamatter?"

"Something you said." Trip chewed his thumbnail. "Defenses. You do monsters, right?" He pointed at the incubus drawing. "If you were gonna give him an archenemy, who would it be?"

"Well, I'm not a writer, but in movies they say you look at your bad guy. Greater evil."

"Like Hitchcock."

Silas nodded, pleased that he'd remembered. "Give Scratch someone to fight." He prodded Trip with a blunt finger. "You pick your poison and the story will follow."

"I've only got, like, the first eleven pages. Setting. Love interest. No villain yet."

"He'll turn up. They always do." Silas yawned and stretched.

"Would you be willing to read what I got?" Trip shifted from one foot to the other, and the words tumbled out as if unbidden. "If you want, I mean. Just to eyeball it and see what pops out."

Silas batted away cobwebs of hesitation. How tough could it be? "Sure."

"Y'don't have to say yes. 'S'just… until I have a script, I'm frozen. You sure?"

"C'mon. I wanna read it. Hell, I'm gonna be in Arizona more than a week on location, so I'll have lots of time." That felt grown-up too. More than a trick. He knocked their shoulders together and smiled at the evening they'd had. "I bet I can come up with one or two scary ideas for you."

Trip sat up and crossed his legs. "Seriously?"

"Seriously."

"Thanks for staying over. Staying the night. It started out as a terrible idea, and then it wasn't at all."

Silas shifted closer. "You are most welcome, Mr. Spector." He let his gaze roam over Trip's rosy mouth, his huge eyes, the jutting collarbones. "Truth."

Silas laughed, and Trip laughed in response.

He'd love to take Trip out on the town, just to test those waters, but it seemed unlikely. The black television screen on the wall reminded him about his dumb show and the *Undercover Lovers* party next month.

"What?" Trip fell silent, and a big dopey grin stayed on his face. He ran a possessive hand over Silas's flank.

Rigid with desire and decision, Silas crossed his arms over his chest and jumped off the roof, praying the wind would catch him and he'd fly. "Would you like to go to a red carpet party?"

Trip looked confused. "Party?"

"Yes. A social gathering with booze and outfits? You mighta heard of 'em." Silas grinned.

"Jerk." But Trip chuckled.

"But this'd be business. I have to go to this big Showtime shindig for the buyers and affiliates. Black-tie nonsense. But I'd like you to come with me." Silas neglected to mention that the party was in *April*, two months away. He'd never done that before.

"Black tie."

"You don't have to wear a tux." He clenched his fists so they wouldn't shake.

Trip ducked his head and smiled. "I'd love to."

"Good. 'Cause I'd sure love to *see* you in a tux." Silas shook his head fondly.

"I meant I'd love to come. I have the tux I wore to Ben's wedding, if that's okay. It's probably out-of-date and everyone will laugh at me."

"Not everyone. I'll try to get it off you." Silas kissed his cheek. "Good. Thanks." Making a date that far in advance gave him a fluttery *trapped* feeling he chose to ignore.

"Thank you." Trip cupped his hands under his lean thighs. "I didn't expect that."

"Neither did I. I usually hate industry shit, but I…." Silas took a decisive breath. "I like doing most anything with you, it seems."

"Well, when is it?"

"Oh God! I forgot. Not till April. The twelfth. God, I'm sorry. Awful."

"I bet I can squeeze you in." Trip blushed and smiled so wide, his rosy cheeks hit his eyes.

"Likewise." Silas kissed him again. He eyed the pile of pages on the end table, marked up with red pen and panel doodles in the margins.

"Maybe you'll find a little evil I can use."

Silas rubbed Trip's side. His blunt cock flopped onto his inner thigh. "You know the style. You know the world."

Trip fidgeted. "I gotta finish the script before I ink the interiors. Anything could change. I don't know enough about *him*."

"Scratch." Silas asserted proudly. He loved how that title had just woven itself out of the spark between them. That's what creating, what dating, should feel like.

"Scratch. Yeah." Trip agreed with obvious pleasure. "I just need my bad guy."

"You'll find him one of these days."

Trip kissed him. "I guess I'll have to keep looking."

10

THERE'S a moment when gay guys have dated awhile and feel like they're cheating on every guy they still haven't had a chance to bone.

Is he a fuckbuddy or a boyfriend?

Over a week had passed while Silas managed to avoid reading Trip's script in Phoenix, because he was terrified he'd hate it or that he'd sound stupid. Since he'd gotten the damn thing, he'd twisted the paper into a rumpled tube, as if he could wring an opinion out of it.

He couldn't *not* read the script and say nothing or slather on a bunch of fake praise, else he became an instant dick—and he didn't want that. Now the twelve-odd pages for *Scratch #1* felt like a uranium cinderblock in his backpack: toxic and unwieldy. He'd never let anyone trust him that much, and now he knew why.

Guilty as all get out, he kept dodging Trip's messages for fear he'd have to confess his failure. After weeks of talking and texting almost daily, Silas knew his sudden case of incommunicado was bound to confuse Trip.

After getting home to his apartment last night, Silas knew he should go see Trip, but the *Scratch* script paralyzed him as surely as a spinal injury. He'd convinced himself he was too tired to think and had gone to bed. And this morning he'd gone right out to the *Undercover Lovers* set without so much as a heads-up to Trip that he'd returned safely.

Outside, snow fell in fat flakes that muffled the city. Riding the Q from Queens toward Chelsea, Silas sat with his stomach in knots. He stared at the pages Trip might as well have written in ancient Kryptonian. In the past, he would've taken this kind of pressure as an excuse to bail... but not this time. *Not this guy.* So he bit the speeding bullet and texted Trip that he'd bring groceries over to make dinner.

Splash's happy hour was in full grind when he stepped inside and stomped his boots. The dancers took Speedo-showers on the bar, roid-rage bartenders poured bottom-shelf cocktails, and a scattering of lonely queeroes of all ages gossiped about nothing before they went home to watch RuPaul.

Silas dropped the rolled script on the bar and zipped his backpack. He'd wrapped his damp gym clothes in a towel, and after this, he needed to haul ass to swing by Whole Foods before he went to Trip's apartment. Maybe he could just bluff his way through with vague praise after he cooked. The script had become an angel with a flaming sword. *None shall pass.*

At the side bar, Kurt chatted animatedly with one of the ripped bartenders who moonlighted in porn. He had slept with about a third of the staff, namely the ones who rented by the night and shot HGH.

While he waited, Silas ordered a Heineken and claimed two high stools. Though psyched to see Kurt, he didn't have much time before he needed to split. He swigged the beer, then checked his watch as Kurt's cool hands gripped his shoulders.

"So Goolsby... for the season three affiliates party." Kurt tilted his bearded head side to side to side like a child working up to a big lie. "I was thinking we could do matching suits. My treat. *Undercover Brothers for Unbored Games.* Maybe make out for the paps for bonus points."

"No." Silas winced. He'd forgotten to say anything to Kurt.

"Incest plays great with the chat shows."

"Sure, but I have a date already. I'm bringing Trip."

The grin on Kurt's face shriveled.

Silas steeled himself. "I sorta figured you'd figure."

Kurt shook his gray head. "We go to all these events together."

"Kurt, it's a joke to you, and he'd enjoy it."

No response. Great. *Fourth-grade playground here we come.*

Kurt scowled. "Does he even want to go?"

"The whole thing happened by accident. We were in—"

"Spare me."

"Kurt, the food sucks, the buyers are horrible. The stars will ignore us anyhow." He shrugged. "I just would like to take him to a red carpet thing so he can see that side of what I do."

Maybe a swanky party would make up for ignoring the script and his silence for the past week. *Or not.*

"I think you're trying to wreck this. I think you know the two of you aren't compatible and you want to move things along. You sure you aren't getting bored?"

"I like him. I more than like him. It's been a month."

Kurt shrugged like a movie musical Frenchman. "He wears glasses."

"Just to read." Silas looked up sharply. "How did you know that?"

"Silas... you always-but-*always* get screwed up over the quiet nerdy ones."

"That's not—that's... true, actually. Isn't it? Jesus. I do." Silas widened his eyes in horrified recognition.

"If they're confident and social, ripped or rich, you could give a what-what, but another uptight dork with a pocket protector and a fat man candle? *Bink*: you spackle your tackle."

Without thinking, Silas picked up the *Scratch* script and twisted it tighter in his hands. "That's oversimplifying a lot."

Kurt closed his teeth. "Goolsby, after like nine hundred years, I know you pretty well. No way are you gonna be able to stay faithful to some uptight head case who can't go to the Saint with you and check your prostate on stage with a zucchini."

"I'm not that guy anymore." Silas doubted he ever had been. "None of that matters."

"People don't change. Perspectives, maybe. Knowledge. But we don't alter our DNA because someone punches some imaginary reset button nine inches inside of us." Kurt tapped at the wall. "I am pointing at the actual reality of your life, Bubba."

"Right." Silas hated being called Bubba. Kurt knew it and did it to make him feel fat and inbred. "He's not closeted. Well, reclusive. He's proud... just not *loud*."

"Okay, fine. Sure. You're free to be a hermit if you want. Even fuck a hermit. I'm just saying...." Shrug. "Do you have anything in common other than his jumbo doodler?"

Silas frowned but didn't take the bait. "Yes? No? He's... I don't know how to explain it."

Kurt took a swig. "I just did."

Silas tossed the script back on the bar amid the graveyard of glasses. "Trip is...." He fell silent. *Is what?* How could he explain something he didn't understand? *Trip is stubborn... cautious... kind... neurotic... kinky... sad... funny... seductive.* For a nanosecond, he saw Trip's dark eyes while he tortured them both with his beautiful boner and the high cheekbones that made him look happy even when nervous. "Super. He's just more guarded than I am. Y'know? Clark Kent! Once you get the glasses off—"

"Perfect. A prude and a slut. Sounds like a fabulous idea."

"Fuck you." Silas barked a nonlaugh, half-offended because Kurt didn't seem to be joking at all. "There's no mistake that I'm trying to undo. This isn't a problem I'm trying to solve. It's a happy possibility."

"Goolsby, you been with porn stars!"

Silas snorted. "Brent sucked! Even you said so."

"But you see what I'm getting at?"

"Let's see. Dating a burnout who tricks at WWF matches is a rotten idea."

"Silas—"

"Oh wait! Maybe I learned that spray-tanned nitwits who live on canned meat can stun animals with their farts. Literally. Empirically. My super's cat still can't open its left eye."

"That doesn't mean that every twinky-dink is the Holy Grail."

"Kurt." Silas crossed his arms, feeling angrier than he should but knowing somehow this argument mattered. "If living on the elliptical and wearing the right swimsuit and using the best gel for your Grindr picture makes every homo so incandescently happy, then why does Chelsea look like a bag of angry Doritos?"

"Amen." Kurt raised his glass.

"V-shaped. Bright orange. Fake spice. Musky. Stale." Silas glared at the interchangeable men around the room. They were supposed to seem hot, but he couldn't muster curiosity, even. "Doritos!"

He glanced at his watch. He needed to finish up this beer and catch a cab or he was going to be late getting to Trip's place. He still hadn't figured out what to do about the script. "Funniest thing, I turn into a gentleman around him. I mean, I'm me... but I do all these things that my folks woulda loved. At first 'cause I tried to charm him, but the more I did it, the more real it felt."

"In a month? Took you this long to get this fucked up." Kurt drummed his fingers on the bar top.

The little barback swiveled to see if they needed refills. Silas grunted in the negative and winked in reflex, then smacked himself mentally. *Stop it.* Why did he do that shit? *Old habits die hard.*

Kurt sat and stared, waiting for him to say something. Then, "Uhh, Goolsby. That was a joke. You're broke and from Alabama-stan, but otherwise you're the least fucked-up person I know." He spread his hands as if sculpting Godzilla out of the air. "I just say no way is comparing secret decoder rings with some closet-case pity fuck gonna work for you."

Silas grinned. "Two words." He let the animal satisfaction steal over his smile. "Nerd sex." He thought about Trip inside him, taking charge out of nowhere with a smile on his face.

"That's a good thing?" Kurt looked uncomfortable at the very idea.

"Things get any better, I'd have to hire someone to help me enjoy 'em. There's just—he—I feel like I have all these options I never noticed. Like my life isn't a concrete box."

"No, dear." Kurt patted his arm and simpered, "It's a *pine* box."

Silas mock-wagged a finger. "Don't be a douche. I like him. As in, really-a-lot like him. You'd like him. Hell, the two of you are a lot alike, though it'd kill y'all to admit it. He's your *not*-evil twin." He sipped his beer. *True.* He'd never thought about it until now.

Kurt spread his fingers. "Silas, a fish and a bird can fall in love, but where will they live?"

"I'm not a fish."

"C'mon, Goolsby." Kurt rubbed his eye.

"Then he's not a bird!" Silas felt angrier than he should.

"How about a dish"—he poked Silas's chest—"and a nerd?" Kurt jerked his thumb back at the snowy street outside, where, presumably, Trip committed some egregious taste-crime no card-carrying homo could tolerate.

"Ha ha. Asshole."

"I'm asking a real question."

"That has no answer. Because I'm not a fish or a bird. I'm a man. He's a man. I may lo—"

"Don't say it." Kurt held up a perfectly manicured warning hand. "Don't you say that fucking word unless you want me to dissect that shit into atoms. Look, date whoever, fuck whoever, but at least go for someone who can spend time in your life."

Silas said nothing.

The barback toddled by to pick up some of the bar rubble from in front of them. The bottles clinked together, but they ignored him.

"I respect every man's need to have a kinky fetish that drives him to addiction, sweatpants, and irrational ruin."

"That's my weakness." Silas picked at his cuff. *Peter Parker. Clark Kent.* "Nice guys."

"Drips," Kurt scoffed and spread his arms. "What?"

"No." Silas squinted at the rows of uplit bottles in frustration. "Isn't the wrong move sometimes the best way forward? I mean, are all mistakes bad?"

No response. The bar crowd muttered and squawked around them. At first Silas thought his friend hadn't heard anything he'd said.

Kurt stroked his salt and pepper hair with a careful hand, not touching so much as grooming himself. "Fine. He's going with you to your big hairy opening." He had dropped his gaze, and he didn't mouth off. "I shouldn't have said anything. It's your funeral."

"Have you ever been with someone because they just kicked your ass? I don't mean nagging, but like talking-walking-sleeping-being with them makes you want to upgrade your whole life?"

To his surprise, Kurt didn't have a snappy comeback or a bitchy comment as he twirled his empty glass on the bar as if he knew more than he wanted to share. He closed his eyes for a moment. "No."

He's lying. Silas remembered seeing his best friend like this, but not when. He sat back, surprised. Kurt looked as though he'd been ready to step off a skyscraper ledge and then yanked his foot back.

What is he hiding?

Splash hummed around them. The sconces warmed the walls, and the scatter of glasses witnessed the argument. For a second, Silas wondered what the furniture would say if they could share an opinion of everything they'd seen, which was plenty. Maybe the room would know how to read the *Scratch* script. Maybe the room would understand why Trip calmed and confused him.

"Do I get to meet Prince Charmless at some point?" Kurt didn't meet his eyes.

"It's only been a month." Crazy to think. "You will." The thought sat perfectly with him. Trip had been asking about his friends, and Kurt's bark and bite were miles apart. "You'll meet him at C2E2. You're going."

"Obviously. Pavilion."

"Trip's gonna be there." The Chicago Comic and Entertainment Expo was a major pop culture convention each April; not as horrible as the San Diego or New York ComicCons.

"Are you?"

Good question. Silas hadn't discussed it, but rather than give Kurt more fuel, he made the decision at that instant. "Yeah. I never been. Thought I might tag along."

Kurt sulked and kept his yap shut.

"Trip will be in Artist Alley selling sketches and original pages." Silas shrugged. "We don't have to wait until then, Kurt. He's dying to meet you."

"Five more minutes." Kurt inspected his phone and frowned. "Ziggy said he'd drop by."

Ziggy? Silas glanced again at his watch and slugged back the last of his warm beer. "I really gotta bolt."

Kurt nodded and dropped the subject so hard it practically dented the floor. "Get a load of Nick Fury. Ten o'clock. Eye patch and skinny jeans. Whaddayasay? I'm betting post-rehab crystal queen with a sock fetish?"

He must have spoken too loud. The eye-patch guy gave Kurt the finger.

"C'mon, man." At that exact moment, Silas noticed the rolled script had vanished off the bar in front of them. His mouth went dry and the blood drained from the top half of his body. "Where'd it go?"

"Get outta here." Kurt summoned his roving bartender, making a finger lasso over his head to signal he wanted another. "Help is on the way."

"Oh shit." Silas stood and leaned over the bar to see if it had fallen behind. "Kurt, where's the fucking script?"

Kurt shot him a side-eye. "Goolsby, I didn't see a script. Just call your agent and have the production office send a new PDF."

"Not for the show! Not for the show." Silas crouched and checked the floor around their stools, seeing nothing but expensive shoes and trousers. "Jesus fucking—"

"What's the big deal?"

"I had twisted it into a tube, and I guess it fell." His shaky hand floated to his mouth. His stomach had gone wobbly and hollow.

"Silas. Calm down." Kurt's perfectly plucked eyebrows drifted together in irritation.

"Trip gave me a script to read, and I've—oh my fucking God." Silas sat down, right where he was on the floor, peered at the forest of legs around him, and didn't care how crazy he looked. "I'm supposed to go over there right now to talk about it. I'm ten minutes late already."

"Not the end of the world. Just tell him what you thought and get another copy."

But Silas hadn't actually figured out what he thought. He hadn't read the fucking thing for fear he'd think the wrong thing or prove himself an idiot. And to ask Trip for another copy would make him more of a heartless prick than he already was for avoiding the poor guy for a week. *I'm an asshole.*

His pocket rang: the *Spider-Man* theme by the Ramones.

Trip.

Kurt cast an eye around the crowded bar. "I'm gonna go take a piss so you and Drip can have some privacy."

Silas peered through shins, and his phone sang against the floor.

"Uh, I think that's for you." Kurt got up and drained his glass before he walked away. "And I'll bet you a new tuxedo that it's still a wrong number."

Silas answered the phone.

TRIP hung up and dropped his cell like a maggoty trout on his messy bed. *End call.*

"Whatsamatter?" Rina stopped chewing on her hair.

"You tell me." Trip flipped his hand at her, expecting her to understand.

She had just finished boxing the wedding dress from the OutRun Organ Trail. After her website hit twenty thousand views of her New Year's zombie video, she'd auctioned off the mud-'n'-blood-stained gown to a lucky fan in Florida. She'd give the money to a global literacy campaign. "Silas on his way?"

Trip stalked to the window that overlooked Greenwich buried in dirty snow. Wide flakes fell straight through the windless air to the pavement. "Not anymore. I knew it."

Rina regarded the phone. "I don't understand."

"Ditto."

"Maybe he got stuck at work." Rina often pulled all-nighters on deadline, so she could sympathize.

"No idea. It sounded more like he got stuck in a happy hour with his fuckbuddies." Trip shrugged. "Doesn't matter. At least he claimed it was work."

Rina shrugged. "He works on movies. He went on location, and he can't text or call a bunch and now they've run over schedule. He rescheduled so he wouldn't stand you up."

"Okay."

"He's called you this week."

"No. Well, he texted from Arizona. I just assumed he'd get back and want to see me." What had they said to each other? Inchoate anger fuzzied his thoughts.

She bugged her eyes. "He does want to see you. He just tried to reschedule a date with you, and you acted like he'd handed you a bag of snake turds."

"He's been back from the shoot since yesterday."

"He's prob'ly catching up." Rina swatted his chest. "He likes you. He cooks actual food from the earth for you. *Bellaco*, don't get crazy. Why are you acting like he's a bad guy?"

"I gave him a script." He dropped his eyes.

"No shit. You keep expecting him to act out this whole scenario—"

"No! Fuck off. I mean he offered to read the rough draft of the demon comic thing. *Scratch*." He hadn't told her the new name, and she didn't react to *that*.

"Oh no." She inhaled sharply. "Trip Spector."

"What?"

"You don't give your new boyfriend a script to critique! That's awful."

Trip coughed and felt stupid. "Why?"

"What if he gave you something to critique? Would you be able to give him notes? Too harsh and you're a dick, too soft and you're a moron. He's prob'ly immobilized. Talk about death ray."

Shit.

"Worse... what if you thought it sucked—*not saying it does*—but if you dug him and wanted to make sure you didn't fuck anything up."

Trip nodded and grimaced. "I'm an asshole."

"You're an artist. And you were raised by wombats with a personality bypass. Two strikes."

Trip's parents *had* messed with his head, but he crossed his arms and scowled. She didn't understand. Rina's parents crowed about "their little best seller." Her entire extended family pimped her novels with religious fervor. "That's not fair."

"Boo hoo. What is this 'fair' you speak of? Unless you're going for three strikes, I say you stop deciding what he has to do that makes him worthy of your attention. Do you like him or not?"

"What's it matter if I like him? He's avoided my calls."

"*Papa*, you lobbed a fucking artistic grenade over the wall at this nice guy, and you're bitching 'cause he didn't pull the pin?"

Trip turned on her. "I just talked to him a minute ago and he's at a fucking bar with that friend. The Unbored asshole.... Kurt video-game whatshisname Zillionaire. That doesn't sound like working. He sounded like I'd caught him doing something. Guilty!" An accusatory finger.

"So... you're pissed because he didn't come back from Arizona and immediately sit down and line edit the stump of your sex demon script for you."

"No." He exhaled. "Fuck you."

"Or maybe you're mad because he didn't invite you out to go drinking while he's gushing about you to his friends and getting the same fucking advice you're wanting from me? Like you're doing right now?"

Trip found himself looking at her coat that hung on the back of a chair. The snow on the buffed leather had melted into dirty water. *Oh.* Abashed, Trip looked down at himself.

"For four years you been cutting the Unboyfriend slack for way worse headfuckery, and a couple weeks with your hot zombie, one rain check and—*pow*—he's Doctor Doom."

"Maybe." Trip blinked. *Fuckety-fuck.* Maybe he'd projected his history onto this poor guy. Cliff had strung him along for so many years he was hypersensitive to the signs. Silas had that same easy, loping sexiness that made Cliff so appealing. That didn't mean they were the same man. "When you put it like that."

She had a point. Of course, Cliff flirted, too. Why didn't that bother him? *Because we aren't together or apart.* The limbo kept it tolerable. How much of the fun he had with Silas involved a fantasy about the boss he'd never snag? He'd used Silas to act out his fantasies, but now Silas meant more to him than that. *Ugh.* He tried and failed to not feel like a dirtbag. *Maybe for the best.*

Trip glanced at the portfolio of his Scratch sketches. The staple mocked his pain. He still didn't have a villain. *But plenty of bad guys.*

Working from the partial script, he had the first twelve pages drawn, but the incubus had stayed fuzzy in his mind and on the page. Scratch morphed and mutated as little slivers of porn and models and fantasy congealed under his pencil. When the character embodied all his sticky, angry fantasies about Cliff, he changed tack and Silas snuck onto the panels.

He sniffed hard.

Always with new projects, Trip scavenged his life for details and then repurposed them. With this character, his emotions drove his hand. The two versions of his incubus wrestled on the paper. Out of spite, part of him wanted to debauch Cliff's rangy swimmer's body and apple-pie good looks. But then, the first splash page manifestly showed the barbarian's build and sloe-eyed gaze he associated with Silas, and the warm sexiness softened the creepier elements in the plot.

"I'm asking some basic questions here." Rina counted on her short oxblood nails. "Hot guy: sweet, smart, funny. He eats organic. Cool job and a comic dork. And the sex is great." A suggestive smile.

"Fuck off, Sabrina. I'm not talking about that."

"I wasn't asking, *cabron*. I can see that the sex is good. Whole month you been walking like a cowboy with a hundred bucks in his pocket. God save me from a man like that...." Rina flashed a slice of teeth. "A guy you could go to hell with."

"No hell for me, thanks."

"Trip, he goes away for a week and calls you."

He blew his nose. "Not calls, but yeah. He texts and e-mailed a couple times."

"That's normal!"

"So I'm a freak."

"Trip Spector, don't you put words in my mouth. You're not a freak. You are a-*lone*. You been by yourself for so long, you expect everyone to play by rules you made up in your head and wrote in invisible ink."

He dropped down onto the couch and picked at the cushion's threads. "All I'm saying is that the thing has probably run its course. We have fun, but he's not gonna get serious, and I shouldn't get serious about someone who will never settle down with anyone."

"He told you that." She looked dubious.

"Not with his mouth, but… yeah. I don't think he has real intentions with me. Jillian thinks so. And Ben. Hell, even Cliff thinks so… but Silas and I just have fun."

"Fun? Say it isn't *so!*" Rina gasped melodramatically. "The shame! The horror…." She fanned herself like a granny in church. "Two homo-*sex*-shuls having a gay old time and yabba-dabba-doing it on every flat surface because they like each other." She snorted with laughter.

"Yuk-yuk. Thanks. Totally unfair. Why is it when you have a guy who's commitment-phobic, you always say to run, but I'm s'posedta hunker down?"

"Because he's not phobic. Every single thing he's doing is committed."

"Not committed to me."

"*Papa*, don't start writing out how you want this whole thing to go. Or better yet, if you're gonna write *this* script, then you better give him a copy so he knows what his lines are."

Trip wiped his nose. She *was* being unfair. Rina usually had a no-nonsense approach to dating: guys were right or wrong for her and she didn't tolerate fussy bullshit. "Sometimes one and one make two."

Rina smiled. "You're right. That's exactly right." *Sesame Street* voice. "And two is bigger and more complicated than one, for boys and girls. One plus one is a relationship." She stared at him without blinking.

"That's not what I meant." He blinked and scowled. "Okay, sometimes one minus one makes zero."

"Then you better make sure he's nothing before you start subtracting."

11

Never in his life had Silas had anyone he wanted to call on Valentine's Day, and Trip wouldn't answer the fucking phone.

Silas had screwed things right up on so many levels. Old habits and exhaustion had steered him right back into the kind of shit that banana-peeled every boyfriend in his pathetic history. He didn't even know which apology to make. After he lost Trip's pages, he'd managed to locate them, but too late to make a difference. Another week had passed incommunicado. *Not good.*

Years ago, he'd gone out with a slinky waiter he'd picked up at a Moroccan restaurant. They'd "dated" for about a month in the winter and had slow, sloppy sex that took hours while the radiators clanked and spat. Silas had wallowed in the hookup because his heat was out and this fuckbuddy had a super who kept the boiler dialed to tropical. Both in their early twenties with bullshit jobs and serious stamina, they'd call in sick to work and watch cartoons when they weren't breaking commandments. They'd fuck and sweat and fuck and sweat... and drink quarts of orange juice from the health-food store downstairs. Perfect winter distraction.

Then one night, they'd screwed for two hours, rinsed off, and when Silas had climbed back onto the futon, the Moroccan had given him a big bouquet. "Happy Valentine," without the S because his English wasn't so great, but he worked his ass off to fit into his new country. "Valentine" as in one "special person" instead of Valentine's *day*. And—*ohcrap*—those soft puppy eyes wanted Silas to have something romantic in his rough hands to give back.

Argh.

Silas hadn't realized February had already rolled around. For one endless, embarrassed second, he'd known for certain this pretty waiter believed he'd come over on St. Valentine's Day because he imagined a tender romance had bloomed between them. To his eternal shame, Silas simply wanted his muffin stuffed hard with a thick North African club.

Horrible.

He'd never gone back to the apartment, not because he couldn't, but because he'd used the poor guy and his father would have whupped his butt for treating another human being like that. How does anyone apologize for being so callous? Now he couldn't even remember that waiter's name.

I'm sorry I treated you like a dildo.

Eight years later, he offered a metaphorical bouquet to Trip, who now thought he was *that* guy: the asshole who used someone like a Fleshjack. For anyone to think that seemed gross; for Trip to think that made him want to binge eat until he ruptured and died.

His mama believed in apologies and gratitude. You screwed up, you said you were sorry. All he wanted was to get Trip on the phone so he could make amends. He'd messed up the script thing, but he'd fallen into his own crappy habits. Going out of town and then hiding hadn't helped. He'd gone silent. He'd panicked.

Silas had spent most of his adult life in the secret club in which casual dating persisted as a mildly athletic hobby. All metro queers had slept with each other, all knew each other and kept each other's secrets... but committing to one guy became a white flag of surrender waved by men too worn-out or damaged to stay in the game. The truth was, he didn't dread ending up alone as much as ending up chained to the wrong person.

He'd left two voice mails, texted, and e-mailed. He didn't care if Trip thought he was nuts, because the chance to apologize had become more precious than anything he could imagine.

The night he'd canceled with Trip, he had gone through garbage at Splash for three hours, up to his thighs in sticky and sweet shredded paper and clanking bottles. Their dumpsters had smelled like hobo vomit, but he had dived in. No way were Trip's pages going to vanish because of his fuckup.

Even if Trip didn't know what had happened, Silas would.

I'm sorry I treated your work like a rehab diaper.

On Valentine's morning his phone rang: Tiffany.

"You're not going to believe this shit."

Silas grunted. "Probably not. It's 9:00 a.m."

Tiffany sounded breathless. "Yeah. Remember that guy from the park? New Year's. That doctor guy. I found his card. Remember? He left his deets and I lost 'em."

"What?" He pressed his eyeballs. The universe had a nasty sense of humor. "It's okay, I don't—"

"The hottie from the zombie run." Rustling. "Trip. The card says Big Dog, and on the back he wrote his name and number."

Silas laughed. "That's a lousy idea."

"C'mon. It's Valentine's. Grudges don't count. Write this down." Then she recited the number Silas already knew by his heavy heart. "Everybody wants a Valentine."

Silas hung up and studied the digits he'd written down for no reason. Maybe Tiffany had a point. Trip had to forgive him on Valentine's Day.

I'm sorry I didn't know how to help you.

He decided to call and not leave a message until Trip finally picked up. By now, he needed to know what had happened. Trip cold-shouldered him. Silas groveled for forgiveness. *Never the twain shall meet.* Unless he did something drastic.

Silas stared at his clock. Still way too early to call. For ninety minutes, he paced in his apartment, scripted out the words he'd use. The date he'd offer. He'd beg and cringe to make his complete shame clear. The manifold proofs of his regret and awareness.

Confident at ten in the morning. By noon, cautious but still ready to give it a go. By three, he worried Trip wouldn't pick up. Maybe he had his ringer off while he drew or wrote. Maybe he'd gone out with his girlfriends or that Cliff and told laughable tales about the overeager muscle bottom he'd scraped off. Maybe he'd moved on, gone on a date with some cooler, thinner, smarter, calmer, S-less Valentine who made him happy instead of a miserable sack of shit fritters. Or maybe Trip sat alone and disappointed on the couch, watching *The Dark Knight*.

Silas couldn't even call Kurt for advice because Silas wanted something Kurt didn't understand.

I'm sorry I expected you to fall for my same old rigmarole.

In the past, he'd have cut bait the minute things got heavy, but somehow everything with Trip had been heavy since they'd met at the zombie run.

Was he serious about Trip or not? Why did all this matter to him? And if it didn't, why didn't he just ball it up and toss it like he'd done with so many other perfectly fine guys?

Because Trip was not perfectly fine for him.

Perfect.

Supposedly, they still had a date to go to the Showtime affiliate party together, in a couple of months. *No time like the present.*

By six, words felt worthless. Was there anything salvageable enough to make it worth camping out on Trip's stoop like a stalker? A lifetime of being the ugly fat kid from Shitkick, Alabama, had left no leeway on that front. Agonized by the wait, Silas knew he wasn't strong enough to stand on the street with a drip on his nose watching Trip hate him.

I'm sorry it's taken me so long to see you clearly.

By the time dark rolled in, he'd reached some kind of horrible impasse, like a stupid walrus pining over a seagull. He mixed an oversized salad of dry romaine lettuce because he needed to eat. It tasted like weeds.

Then the idea hit him.

Trip deserved more than a fucking card, or a date, or a string of sentences that said all the right crap. Instead of scrabbling around to figure out what Trip wanted to hear or what he could do to prove himself worthy, Silas decided to give Trip what he really deserved.

A gift.

Not something expensive or fancy. Not some jokey trinket to break the ice.

Trip had said something the day they met in Central Park. *"You're really gifted."* That's where the spark started. Two artists alone in the woods, surrounded by fake monsters.

And I'm so sorry I wasn't ready for you to be so wonderful.

Silas smiled at the memory and missed him. At some point Trip Spector had started to mean more to him than a lean body on top of him on cold nights. Trip just kept on pulling rugs out from under him and making all the dim corners of his life seem empty. Maybe he didn't understand yet how much Silas had changed.

If Silas cared at all, if this guy meant one fucking thing to him, the time had come for some swooping and saving.

Some mistakes are worth making.

No bed tonight. His feelings had flip-flopped so completely that he felt as if his heart were dyslexic. *Yearning disabled.*

His father had always said, "Nothing lost that can't be found." He just needed to go look. *I can do this.*

He went to his desk and pulled out the photocopy he'd made of Trip's stained script, worse for wear but still legible. He pored over the half-written pages and the panel descriptions, tried to see what Trip had built behind his closed eyes. Some of it was there, but some came from hints Trip had let slip.

Silas took a deep breath and shut his lids as if playing hide and seek with his future. *Ready or not, here I come.* What could he give Trip that would save them both a whole bunch of misery and mistakes?

Trip would be signing *Hero High*'s new issue at Forbidden Planet on the twenty-fourth. He'd seen the *Time Out* ad on Trip's corkboard a couple of weeks back, and Trip had complained about going. Silas would fucking stand in line if he had to.

His mind snapped and churned like a piranha tank. In his mind's eye, he saw the sad Moroccan waiter and that sad bouquet of deli roses. At 9:17, he decided to give up and leave a Valentine's message, however unwelcome, because he was fixing to come apart like a ten-dollar suitcase at the bus station. His hands sweated as he dialed. His scarred fingers smeared the face of his phone. In his own ears, his voice sounded breathless and worried, but so it was.

But I'll never-never-never in my life be sorry for knowing you or needing you.

"Hey, Trip." A cough. "'S'me. Uhh, Silas. And I wanted to say hello. Silas Goolsby, I mean. Actually I want to say I'm sorry. But I figured I should start with hello and then I could get going on the sorries because there are quite a few which I owe you. And—I'm thinking about you. Umm. A bunch. All the time. You might be out tonight, but I wanted to say I miss you and—" He cleared his dry throat quietly. "I hope you have a wonderful Valentine."

Valentine. Only after he'd hung up did he realize he must have immigrated to the land of lonely, deluded fuckbuddies at some point, because he had dropped the S too.

CLIFF had summoned Trip to the principal's office at *Hero High.*

Rather, he'd demanded an emergency editorial meeting at Big Dog, on Valentine's Day no less.

Same diff.

On the train, his eyes started to smart, so Trip popped open the Allegra bottle, rattled a pill into his hand. His first in how long? He spitswallowed it.

As soon as he came through the door of the midtown office, Kimmie waved him back to the office where Cliff paced red-faced around a scatter of inked Bristol boards on his desk.

"Emergency?" Trip knocked on the doorframe as he stepped through. For once, the moldy recycled air didn't clog his lungs instantly. "There a problem?"

Cliff obviously wanted some kind of rescue, else why had he shown up all flushed from a run, wearing sweatshirt and shorts in the middle of February?

"Sex maniacs, bro!" Cliff turned and scowled at the waterstained ceiling. "Fucking South America." He waved his hand at printouts on his desk. "See for yourself."

Trip leaned closer over the inks. *Yep.* The Mighty Mites had wandered into the Land of Kinderslut again. Because Cliff constantly cut corners and leaned on young foreign artists with hellish deadlines, the racks and tackle always ballooned and the costumes shrank in the wash.

While Cliff geared up to beg, Trip shifted his portfolio and backpack. He had the odd sensation he was watching the Big Dog offices from above. He could predict the way this maneuvering would play out, like chess moves, and for once, Cliff's tizzy left him unflustered. In one sense, he missed the simple pleasure of Staplegun soft-soaping him. Still, four weeks after Cliff had swiped his *Campus Champions* idea and given it to that child, watching his Unboyfriend squirm gave him a steady intravenous drip of contentment.

Now he was relieved Cliff had hijacked the new project. Compared to *Scratch*, it seemed like an insipid rehash of about fifteen other titles. Let some other pathetic wannabe corner the market on anodyne pastel co-eds.

Cliff scratched his sweaty head and licked his lip. "I can cover most of these with balloons when we letter... but a couple of these are like *Sir Juggs-alot.*"

"I don't have time, Cliff. I'm already finishing pages on two books." He put his sketchpad on the desk and lowered into a chair. "I can't squeeze more hours outta the day. I gotta sleep sometime."

"Please." Cliff gazed up through his eyelashes and bit the inside of his cheek without shame. He literally bumped the edge of the table with his fat basket, and Trip had to look. *Neanderthal brain.*

The wad in front of him trapped Trip's gaze for a split second, but he didn't soften or step closer. "Full fee, Stapleton. You're paying me my full quote. What IDE and Image pay me. No shit about it, either. This is me saving your penny-pinching ass at the fifty-ninth minute."

"Deal." Cliff gave him a thumbs-up. "And it's just the one splash page. Tomorrow if you can swing it." Blink. Sexy smile. *Asshole.* Cliff's chrome had flaked off.

"Tomorrow?" Trip reached across the table and spun the drawing around: a doublewide splash page. "Wait...."

"Twelve and thirteen. I guess that is kinda two pages." He perched on the desk on one round buttcheek.

Trip blinked, breathed, and didn't say anything.

Cliff flashed the five-hundred-watt smile and circled his chair to lay big hands on Trip's shoulders. Kneading them gently and well, he leaned down. "Ohh-kay. I can pay for two. Or I could blow you a little."

Ha ha.

The black-and-white page depicted a crowded lockered hallway, packed with squeaky clean multiethnic students on their way to class. The main scene showed a pert blonde kissing Alphalad. In the foreground, Princess Quantum pouted, her arms folded under her cleavage as she roasted with jealousy and gave them the third-wheel side-eye: a teen superhero love triangle.

"I mean, dude...." Cliff pointed and sniffed. "Eugenia almost has nipples, and Alphalad's packing a superstiffy. These fucking Brazilians."

"What stiffy? I don't see anything stiff on him." Trip put his face closer to the inked board. "Or nipples. I think your mind's in the gutter."

"His *bulge* is in the gutter." The space between the panels, he meant, and no, it wasn't. "Like a possum in his pants. Jesus." Cliff tapped Alphalad's crotch with his tan finger. "Or a gigondo gonad-wad. He could get her pregnant if he sneezed."

Trip scanned Alphalad's basket again, unable to detect the gruesome cockmonster. "Cliff, you're overreacting. I don't see an erection. Maybe the angle of the zipper is a little wonky. And maybe, if you're trying, the shadow makes some camel toe. If you're an incorrigible chicken hawk and you squint."

"Well, check out Eugenia's headlights front and center. Princess Quantum's lactating like a sow." The brunette, he meant. C-cups yes, nipples... not a one. "Nips of steel."

Phantom nips, apparently, because Trip spotted nothing erect under her sweater, just another bland googly-eyed teen Barbie drawn in a country where artists worked cheap and sexism still seemed sexy. *Whatevs.* "You're paranoid."

"No. I'm cautious. *Walmart* is paranoid. I can't have a Million Mom March against *Hero High.*"

You should be so lucky. Sales would explode as kids assumed this dumb title was racier than it was.

Cliff tugged Trip's portfolio closer and swiped through the newest artwork... making obligatory whistles and hisses of ass-kissing praise.

At twelve, Trip had dreamed about the perfect bodies in *Spawn* and *Hellblazer.* He imagined the sad gay kids, trapped in shithole born-again towns, dying of shame and boredom, dreaming of a never-never land of superpowered Lost Boys with tantalizing bulges, battling Captain Shnook. Trip couldn't fly in and rescue them with his miraculous pencil, but maybe the next best thing.

Why couldn't Alphalad have a mastodon wang? Why couldn't he have super speed and be a power bottom?

"Tripwire, you gotta save me here." Cliff's huge cocky grin and sad smile offered the same blank Trip had always filled in without a second thought.

Any self-respecting artist would've said no. Any shrewd queer would've felt pissed at the blatant metrosexual will-he, won't-he come-on. Any rational adult would've said you don't pay me enough and this comic is a bland rip-off of comics with tighter writing and sharper audiences.

Not me. Trip would fix the fake problems on Cliff's double splash page and then use that money for *Scratch.* Buy himself a little wiggle room. He needed a couple of weeks to finish the issue one script and get some tight samples drawn. Silas blowing him off had only steeled his resolve.

In the back of his mind, Trip formulated a plan. Con season would gear up in the spring, and for nine months, he'd sit in convention halls across America with hundreds of indie comic publishers who'd jump on *Scratch,* who wanted things a little raunchy. What he needed was a package: script, concept pages, finished interiors, a slick workup of the series arc.

Cliff froze on one of the portfolio pages. "What's this garbage?"

"Hey!" Trip stiffened and stood up. His sinuses throbbed. "Fuck you, man. They're not garbage."

Then Cliff slid one loose page free: a random scatter of faces, limbs, and poses... too manly and suggestive to belong. *Oh shit.* The incubus drawing from his lunch with Rina: a three-quarter face and a head to toe. Silas retooled for hell.

Scratch.

How did that get in there? *Stupid.*

"Oh. Sorry. That fella's not yours." Trip circled the desk and plucked the demon out of the pile. "He musta snuck in." He frowned, and his heart chugged as if Cliff had caught him masturbating at his desk. He should have been more careful. Thank God it was one of the Silas sketches and not Cliff with horns and a thick uncut bazooka. He'd never have lived that shit down.

"As bad as the Brazilian crap." Cliff scrutinized the bulging crotch and dashing demonic profile. "I don't like it."

A cold lizard of shame crept across Trip's belly as he sat down again on the edge of the chair for the inevitable scolding. "You don't have to." His eyes itched for the first time in weeks.

"He has pubes. And nipples? Jeez."

"Not for *Hero High*. For me. Just playing around with an idea. A different title."

"So now, you're, like, *cheating* on me?" Cliff sighed and leaned back. *Blink.* "We're not enough for you?" His voice got husky, and his biceps stretched the T-shirt as he leaned forward.

Trip avoided his sexuality at Big Dog. His queerness was the elephant in the room, and however much Cliff joked, the reality had hovered for four years without landing anywhere. Comics could get weirdly bigoted, even now. Those old-school companies still had morality clauses.

But... why did Cliff wear his clothes so damn tight, unless he *was* gay? Why did the Unboyfriend hang all over him all the time and flirt constantly? What was Trip supposed to think?

Button, button, who's got the button?

"Six months from now, we're gonna get scooped up by DC or Marvel, and you don't wanna get left behind. Right? We're so close." Cliff's sweatshirt smelled a little straight-boy musty, as if he'd worn it to the gym a couple of times without washing it. "I guess I don't like you playing with the other kids." Cliff ran a hand over Trip's scalp and squeezed the back of his neck. "I want you all to myself." *Cock-and-bullshit.*

"Fuck off." The feathery scrape of Cliff's fingernails made Trip twitch. He fiddled with the zipper of his jacket. *Ugh.* His skin tightened in lust or disgust. "I'm not saying it's definite. I'm just doodling, y'know?"

"Indie comics are a dead-end road, man. If you need more work, I got plenty for you."

Trip sighed in exasperation. *Shit.* Now Cliff thought he needed to chisel work. "I need to have some fun. Like a creativity break. This'd just be a little thing I did on the side."

"C'mon!" Cliff leaned over to scrutinize Scratch's assets. "Everybody's gonna expect that. A comic with boners and boys. Lame! Where's the surprise?"

Trip looked away from the whole package and rubbed his pinked forearm. "It was just a thought."

"No shit. I can tell the kinda thoughts you were having, bro." Cliff squeezed Trip's knee hard enough to make him flinch. For reasons he didn't analyze, the tingling grip made his cock chub. "Someone needs to do the gooey mambo. Trust me. If you wanna jerk off to it, fine, but gay titles don't have enough market share to make sense. There's no business model."

"I didn't say he was gay."

Cliff favored him with some choice scorn. "He looks gay."

In his head, Silas winked and laughed at him in Scratch's husky voice. "How do you look gay? He's a muscular male. Hi? That's every superhero comic." A blush crawled up his throat.

The Unboyfriend tapped the swell of Scratch's glutes. "No cape. Ripped up. Massive ass and junk. So sexually confrontational I can, like, smell your blue balls from here." He grimaced, then pretended to wipe the page and flick the finger at Trip. "The Mighty Mites don't look like this."

"They're fourteen, Cliff. Gimme a fucking break!"

He flashed a prom king smile and chortled, "I'm kidding."

"I'm not. How does he look gay?"

"Well, you're gay, so… duh." There. Cliff had managed to say it out loud for once. He cracked his knuckles.

"Duh, what?"

Then Cliff got very chummy, almost baiting him with loose affection. "Dude, dirty comics don't make money. Queer books are like kryptonite… they take money away from you by proximity. Feel me, Harry Bush and Tom of Finland didn't license anything to Hollywood."

"I can't believe you know who Harry Bush is." And Trip couldn't; even gay guys who loved the iconic drawings had no idea who'd drawn them. Harry Bush had been one of the kings of the midcentury skin mags.

"Those old pervs did that shit for love." Cliff reopened his hands to the ceiling like Solomon dividing the baby. "Listen, do you know what *amateur* means?" He said it with a bad French accent.

"Uh, yeah. Thanks. I'm not an idiot." A hard pellet of anger lodged in the back of his throat, too deep to hack out.

"No, I mean in French, dumbass. It means 'love of.' It means some dumb fuck who slaves away for love. *Amat.* That doesn't cover anyone's mortgage. Or buy cheese doodles. Or pay off student loans." A meaningful stare. Cliff knew exactly how much debt Trip had chipped away, and for how long. He also knew Big Dog paid Trip a pretty healthy income to whip up *Hero High*.

Trip took a long breath and wiped his swollen nose with deliberate slowness. "I'm a professional. I'm working on an indie comic because I want to stretch myself." Trip had never seen Cliff so agitated or sustained such calm himself in the Big Dog offices. Stupid really, because he suspected Cliff's whole shoot-for-the-moon plan depended on him. Trip's high-detail artwork allowed Big Dog to seem fancier than it was.

Cliff shrugged and tried to sound casual. "You're bigger than indie." He curled quotey fingers and sniffed at the incubus drawings as if at a used condom. "Comics for a small group of people."

"Gay people are a small group?" Now Trip wished he hadn't agreed to redraw the fucking splash page in twenty-four hours. He could still walk out. "Cliff, I've got an opportunity to do something on my own."

His editor snorted and spread his thighs with the fratboy snicker: *Hrr-hrr-hrr.* "Yeah. That's called masturbation, and I'm pretty sure you're already doing that plenty, bro." Was he mocking the torch Trip had carried for four years?

"Fuck off. A book of my own."

Cliff stopped laughing, stopped smiling. The torch guttered. "What?"

A cool pleasure slithered through Trip as he watched this cocky motherfucker squirm and doubt for the first time in, well, ever. For three seconds, he suspected Cliff and he both knew *exactly* what was and wasn't ever going to happen between them. Trip forced his voice into casual chitchat mode. "Not full time. I mean... no way it'll interfere with any of our stuff, but something for fun, y'know? To get my mojo going again. I been real frustrated—"

"Wait a sec. Wait a sec."

Trip didn't wait to hear the bullshit logic. "Y'know? Needing to cut loose. Like you said. And it's—"

"This is big business."

"Going really well, actually. Not big. This would be an independent book. More Vertigo than DC. Totally niche. But it feels great to let my hand go."

After wiping his sweaty forehead, Cliff mapped out the future with athletic hands. "Mass media doors are waiting to be opened. *Hero High* would make a great cable movie. Something on Lifetime? The kind of wholesome American entertainment that will end up on lunchboxes across America."

"And Scratch *won't*. That's what you're trying to say. In case I had expected a rush on sex demon merchandise for sixth graders?" Trip's exasperation crept out. Maybe Cliff carried a kind of torch as well: for a shortcut, a secret handshake, overnight success.

"So work with me." Cliff leaned forward on his elbows. "Be serious. Comic books make serious money."

"Great. But I'm not under exclusive contract. I'm not gonna just sit at home like a monk. I want to draw. Big Dog doesn't own me. And until Mr. Big-time Movie-pants pays me, he doesn't own me, either!"

"Trip, I wanna sell out. You wanna sell out. They just gotta pay us for the privilege. A big licensing deal will put us on the map. Money, control, access. One deal and we can write our ticket. The big time."

Trip scowled at his knuckles. All this *rah-rah* sounded... wrong. Silas never talked about movies like this at all. Actually, come to think of it, Cliff's version of movie production seemed like *People* magazine bullshit. Silas had gossiped about film school interns on the set who swore that *Spielberg was drooling*, had a *thousand projects* in development, *a deal away* from the big time.

Without thinking, Trip stole the words and pretended they were his. "Man, a thousand projects get optioned and kept on life support for years. Studios write checks so they can keep their D-girls and bitch over Cobb salads."

Dead silence.

Cliff goggled at him as if he'd coughed up a toy poodle onto the desk.

"Cliff, I'm not a nimrod. I mean, I follow the trades." Trip shrugged.

"You do?" His editor stared in bafflement at the desk as if the imaginary poodle had taken a crap and then danced on its hind legs across the Bristol boards.

For the first time, Trip felt in control in this office. "Well, not directly. But I pay attention to people who read the trades."

"Who wanna use you? Like an agent?" Cliff narrowed his eyes. "Who have you talked to?"

"Cliff, I can't only draw this weeny-bopper shit 24/7." He flapped his hand at the *Hero High* banners and merchandise all over the jumbled meeting room. The collected junk of the company's eight years of comic cons angling for acquisition.

His Unboyfriend nodded with veiled condescension. "Go with me.... If it got out that the genius who draws the Mighty Mites did kinky shit on the side...." His voice trailed off into the pitfalls and poison ivy of Trip's career path.

Oh. Surely Cliff didn't expect him to live in fake, cardboard, no-budget, half-assed not-quite-Oz for the foreseeable future to save a buck and close this deal? *Somewhere... there's a land of lollipops and rainbows.* His stomach turned over.

On the table, Scratch's world-weary leer stared back at him with hazel eyes. *Not hazel.* But not Cliff's eyes ever again.

Cliff flexed his hand and rubbed the thick wrist. "And then you got the Fundies marching up your ass because you showed a wang. Worse! Wang and fang. No thanks. Keep that stuff in your pants for now." He opened his hand. "I mean, hey, Alan Moore had to do *Swamp Thing* before he got to do *Lost Girls*. Once we're done here, you can really cut loose. Crazy as your gay heart desires. You won't have to draw a straight *line* if you don't want."

Cliff's shirt rode up to reveal his abs, but seeing the calculation killed the effect. What would have looked like temptation dissolved into a strip of hairy skin.

"I'm not Alan Moore. And my gay heart is fine, thanks." Trip reached across the desk and dragged the damning page back into his lap. He examined the sly seductive brow and the exaggerated muscle. What if it was all worthless? What if he fucked up his job here and Cliff gave all his work to Dee? Cliff had shamed him, the way his parents had when he'd fought back. As soon as the humiliation spiraled through his veins, anger chased it. "I'm not going to kill this because of some possible deal that might never happen."

Cliff's soft fingers closed into a loose fist. "Okay. But don't say I didn't warn you, Triptophan."

"You've warned me." Trip refused to go, dissecting him. "I'm fully warned."

Scratch smoldered there, ready to liberate the lost and the lonesome from lives of surreptitious porn-trolling. *Got an itch?*

Trip spoke calmly. "I'm getting your work done. I've delivered the next two interior pages early, and I only got this double splash to clean up Brazil's imaginary mess." He semishrugged, enjoying the lazy power he felt.

Cliff's gaze snapped up, icy in the open fratboy face. "And what if I put my foot down and told you to stop?"

Boom.

"I would tell you—" Trip swallowed to make sure his mouth wasn't dry. "To blow me. A little." He pretended to smile.

Cliff pretended to laugh. He fidgeted with the pen in his hand, capping and uncapping and recapping it with his left hand: *clickitaclick-clickita-clickit.* "Right."

After all these years of Trip acting like Cliff owned him, they'd both forgotten that nobody owned anybody. Trip stood up for himself and *poof*—they were just two hairless apes with a passing familiarity, and *Hero High* was just colored shapes on mashed wood pulp, held together with two splinters of bent steel.

We have the gift of bullshit.

Trip nodded and made a mental note to thank Silas, and instantly erased the thought because Silas was on his shit list for balling him and tossing him. Silas wasn't wrong about much.

Clicka-clickit-clickita. Cliff's pen finger twitched.

An awkward few seconds of silence hummed between them under the fluorescents. Scratch stayed put on his page, watching them with sly eyes.

Trip glanced up to find a Cliff he'd never met before taking his measure.

Cliff sucked his upper lip and nodded. "Fuck strategy. Fuck loyalty." *Clickita-clickaclick.* "Huh?"

"Loyalty?" Trip plucked the goddamned pen out of his hand, just to stop the clicking. It was hot from Cliff's skin and a little gummy. Someone was sweating and it wasn't him. "You hire some intern with a cow's hand to draw a book I drafted. You drag me in at 9:00 a.m. to fix a fuckup in twenty-two hours. A fuckup I predicted and you marched yourself into. I'm cleaning up your mess, Mr. Stapleton. I'm the cavalry."

"Get those pages to me by Tuesday." Cliff pushed files around in a tacit signal for Trip to clear the fuck out.

The Unboyfriend has spoken. The Unboyfriend is displeased.

Trip crossed his arms and didn't budge.

Cliff glowered at the demon that had snuck onto his desk in the middle of all the Mighty Mites. "And don't waste time on this homo-baloney."

He sneered at Scratch's sneering face. Scratch won that staring contest hands down.

Fuck you, Staplegun.

"Well, boss, until you're paying me for this book, you can't tell me to do anything on it." Trip kept his tone light, but he'd never said no to Cliff before.

Again the cock-and-bull fratboy laugh Cliff thought would cajole him into line: *Hrr-hrr-hrr.* "Promise me you won't be stupid about this."

The disdain on Cliff's face had quite the opposite effect. Trip's protectiveness of his strapping sex demon surged inside him. He wished he could call Silas and thank him, but instead he took pride in not crumbling.

Fuck you, Unboyfriend. In fact, all the unboyfriends could go fuck themselves.

Suddenly, Scratch made his fingers itch, and he wanted to draw nothing else for the rest of the night. Dreams don't cost anything. He'd finish the character models, at least. He offered a silent vow to himself that he'd get the sections and masters done by Sunday so he didn't lose the thread of the original excitement he'd found with Rina. He could summon Scratch all by himself.

"Good boy. We're gonna sell to the big guys, and then we can write our ticket. You and me, right?" Cliff got up, wrapped an arm around Trip's neck, and squeezed him close in a jocky hug and kissed Trip's head with a wet smack. "*Mwah.*" He poked at the drawing.

A small poison bubble of irritation slipped up Trip's spine. The sight of Cliff's perfect fingertip thumping Scratch's two-dimensional crotch, trying to pound it into Ken doll impotence, unlocked something in him. For a moment, he thought he might say something insulting just to get it out into the light where it belonged. Instead, somewhere in the cluttered closet of his soul, a decision made itself, and made itself known to him.

He'd draw his beautiful demon... and no one on this fucking earth would stop him. Without Cliff ever knowing it, he'd just lost the chance to be a hero in the new comic. Without Silas ever knowing it, Trip would capture his good bits on paper as raw material and make magic. Delicious decision.

Before he faced Cliff, he schooled his features into pleasant blankness. What had Silas said? *Sometimes you do it to teach them a lesson.* "Gotta split." He didn't wait for permission.

"Hey." Cliff tapped his phone. "You got the signing on the twenty-fourth still. Forbidden Planet? They have a new location." Cliff stood there, practically daring him to try and get free, knowing Trip hated confrontation. And allergens. And change. The flirty team-captain bullshit seemed like a mechanical oxymoron. *Rote charm.*

Pretty ugly. Definite maybe.

Had Trip just not noticed before, or did a couple of amazing dates with a certain makeup artist make him an expert on the male animal? *I'm not that hard up, am I?*

When he pulled back to meet Cliff's stare, even the chummy smile seemed like a white lie.

Trip tossed the pen on the desk, grossed out by its anxious warmth.

"Two of us are gonna take over the world." Cliff ladled charm over him like high-fructose concrete. *Which two?*

Trip gazed at Cliff from the doorway, inhaled and exhaled so he didn't start telling the truth.

Don't postpone joy! In his mind's eye, he saw Silas's rugged, beaming face outside his building on their first date and decided to lie out loud so he could be true to himself.

Cliff met his stare. "Don't quit on me now."

No. Trip looked up. *Pressure.*

"Of course not." Trip shook his head and pretended to grin. "I'm all yours."

And for the first time in four years, he wasn't.

12

AT FORBIDDEN PLANET, Silas lined up with his fellow geeks, hoping for an autograph but bracing for a punch in the mouth.

These weekend promotions were usually well attended. This close to Union Square, the pop culture emporium got plenty of co-ed foot traffic. The store had recently moved into this new space, a single rectangular room with rows of high shelves stocked with comics and collectibles. This new store was less cluttered than the old, but smaller as well. The legendary window displays were scaled back to fit in a single cube of well-lit Formica with hardcovers and movie merchandise. Wipe-down convenience had replaced the funky trash-'n'-treasure vibe.

New York had warmed up for the last few days of February, and Silas had dressed up a little in chinos and a salmon pink shirt that made his eyes blaze. He carried his backpack over one shoulder and a bag of groceries in one hand. In a comic book store filled with T-shirts and Doc Martens, he might have stood out, but that was, after all, the point.

Seeing Trip, even forty feet away, filled Silas with a strange relief and pride. He let out the breath he'd held, then took another, bought the new issue of *Hero High*, and waited in line. He stared at the magenta and tangerine cover of a superpowered pep rally and listened to adult fans gabble about Alphalad and the final mastermind exams. Trip might not love the Mighty Mites, but these folks did.

Maybe that was the real deal: no one can judge someone else's heroes. For all its tackiness, *Undercover Lovers* might rescue marriages coast to coast. Browsing the bright jumble of Forbidden Planet, Silas's gratitude grew—he worked at something he truly loved. Even junky fantasies had value. Anything could change a life.

Art is important, but importance is not.

The line humped forward. Trip's eyes looked insomnia-bruised, but he smiled and joked with his aficionados, signing their purchases as the frothy tide of enthusiasm broke against his table.

He looks sad.

As Silas got a few yards closer, he picked up Trip's voice, first the pitch and then actual words as he answered questions. He was warm with the fans, funny and respectful. Again, some slipknot inside of Silas strained, loosened, and fell into coils of rope. Just the sound of Trip chatting about deadlines and Prismacolors relaxed him.

A cheerful clump of middle-aged cardigans got finished and left, and at last Silas got a look at Trip directly: pale arms, black stubble, the familiar gestures with his ink-stained fingers that animated his conversation. The lean line of muscle from his shoulder up to his freshly cropped skull made Silas smile and swell with longing. *No inhaler.* Apparently, Trip's allergies weren't bugging him.

By the time Silas stood a few feet away, his guilty nerves had traded places with anticipation. And then the girl in front of him stepped away.

It's a bird... it's a plane....

Trip didn't see him until he stepped right up to the folding table. At least he didn't seem angry when their eyes met.

Silas put the comic in front of him and smiled shyly. "Hi."

And miracle of miracles, Trip gave a little puff of dry laughter and uncapped his silver Sharpie. "Greetings, Mr. Goolsby."

"You doing okay?"

Trip checked him up and down a second and nodded. A smile snuck across his face. "You look...."

"You too." Silas let go of the breath he'd held.

For a couple of seconds, they just stared their fill, and that felt pretty fucking spectacular.

A short, square woman in a Forbidden Planet shirt jogged Trip's elbow and glanced at the line of comic hounds behind him.

Trip turned and tilted his head to listen to her mutter something, exposing the strong sweep of his long neck, and then he gazed back with those huge, dark eyes, right into Silas's. "How would you like me to sign this, sir?" He wobbled the pen in his fingers.

"Hmm. Okay. Umm." Silas peered at the ceiling and back. "To the stupidest schmuck in New York...."

Trip snorted and took dictation without protest. A smirk teased the corners of his rosy mouth.

"I forgive you for being such a twunt and promise to let you make it up to me with extended kinky sex, carbohydrates, and cash prizes." Silas watched the words appear upside down in scrawled silver. "Exemplary penmanship, Mr. Spector."

"Thanks." Trip didn't seem too mad. "Anything else?"

Some kid behind Silas grunted in irritation. "Is he writing a novel?"

"Wait for me at the door so you can cook me dinner and grovel at great length and girth. X-O... Rectum N. Spector."

Trip wrote every word, although not much of the cover was visible when he finished. He handed it back to Silas. "Thanks."

"Back atcha." Silas smiled back stupidly but ducked out of the way before the Forbidden Planet minion chewed them out again.

From across the room, Silas watched Trip shake hands and answer questions, feeling a lazy, borrowed pride at how beautiful and talented Trip was without realizing.

That's my job from now on: to realize it for him.

After about ninety minutes, the jabbering crowd petered out, and Trip crossed the room with his portfolio. "Always takes forever to get them to go." He contemplated the zealots who lingered at the table where he'd signed. The staff patiently herded them away so they could fold and stash the furniture.

Trip wrapped his scarf around his long throat. In the navy sweater and knit hat, he resembled an undercover cop in a '70s thriller. "I got your message. Valentine's, but I was in a dicky mood that night. Too ugly. I should've—"

"Doesn't matter." Silas licked his chapped lips. "Have you eaten?"

"Couple Snickers." Trip shrugged. He looked nervous and tired. "Oh, and a half bag of Combos. Pepperoni-Ranch."

"No, goofball. I mean biodegradable food. From the earth. Never mind." Silas shouldered his backpack and gestured vaguely with the groceries.

Trip considered him for a moment, then started walking toward the door. "I'm listening."

"Is this okay?" Silas led the way across past shelves of figurines. "I thought you'd let me get away with a little retcon if I explained myself."

Retcon, as in retroactive continuity, was what fans called the moment a comic book shamelessly rewrote its own history and hoped no one caught on. Some retcons ruffled no feathers, replacing old cheeseball origin stories or gimmicky Silver Age teams. But some changes drove the devotees insane: clones and twins, personality flips, fake deaths, making up powers on the spot... any tweak that violated the core of a character. For the big heroes, retcons were a function of hundreds of writers fiddling with them over decades... shit happens and times change. For sidekicks and villains, they usually represented a last-minute edit to fix an unforeseen problem.

Silas held the front door of Forbidden Planet open to let Trip step out onto Broadway. The damp late-February air had cleared the Sunday streets.

As Trip walked past him, he stopped on the threshold and paused. "How much retcon we talking?"

Shrug. "A couple days tops. The right minute would probably do it."

Trip looked down at the sidewalk. "I used to wish life had retcons. An undo button. Do you know how much of my shameful past I'd change if I could?"

"I missed you, Mr. Spector. Somethin' *awe-ful*." He ladled on the twang and loved Trip's reaction to it.

"Mmh. Nice." Trip bumped their arms together. "Retcon: I never gave you the *Scratch* draft."

"No dice. You did. And I fucking loved it. So you can't take that away. Sorry."

They walked past the Strand and hung a right onto Twelfth.

Silas switched the backpack from his right shoulder to his left so they could walk closer. He didn't take Trip's hand, but with their arms bumping like that, he could have. "Retcon: I should have just called you every night from the set. I would've but I didn't want to freak you out."

"Nah. That's fair. You were working and I needed to get the script finished and it's actually better to pine a little."

"Pine?"

Trip blushed as he stared at his shoes. "Yeah."

"Oh. Well, then, no." Silas inhaled. "Retcon: how about before I went to Arizona, I told you how I felt and then you did the same?"

Trip stopped and looked him square in the face, unflinching. "How did you feel?"

Silas opened his mouth to answer and shut it. The light changed, but neither of them moved.

Trip crossed his arms and hugged himself. "I missed you every fucking second, Mr. Goolsby. I thought about you in bed, on the train. Because of you, I put Big Dog on a leash and started *Scratch*-ing for real. And I didn't say anything because I thought you saw me as a good time. Y'know? Laughs and a big schwanz until your next ex comes along."

Silas touched his arm. "You aren't a good time."

Trip's shoulders stiffened.

"No! I mean…. You're not a *time*. You're the best thing that ever happened to me, Trip Spector. I've never—" Silas regarded the stars tiptoeing across the clear sky overhead. "It's all new turf. No secrets. No plan. No map. Just treasure."

Trip grinned. "Me too."

"Lucky. And I don't know what's coming. But right now I feel so goddamn lucky to have a second chance that I don't want to jinx anything."

As they walked, Trip put his hands in his pockets. "You know how some people collect toys or comics and they leave 'em in plastic? On eBay or whatever."

"Mint on card."

"Yeah. Like having them pristine and sealed away for display is better."

"Collectors pay more." Their elbows bumped again. "Costs more because kids haven't played with it. Dog hasn't chewed it."

"I've let my whole life stay mint on card; so my friends keep telling me." Trip glanced over. "I been so afraid of dings and scratches that I'd rather hang in a case under plastic. Collecting myself, sorta. I didn't mean to, but I've got this habit."

"You get plenty rough when you wanna."

"Maybe." Trip twisted to look at him. "But you don't leave *anything* in the wrapper."

They crossed Sixth Avenue.

"And that's good?" Anticipation took root in Silas.

"That's amazing." Trip waved the air between them. "I listened to your Valentine message about a hundred times."

"Yeah?"

"More, maybe. I should have called you to apologize back. I knew exactly what you were trying to say and I wanted to say it back, but I was too... stubborn. Stupid." Trip wrinkled his nose. "Sad."

"I thought you might have a date. A Valentine." No S, but now he'd omitted it purposefully.

"Yeah, right."

He turned, and they stood smiling at each other under the trees that arched over West Twelfth Street.

"Hi." Silas ran his hand through his messy hair. He hefted the Whole Foods bag. "We got tilapia, ginger, peppers. And they had killer broccoli."

"No Twizzlers?"

"Agh!"

"Joke." Trip rubbed his arms. "Do you know that I don't sneeze or scratch half as much? I mean, nearly as much as I used to. I still take a couple antihistamines, but my allergies were almost gone. Somehow you fucking rewired me."

"I'm glad. I like you healthy."

Trip perused Silas: his eyes and his mouth and his hands. "I dunno."

Silas stepped close. "Well, I force you to eat better and make sure you get more than three hours of sleep a night." He glanced up at the pocked sky. "I should have made plans with you when I wanted to."

"You did." Trip scoffed. "You made plans."

"But special plans. I don't know how to explain. I followed this imaginary playbook because I thought I needed to... that you would—"

"It doesn't matter now."

Silas disagreed gently, "Matters to me."

Trip rocked from side to side on the curb before he replied. "Retcon: I shouldn't have expected you to fix my script. That sucked." The streetlights overhead cast their eyes into deep shadow, but a wedge of white appeared when Trip smiled. "It was a crappy thing to ask." He closed one eye.

"Not our shining moment, no." Silas frowned. "But then I lost it. Yeah. Sorry. The script, I mean, not lost my shit. Of course, then I did, both. Your script vanished because I'd carried it around with me, and then I had to spend three hours digging through a dumpster until I found it."

Trip chuckled. "In the garbage?"

"Man, *bar* garbage. I wasn't gonna leave until I found it. Smelled like cherry lime barf when I dredged it out."

"I never should have saddled you with my BS."

Silas frowned. "I wanted you to. Honest. I was honored. I admire you so much, and then I froze, which terrified me, and that made it worse."

"My fault."

Silas stopped and opened his palms. "It made everything real, I think. We'd had a good time, and then it was…."

"Bad?"

"Wonderful. Terrible. Bizarre. I dunno."

Trip shrugged. "Real."

"Yeah." Silas smiled. "Usually I'm looking for a way to keep things simple."

A cab went by them at the Village Green. Trip paused to watch it pass and spoke before he turned back. "Definitely not simple." The cab swerved downtown at the little fenced garden at the end of the block.

Without asking permission, Silas leaned in and kissed Trip's throat just above the clavicle.

Trip stood rigid and eyeballed the empty block around them.

"Sorry."

"Don't be. I'm sorry for being so afraid of everything."

Silas spoke gently. "You know… you're going to have to get used to the idea of being worth looking at. You are, y'know."

Trip relaxed his shoulders. "And you need to stop feeling like all you are is something to look at. And you can pretend all you want that your gast is flabbered, but you know it as well as I do." He rubbed his mouth. "You wanna grab a cuppa coffee?"

Silas shook his head. "Huh-uh."

"You hungry?"

"Not really." Silas licked his lip.

Trip shoved him. "Asshole. I want you to come home with me. I'm trying to be smooth, Mr. Goolsby."

"Well… tough, Mr. Spector." Silas snickered. "Come back to mine and let me make you a biodegradable dinner and take you to bed." He held his hands open. "Please?"

"I can't."

So much for charm. "Oh."

"No, I need my clothes and my portfolio because I have a meeting at Big Dog tomorrow."

Silas let out the breath.

"My place?" Trip shifted his weight. "Rain check on yours."

"I'm starting to think you have a phobia about my apartment. However…." Silas shrugged and sighed contently. "If you promise to pillage and plunder me mercilessly, I am willing to consent to this indignity."

Trip grinned back. "I'll do what I'm able."

"Retcon not included."

When they reached Trip's door, three youngish guys were huddled sharing a joint in front of Johnny's Bar. The shortest raised his chin in greeting, and Trip nodded back.

Silas stood back while Trip unlocked the entrance door and then followed him up the narrow flight of stairs.

"They have three dollar beers, so students kinda gather. Better than doormen, security-wise." Trip's perfect butt shifted under his pants.

Silas took his sweet time climbing. "Mmm."

On the little landing, Trip spun and unlocked his apartment door while Silas waited a few steps below. "Are you cruising my glutes?"

"Yessir."

"No comparison." With a *crick-crack*, Trip flung the door open, but as he turned around, Silas dropped the backpack and the groceries and unbuckled his pants while standing at the top of the stairs, exposing his packed purple briefs.

"Silas!" Trip hissed in shock.

Silas rubbed his mouth and swallowed. "I missed you."

Trip dropped his portfolio just inside and tapped the door. "Come inside."

"In a second." Instead, he sank to his knees, shoved his backpack and the groceries at the threshold, and crawled toward Trip across the creaky hardwood landing.

Trip glanced down at the front door and whispered, "The guys'll—"

Silas pressed his face against the high, hard curve behind Trip's zipper. "I can't wait."

"You're crazy."

Silas laughed and nodded. "Please. Please let me."

Trip braced his hands against the open doorframe. His eyes grew wide and dark, but he didn't say no.

"I'd suck it down there on the stoop if you'd let me. I'd love that. Eat every fucking drop kneeling on the concrete so they could watch you use me, put your jazz in my mouth."

"Je-*sus*." Trip rubbed his mouth and his hot crowbar pushed at his waistband. "Things you say."

Silas hummed. "Make me."

Downstairs the voices on the stoop called out to someone. Trip's shaky hands tightened into fists.

Silas eyed him hungrily and coaxed in a hoarse whisper, "Stay here. Don't hide." He licked his wet, loose lip and chewed lightly at the stiffness through the denim.

Trip groaned but made no move to either stop or help. He gripped the doorframe, his fingers white-knuckled under the ink stains. He opened and closed his mouth.

"Shh. Let me have it." Silas took a deep satisfied breath and nosed against the rigid bulge. "I missed you so much." Trip cautiously pushed his hands into Silas's hair. "Yeah?"

Their breathing and the laughter of the guys downstairs were the only sounds in the low-ceilinged stairwell.

Trip whispered. "You wanna get caught?"

"Naw. I wanna give in. That's my..." He glanced at Trip's erection again. "...weakness."

"Okay... okay." Trip's legs tensed, but he fumbled with his buckle and zipper until he exposed his gray briefs and the dark spot punctuating the front. "I have a goddamn wet spot." He flipped the front of his briefs down and the lazy length of his cock swung free.

Silas didn't bother to nod. He leaned forward again, but Trip stepped back into the dark apartment. Silas squeezed the base and Trip's cock flushed dark red and veiny. "Fucker."

A pearl of precum welled at the plump crown. Trip wiped it with his thumb and offered it. Silas grunted and knee-walked forward, then sucked the entire salty thumb down to the flesh of Trip's palm. The thumb scraped at the back of his throat, but he made a real show of sucking the thumb hard.

"Okay. Okay." Trip reached down and clasped his shoulders. "C'mere."

Silas rose and his pants fell to his knees. He shoved down the purple cotton so his broad cock bounced in front of him.

Trip glanced at the stairwell. "I get it. I think. But you got a streak in you. Exhibitionist."

Silas pushed the elastic of Trip's briefs under his nut sack, then scraped his belly with rough fingers. "'S'good to me."

Trip jerked and spun him so they faced the street downstairs, his stiffness wedged between Silas's bare cheeks. "You're so...."

"What?" Silas gasped.

Trip reached around his chest and plucked at his stiff nipples through cotton. "Strong."

Silas rolled his head back onto Trip's shoulder, pushing his chest forward.

Trip snaked a hand under the collar of his knit shirt and over the muscle, fishing for the firm tips.

Silas flinched. "You could make me come like that." His glutes gripped Trip's cock.

"Yeah?" Trip pinched down, milking a hiss of borderline discomfort, but Silas didn't complain.

"Mmm." Silas breathed through his mouth. He pushed his hips back insistently. "For real. So sensitive." *No kidding.* Sweat bloomed as he ground against Trip's weight, his skin hot as a griddle.

Trip let go and cupped the square pectorals. "When I was in college, I had a boyfriend who had a thing for nipples. He would just work on them and work on them until I lost my gourd."

Silas panted and ground back slowly. Trip extracted the hand and then rucked the shirt up over Silas's torso.

"I dunno what to do with you." Trip licked his ear. "One of these days I'm going to tie you down in my secret lair." He bit the lobe and squeezed Silas's neck hard. "And then what're you gonna do, mister?"

"Let you." Silas gasped and didn't close his mouth.

"You would, wouldn't you? Full permission." Trip ran a hand down Silas's back till the digits pressed against his butthole.

Silas hissed and held his breath.

"You'd let me hogtie you. I bet I could make you come with just my fingers in your butt. Huh?" He pressed two hard against the opening. "Two or three?"

Silas pushed back.

"Hungry." Trip ran his chin over the abused skin of his neck.

Silas swayed forward with his hips, and the ruddy jut of his erection drilled the air. He gazed back over his shoulder with lazy admiration.

"I don't even think I'd need to help. I'd just push inside, and you could fuck yourself on my hand."

Trip's feverish patience drove Silas out of his mind. Instead of breathless fumbling, sex with Trip always had a razor intensity, as if he were memorizing something under the skin, but doing it with his whole body.

"Gawd." Silas closed his eyes and flushed bright red. "So much for nice Jewish boy."

Trip kicked the backpack and groceries inside, pushed the door shut, and pulled Silas farther into the apartment toward the sitting area and an overstuffed armchair large enough for both of them.

Lube on the end table told Silas plenty about what Trip had done to keep busy the past few weeks. Trip dropped into the chair and pulled Silas onto his lap, one lean arm around his waist.

"Too heavy!" Silas protested but couldn't stay on his feet. "Wait—"

But Trip wouldn't. His pole reared up, rested against Silas's balls. Trip ferreted a rubber out of an end table drawer and handed it to Silas. "And you better grease it or you'll be sorry."

Silas pumped lube into his hand and rolled the latex down the broad tusk that reared under him. Silas reached to line things up and stopped at his entrance. No way he could take Trip without any prep.

"Easy, fella." Trip kissed his neck. "I gotcha."

Silas juddered. His butt ached, and his heart thumped as he bore down, tried to open himself by force.

"Hush." Trip scraped those elegant hands over his skin, ungently. "You're not going anywhere."

Silas hissed and clamped his mouth in frustration. If he could stretch himself, he'd be able—

"Shhhh. You're fine where you are. Who's rushing now?" Trip's lips were against his throat and the narrow hips flexed under him a little. Trip stroked his thighs, pale skin on tan.

Silas relaxed a little, easing back.

"Stay with me." Trip nuzzled at his shoulder. "You smell so good." He took a deep breath. He slid fingers between their stacked legs and tested the point where they intersected. "You feel that?" The knob was half-inside but wouldn't budge.

Silas groaned assent. It burned. Lube ran down his inner thigh. He gripped the plush arms of the chair.

"I need to be inside you, but I got all the time. You taught me." His stiffness flexed. "Alla time in the world for you, man." He stroked the hole and his own hard-on.

Silas gasped. His butthole rolled open and he pushed himself down. The welcome pain took his breath away. His eyes smarted.

"C'mere, big guy. Give it all to me. Gimme all of it."

Silas slid inch by exquisite inch onto the hot spike, impaling himself until he sat directly on Trip's lap. "Whhuuhhh."

"There it is." Trip wrapped his arms around Silas and completely pulled him back to rest his full weight against Trip. "Let go. Let me have all of you. Lean back." He rocked his pelvis and slid out a few slow, punishing inches.

Warily, Silas lay back on top of him and tried to catch his breath.

Trip squeezed his ribs and rocked back into him.

Silas gasped. "Nhhauuuhhh!"

Trip slipped his arms around the armpits and up to the back of Silas's neck, sort of a half nelson.

"*Ungh.* Trip." Silas purred. "*Guh.* Go slow, go slow." He twisted to bring their mouths together, but the angle was wrong. He braced himself against the sides of the armchair and twisted left.

Trip shifted in the other direction and leaned forward to kiss Silas properly, nursing at his tongue. He jerked his hips sharply to make Silas see sparks.

Much better.

Silas flinched and opened his eyes. His own hardness was wrapped in Trip's roving hands for the moment. "Ahh—yeah... even slower if you can. Let me feel it. Make me feel it."

Trip obliged happily, dragging his cock out with obsessive patience....

"Tri-ip." Silas shook and squirmed against the snaky strength of that torso. His oozing hard-on bobbed before him.

"Grunt for it. You're so beautiful like this." Trip twisted Silas's mouth to meet his. "You're pulling me back inside. You feel that? Your body wants it."

Silas moaned. His cock was inflexible against his bent thigh, and a strand of sap draped from the crest to his creased belly. It bounced with each thrust, and he arched his back to drive Trip deeper. "Touch me." Silas loved that breathless, skewered feeling of being taken. *Manhandled.*

Every third or fourth thrust, Trip ground his hips, drove impossibly deep and pulverized that place inside Silas that made his eyelids close and the breath rush out of his lungs. The squelch of it should have embarrassed him, but it didn't.

Without warning or comment, Trip tipped him out of the chair and forward onto his stomach on the rug, then flipped him over so they faced each other. His veiny cock swung slick before him. "Y'okay?"

"H'yup." Silas stared at the branched vein that ran over the top of Trip's shaft and then wrapped to the left. "Please." He hissed, bent his knees, and pulled his legs back against his chest, exposing himself without touching his boner.

Trip squinted experimentally and pushed demanding fingers into the sloppy, swollen hole. "So open. I love it wet like this."

He squirted more lube into his hand and angled that chunk of meat back toward him. Trip shifted forward, and the stiffness slipped past the hole. Their hands fumbled for a moment as they lined things up and then—

"*Awwhh!*"

Trip speared him in one brutal thrust that knocked the breath out of him. The stretch stayed just this side of impossible. He stayed buried and worked his hips in a tiny spiral.

Silas whispered and choked. "Again." His cock was ruddy brown and crushed between them.

Trip pulled back, rammed home again, sheathing himself. Sweat dripped from his pale chest.

Silas hooked one leg over Trip's arm and drew it to his own ribs, so that Trip fucked him sideways at a slight angle, cradled and drilled him at the same time.

Trip planted himself hard and took his sweet-ass time pulling out. "Wow."

Silas shook his head in wonder. "I can't...."

"Then hold on to something. I'm just getting started." Without warning, Trip slammed his pelvis against Silas's and the full length—*ohmygod*—drilled into him to the root.

Silas took exactly no seconds to pull Trip closer and brace one arm against the wall.

"So sweet inside." Again Trip drove closer.

Silas's eyes watered. Gooseflesh puckered his skin and his nipples burned. The tender ferocity short-circuited something in his brain.

Again. As Trip slid free, he closed his lemur eyes and a grin haunted one corner of his soft lips. The fatness slithered out with exquisite delay. Trip's shaft felt thickest in the middle, like a torpedo, so it slipped in easily and stayed lodged a moment after it touched bottom, but the middle breadth took effort.

Silas grunted each time Trip touched bottom, and his gaze stayed nailed to the juncture of their bodies and the wet slap of their skin. "Trip." He shook his head in slutty wonder.

Trip dragged his boner nearly free again, stopping just at the swollen ridge. He waited for several heartbeats, feeling the pulse where they intersected.

Silas offered his neck to Trip's mouth and squeezed him closer. Another two or three thrusts and he would be a goner. Nectar welled at the tip of his cock, then cast a glimmering thread toward the crisp hair of his abdomen. His ass clamped involuntarily, and Trip squawked in surprise. "Sorry."

Trip ground deep a moment, stretching him.

The delicious, relentless itching built until Silas couldn't breathe, couldn't think. His cock swelled perilously, rigid and trembling with the crazy rhythmic pressure from inside and out. "Wait. Wait-wait. Too soon," He begged and gasped. "Go slow." His eyes drifted shut. "Take your time. *Aaggggh.* Make me feel it."

"Not hardly." Trip's eyes twinkled as he strained forward to press his forehead against Silas's temple. "Slow?"

"Umm."

"How… slow?" Trip drew out again, gradually, and then rather than slamming, thrust with equal, evil patience.

"Hey," Silas almost whined. The panicked tickling sensation took him over again; his legs twitched and his toes bunched hard as he struggled toward his release.

"Hey, what?" Trip gritted his teeth and inhaled. His heart knocked at the side of Silas's ribs. "Hey… what?" Still he took his time, skewering Silas gradually.

Horrible. Perfect. Silas could scarcely get oxygen into his lungs.

"Make me…." Silas gripped the slim hips in tense fingers, delaying it even further. The belly of the shaft slid over that crazy place inside him that made his head fall back and his mouth fall open. He sobbed and panted insensibly. "*Guh-ungh.*"

"Good?" Trip whispered.

But no words came out of Silas's mouth, so he answered with a crooked nod. Even moving his head took effort while that monster held him open and his prostate struggled to keep its molten cargo.

"Good." Trip petted his belly in lazy circles. "Good."

Silas's skin itched uncontrollably, as if a million eyelashes grazed his limbs. His mouth had dried and the syllable he managed didn't make a word. "H'yuh."

He squirmed in the sweat that poured off both of them, and the spit from kissing too hard smeared into their stubble. *Beast.* Frantic but unable to stop himself.

Trip lifted up to stare wide-eyed, presumably at where his blunt truncheon sawed in and out by degrees. He reached down and palmed the heft of Silas's sack for a better view. He smiled. "Wow."

"No—*hffft*—kidding."

Trip fell forward and slipped his arms up the wet planes of Silas's legs, folding them back until his knees pressed against his broad chest.

"Closer." Silas gathered the lean torso into his arms, cradled him close, and squeezed Trip into him with thick thighs. The heavy cock gouged ecstasy from his clenching ass.

He'd never felt so alive, so aware of every part of his body.

Between Trip's stomach and his own hip lay Silas's blood-hot club, trapped at a freaky, almost painful angle. He hunched hungrily against the wet skin. The scalding pressure stood his hair on end. The squeezing, fluttery tickle inside his ass swirled outward, licked his abdomen, his nipples, and his groaning mouth. He clutched at Trip's slippery arms.

Almost. He was almost….

Trip grunted and humped against him in short steady strokes. His eyes narrowed to slits, his mouth open.

Silas barked and arched, "I'm nearly—" *Flying.* A sharp gasp and his eyes blazed wide.

Switt. Swiiit-thwit.

He bowed hard as the lava burst from him onto his face and shoulder and Trip as well. Somewhere above him, Trip yelped and squeezed him hard at the same time before he fell forward.

Oh God. Together.

His spooge was so thick it made pattering sounds as it hit skin and floor, and his ass clamp-clamped on Trip, buried to the root, skewering him to his core. Trip twitched and gripped him so hard Silas could scarcely breathe.

Wild with release, Silas roared and squirmed and curled to get their bodies as close as possible, to mark his territory. He licked their salt off Trip's sternum and wrapped him close with wet arms and thighs, fusing their skin and wiping the cum between them like scalding syrup. *I missed you.*

"Thank you." He wiped Trip's damp chest and sighed in relief.

"Was it too much?"

"'S'super, man." Silas smiled to himself drunkenly as he reveled in the wet skid of Trip's corded arms looped around his trunk, grinding close as he dared.

"Fuck off." Trip giggled. "You're Superman."

"Then you gotta be Clark." Silas chuckled. "No wonder Superman always had Clark Kent inside him."

"Truth. Poor Lois Lane." Trip laughed once, laughed again; then his eyelids drifted closed.

Silas kissed his stark collarbone and let his head drop back as he tried to catch his breath. "I think you gave me a hickey."

Trip shivered a moment and hunched deeper before he carefully glided free. "Good."

Silas gasped at the loss and the sting. His cock nestled in a cocoon of hot jam, but the crazy, shaky bliss wouldn't leave him.

"Mr. Goolsby." Trip patted him with wet hands anywhere he could reach. "What the hell did you do to me?"

What didn't I do? Silas shrugged a shoulder and winked. "I—" He looked across the slick slope of their bodies. "—am just getting started, Mr. Spector."

They must have dozed for a while, and Trip must have pulled a blanket onto them, because Silas woke up tangled in pale limbs and hypoallergenic fleece.

The clock said 1:00 a.m. Outside, the moon hung high over the Village, exactly the color and texture of unpainted latex.

He didn't want to wake Trip, so he stayed put. He enjoyed the gentle weight stretched over him, the rise and fall as Trip breathed. Occasionally he stroked Trip's back.

"Mmm. Love how they feel." Trip's drowsy words were smushed against his chest. "Rough." He wriggled to his side, with only his naked leg thrown over Silas.

Silas spread his fingers and frowned. "My fucked-up hands."

Trip gave a slow, appreciative whistle. "Nuh-uh. Sexy."

"I always tell people I got it doing construction. Working with toxic waste."

"You mean like acid?" He balanced his chin on Silas's pec.

"No. Like Kim Kardashian."

Trip snorted, then immediately covered his mouth.

"Don't hide." Silas reached for Trip's wrist. "I love seeing you laugh." He laced their fingers and planted their hands in his lap. "Don't hide it."

Trip nodded and kissed Silas's knuckles, then traced the marks. Trip turned his palm over. "These are scars, huh?"

Silas twisted and stroked Trip's ribs. "Summer I was fourteen, I put up a barbwire fence on my uncle's farm over vacation: cedar posts. Big ugly Finn, he was. My parents knew I was gay, but my uncle wanted to 'make a *man* outta his fat-ass faggot nephew.'" He spat Uncle Roosa's words. "A month that took us. And my hands bled every night. Sunburn and splinters." Silas didn't bother to fight the rasp that seeped into his voice as he talked about home. He could almost hear june bugs.

Trip ran light fingers over the weathered roughness. "They're not cuts, though."

Silas shrugged. "Naw. Not exactly. Kept getting infected, and the clinic was too far, so my aunt soaked 'em in a bowl of hydrogen peroxide. I lost twenty-two pounds 'cause I kept throwing up in the heat." Silas rubbed his palms together so the skin whispered.

Trip crooked his head closer.

"My father almost killed him when he found out. For real: tire iron." He snorted mirthlessly at the memory of his big ole dad screaming and chasing his brother around the sweltering yard while his mama fussed over his raw fingers. "A great day." He grinned. "I mean, I was never gonna be a hand model, was I? Alabama?" He squeezed a loose fist.

Trip frowned but said nothing. His eyes said plenty.

"Rest of break, my mama cried and tried alla home remedy shit to fix 'em. Arnica, aloe vera, witch hazel. They healed up eventually. Learned to moisturize, that's for damn sure. Almost by accident, I started fixing my acne. Football. Humping the bed. And somehow, I started doing makeup for plays and sculpting and got the hell-'n'-gone out. My asshole uncle." He stared through the bricks at the memory.

Trip laced their fingers.

"You like 'em." Not a question.

"Ungh. You kidding?" Trip pressed his face into the palm. "I jerk off thinking about 'em." He let his head fall to the side to let Silas run it over his ear and throat and chest. "Weeks now."

"He died of stomach cancer a couple years back. I didn't go. Not even to piss on the grave." Silas scowled. "Still hate the smell of cedar."

"Know something funny?" Trip tipped his head all the way to the side like a little boy. "First date. Your hands were one of the first things I noticed. So beautiful." He pulled the hand to his mouth and kissed the palm.

Silas examined the rough marks. "I wouldn't fix 'em now. They're part of me."

"Good. I think they're the—" Trip kissed the back. "—sexiest paws I've ever had on me."

"Idle hands and all that." Silas squirmed against all that lean muscle and smiled. "Maybe it's 'bout time for me to apologize to you again."

"I hear tell Alabama boys get awful horny."

"You heard that?"

"Yup." Trip nosed him doubtfully. "Somewhere."

Silas grinned and nuzzled his ear. "Well. That might have been true, once upon a time." He sucked the lobe and pressed his teeth to it.

"Yeah?" Trip rumbled. "Once upon a time?"

"Well…." Silas rolled over on top of him. "Twice if you're lucky."

TRIP didn't wake until the noise from Greenwich woke him. He flicked a curtain and daylight roared in, shaggy and fierce as a lion. Not quite March, but good as.

They must have fallen asleep again at some point; when, he couldn't say. They'd migrated from couch to bed to tub and back to bed in the course of the night, his dick raw and his nuts drained to a dribble.

The clock read ten-something. Silas wasn't in bed, which made Trip anxious until he heard someone humming and poking around in the kitchen on the other side of the studio. He smelled butter. His bed had no view of the rest of his apartment, but hearing Silas in his space felt so right, he dozed off again.

Trip woke for good curled against Silas, who raised a thick hand to Trip's face and ran a thumb over his lip. Grinning, Silas leaned in for a quick kiss. His stubble was so long now it felt tickly soft. "Hi, stranger." He smelled like cookie dough.

"I think you—" Trip got a grip before he said something embarrassing. "You'd look handsome with a beard."

Silas's face was gentle and unguarded. "Yeah?"

"Well, you're not too hideous without one." Trip leaned forward slowly for a kiss.

"I been wanting a secret identity. Maybe it'd disguise me better." Silas brought their mouths together, a warm dry press that ended in smushed smiles. He twisted and snagged a piece of buttered biscuit. "Check it: cooking occurred." He offered a bite, which Trip accepted.

They smiled and chewed. An easy silence settled over them. Soon the plate was empty and the crumbs licked away.

Silas took a breath, and took a moment as he twisted a fistful of the satiny sheets.

They'd spent the whole night together, and still Trip itched to share more stories, for them to know each other better. A million secrets crowded into his mouth to be shared, but he still couldn't read Silas.

Finally, Trip nudged him. "What's up?"

"On Valentine's, I read your script about a hundred times. Studied it, actually. And tried to see what scared me." Silas crimped his mouth. "'Cause maybe it scared you too."

Trip laughed. "Probably."

"I think I figured something out. I brought you a present. Like a Valentine." Silas stretched over the side of the bed. "I thought and drafted. The way I'd build a proposal if I was on a movie."

Trip blinked, a little off-balance.

Silas twisted back, cradling a sketchbook and a charcoal pencil. "Film people just say 'monster,' and they've got no fucking idea what that means. Writers or directors. I dunno. *Alien* was designed by an artist." He opened to a blank page.

"Giger knew how to scare people."

Silas's charcoal flashed over the sketchbook. He frowned in concentration, but he didn't look up. "People think that if you stick scales or fangs or horns on something, that makes it scary. Duh. It's not like Bambi or Nemo terrorizes anyone. It's fucking context."

Trip squeezed Silas and hooked his chin over his shoulder to watch the drawing take shape before his eyes. A massive hammer, the size of a barrel at its business end. And a scarred hand holding it. A pilgrim, maybe. Sorta *Little House on the Prairie*, but with manly shoulders and a scarred mouth.

Silas muttered, "'S'bullshit. The best villain is the thing that proves your hero wrong. Whatever murders hope. Y'know?" He bit his tongue like a little boy. His strokes carved the page into segments: dark and bright. "Monsters don't wreck the world by smashing it. They corrode everything around just by existing. Right? Like acid."

The charcoal slashed at the paper so that the clothes darkened and lengthened into formal robes carved from shadow. The hateful hammer showed a stark Christian cross on the flat surface of its head. The handle was as long as the grim gent holding it. A monk? A priest. *Too boring.*

"Okay…. I thought about *Scratch*. What he needs is something to fight forever. But he can't be a modern, because Scratch has to be old. History's romantic anyways. A little sadism, so you can get twisted from time to time. And you want your bad guy to be a little sexy, too, 'cause I'll bet you a hundred bucks you're gonna get him shucked bare, too, at some point."

"Hey!" Trip squawked

"Don't sass me, bub. You—" He pinched the head of Trip's cock gently. "—are a kinky sumbitch. This has been established credibly."

Silas was right. To sustain itself, a comic needed a cast. Scratch needed to meet his match.

"Every hero needs a nemesis. Batman and Joker. Professor X and Magneto."

Trip winced, clamping his mouth as he tried to articulate the thought. He tapped the sketch. "But he's not like a straw dummy or a dumb porno cartoon. Not like a 'super' villain with tights and a lava pit."

"Plus it gives you more story to write down the line."

The antagonist who emerged from the charcoal strokes had the scary daddy vibe of S&M cartoons, but under the robe he wore homespun clothes from another time. A crazy Dom? An executioner? That seemed too Silver Age. And a big-ass handle in one knotty hand. "But why the hammer? Thor has a hammer."

"Not like this one."

A carpenter? A maniacal blacksmith? A Hammer Horror Easter egg? The drawing leaked menace onto the paper, ramrod posture cut in stark shadows.

Silas smudged a puritan collar into place and a weather-beaten face, pocked with shadows: an insane Yankee witchfinder.

Trip touched the paper. "A judge." And it was: a looming ye-olde-timey magistrate straight out of Salem. He had a lipless, self-righteous sneer; robes hung on his ropy muscle. "Jesus."

"But not Vincent Price. I mean. He's scary and all, but his *Witchfinder* always feels prissy to me."

Trip protested in a higher pitch. "I love that movie."

"Yeah, but do you want to fuck him?" Silas looked askance, really asking the question. "So we want something more on the border between kinky preacher and abusive uncle."

Trip stared at the pad in his hands.

A gorgeous grin lit up Silas's scruffy face as he wedged in the buckles and the starched cuffs. "I thought about the touching thing. What you said, that your demon has to touch people, so I figured it would need to be someone who kept folks apart."

"Fuck, this is smarter than any of my concept drawings." Trip tapped the grim puritan figure. "That right there is a successful series waiting to happen."

Silas built up the boots over the calves, gave them square toes and modest buckles, like something stolen off a dead soldier. His pencil crept over the stern jaw, adding bristly muttonchops.

"And he even has a prop, like you wanted. A weapon for the fight scenes, so you don't have to use glowy superpower hoo-hah to fill the panels." The judge gripped the giant hammer with tight, pale fists. "I pulled a bunch of groovy Salem research." Silas added lettering to the carved handle, *Thou shalt not....*"

Suddenly Trip realized what he was seeing. "A fucking gavel! It's a gigantic gavel."

Silas bowed his head and smiled. "Ivory. 'Cause he's fulla crap. See? Fucking hypocrite. In the script your guy rules the Horn Gate, and this thing's like the sledgehammer of bullshit."

"Boy, do you know me." Trip tapped the page where the judge glowered back at them, barely trapped on the page. "He's my villain." He blinked and plucked at his lip in embarrassment. "Genius."

"Yeah?" Silas turned his face toward Trip's and pressed closer, scrubbing their chests together a moment. "Well, I do have a thing for sexy monsters."

"Fuck off." Trip shoved him playfully. Magnetically, the page full of scowling Judge drew his eyes and hands again. Trip found his voice. "He's so...." A warm smile. "Horrible."

Silas scowled, as if about to defend his work.

"No, I mean... scary, ugly, and I still just-a-little wanna fuck him. He's *my* monster. Phobia. He is. He's the whole deal." Trip sighed in satisfaction. "Like... a punishment, but I'd still jizz myself. Harsh daddy with a jumbo tool."

The worry between Silas's bronze eyebrows seemed to melt into relief. "I'm really glad."

"Oh hell yeah." Trip rubbed the page with the flat of his palm. "Exactly what the story doctor ordered. He feels kind of, I dunno, important and serious, even. He's gonna make the whole book seem cooler than it really is." He looked up. "Why didn't I think of this? Him."

"You did." Silas opened his hand. "You been dancing around this fucker for a month. I just heard you do it. The whole time you been hunting for your demon story. Think about it: Sexiness. Punishment. Rules. Shame. Judgment. You kept saying it. So *he* is my Valentine present."

"I didn't even hear myself." Trip wagged his head slowly, like he'd woken from an oxycodone coma. "And you listened."

"Well, yeah. I kinda dig listening to you, y'know?" Silas's devilish gaze shone and shifted.

Trip covered his mouth with his hand and prayed it wasn't shaking. His eyes pricked. *Why am I sad?* He swallowed, unable to process. Not sad. He swallowed again. "No, I mean…. You paid attention to what I said."

"Of course I did." Silas looked away.

Trip touched the page again. How many hours and hours had Silas bent over this book? How had Silas known? Had anyone ever taken the time to read something he hadn't written yet? Trip's breath wavered high in his chest. His fear and faith and gratitude gathered in him sure as a sneeze but had nowhere to go, no safe release. Instead he just waited for Silas to understand, since he obviously did.

Silas blinked. "At one point I was gonna cut off a hand."

"Yeah?" Trip watched Silas as he spoke. For some reason, everything Silas said sounded like a fabulous idea.

"Make it a scarred stump, but I didn't want to box you in."

Trip covered the right hand with his thumb and squinted. "Right. But I love the stump idea. Awesome to draw." He flipped onto his back and reached for the sketchbook again. "So how many of these did you do?"

"I did a couple." Silas sounded sheepish as he turned the page to reveal a side view of the gavel in high relief. "This is a sketch, but I did a full character design. Y'know, in case you liked it. Costume pieces, even."

On the subsequent page, he'd drawn a loving close-up of the buckled shoes. The clerical collar, the mildewed robe split wide enough to show skin. The next illustration showed the judge naked from the front, side, and back: gray-fuzzed chest, ropey muscle, tight foreskin, swollen joints.

"The Judge." Trip chewed his lip. "Mr. Goolsby, I think you just finished my script for me. I know what the second half is, now."

"For real?" Silas ran his finger over the three-quarter. "I did a real 3-D section, if you want. Nudes and all, angles and elevations. He has a whole workup, just like I'd do for Kurt on a game. But only if ya want." He held his hands up. "I give you full permission to use or ditch or alter anything. He's a present." Grin. "For the future."

Trip opened the cover, and there was the Judge again, this time rendered in serrated marker, a close-up three-quarter of his grim Yankee face and a full-length study of him scowling in his robes with that pitiless gavel in one grizzled hand.

"Ugh. *Nar*sty. Even naked, he's a bible beater." The figure radiated stern, dick-shriveling displeasure.

"Zero sense of humor, right? And I put scars on his whanger 'cause I figured that'd give you shit to explain later." Silas flexed his knuckles. "Plus I figured anybody this uptight would have huge balls."

Trip laughed. They rode high like anxious tangerines behind the short, thick penis....

"Neck down, he's a ringer for my shitbag coach in high school. Coach Harden." Silas side-eyed Trip. "Yup. Homophobic, racist, born-again asshole. Terrorized the queer kids. Fucked the new teachers. Naturally, I had an awful crush on him. He got busted videotaping the girls' showers. Prick."

Trip goggled at the paper. "Wait... you had a crush? On him?"

"Well, not this scary monster version. He was very... I dunno... aggressive. Butch. His dick was always half-hard, like he needed to jab it somewhere wet, pronto. And I was this little butterball with bad skin and an underbite, uglier than homemade soap."

Trip scrutinized the Judge's knotted cock, as if the scars and veins drew some kind of map. All of it felt potent and personal, as if Silas needed to confess something to him and this was the best way to get it out on the table. He'd need to chew on that for a bit, but somehow, this monster needed solving. The rough hands, the hairy legs showed obsessive precision. "Does this mean I need to start carrying a big ivory hammer to get your attention?"

"You got one already." And without blinking, Silas took a handful of Trip's engorged shaft. "Where do you think I got the idea?" He giggled and bit Trip's neck, taking bites of laughter out of him. "Slam that monster down on me while I beg for mercy." Again a flicker of something serious and deep in his eyes.

Later.

"You." Trip gripped his erection roughly, making the ropey veins bulge and the head darken to plum. "Have been." He smacked it against Silas's thigh. "Judged."

Silas watched as if hypnotized; his tongue slipped out to wet his lower lip, but he never blinked. His own erection strained, trapped inside Trip's too-small sweats.

Trip eyed the heartbeat as it drummed in the hollow of Silas's throat.

A ray of buttery light snuck through the dusty windows and landed on Silas, gilding his hard haunch. He noticed and slapped his butt, grinning innocently. "That's God giving you a hint, Mr. Spector. I think a little sodomy is indicated."

A drip of precum fell from Trip's crown onto the sunlit flank. They both dissolved into snickers.

"Jeez. You're welcome!" Silas gave him a quick peck on the nose. "I'm gonna squirt in your pants."

"Hold that thought." Trip held up a knobby finger and hopped out of bed.

Trip trotted to his clothes closet and stuck his arm in, fishing for the little hook on the wall behind his suits. *Got it.*

"Whatcha doing?" Silas dropped his knee toward the sheet and his balls shifted in the golden light. He-Man sated.

Trip came back to the mattress. He held out his hand. "So you can get in. Is that okay?"

"What is it?"

"Key." Trip gestured toward his front door. "For you."

"I never—" Silas shut his mouth suddenly and exhaled. "Yeah. That's okay. I need to get you one. You should have one too. For me... my place."

"Well, you didn't shut me out. I did. Yeah? A key might keep me honest."

"I want to, though." Silas weighed the little piece of metal in his hand. "I never had two keys before."

Trip crawled back onto the bed, right over Silas, until they were nose to nose again. "Well, this is purely selfish. Maybe some night I get home and you're in my bed asleep. I would fucking love that. No more waiting on the stoop in the cold."

"Oliver Twisted."

"Leave your clothes here. I got pens and paint." Trip pinched his nipple. "I want you in my bed. I want you in my life. I promise to come over to yours. I don't want you to vanish, Mr. Goolsby." He whispered, "Deal?"

Silas stared back and whispered, "Deal." His eyes gleamed, wet with secrets. He ran a hand over Trip's chest. "So beautiful."

Then Trip shook his head and Silas nodded, at the same time. And Trip had the strange feeling they'd both told the truth, that both answers tangled in a way that left them inseparable.

Like us.

All at once, Trip wanted the whole future with Silas like a kaleidoscope jumble... all at once, afraid of nothing, side by side, walking forward. *All at once.* He wanted them naked and sweaty. He wanted them dancing in suits. He wanted to share dinner with their families at one long table. He wanted to hold hands on the Brooklyn Bridge. He wanted to sing at the top of their lungs on a road trip to Cape Cod. He wanted to feel, with lazy fingers, his semen leaking out of Silas. He wanted them drunk in matching costumes at Comic-Con. He wanted to draw and laugh and be unafraid out in the world with everyone watching, for once. He wanted to curl up with Silas in their warm bed, kissing his face... his sweet, scruffy, sleeping face... but lightly, so he wouldn't wake.

I love him.

A tear slipped out of Trip's eye, but he ignored it because their cheeks were too close for it to embarrass him. Silas's blunt erection ground into his pelvis at a funny angle, where their bodies fused.

Right then, right there, he loved Silas so much he didn't care if Silas loved him back, just the loving was enough.

"You okay?"

Trip nodded, though Silas couldn't see the movement.

"Good." *Scratch that.* Apparently his spidey-sense was working overtime.

Cowed, Trip looked back at the Judge on the end table, scanning the buckles and stitching, the hooded eyes and the horny hands, a hundred thoughtful details in the drawing. *Must've spent two weeks on it and then some.* "Can I really use him?"

"Yessir. I drew him for you, didn't I?" Full Alabama. Silas grunted and reached over. He closed the sketchbook and patted it proudly. "I give you full permission to exploit that rigid fucker every which way you want. Put him through hell."

Trip ran a hand over the pencil. He almost felt the hours and hours of the fierce attention and affection that cooked off the page. What had Cliff said? Amateur meant slaving away for love. Emotion throbbed in each line that sliced the page into self-righteous villainy. *Silas did that for me.* He took a shaky breath.

"Nap?"

He nodded, then chuckled, because again, Silas couldn't see him.

"Excellent." Apparently Silas didn't need to see him to know. Those hands urged him down so their faces lined up.

Trip peered into one soft hazel eye and then the other; both sparkled with gentle humor. If Silas noticed the redness in Trip's eyes, he didn't say so.

Finally Silas whispered, "I'm really glad you like him."

"I love him." Trip snapped his mouth shut before he went further. *Keep it together, brainiac.* "You kidding?"

"Good." Silas wrapped one loose, brawny arm around him and hooked his chin over the top of Trip's head, cradling him puzzle-piece close.

Trip kissed him between his pecs and pressed his face there, not looking at the scary Judge or his handsome hero anymore. He whispered it again. "I love him."

Somewhere above him, Silas pressed a kiss to the top of his shorn head and sighed. "Me too."

13

EVERYONE has their own shit sandwich to eat, and the bread makes a big difference.

Kurt liked to hit happy hour at Splash on Musical Mondays, not for love of showtunes, but because the gay geek community tended to converge to get trashed and sing along.

Silas went early to the Unbored offices because he wanted a friendly pep talk, even though Kurt wasn't keen on his newest infatuation. Trip would never meet or agree with Kurt's idea of a catch.

Unbored Games covered a narrow floor of an old piano factory on Lafayette, just north of Houston Street, because that's where the cool kids congregated. Office space in Brooklyn would have been way cheaper and newer, but Kurt loved razzmatazz, and his investors were outer-borough-phobic. He'd taken the lease on a third of the space back when he could scarcely afford it and gradually expanded—fueled by Red Bull and ruthless ambition—to devour the adjoining square footage like a digital amoeba. In nine years, Unbored had gone from bootstrap origins to one of the companies to watch in Silicon Alley.

The elevator opened right into the workspace, a point of pride with Kurt: having the entire floor and all those windows looking out over NoHo. They were high enough that the view was mostly puffy silver horizon, and down below the traffic's faraway rumble sounded like the Adriatic Sea.

Silas parked his ass in a reception area papered with framed awards and launch posters that were supposed to intimidate showbiz types. He *was* a couple of minutes early, so he paddled through his text messages. Two from Trip put a smile on his face. He resisted the urge to reply immediately.

On the other side of the open space, Kurt laughed and said something from his corner. Curious, Silas headed back, following the wall of arched windows. Before he'd gone three yards, shouting stopped him:

"—because they're cunt-noggins!" The male voice sounded angry.

Jesus.

Kurt's opponent sat with his back to Silas. Tangled waves of light-auburn hair fell to his shoulders. Who talked like that to a CEO? Kurt glared at the seated figure, red-faced, his mouth working but no words emerging to ease the crackling tension.

Christ. Had he roller-skated into the middle of open-heart surgery by accident?

Kurt wiped his face and stood, revealing an impeccable three-button Burberry suit, but he'd yanked his gold tie hard to the side and unbuttoned his collar. He didn't retaliate. Obviously he needed this sloppy nutjob to like him, whoever he was.

No suit. Of course, in game-world, that didn't mean much. Video game studios had little use for corporate drag. They usually aimed for "ironic slob" as a uniform. The seated adversary could be anyone from an investor to a writer to a deranged blogger.

Silas sauntered closer to Kurt's lair to get a gander at whoever had him so ruffled.

Shoulder-length hair and a faded green T-shirt, so no venture-capital drone. So many geeks jumped in after school and forged hundreds of international best sellers in garages and basements. Billions of dollars built nerd heaven. Games already earned *way* more money than Hollywood, with way less scrutiny.

Kurt glimpsed and noted Silas minimally, but his canned charm sprayed steadily on his crazed guest until—

"Blah-blah." The long-haired fella flipped Kurt off and snorted. "Bullsh-shit."

Kurt held up both hands as if white-flagging. "I get it. I'm hearing you, but we just don't have a market that'll support that kind of project." He grabbed handfuls of his bedhead and tugged it into bizarre spikes he didn't smooth down. "A gossip game? Hug wars? Get real, Ziggy."

Ziggy.

"Do you think I-uh'm as retard-ded as the rest of your slay-aves?" Ziggy's voice halted and swerved with some kind of impediment. Not a stutter, but as if he couldn't control the consonants.

"I'm taking you seriously. I trust you more than any—" Kurt pleaded.

"More th-aan nothing. More than your *di-hick*!"

This Ziggy person gave a wheeze of choked nonlaughter. He swiveled his skull to an odd angle, making his auburn hair float like hot Einstein. Maybe he was just one of those hardcore playtesters who communicated in grunts on a *World of Warcraft* headset in the dead of dorkness. "I didn't say *Hug Wars*. I said let's be smart."

When egomaniacs collide!

Silas tried to read the back of the man's tousled head, wondering what he'd walked into. Maybe this was a project lead for one of the big studios. Xbox Live had pushed for a lot of independent content, but why would they fly to New York? Why was he baiting Kurt?

"Ah-ah…. Item." Ziggy jabbed a pale finger at Kurt. "No one elss-sse has any-fucking-thing like it. The tech supports a who-hole other kind of interaction, duh-uh-umbass." His neck twisted as he spat the last syllable out. His chest rose and fell hard. "Quit wax-inng your crack-hair or you get scoo-scooped."

Kurt didn't put up with that kind of belligerence from *anyone*, so this nut was definitely important to the company: maybe press or a co-branding partner. Some Hollywood jag-off with an expense account?

Ziggy had a narrow build… early thirties, maybe. "Or wa-wait! Fuck buyout! Duh! We can just license the hardware and the protocols. Contracts or what the hell. But you should tie it up, like now. Yester-rerday. The designer doesn't game ee-ven, so he hasn't twigged to what he's got."

"'S'too expensive, man. I don't have the capacity to handle hardware anyways, and it doesn't fit any of our games. Zig, Pizza Hut doesn't sell tickets to *Italy*." Kurt spoke slowly, but the agitation made his voice higher, making him sound about fifteen.

Silas caught Kurt's eye again and jerked his thumb over his shoulder. *Should I split?*

Kurt subtly shook his head "no" but didn't invite him in or introduce Silas to the lunatic lecturing him.

"Gay-*yame* changer. Kurt, you know I'm right. I'm al-wways right about this kind of shit. You're gonna blow the… I duu-uhhnno… future of features." The shoulders bent as he struggled to get his words out, and one irritated hand paddled the air uncontrollably. "If you don't use the… fuzzy *nutsack* on top of your neck."

Silas stifled a snort. No one talked to Kurt Bogusz like that and lived to see daylight. He dropped the magazine and the pretense of waiting and edged a few steps closer to Kurt's corner for a ringside seat.

Kurt stared at his guest without blinking, apparently unaware he'd mussed his impeccable hair.

Even seated, this Ziggy person looked short and slight, but not a kid by any stretch. He showed no signs of being cowed by Kurt in multimillionaire master-of-the-universe mode. "They got gaze deteck-tion coming at Carnegie Mellon. And thoh-hose sisters in Korea have starrrted testing subdermals."

Kurt noticed Silas trying for a better view. He held up a finger and tightened his jaw. Beads of sweat studded his face. Since when did Kurt sweat?

Ziggy ran a hand through his tangled locks and leaned forward in his chair. "I mean half is for animal tessst-ing and the other for OT, but it's low-hanging fruit. Nuh-none of this stuff is for gay-yaming, but it *is*. Duh?"

Who is this whackjob? When had the name Ziggy been mentioned? If Silas didn't know better, he'd have thought Kurt seemed guilty or horny or afraid.

Silas nodded, then looked between them. As he considered Kurt's tense shoulders and Ziggy's messy curls, he realized he'd stumbled onto a kind of secret. Everything crystallized. He knew exactly what was going on, because he'd seen himself in the mirror a bunch after he'd met Trip.

Kurt has a crush.

All this time and he'd kept it hidden. He didn't date, really. Too picky. He said hustlers were simpler than small talk… order from a menu, home delivery. But obviously this Ziggy got under his skin. Silas smiled, tickled at the idea of Mr. No Nonsense getting mushy about anyone.

Silas pretended not to notice Kurt's signal to wait. Determined to snoop, he wandered closer and leaned against a whiteboard that partially screened Kurt from prying eyes. All the other staff must have gone home early.

Kurt shook his head sharply.

Ziggy turned to eye Silas with a face perfectly proportioned like a Tintoretto angel's—*jeebus amoebus*—with a broad nose over a scarred upper lip, a noble chin, and a long throat sloping into proud shoulders, and impossibly thick arms holding battered… crutches.

Crutches?

Ziggy was disabled. He was the ponytail guy from New Year's Eve. Silas struggled to put the pieces together. Kurt had kept him hidden and had some kind of soft spot. He also did work for Unbored? And he obviously gave two wet shits for Kurt's power and reputation.

Kurt came out from behind his desk. "Ziggy, this is my best friend."

"Nnph." The eyes that scraped over Silas were an unsettling pale blue: no welcome in them and no patience, either. Even more classically handsome head-on.

"Silas." He extended a hand to shake so Ziggy didn't have to try to get up. He jumped forward full of the weird guilt he always felt around people who couldn't walk or hear easily. He knew better, but he always felt like he should apologize.

"Fuck's *sake*." Ziggy corrugated his forehead and exhaled. "I'm a fucking c-c-cripple, jocko; I'm not may-ade of thuuhhhmb-tacks." He sneered and pushed himself up awkwardly on the oversized forearms. His hand felt horny with calluses, and he gripped a little too hard, either to prove his strength or because he didn't know how to gauge it. He sank back heavily, letting the chair catch him.

For two seconds, Ziggy's strange eyes cruised Silas without shame: face, torso, crotch… and then jogged his head dismissively, as if Silas passed muster but didn't merit attention. He swung his full flashing focus back to the boss in the Burberry suit.

Kurt looked queasy and hypnotized by his foe. "Ziggy codes and playtests for our adventure titles." His face had pinked at some point. "We were just talking about—"

"The dummmbest fucking piss-taking misss-take this…" His mouth circled the word before he spat it out. "…*homunculus* will ever make." Ziggy pointed across the desk at Kurt with the tip of one thin black crutch. "Bec-hause it's gonna may-ake some uhh-ther asshole rich as a born-again hooker."

Kurt snorted, resigned. "Lemme think on it. All right? I just need to chew on it."

Silas had never seen his friend so passive. Why would he put up with this kind of tantrum from anybody? He remembered Trip's remark about stuff that threw you for a loop. Shitty ideas. *Huh*. He turned to Ziggy. "This a game you're pitching?"

"Kurt, swearrr to *Gahd*. You're gonna regret this until you ahr-are a cold dish on the worm buffet."

Ziggy grabbed the strap of a laptop case and slung it over his shoulder, catching his hair and then wrenching it free without flinching. He lurched to his feet and caught himself on his left crutch just before he overbalanced.

The sarcasm obviously pissed Kurt off, but he didn't snap back. He swallowed slowly and waggled a hand in Silas's direction. "Silas isn't competition, man. He's a friend. A colleague. Character design and concept art only. Chill out."

"Hi." Silas gave a feeble wave, uncomfortable watching these two guys maul each other.

"Perfect." The cold eyes shredded Silas, scalp to toes. Ziggy's deep scowl could have been a muscle spasm. "Just 'cause he's your friend *dzzz*-does not mean he doesn't wanna be a zillionaire. Ahh-amateur hour bullshit."

"Not like that." Kurt grimaced at Silas in apology. "Silas does concept for us."

"For yuh-you." Ziggy snorted and rolled his sulky eyes. "While you get your dick wet inna rent-a-hole. Great." He tipped his head at Silas, swinging the wavy hair out of his face. "Yeah. Goo-ood luck with that." He slammed his palm against a crutch handle hard and locked his mouth shut as if to stop the jerky flow of words.

Silas jerked a thumb over his shoulder. "I can totally take off. If y'all have business—"

"No." Kurt shrugged and smoothed his hair down. *Was his hand shaking?* "Zig has identified an opportunity in some new hardware that senses—"

"Don't yah-yap about it, asshole. *Fuck!*" Ziggy glowered at Silas and flailed for a minute, legitimately about to fall, then caught his weight again on his crutches at the last moment. He breathed heavily and flushed dark; a vein snaked up one side of his classic brow into his wild hair. He spat and muttered, "This is retarded! Know bett-ter. Shouldn't have said *any*-fuck-uhking-thing." His right arm jerked spastically, the fingers knotting and flexing until he seemed to force it back onto the second crutch. "Great. 'Nother whore-no porno-clone to duh-do his lord-shit's bidding."

What's the big deal?

"No." Silas opened both hands as if proving he was unarmed. "For real. We were gonna hit Splash to hang out—"

Ziggy growled at Kurt, choking on the wet syllables. "Asss-loaf."

"Cockknuckle." Kurt didn't blink. He looked wrung-out. "You can't act like that, Zig."

"Don't you... ever say *can't* to me!" Ziggy blinked hard several times. "I thought-tut this was a pri-yivate sit-down." He struggled and shifted on his feet, bracing himself against his crutches, his fists clenched so tightly that his forearms bulged.

"Goddamnit, Ziggy." Kurt pleaded, flapping a hand at Silas like a high-school stoner arguing with a principal. "This is my best friend. Hell, Silas designs all your wacko monsters. Zig, he sculpted the bosses for *Miss Taken* and all four *Chopping Malls*." His last words were loud enough to bounce off the windows, not a shout, but a command. "Stop freaking out!"

Without warning Ziggy did exactly that, as if Kurt had pressed a button. He blinked and took a deep breath. His wolf-blue glare slid over to Silas, and an odd, bashful smile crept across his aristocratic face as though a sitcom mom had caught him sneaking a cookie. "Uhh. Duh." Ziggy glanced at Kurt and back, pursing his lips. "No offin—" He opened his mouth wide and fought with his tongue. "Offense." He blinked.

Silas flashed a small smile back, unoffended and unsure what threat he could have presented.

Ziggy pivoted on the crutch, headed for the hall door. "I was luh-eaving anyway."

"Sit back down." Kurt touched his ashen face, presumably checking to see if the skin was still there. "Ziggy. Don't be a dick. Talk to him."

The handsome programmer slanted his head and took a couple of halting steps toward the door. "Nice to meetcha, bes' friend'a Kurt. Um? Hell-o?"

Silas realized the irritated bark was directed at him and stepped forward, embarrassed by the scuffed crutches and his intrusion. "Don't feel like you gotta bag. I just came to take the boy wonder to dinner." A nod at Kurt, who was rigid with mortification. *Mortified.* "You could come with us."

Silas wanted to watch the two of them at close range. He'd come to talk about his own love life, but this felt way less scary.

Ziggy shook his head, and the reply came out as a single guttural phrase. "Nuh-no-thanks-no." He favored Silas and Kurt with that huge childlike smile, totally at odds with his earlier rage. "Guh-otta, gotta go!"

He moved quickly on his crutches, swung his legs forward in three strides, and went out through the reception area. Instead of pausing, he skipped the elevator and went right to the emergency stairwell. The heavy door *whomped* shut behind him. A few seconds of silence swirled in his wake. Silas watched Kurt staring at the door hard enough to open it telekinetically.

The sun had nearly given up outside, so Silas clicked on the overhead light. Kurt sat down on the corner of his cluttered desk. His hands shook. The old hardwood floors creaked underfoot.

Awkward stillness filled the entire open Unbored space like inflatable felt dinosaurs. *Eek*. Silas watched Kurt watching the door until he had counted to twenty.

"What… the… *fuck*-enstein?" Silas turned, his eyes wide.

"'S'up, cocksucker?" Kurt snickered, as if they'd shared a six-minute hallucination. "Thirsty?"

Silas tried to remember ever seeing Kurt this wigged out and failed to get anywhere close. "Umm? Who the hell was that?"

Frowning, Kurt didn't say anything for a couple of fidgety seconds. He stood, grabbed at his tie, and unbuttoned his shirt farther… not answering the question.

Silas pressed. "That… man works for you? For Unbored Games."

Closing his eyes, Kurt dipped his head absently and sighed. "Programmer. Ziggy originally did freelance code on *Miss Demeanor*, and then I put him under contract. I poached him from a startup that did banking interfaces. Security. *Jesus*." He rubbed his face with his hand and plopped down in his chair, scooted back, and examined the vaulted ceiling. "He dreams in hexadecimal. Genius. He got scouted by NASA in high school. He's got crazy instincts."

"Crazy something."

Kurt tried to rock in his office chair, short bounces that seemed more jarring than relaxing.

"Maybe he had a plan. You could talk to him."

"Silas, that *was* me talking to him. 'S'like juggling grenades in a kitten factory."

"Which game was he bitching about?"

"No game. It doesn't exist!" Kurt snatched at his hair again, then wiped his mouth. He looked insane. "So not just the controller, not just the R&D and fabrication, but a whole other title developed from scratch. A couple years and millions of dollars 'cause he has a fucking hunch? Like I'm fucking Bill Gates on a bonus round."

Silas grinned and spoke softly, "Practice, practice, practice."

"He's the best. Hands down, no competition. I mean…." Kurt frowned and sat forward, his gaze furiously roaming the desk and walls and windows. "Ziggy is a bastard and a lunatic and talks to me like I should shine his boots with my trimmed pubes, but truth is: he put us on the map. Unbored Games grew out of him, and he knows it. That motherfucker is the reason *Chopping Mall* moved seventy thousand units in eight weeks, out of nowhere. Goddamnit." He swatted at his desk, knocked over a twelve-inch model of a cartoon dinosaur in pastel armor from *T-Wrecks*.

Silas righted the dino and watched Kurt, the irritation and yearning written on his face, as he traced and retraced Ziggy's jerky path out the emergency exit.

All those lectures about crappy ideas and awful dates had been Kurt talking to himself. Apparently Kurt's advice only went one way. *Everyone is a liar.* Of course, that meant Silas oughtta take his own medicine too. "So why don't you give it a once-over, at least? At this mysterious whoozits he brought you. The controller thing."

Silas didn't need to talk about his love life anymore. Or if he did, Kurt didn't need to say anything. *All we have to pay is attention.*

Kurt sulked, his own worst enemy. *Who isn't?* "Terrible fucking proposition."

"But are you sure that makes it a *bad* one?" Silas nodded, although he didn't particularly agree. *You like him.* Kurt had a little crush on this demented programmer on crutches… gorgeous, sure, but fucking certifiable. Silas wrapped his brain around that lamppost, but he decided to play it safe. "You trust him."

"If that gimpy nutbag was smart, he'd walk it over to Nintendo or Microsoft or Sony and they'd make him a media mogul. Technology this big, they'd stab *themselves* in the back to get their shitty mitts on it." His thoughts seemed to scurry around his head like mice in a blender. "Prick." Again, he whispered the word like a reverential compliment.

"Wait, I thought he was a genius. He's helping you."

"He is. That doesn't mean I can afford it! By the way… that isn't a metaphor. I mean that I literally can't access enough capital to tackle something that high profile." Kurt tapped at his desk with a *Miss Demeanor* promo pen.

"But he's bringing you a rainmaker. Giving it to you."

"Maybe. Fuck! If I had half a brain, I'd cut him out and pitch this controller to Nintendo myself."

"He knows you better than that. I know you better than that."

"Ridiculous."

"Obviously he didn't think so." Silas crossed his arms. "If Ziggy is so fucking smart, why isn't he sitting in an office at Apple right now? Why bother coming here at all?"

Kurt's gaze flicked over the expensive view outside. "*No* fucking idea."

"Well, genius…. Maybe you should find out."

14

TRIP forgot how to sleep alone.

Beginning of March, Trip managed to finish the first *Scratch* script with the Judge firmly in place, practically thumbnailing it as he went. The pencils and inking the last half would take longer, but now he had a map.

Somehow, Silas blended easily into his bizarre life. They pretty much lived at Trip's because of his allergies. At first, Silas griped about Trip's snacky crap and stocked his boyfriend's fridge with things that actually expired. He ran home for clothes. Trip's asthma faded. Even as spring sprung, the pollen count never spiked somehow. No hay fever, nothing. Little by little they fell into an easy rhythm. With Silas out to Silvercup for day and night shoots on *Undercover Lovers*, the sleep and meals got wonky, but between the Mighty Mites and *Scratch*, Trip drew so much that their impossible schedules wound up working.

On March 16, Trip started on the remaining interiors and decided to go for broke. *Scratch #1* turned out crazier and kinkier than anticipated. Amazing how something he cared about flew out of him while his *Hero High* assignments trickled onto the paper.

Trip's worst problem? The more time they spent together, the more the sex demon resembled Silas: face, body, personality, raunchiness. All traces of Cliff had faded. He kept the sketches hidden, too embarrassed to unveil them, while he tried to work up the nerve to come clean. He'd never lost control of a character, but Scratch stayed a dead ringer for Silas, full stop, end of debate. At the same time, he fucking loathed the idea of sharing Silas or putting his body on public porno display. The cover-up got tricky as their day-to-day lives overlapped more.

Whenever Silas got too close, Trip flipped pages and closed his sketchbook. Silas joked about his secrecy and paranoia but didn't give him much grief. *Soon.* Once Trip finished the book, he'd confess. Hell, Silas kept secrets from him: all those ex-boyfriends and the *wham-bam* partying he did with Kurt. Trip decided to bide his time until the opportunity presented itself. Which was worse: Silas hating or loving the idea ? And then one night Silas didn't come home to sleep. And he didn't answer his phone. The text said "night shoot."

Friday afternoon, Trip fell asleep on the couch waiting for Silas. Middle of the night, he'd woken up and worked on *Scratch* pages, as he pretended it wasn't weird that his texts hadn't gotten a reply and Silas hadn't called.

About ten the next morning, a key tripped the lock. Rain pelted the streets outside.

Silas trudged in dripping and dropped his bag. He looked wiped. "Ugh. Hey."

Trip didn't say anything, just waved hello. Obviously, Silas had worked all night. But then, maybe he'd gone out with Kurt and his bar friends, without boyfriend in tow.

"Tried to let you know. We shot on the street and my phone died. Sorry."

The radiator hissed like an evil teapot dragon in the corner.

Trip put his pencil down. "Got nervous."

"It's too hot in here. You're gonna get sick." Silas wiped his sweaty neck. "Open a window at least, so you've got some air."

A tendril of irrational jealousy climbed up Trip's chest. He had hidden *Scratch* from his boyfriend, the same way he hid porn from his parents. "You have fun?"

"I'm glad for the time and a half, but it sucked. Paul was sick, so I had to assist Tiffany. God-awful weather. Director wanted a thousand takes... actors pissy in the rain."

Sneaky anxiety congealed between them.

Silas must have noticed the chill. His shoulders sagged. "I need a shower." He headed toward the little bathroom.

Trip stacked his sketchbook and tablets in a neat pile on the kitchen table beside his portfolio. "I figured you were out with Kurt and forgot to call."

As if rewound, Silas backed into the room. "What are you talking about?"

"C'mon. He avoids me, talks shit behind my back when he lures you out to play." Trip drummed his fingers. He'd seen enough of the texts that he despised Kurt on principle. "He's got some unrequited thing, and then I come along."

"What thing?" Silas wiped his stubbled face. "Um. Yeah. Kurt is not jonesing for me." He scowled. "Let's be clear on that. He's not my fuckbuddy and he never was."

Was he being paranoid? "He wants you to be."

"Bullshit. He doesn't want me. Any more than Cliff Stapleton wants you."

Trip glanced up sharply. Where had that come from? *Projection.* Even though he didn't feel the least bit asthmatic, he took out his inhaler and huffed a big dose of bitter humidity. "Everyone wants you, man." The paranoia spilled uncontrolled from his mouth. "Kurt keeps you close because he's hoping—"

"No! No, actually he wants to get blown by fitness models who do as they're told and take money off the nightstand. He only pays for sex and only from people who don't give a fuck who they fuck. I'm nowhere near his standards. We joke about that shit. And why do you care who he's boning anyways?"

Trip latched onto the deflection. "You expect me to believe Kurt Bogusz never made a play for you?"

Silas should have answered immediately, but he didn't.

"'Nuff said," Trip growled.

"No. No! We didn't fuck. Kurt jerked me off, once, at the Roxy. Back when there *was* a Roxy for the club kids! That's how long ago we're talking... and only 'cause we were lonely and ex-ing like hell. C'mon."

Trip grew queasy. His nerves had gotten the best of him. He'd sleepwalked into an archvillain's dastardly trap, with Kurt cackling from the shadows. *My hipster nemesis.* They'd never met and now he hoped they never would. "You shouldn't have told me that."

"Attraction is normal. You and Cliff musta screwed around at some point?" His eyes flashed.

Trip blushed and blinked. Had he given that impression? "No. No." *Not even a hand job.* Irrational shame pierced Trip.

"Oh." Silas looked confused.

"We just—that's why he's the Unboyfriend." Trip licked his dry lips.

"What?" Silas shut his mouth for a moment and his shoulders sagged. "Trip, you keep acting like you're casting a role. Like I'm a character in a book."

"That's not what I meant." Rina and Jillian already gave him shit about scripting everything. *Guilt or panic, probably.* Any day now, anyone with three bucks could see Silas having acrobatic sex.

Silas waved a hand at him. "I think we're allowed to have privacy. I don't expect you to tell me everything you do." He glanced at the closed portfolio.

Yikes. "Nerves bring out the worst in me."

"Well, thank fuck this isn't your best." Silas chuckled, and that took the sting out of his words.

"No." Trip flinched and jerked away as he stood up. "I keep making these stupid mistakes." He walked away, headed nowhere, and stopped when he reached the window, hating that he couldn't shut the door and freak out at will in his own apartment. "I'm terrible at this. I'm going to snuff you out. I'm going to suffocate you." He didn't turn around.

What the hell did Silas make of him? Walking the perimeter of his crush turned their relationship into an empty cage at a zoo. *Don't feed the lions, if any turn up.* How had he learned to misread his life so carefully? Trip frowned at the sheets of rain outside.

"Go ahead and try. Don't be afraid. Talk to me."

"I'm not afraid, I'm allergic."

"To life?" Silas laughed.

Trip glared so hard he expected his face to splinter. "Yeah. Sure."

"I didn't mean it like that. No."

"I am, though." Trip scowled. "Raised by aliens. No social skills. Weird job. Coping mechanisms out the wazoo. Bony pale thing with a huge doodad and too many insecurities." He wiped his leaky eyes with the heels of his hands. "Gah." His nose probably looked like a russet potato.

"Breathe." Silas held up a hand for a couple of heartbeats. "We're so lucky. I mean it. Every day I wake up, and I feel so fucking blessed that we crashed into each other in the park. Yeah?"

What would Scratch do?

"I'm trapped in an embarrassing comic, working for an Unboyfriend who's bamboozled me for years. And somehow, against my better judgment, I've gotten sucked into drawing an X-rated graphic novel starring a porno demon. There are other projects—"

"Trip, you're a little afraid. That's okay." Silas stared straight at him. "I know I can seem flaky. You've seen me flirt to get what I want. You've met a couple loony-toon exes."

Trip spoke low to his hands on the drafting table. "Which makes me jealous. Sorry."

"That's sexy in a way, but it's nuts. None of that shit is real. If I want to be somewhere else, I'll go there. I'm *here*. We're here."

Trip didn't nod, but he didn't interrupt, either.

"That's not who I am. See? You know me."

"I think it's 'cause all this is new. To me."

"To me, too, because I'm not pretending to be anything. No masks. No secret identities. Huh?" Silas ran a rough hand over his face.

Trip knew what he meant. "I like that." He walked back to Silas.

"I've never been with anyone this long. Not ever. Because I don't think I've ever *been* with anyone. I want to be with you, and I'm kinda hoping you feel the same. I like being your big dumb sidekick."

Trip snorted. "Hardly."

"A dynamic duo, then."

Trip opened his mouth to say something and then shut it, as if he'd taken a big bite of an oxygen cupcake. *Why do I care?* He sat down at the kitchen table. "I'm being insane."

"No. You're nervous. Frankly, ditto." Silas pressed a hand to his own heart. "We're nervous because it matters. That's good."

"I know."

Silas stared at him for a couple of breaths. "You do?"

Did he know?

Maybe Silas had changed him. For all his ranting, Trip hadn't sneezed, wheezed, or broken out in hives from the feathers or mold or pollen. And his dick stayed hard enough to hang towels. He fought the urge to mark his territory. A preview of the unhinged jealousy to come when *Scratch* hit the stands flashing Silas's goodies at the world. The book would be done in a couple weeks and the prospect elated and appalled him.

He needs to know.

Trip pulled his feet up and hugged his knees as he scraped his chin across their tops. "Just stir crazy. You didn't call and I thought we had a plan. Big Dog announced *Campus Champions* today, which put me in a fucking mood, I can tell you."

Silas gave a sympathetic blink and sat down at the table beside him.

"Forgot to eat, so I'm grouchy anyways. And so I wasted time on a dirty comic no one will publish when I should have drawn castrated bullshit for Cliff because I need the paycheck." Trip swatted his portfolio so hard it fell to the floor and opened, only instead of *Hero High*, there was Scratch, in all his horny glory, sucking the fight out of the room.

They both froze: Trip in shame and Silas in apparent horror.

"Jesus." Silas blinked and picked it up.

A balls-out three-quarter sketch of Scratch—with his face and torso, his dimple and dick—stared back at Silas.

Oops.

Trip tried to close the portfolio, but Silas slapped a hand onto the page.

"I can explain."

"No." Silas blinked and stood. The chair scraped as he kicked it aside. He flipped the page and another. He flinched and muttered; he stared at his own face staring back from the large page. "You can't."

Trip held out a placating hand. "This seems crazy, I know."

"You don't know. These are—" Silas looked forlorn. "I never—" He opened his mouth and shut it. "I've never thought of myself like that. Not ever in my whole stupid life." His accent drawled Dixie-thick. "That anyone could see me like that." His eyes were wet.

Is he crying?

"You sorta…." Trip fidgeted. "Got under my skin. Which sounds Hallmark-gaggy, I know. But, tough. Once I started, I couldn't stop."

"Don't ever." Silas shook his head. And then he did cry. One tear—*tlip*—hit the picture's eye. He sniffed and jogged his head again, smile-frowning and staring at Trip. "Beautiful." He wasn't looking at the drawing.

Trip stopped flapping around and tried to hear him. "Thanks." Relief soared through him like pigeons scattered by a taxi.

Silas pawed through the eleven-by-seventeen art boards. A demonic talon slashed at his jailer. Scratch curled in a ball in his cold basement prison. One long panel that could've been Silas showering after sex, except for the cloven hooves.

"God…" An entire page of Scratch's impish eyes, the brows flared like seagulls above them. "…damn."

Silas stopped at a large close-up portrait of his face, just Mr. Goolsby peeking back over his bare shoulder, lips parted in sullen invitation… a perfect likeness except for the small horns that glinted at the top margin beyond the blue border of the comic book art board.

Go to hell.

"Is this how you see me?" Silas turned.

Trip rubbed his head. "Those were just me getting him into my hands. While trying to draw this… him. Scratch. I just…." Trip fell silent.

"Such a gift. For you to see me like that. To be able to see myself like that and believe." Head shake. "Believe me."

"Just looked. I looked at you and Horny Bastard kinda took over. I mean Scratch."

"Horny Bastard?" Silas stood there, loose-limbed and trusting. "Is that what you called him before?"

"Wait! No." *Agh.* Worse and worse. "I didn't mean you're a bastard or a sex mania—"

Silas kissed him.

Oh.

"Now, hush. Just let me be overwhelmed and grateful, okay?" Silas tried to pull away.

More excuses scrambled to the front of Trip's mouth like incontinent puppies. "Which is an awful thing to—"

Silas kissed him again, slowly licked his tongue and pulled their hips together, his scarred hands firm on Trip's butt. This time he drew back more slowly, stoking that odd buzzy electricity they always generated. "Okay?"

Delicious languor stole over Trip's limbs and the clock, melting his anxiety. He nodded again, in slow motion. "And his name is not Horny Bastard, I promise." Trip gathered some of the loose pages into a jumbled pile, tried to hide some of the more salacious drafts on the kitchen table. "I should've asked."

"Why would I mind? You changed me into a supersmart sex demon with a magic whangdoodle."

"He's not just you… I borrowed parts. But when it just sort of came together, he had your bones and bits and…." *Keep on digging that grave, asshole.* "I mean, I'm not a fine artist, but you gotta admit that—"

"He looks like me. Hell yeah!"

Trip flinched. How strange and terrifying to silently watch Silas comb through the craziest work he'd ever drawn. *Totally exposed and totally safe.*

"Trip, I'm not upset." Silas leaned forward. "Why would I be upset?"

"I drew you fucking people. A lotta people actually. As a demon! Jesus." Trip spread his fingers and let invisible sand slip through them. "I feel like such a tool. A jerk, I mean."

"Hey, cumming and sneezing use almost all the same muscles, but folks only have issues and guilt about one of them. You want hang-ups, you're gonna have to go elsewhere."

Trip chuckled. "Yeah. I got that part."

"You made me a damn hero." Silas mock-scowled. "If that means I have to be a slutty hellspawn who fucks the truth out of people, I'm *so* down."

"Not a slut."

"I'm not? That's good." Silas sniffed.

"Scratch is instinctive. He works on people's appetites. He eats their pain." Trip slid a loose sketch of legs closer to the others. "The first book he's been imprisoned, and then he gets rescued." Trip realized how that sounded. "Oh—"

"He does, huh?"

"I just mean I'm not kicking the series off with a whole *Smallville* radioactive spider-bite chosen-by-aliens origin thing. Scratch kinda regains his powers. And a nerdy human sidekick helps him get revenge. Isaac."

"Uh-huh." Silas grinned. "A little help from a shy guy with a big, hard talent. I'll buy that." He squeezed Trip's basket.

"Not like—" Trip blushed and started to backpedal. "I didn't assume—I'm not trying to say—"

"I didn't assume, either. I'm agreeing with you, Mr. Spector. Connections are powerful things." Silas kissed him. "Hey. Hey! Look here. Look at me." He lifted Trip's chin.

If Silas was annoyed, he hid it behind a convincing mask.

"I'm just teasing you because I'm so happy. This is the nicest thing anybody ever did for me. I'm honored, Mr. Spector."

Trip swallowed, unable to move.

"I'm a fan, man. Y'see? You made me—I dunno. Knowing that I'm part of it makes me want to buy a thousand copies and send them to all my exes."

Trip pretended to gasp in shock. "You have a thousand exes?"

"No. Well... no. Shut up!" He laughed and dropped a heavy arm over Trip's neck.

Trip let the weight tip them together. "Just sorta happened."

"That's even sexier. Happy accident." He growled. "You can use me in your personal porno creations anytime you wanna." He bit Trip's earlobe and sucked it for a second.

Trip shivered. "Well... porn is interactive. I mean, it's a picture or a story that milks a feeling out of us. They're jerking off, and I figure the character should know it. Which even links back to the incubus touch thing."

"Like, he's gonna watch them jerking off to him. Cool." Silas grinned, all frank kinkiness. Of course he liked that idea.

Trip grinned. "Yeah... like *Deadpool*, but less sarcastic. Very meta."

"Funny too. And sexy." Silas bobbed his head. "I like it."

How weird to be able to talk about a project, a story, a set of sketches with his... fuckbuddy? Colleague? Boyfriend? Muse? *Silas.* How strange to see his new hero staring back at him in the musky flesh.

My own fault.

"We good?" Silas cocked his head. "I mean Kurt and Cliff and the rest of the gooey zoo."

Trip nuzzled his ear and took a breath of his soft scent. "I'm sorry I got jealous." How stupid to bring Kurt up at all, and was his crush on Cliff that obvious?

"Likewise." Silas squeezed him. "Just talk to me. Okay?"

"Deal."

Silas flipped through the portfolio some more, and Trip enjoyed the featherlight smile that played over his mouth as he scrutinized the artwork. *So beautiful.*

Silas had a handsome face, but it wasn't perfect... yet in this moment, in this light, in this room, the planes and lines of that face almost hurt Trip's heart. For an endless split second, the strange conjunction of imperfections shimmered with appeal.

For that one odd moment in the half-light, talking to Silas and caring about Silas and sharing the truth with Silas had made him the most beautiful person Trip had ever seen.

Trip wasn't *blind* to the flaws, but they added up to something beyond explanation. They reminded him of something true about the world that made his chest ache and his fingers itch to draw.

Maybe the clocks had hiccupped. Maybe it was sorcery.

Maybe knowing Silas had something to do with it. And his own illusions and projections. Drawing and drawing him as Scratch, Trip had tried and failed to find the thread that held it all together.

He knew how to draw a "perfect" face, just as Silas probably knew how to build one. Most comic characters were built on the basic cultural expectations of beauty, so much so that distinguishing between certain characters was often a matter of millimeters and angles. Generic beauty operated as a catchall in comics: the lazy artist's friend. Give strong men huge arms and solid legs. Give villains arched eyebrows and crooked angles. Give bold women firm jaws and lean builds.

One tall, dark, handsome champion resembled all the others... they swooped to the rescue beside a legion of boobacious heroines with silky coils of differently tinted hair and barely there costumes.

But now, looking at Silas in the dull amber glow of the lamp and the streetlight shining through the rain outside, how would he draw the exact bend of his cheek and the aggressive slope of his nose in a way that would catch this feeling?

Impossible.

Trip's scrutiny revealed more questions than answers, an artistic cul-de-sac. He stared, and a trail of details beckoned and teased: the low rise of delicate bone behind Silas's small ear, the width of his scarred knuckles when he closed his hands, the lush swell of his lower lip under the thin upper.

On the wall, the second hand advanced by one.

"What?" Silas was watching him.

Trip grinned back. "Just looking at you."

Silas furrowed his brow.

"All—" Trip closed his mouth and opened it for a moment before answering. He smiled softly at Silas. "Good."

Silas dropped his gaze and bowed his head slightly. "You're giving me goose bumps, watching me like that. Your eyes are so dark."

"Scary." Trip's skin flushed with warmth.

"Nuh-uh."

"Sorry." Trip squinted at the window and pulled Silas closer. "I don't want you to worry."

"Why would I?" Silas shrugged one shoulder. "What's the point? Worrying is praying for something you don't want."

"Fair enough." Trip laughed and sighed, loved that he'd fucked up and come clean and no sky had fallen. The girls had it right; he'd gambled and won.

Not such an awful idea.

Silas shook his head at the floorboards. "Y'know, you *could* just take him directly to the fans."

"Who?" After a moment, Trip realized Silas meant Scratch. "Oh." He shrugged. "How?"

"The other pros know you, right? Artists and suits?"

Did they? "Sure." All the creators knew each other because they all ate and drank together those weekends. Plus, the Image and Top Cow teams always came by to say hey. Kevin Kiniry from DC Merchandising invariably checked in to see if Trip would consider illustrating some trading cards or toy packaging. *Hero High* had made fanboys of a couple of Vertigo editors. Come to think of it, Cliff liked to pretend those folks sniffed around Big Dog for co-branding. "Yeah. A bunch of them know me."

"Maybe you should ask some of them for advice."

Trip shrugged. "*Scratch* isn't even done. And those guys aren't gonna help with a queer sex comic."

"How do you know?"

Trip frowned. Truth was, all those guys probably knew he was gay, though he'd never said anything. Nobody's business but his own. Showing them *Scratch* would change the way they saw him, and maybe not for the better. "I don't, I guess."

Silas grinned. "So ask one of 'em. Whoever you think will be cool with the idea."

Sensible, if scary.

Trip glanced back at the *Scratch* portfolio. He was a sexy bastard. And Silas's pleasure in the drawings only sweetened his pride. Even if nothing else ever happened with this crazy book, he'd know he'd done something right because of that tenderness on Mr. Goolsby's face.

Silas leaned over and pressed his cheek against Trip's upper chest, that slight hollow by the clavicle he'd claimed as his. He flipped to the next page; this one showed a head-to-toe profile that emphasized the jut of Scratch's pecs and ass, as well as the square jawline. Then a double page crayon top-down view of Scratch on all fours, the flare of his back exaggerated by the perspective. "God, I think *I* wanna fuck me now."

"You see my problem." Trip groped the lump in his pants.

"Well, I definitely have a solution."

"You kidding?" Trip turned. "You are a solution."

"Yeah?"

Trip shrugged. "Oh yeah." He walked toward Silas and backed him against the table.

"Wait! I don't wanna—"

"Paper." Trip pushed the sketchbook and portfolio off the surface and onto the floor. "It's just paper." He pushed Silas and stepped between his legs.

Silas resisted with a chuckle.

"Oh really?" Trip dipped his head and peered up through his lashes. "I'm not gonna take a no."

Silas slid off the table's edge, without pulling any pages down with him.

15

SILAS needed to rescue Scratch from his creator. Trip might not be ready, but *Scratch* was.

First, he lured Trip out to Silvercup near the end of March to see some of the shoot and hang with him in the trailer.

"Mr. Spector." Silas braced his back against the frame of the makeup trailer door and crossed his arms.

"Mr. Goolsby." Trip ambled across the concrete toward the trailer. He looked exhausted, but the grin on his face grew until it showed teeth. "A sight for sore eyes."

Trip walked right into his shady space for a hello peck.

Silas loved the way Trip held the back of his skull firmly and kept their mouths together for a few breaths. In semipublic, even. He had loosened up about little things.

"God that feels good." Trip stole another kiss. "Hello."

"You better be hungry and horny. I'm nearly done." Silas opened the door to the trailer and let Trip pass.

He cracked his neck and Silas winced.

"Yes, please." Trip dropped his backpack by the door. "Like you wouldn't fucking believe."

Inside, Silas stepped closer and ran a hand over Trip's scalp. "When was the last time you slept, mister?"

Trip twisted his face into comical horror. "No idea. I've got so many pages due. I took a nap at one point."

Silas nodded. He knew better than to ask about meals. Trip's hands jittered, and the stubble on his cheeks was as long as the dark bristle on his scalp. When he got into studio mode, Trip lived on sugar, salt, and caffeine, with occasional servings of processed meat-goo.

"Was the subway crowded?" Silas wiped his hands on the towel over his shoulder.

"Took a car service 'cause I worried about getting lost." Trip shrugged. "Crappy comics pay me well."

Silas fidgeted. *Must be nice.* He covered his bills, but even now, at twenty-nine, he lived his life hand to mouth. Showbiz had never paid steady.

Trip blinked at him sleepily. "What are you making?" He glanced across the table at the buckets Silas had plonked on the floor.

"I'm repairing, actually. It's a cowl." Silas picked the hood-thing up with one forearm inside it, a faceless head and neck. "I should have cast in silicone, but we didn't have time and it's more expensive."

Trip shrugged. "Freaky."

"I rushed and it's humid, so I ended up with huge steam pockets. Moisture builds up in the molds sometimes… it leaves ugly pits and crimps when you're baking your foam. So I spent all morning repairing shit because I rushed yesterday."

Trip grimaced in sympathy. "Sorry."

"Not your fault. I'm almost done, if you wanna siddown." Silas wiped his chair off with his towel. "Five minutes tops. I thought Francesca would take longer to show you around."

"She was great. Then they asked to clear the room."

"Nudity." They were shooting Leigh Ann's lap dance for the mob boss. She'd worked with the choreographer for two days, and Silas had spent fifty minutes getting her holographic body glitter right because he loved her so much.

Trip grimaced and shivered. "Ugh. In front of a crowd. I could never."

"Yeah. Actors get thick-skinned quick." Silas bent over to dig in his kit. "I have a surprise for you."

"No way."

"It's nothing serious. I goofed around with a batch of PlatSil, and I had an idea. They need paint, but I wasn't sure about the colors."

"What are they?"

Silas held the little appliance over the bridge of his nose. "Scratch's horns. I thought if you ever wanted to cosplay Scratch at a con, you'd have a set of good horns, teeth, claws, y'know?"

"Cosplay?"

"Dressing up as characters at a public event. A great way to promote a new title too. Like Miss Rina's zombie wedding."

"I could *never.*" Trip gaped in horror. "That kind of attention would freak me out."

"Actually, that's what gave me the idea. I thought that the costume might buffer everything. It would promote for you, and you'd be off the hook, sorta."

Trip seemed hypnotized by the texture. "How do you—" He picked up the horns and rested them against his forehead.

"You build it for the face. Usually when I'm experimenting, I use a cast of my head so I can test it on me first." Silas winked. "That's why I'm such a badass every Halloween. If you're game, we'd have to do a mold of yours with Alginate."

No immediate protest. "Doesn't feel like I expected."

"This is silicone. It feels organic. Or at least not like rubber." Silas smirked and rumbled in his manliest voice. "Are you denying the snazzy of that?"

Trip regarded him uncertainly.

"The Tick?" Silas gawped. "C'mon! Greatest television ever devised, I'm telling you."

Trip squeezed the horns.

Silas leaned closer. *Not too shabby.* "Foam latex rots, so I'm gonna run most of it in silicone, for the translucency. Takes a little longer, but it won't read 'cheap Halloween mask.'" He pawed through his kit for a Bondo canine and held it up. "I can recycle the teeth and claws with a couple modifications. The real issue will be painting, because I won't have a team, but I can prepaint a lot before application. I'm good at dressing up."

"Does it hurt?" Trip eyeballed the chair with suspicion.

"Not at all." Silas tapped the spatula against the bowl. "The most uncomfortable thing is that you have to lie there while it sets up."

C'mon. C'mon, man.

"And these are for the fingers." Trip picked up the little firm silicone thimbles. "They aren't sharp."

"Naw. It's just for the look. They go over your fingertips to cover your nail beds and give you his talons."

"So I wouldn't be able to draw or sign or anything."

Silas grinned. "I didn't say they were for you."

Trip's mouth opened into a little shocked ring.

"If you wanted a set, I'd cast 'em special." He pressed the silicone against Trip's forehead firmly so the translucent horns sprouted there.

Trip beamed. "Awesome."

"They'll fit and angle better if I cast a set for your face."

Trip laughed. "Like a spell?"

He snickered. "No, Mr. Spector, like foam latex."

Trip hugged himself. "I couldn't."

"Then what about some help? A couple minions to work the convention hall. I could call in favors."

Trip shook his head. "It's not that easy, though."

"You don't have to be a one-man band. You have a support team, right?"

"In theory."

"For the artwork?" Silas knew the answer to this, but he wanted to sit and listen to Trip, watch his mouth move and his eyes stare past the wall into wherever his ideas lived.

Trip's nerves appeared to have settled; covering familiar turf seemed to put the full weight of his attention directly on Silas. "Well, I'm not the real honcho. But Big Dog only hires me for pencils and ink... and sometimes not even for the whole book. I thumbnail the artwork and then render it in blacks so it can be colored."

"So someone else decides what the colors are?" Again Silas knew the answer but pretended he didn't so he could hear that angular voice gently explain things.

Trip shrugged. "Well, there's a script. The writer sometimes tells you. And when it's an existing brand, like the Mighty Mites, the uniforms have preset designs. Editors get involved. Color can wreck a great pencil, or it can save a shitty one. After a while, you get to know the folks you work best with. It can get...."

Complicated. "Yeah."

"Complicated."

Somehow, knowing Trip's next word before he spoke... delicious, like the crunch of fresh-baked bread and peach preserves.

"So... script, then thumb, then pencil, then ink, then color. Right?" Silas used shears to clean the seams of the cowl while he enjoyed Trip's happy attention on him and the calm that lapped between them. "It all sounds pretty complicated. Do these colorists live in the city?"

"I wish!" Trip's laugh burst from him, clean and sharp as scissors. "No. Two brothers in Vancouver. And Wavenna in Turin for more natural stuff. But Dolores is my favorite. She's in Uruguay. I swear she can read my mind. I don't even speak Spanish and sometimes she feels like one of my closest friends."

"You're lucky."

"Yeah."

"I mean, to have that kind of connection. I get called out to work shoots, and I have folks I work with pretty regular, but I don't belong to a team. Or I haven't gotten successful enough that I can even have a team to belong to. FX is pretty clique-y."

Trip gave him an awesome squeeze. Silas didn't move, hoping the hand would stay.

"Hell, all I do is glue and paint shit on people. Dream up boogeymen I can't afford to build." Silas knocked on his skull. "Sometimes I feel like I'm still doodling naked werewolves on my algebra notebook."

Trip squeezed the fake horns again, like oversized nipples. "Did you really draw naked werewolves—?"

"Duh! With boners." The dimple reappeared in Silas's cheek. "Wild and woolly, man. At Savini, I got to build a naked werewolf with a hairy penis, but when my teacher found out, he trashed the photos."

Trip closed his eyes and pretended to scold him. "Silas."

"Well, I had a blast designing and building him. And the class loved it."

"D'ja get in trouble?"

"I had to pay for some of the supplies." Silas shrugged.

"And I'll bet you dated the model."

"Hey!" Silas laughed. "I did not."

"Because he was straight?"

The jealousy still bugged Silas. He heard the spidery suspicion in Trip's voice.

"C'mere." Silas took Trip's hand and led him to the battered couch at the side of the trailer. Actors had left a scatter of unfinished crosswords and folded sides from scenes they'd shot this week. "Siddown a second."

"I'm okay."

"Well, I'm fucking whipped, so sit with me a second." Silas tugged at his hand until Trip sat down and leaned into him.

For a few moments, the only sounds were their breathing and the hum of the little refrigerator.

"Mr. Goolsby…." Trip sat back and opened his hands. "What would you do?"

"With *Scratch*?"

"Yeah. I mean, what if you had the start of a book and weren't sure what to do with it?"

Silas shrugged and spoke with complete candor. "You don't want someone giving it away or fucking it up. So you keep hold of the rights. That'd be my number one priority."

Trip wrung his knuckles like a rag. "I wouldn't know where to start."

"From *Scratch*." Silas shoulder-bumped him. "What publishers handle erotic content? Who would dig the occult angle? Class Comics? Prism? You must know people."

"I dunno. Cliff handles all that shit."

"So do a little research. Me, I'd go to a comic convention and pitch it to companies with a solid track record with sexy titles."

"Go public?" Trip scrunched up his face, his mouth warped with misgivings.

"Well, he ain't a shy critter." Silas held the horns near his hairline. "It's a gay title. And there are a few gay-friendly publishers that know their way around a bare demon dick."

"Come out proud." Trip twisted his hands together.

"If you want." Silas spoke gently. "I mean, we already talked about you taking him to a con."

"I thought you meant just to ask advice." Trip looked fretful. "Sounds like a huge gamble to me."

"Sure. But where's the harm?" Silas crossed his arms: stubborn farmboy. Trip liked his chest, and if he had to *flirt* Trip into making a bold move... he'd had tougher jobs.

"I don't even have all the interiors done. I've only had the Judge a month." He smiled at Silas.

"Who says you gotta have it finished?" Silas drew a shape with his blunt fingers midair. "You just want to connect as many of the dots for them as you can. The story is in the spaces. 'S'like comics. Any story really. Give them sexy gaps to fill."

"Gross!"

"Not that. But you gotta seduce 'em a little." Silas brushed Trip's cheek with a thumb. "So maybe a little, yeah."

"You think I can sell an unfinished project?" Trip rested his arms on his knees. "*Scratch*, I mean."

"It's not that unfinished, Trip. Look, if I see two drawings, a full glass and an empty glass, the order tells me what happened. The action happens between the panels, in the gutters. If the full glass comes first, then the glass pours out in that space. But if the empty comes first and then the full, then in between those panels someone filled it."

"I love that." Trip grinned and pressed his arm.

"Film's the same way. It's just a whole string of pictures. They run through a projector so it tricks your eye into thinking they're moving, but they're static. The moving is something that happens in the gaps."

"Big Dog does that all the time. Actually, I think I do that—"

Cliff, he means.

"Everyone. We all do. That's art, man. Make good dots and help folks connect 'em. Help them see the whole package. The real juice runs in the gutters."

"It's a mess, still. Nothing polished. My flats are rough." Trip ran a hand over the hair on Silas's head and smoothed it down again.

Silas considered him. "You don't have to stay a solo act your whole life."

"Like Dolores would ever color a gay romance." Trip's face clouded.

"Why not? Your publisher would set up a team. It's a gig. She digs you. How long you got left penciling Issue 1?"

"Couple weeks? Maybe three. I owe Big Dog interiors and that slows me down."

"Well...." Silas turned to face him squarely. "You got character models for Scratch, Isaac, and the Judge. A sheaf of panel pages. All the thumbnails. A couple cover alternates waiting for you to squirt your magical eye jizz. That's enough of a package to show to friendly publishers."

"Behind Cliff's back."

"What back? Trip, he knows you're drawing it. He also knows that other folks wanna work with you. He could've signed you to an exclusive on that *Campus* whatsit and he didn't... just to save a buck. He's relied on your loyalty for the past four years to keep you dickless and shackled to *Hero High*. You're his star."

"Twinkle, twinkle."

"For whatever reason, you gave him permission. If he won't hire you, then someone else should."

"Every comic is a criticism of every other comic." Trip sighed with certainty. "*Scratch* reads like a fuck-you to Big Dog."

Silas grinned. "Which is why you want a company who doesn't have suit-itis. You wanna keep the new book separate, or else they'll spend all their time trying to make it into a cliché."

He watched Trip turn the possibilities over in his head. Silas imagined his anxiety about unveiling the big demon at a con, but a miniscandal could launch a "very graphic novel" toward the right audience in a major way.

"Y'know...." Trip hugged himself. "I have a fanbase."

"From *Hero High*. Those are not the same folks that want a big homo-hocus-pocus title from Trip Spector."

Frown.

"But hear what I'm saying. If you're throwing a black-tie dinner party, you want to invite the guys who own a tux. *Scratch* already has a fandom, even if they don't know it yet. We just have to invite the folks who have the right itch."

"It feels wrong. Too soon."

Silas dropped his arms and put his feet square on the ground so he could lean forward and use his hands to make his case. "Trip, if you want people to buy the book, they have to know it exists. What about C2E2 in Chicago?"

Trip dropped his chin. "In a month? There's not enough time to plan. We don't have any swag. No printer will—"

"Hey!" Silas laughed and drew a finger across his throat. "Hey. Hey. It's not Iwo Jima. I didn't suggest this to wig you out."

Trip shifted in his seat, obviously hating the idea of putting his racier work on display. Even with his pride in the project, *Scratch*'s frank eroticism was new turf, and he likely had anxiety about fan reactions. He sucked on his lower lip. "Ugh. I hate this part."

Silas wondered if he meant the business part or the erotic part or the demon part or the gay part. He took a breath and let it out, wanting to help. "Are you nervous because of Big Dog or because of your audience?"

Trip squeezed his skull and sighed. "There are plenty of cons that could launch Scratch. When he's ready."

And when will that be?

Trip elaborated. "There's this Bent-con thing for LGBT comics, but that isn't till December. Maybe we wait until then."

"You're gonna sit on *Scratch* for nine months?"

Trip pinched the bridge of his nose. "I just wanted to do something new."

"And you did. Awesome." Silas spoke slowly. "So... what if you and I pooled our know-how."

Trip laughed, and a little puff of anxiety escaped. He wiped his face. "Howzat?"

"Easy, I could build a couple badass incubus makeups, and we could Scratch-bomb a comic con." Silas held up the fabricated horns again and eyed Trip. *I double-dog dare you.* "Even if we couldn't afford models, I know plenty of buff actors who'd help out."

Trip looked at him sharply, an odd expression on his face. "I don't think that's a good idea."

"It'd sure get attention."

"Only Marvel and DC really know how to do that kind of promo at a con. Booth babes and all. They're owned by movie studios. Otherwise it comes off like craft-project creepytimes." He scowled.

"But I'm the guy they hire. Y'see? It's just a great way to get people talking about the book."

Makeover.

If he could get a couple of fellas made up as Scratch, the rest would be gravy. He wanted to find his new audience, right? Trip's sexy anti-hero walking around a big event was bound to rustle up publishers and a legion of eager fans.

"I think Scratch sells his own book better than anybody. Turn him loose on a convention and see what shakes loose."

"'S'too much. Too fast." Trip sneezed and sniffled.

"The thing is, most of what you did is so elegant. I'll paint, but the character is pretty clean effect-wise. I'd run a brow piece. Hands. A plug to erase their navels."

Trip hugged himself. Silas wavered. This wasn't landing the way it was supposed to.

Silas shrugged. "Hell, I'd do it. It helps that he's got my face and body."

"No." Trip's forehead creased.

"But why? I love dressing up."

"Well, for one thing, for all of Issue 1 Scratch is balls-naked."

"Twist my arm." Silas grinned.

Trip flushed.

Wrong tack. "We can easily come up with some kind of demonic fig leaf that covers my bojangles." Silas kissed him.

"Ummm. Y'don't need to get your junk out to sell my graphic novel." Trip held up a hand like a traffic cop.

"My daddy would say you gotta play to your strength. Scratch is a big, bold character and that means a big, bold move." Silas opened his palm, weighed the air. "If that's what you want."

"I want to. That's the sick bit. Part of me wants to unleash *Scratch* on the whole goddamned world. When in doubt, freak 'em out."

"Is there anything else you wanna be drawing? Anything that gets you juiced?"

Trip frowned, and then he blinked like a starving dog. "No. Fuck."

"Then let's figure out a way to keep your *Hero High* gig safe and also let *Scratch* loose." Silas held the horns up to his head.

Trip relaxed a little and a breath escaped him, as if pursued. "You're awesome. And crazy. And gorgeous. But no."

"Crazy?"

"You're a lunatic."

"*May*be." Silas kissed the side of Trip's head. "But if I gotta draw the moon, I wanna give it a mustache."

Trip leaned into him and sighed. "You have this way of making anything seem reasonable."

"Yeah?"

"You make everyone brave. You don't even know, but you do."

Silas thought of Leigh Ann and Benita in this trailer, not ten feet from where they sat. The ladies had said something similar. Maybe that was his superpower. "So I'm like a spiritual jockstrap."

"Fuck off." But Trip was smiling as he pushed Silas away. "You're the hottest, smartest dork in the multiverse, and you know it."

"Just think about it." Silas looked him straight in the eye. "My opinion, I think *Scratch* is more than ready, and you should launch as soon as possible."

Trip stifled another sneeze and wiped his nose. "In Chicago."

"If you want. Somewhere. That doesn't matter." Silas frowned. "I think this book could be bigger than you can imagine. Kurt always says that all markets are driven by hideous ideas. Crazy risks."

"Or career suicide."

"What?"

Trip ground his teeth. "Nothing. Kurt gives you an awful lot of advice."

"Well, what do I know? He runs his own company. I just glue shit on people's faces and go to the gym three days a week."

"H'yeah."

"I'm saying. Kurt's just right more than he's wrong. He's my friend."

Trip muttered at the floor. "—oyfriend."

"C'mon. He's not my boyfriend."

"He's your fucking *un*boyfriend." Trip crossed his arms.

"What does—?" Silas turned. "Are you still jealous of Kurt?"

Trip picked at the cushion on his lap. "Let's see: he's rich, smart, handsome, and he comes up in every conversation we have because you idolize him."

"I don't."

"Respect him, then." Trip shrugged but wouldn't lift his gaze. "I get it."

"Sorry." Silas blanched. Did he talk about Kurt that much? "But I have no interest in Kurt."

"F'you say so." Trip then sat silently, scowling at his smudgy hands.

Silas squinted but let it drop. Kurt might've done something or said something? *No.* Trip had never met him. He'd put it off each time Silas offered.

"I get it, though. Annoying as hell." Trip winced in slow motion. "I never understood what they meant."

"Sorry. Who?"

"Not you, the unboyfriend thing."

Unboyfriend? This wasn't about Kurt. Silas knew there was some kind of relationship calculus he needed to untangle, but fuck if he knew how it worked.

"I think I have a headache." Trip ground his temple with the pads of his hands, petting himself firmly.

"It's your call. This is a risk and you shouldn't take it till you're ready." *Where did that come from?* For the first time in his life, Silas was trying to see the situation from the other guy's perspective. Usually he just made messes first and apologized after, but Trip didn't need more complication and bullshit.

Then again, maybe Trip didn't want to share Scratch with anyone just yet. Maybe he was too dirty, too scary, too personal. Silas didn't want to headfuck his boyfriend, but he didn't want the opportunity to be put off forever. *Different tack.*

"You're right."

"Whuh?"

Silas leaned forward carefully. "Maybe this is all too much. You'd be better off waiting until everything was in place."

"Wait-wait. I thought Kurt said terrible plans were—"

"You're a writer. A creator." Silas tried to catch his eye. "You make things up because you have too much imagination to hold inside your body and it spills out."

Trip snorted.

"Kurt is my friend and he's very razzle-dazzle. He's also pompous and annoying and lonely as hell. I'd love y'all to meet. I wanted that, but I didn't think you had any interest. See? Y'gotta lot in common besides me. Don't you for one second think that I'm hiding anything from you. Open book right here. No secret identities. No masks. Just me."

Trip glanced up then, his soft brown eyes almost black. "Idiot."

"Never said I was smart."

"No. Nothing. Me." He sniffed. "Jillian has told me for years. And Rina. Unboyfriend, I mean. Doesn't matter."

Silas knew it mattered, so he didn't blink, but held Trip's gaze as gently as a baby bird. *What are you seeing?*

Trip looked down at the battered couch and the coffee table full of dead scripts and unfinished puzzles. He rubbed his eyes and heaved an exhausted sigh. There were dim circles there that hurt to see. Trip probably hadn't slept since the last time Silas had stayed over. *Three nights ago.*

"I am not trying to lure you into my elaborate Batcave of Hollywood craziness." Silas jabbed a finger at him. "Or if I am, it's 'cause I wanna be your strapping sidekick."

Trip smiled and sat.

Silas joined him. "And I reserve the right to be completely fucking wrong about everything." He knew the word for what he felt, wanted to say something irrevocable, wished for the guts he pretended to have. Except, once he said *that word*, all hell was bound to break loose. "That demon is your deal, Mr. Spector."

"I know." Trip rocked forward and kissed Silas on the chin and then squarely on his mouth. "I know he is."

Silas leaned back against the crumpled arm of the couch, which suddenly seemed like the most comfy spot on the planet. He poked Trip in the tit. "Scratch is not any kinda mistake, even if he is a very, very naughty idea."

"Very bad. Needs a spanking." Trip reached around and gripped Silas's buttcheek.

Silas yelped in surprise. "I'll be damned."

"Save me a seat." He inhaled deeply. His eyelids seemed heavy.

"Anybody fucks with you, they're in some deep Alabama shit." Silas made the words full backwoods trucker. "Idjits gonna end up pregnant in cutoffs, working for my daddy in a bait shop." *Shaaahhhp.*

A snuffle of laughter. Trip muttered "Bubba," but for all his sarcasm he seemed grateful for the *Hee-Haw* BS.

"C'mere." Silas wrapped his arms around Trip's lean torso. "I gotcha. I gotcha." He kissed Trip's temple and sighed. *Just a couple minutes.*

Trip pulled his knees in and went slack. Second by second, minute by minute, Trip's breathing slowed. He pressed a hand over Silas's heart and nodded, then nudged his head closer.

"Hey," Silas whispered. "You think you can fall asleep?"

He already had.

THE day Trip finished, he told no one.

He'd drawn and inked all twenty-four pages of *Scratch, Issue 1* in eleven insane weeks, but instead of cracking a beer or shouting from the rooftop, he walked over to the river and stared at all the water trying to find the sea.

When he got back, Trip padded into his apartment and dropped his backpack in shock.

Lights on. Low music. The apartment smelled like roasted eggplant. Silas reclined fully naked on the couch, knees bent so his heels pressed into the cushions. His ass was tipped up, exposing his trench. He pushed back into the cushions as he polished his erection with one hand.

Trip took a couple of quiet steps closer. He'd forgotten Silas was waiting for him. Trip opened up and let a big grin out.

The hypnotic humming calm Trip associated with his boyfriend stole over the room and him. Time expanded as he ambled toward Silas, the hands milking languid pleasure out of his stiff joint. He knew exactly what it tasted like, what made Silas holler and hiss, what they both wanted. The warm spicy air hung suspended, like honey drizzled over them.

Silas didn't open his eyes. His fingers pushed down under his balls and plunged inside his hole.

Trip wet his lower lip. His aching dick firmed up with a sluggish throb that matched his pulse.

Silas tightened his eyes and dug deep at his ass, struggling to reach the right spot. Unashamed, he raised his knees still farther and grunted as he worked to find the right angle. "Mr. Spector." Silas opened lazy eyelids and licked the corner of his mouth slowly. "Jus' thinking about you."

Trip bit his lip, stupidly, as he watched Silas drive his greasy boner into his fist. The slither of the lube was the only sound he heard other than his own heartbeat *whump-pump*ing in his ears. "Need some help?" His voice came out hoarse.

Slow blink, slower grin. Silas hunched his hips and crooked his head at Trip's buckle. "'F'you want."

Trip shivered at something happening inside him. He had never encountered such openness or anyone so frank about their appetites. He wanted to match it and worried he couldn't. He hoped his caution didn't come off as boring or childish. At the same time, Silas would speak up if he had a problem.

Silas sped up his stroke. "I can wait, if you want. Or you can watch." The hand at his hole strained as he twisted his wrist hard. His head dropped back. His cock flushed a rosy tan. "*Faugh.*"

Fluttery embarrassment knotted Trip's insides. He fought the impulse to laugh or hide. The tip of his tongue snuck out to taste his upper lip. Silas used some kind of lotion that snicked and popped as he fucked his hand.

"I been edgin' forever, chokin' my squirrel. I tried to wait." Silas tensed his toes and angled his hips, spearing himself in a rhythmic grind that splayed his hand against the swell of his ass. His sweaty forearm flexed as his eyes dropped to slits. "C'mere."

Trip walked to the edge of the rug. The musky vanilla and markers scent got stronger. He stared down at all that rough hunger that rendered him invincible. He could ask anything, do anything. His heartbeat slowed to dull percussion, and he traced his mouth absently. The buzzing, feverish heat stole over his limbs. He peeled his shirt over his head and let it fall. Without questioning the impulse, he bent his knees and crouched in front of the spread tan thighs. *He's mine.*

Silas jerked faster, and the rosy pouch of his balls jumped, the caramel fuzz around his hole smeared into dark fringe by the lube. The mushroom cap deepened to a dull salmon-brown. "C'mon. C'mon."

Trip brushed his right hand over the back of one thick thigh, and Silas flinched.

"Please."

Trip skimmed his hands down the back of Silas's hoisted legs and stroked the skin.

"Trip." The word hissed out in a pained plea.

He slid a finger beside Silas's, then pushed into the sucking, greasy heat of his ass.

"Oh!" Silas tipped his pelvis sharply and smiled. "*Yuh.*"

Trip sucked at his lower lip, then put his face a few inches from the perfect pink swirl that swallowed their digits and held them together.

Silas panted and nodded urgently. "Put that thing in me. Stick me, man. I can't go much longer."

Trip studied his erection trapped behind his trousers as if it belonged to a stranger. They'd gone through all his condoms. "Gotta rubber in your bag?"

"Naw. Then just jerk it."

Trip yanked his buckle free and dragged the zipper and his briefs down. His fleshy length looked dangerous and the skin uncommonly pink.

"Lemme feel." Silas stared at the blunt erection. "Fuck. Please, man. Just ride the outside." He slid his fingers out and gripped his cheeks to expose the hungry knot of muscle flexing there. "Let me feel it."

Trip knee-walked forward, then rested the underside of his boner right on the scalding iris.

"Ugh." Silas stuck out his curled tongue and the tip touched his upper lip.

Trip ground his hips and humped the hole a couple of inches each way, dragging his shaft over the firm ridge. The lotion had vanished into the tawny flesh, and the rough rub turned his cockhead shiny on the upstroke.

"Gawd. *Agh*-umm." The Alabama croon coming out of Silas made him sound like a ruined farm boy. "Chunka beef, man. So damn fat. Let me feel it right there."

Trip spread Silas's cheeks wide with his sweaty hands and humped the trench. He couldn't get purchase on the hips. Trip muttered, "Can'stop." He bumped his crown against the stretched opening, then slid his full hardness along it.

Silas scooted back into the cushions and drove his hips into Trip's hands. The lube he'd used had left him impossible to hold.

Trip leaned over him to stay in contact as he massaged the round haunches. More than once, he managed to slide a finger inside… a quick, slick *in-out* that forced hisses and hunches out of Silas each time. He reared up, kept one hand at the entrance, and ran the other up Silas from pubes to throat.

Silas yelped in apparent surprise and suckled at Trip's tongue lazily. He rubbed their slippery chests together.

Trip nuzzled at Silas's upper lip, then his jaw, then his gasping throat, rasping across the soft bronze stubble and leaving a trail of spit. He chewed softly at the muscle, teasing it with his canines till Silas shook and pleaded in that husky rumble.

"God." He squirmed and purred under Trip's stained hands. "Make me." He craned forward, lifted his chest to meet Trip's touch. His crack exposed, his eyes fixed and feverish.

Trip swallowed, hypnotized by the pleasure of dominating someone so manly. *No apology, no shame.* He pressed one hand over Silas's scruffy face, crushed the rugged profile into the pillows. The more he pushed, the more Silas sobbed and arched and struggled against him.

Silas trembled anxiously, and his forehead crinkled. His free hand twitched midair. His busy hand sped up, and he whimpered. "Can't—"

The greasy ring went crazy against Trip's cock, flexing and yielding against the underside. Trip slid his fingers inside the oily heat again and spread the ass-flesh open, rode it with his full stiff length. *Mine.*

Silas choked. "Can't wait. Can't—*Gawd.*" He made short, sharp jerks with his hips, and his blunt crest darkened to a dull rosy-brown.

Trip bent closer. "You got something for me? You saving something?" Two of his fingers slipped over the sweaty cheekbones, and Silas sucked them into his mouth with wet abandon. "Almost." Trip pulled out and petted Silas, his flushed cheek and the sweaty cowlicks.

Silas wheezed and twitched. His hole clenched rhythmically against the belly of Trip's erection. "*Shh-huh.* H'yeah. *Truh—*"

Trip rubbed his palm over the sloppy knob until the frantic stroke of Silas's rough hand bumped his out of the way.

Silas bowed off the couch. His torso flexed and his head rolled senseless. Blobs of thick white goo bubbled slowly out of the wide cap and fell to his furred belly in a copious puddle that ran down his ribs.

Trip laughed and stroked Silas's broad chest. Silas's taut lips melted from a silent roar to a huge open smile.

Part of Trip wanted to race to jerk himself off, but the smarter half of his libido knew Silas would make his waiting worth it.

Silas panted and relaxed by slow degrees, lowered his hard arms to the couch. His head fell back. He flexed his round butt and clasped Trip's girth in a damp grip.

Trip examined his own straining boner and gulped. He lifted a mischievous stare. "Now look what you did."

"What we did. Fresh churned nut butter." Silas dabbled his fingers in the soupy mess on his abdomen and sucked them clean. "*Mmth.* H'yeah, bubba."

"Bubba?" Trip ground against him again. "I thought you didn't like—"

"I don't. But I wasn't talking about me." With his warm cummy hand, Silas took hold of Trip's firm cockhead. "All it means is 'brother.' And brother, that was just what I needed." He twisted his wrist, and the hot slide of his semen made Trip flinch.

"Got a problem, there?" Silas stroked him with feathery lightness. "What are you needin'?"

Trip's cock jumped. "Not sure."

"Lemme guess." Silas slicked his steamy load onto Trip and scoured the top, twisting his palm over the plump apex.

Trip spasmed and thrashed. "Whoa!"

"Y'don't stay still, you're gonna hurt yourself." Silas milked the erection languorously. He didn't stroke it, just gripped Trip's hog with casual ownership and squeeze-squeeze-squeezed patiently like an external heartbeat.

Trip's stiffness swelled so rigidly the veins stood in high relief. "Not fair. Your hand."

"Rough." Silas milked the meat rhythmically with his scarred, spermy palms. "Best lube in the damn world."

Trip fought the thought that put in his head. *Greasing myself with his load to pound another out of him.*

Silas held him fast, gripping his cock insistently.

"Wait…. Ungh." Trip hunched into the delicious fist. Instead of fighting to get free, he leaned and stole Silas's mouth. He pushed his hand into the calico thatch and held Silas's lower lip against his to nurse at it, taste the slow honey slip for as long as he could without taking a breath.

Trip's orgasm floated up to him like cinders swirling from a bonfire. The scrape of skin and the electrical shimmer within expanded until the scorching jism erupted from him over Silas's thumb and wrist and ran like hot wax.

"I… think…." Silas sat back on his heels. His hand glistened with Trip's seed. "We need to go buy some more condoms or I cannot be held responsible."

Trip twitched and relaxed by increments.

"I almost blew again. When you went." Silas blinked and wiped his chin. "Boy, do we fit together." He kneaded his boner gingerly with the sticky hand.

Trip felt drained, probably for the first time in his life. Not like his balls were empty, but as if someone had scooped his entire body hollow and refilled it with drowsy bliss.

He'd always thought of sex as something he got away with, but Silas brought all his enthusiasm into the bedroom and had this way of giving him exactly what they both wanted. Trip slid right into the honeyed heat that hummed between them.

Hand in glove.

"You okay?"

Silas coughed and held Trip still with one big paw. "Whoever told you that you were uptight was a fucking moron."

Trip took a deep breath of the starchy air, suddenly hungry. Perfect opportunity to show Silas the finished interiors, but Trip left *Scratch* covered and concealed on his drafted table and he said nothing. *Not just yet.*

16

WHEN faced with a well-meaning firing squad, bring on the showtunes and gore.

For their first group outing, Silas offered to take Jillian and Rina to a matinee of *Evil Dead the Musical*. Tiffany had called him with free tickets to give away because she'd built effects for this revival. Between zombies, belting, and demonic possession, he figured any ice would get broken. Silas didn't see a lot of theater, but this and *Toxic Avenger* had been a blast.

Unable to find a taxi, they'd walked uptown in cottony fog that hung so low it blurred the tops of buildings. Silas carried an enormous golf umbrella, but the sky refused to rain.

"I didn't get us tickets in the splatter zone."

Trip swung around. "The *whuh*?"

"Well, there's bloodshed. A lot. And the first few rows get pretty messy. Hardcore fans fight over those seats. You said the Stones are horror buffs, but it seemed safer further back."

Trip made a face and bobbed his head. "Jilly will be annoyed. Rina will be relieved. Max and his dad will probably sneak closer after they kill the lights."

The only hesitation Silas had was about Jillian's son. The show's carnage was goofy, but *Evil Dead* got pretty gruesome. Trip had assured him the Stones did regular slasher marathons and Max tended to fall asleep during them, so Silas went with his gut.

New World Stages was a large off-Broadway multiplex off Eighth Avenue housing a bunch of smaller theaters. When they arrived, Silas grabbed their tickets at the booth and found out Trip's friends had already claimed theirs and headed downstairs.

In the bar area, Trip waved at a foursome who stood at their table: A stocky man with his hand on the knee of a pixieish brunette. A little boy talking with his hands to the group. And from the back, a *va-va-voom* woman with a bodacious body poured into a violet-brown knit dress.

Unfamiliar nerves gripped Silas about ten yards from Trip's closest friends. *Don't screw up.*

As they reached the table, the pixie froze, her hand angled in the red streak in her hair. She opened her mouth and hacked, but no sound came out. Her eyes flashed, blinking rapidly, and she twitched silently and violently.

The dad didn't seem to notice, and the other woman fanned herself with a postcard.

"Umm, guys?" Silas walked toward her.

Pwamm. She crumpled to the floor as if having a seizure. Her eyes flickered white and she convulsed.

Silas crossed the fifteen feet rapidly. "Hey!" He squatted beside her and pressed his hands to her heaving ribcage.

Just as he opened his mouth to call for help, the kid turned to her and said, in a bored little-boy voice, "Mom, don't be embarrassing."

She stopped spasming instantly and flipped her head to Silas, her grin wicked. "At least the floor is clean. That's a very good sign in the American theater."

Joke.

"You people are strange." Silas rocked back on his heels.

Trip leaned over and muttered into his ear. "I warned you."

"Hey!" The little boy huffed in irritation.

Silas offered the fake-dead lady his hand and helped her to her feet.

"Jillian Stone. Hi, And these fellas are mine." She put a hand on her husband's and son's heads. "Ben and Max."

Silas shamelessly aimed his dimple on Jillian. "You know…. If you'd had a blood pack in your mouth and bit down as you—"

Her husband groaned. "Don't give her ideas."

"Nice to meet you, man."

"Ben Stone." His handshake was firm and dry.

"I'm Rina." She looked Greek or Hispanic and snuck little happy glances at him holding Trip's hand. *I like her.*

Silas took off his jacket and smoothed his hair, still damp from their foggy stroll.

Trip held up his watch and went around the circle. "Bathroom?"

"Lord, yes." That was Rina.

Trip squeezed his hand but didn't let go. "And the boys'll go find seats. Max?"

The kid nodded solemnly, incredibly well behaved. Ben gave his wife a quick hand signal like a baseball pitcher.

Jillian and Rina tottered away on their heels, heads tipped together as though gossiping. *About me, probably.*

Ben seemed more fidgety and tongue-tied. Probably not super outgoing, so Silas made a point of walking with him toward the *Evil Dead* doors. 'S'hard to be the straight guy in such gatherings.

"Thanks for scoring the tickets. Max and I don't see a lot of shows, but Jilly loves 'em." Ben pulled off his jacket.

"Glad y'all could make it."

They proffered their tickets, and the usher walked them down to their seats. Silas perused the ceiling and walls. *Yep.* They'd rigged the blood spray to come from most directions for those first three rows. Good thing he'd opted for the tenth.

Silas entered the aisle first so Trip could sit closer to the rest of the gang. "Trip said you're an *Evil Dead* fan." He sat and turned back to Ben.

Ben had just sat down. "Sam Raimi fan. Hardcore. *Spider-Man* too. Right?"

"Same. I loved *Xena* and *Hercules*, too, back when. Snarky barbarians."

Max hung back to enter last. "Can Mom and Rina sit here?"

Ben eyeballed Silas a moment. "Bruce Campbell is the greatest actor who ever lived." He laughed and seemed to relax. "Manly snark." He pointed at the gory program art. "Death is not just for dead people. It can happen to anybody." His voice sounded like Dudley Do-Right, idiotically rugged.

Good gravy!

"Are—" Silas stopped moving and let his mouth fall open, then beamed. "Did you just say...?"

Ben spun. An identical beaming grin appeared on his face, and he tucked his chin to announce. "I hate broccoli, and yet, in a certain sense—"

"I *am* broccoli!" Silas shouted along with Ben. They stood and embraced each other over Trip, thumped backs in a butch display that turned a few heads around them. *Fanboy mind meld.*

"Umm, guys." Flattened into his seat, Trip looked at Max, who shrugged.

"Crazy." Ben poked Silas in the tit.

They sat again, and Ben swiveled on Trip with incredulity. "*The Tick* is comic gold. The guy who played Bat Manuel ended up as the—"

"—mayor in *Dark Knight!*" Silas high-fived him, and robust cackling and snorting ensued.

"Dad. Stop." Max glowered. Grown-ups were embarrassing.

"Did you just steal my boyfriend?" Trip jabbed Ben.

Silas blinked at the ceiling. "You're talking to someone who believes that *The Tick* is the single greatest sitcom ever broadcast in the United States."

"*The Tick?*" Trip frowned. "I didn't know that. What about *Conan?*"

Silas waved the distracting thought away. "Sure, yeah. Barbarian movies are my comfort food. I have a shitty day, I come home and go through the Deathstalkers,

Hercules, Amazon Queen flicks like *bam-bam-bam*. But *The Tick* is like the best of both worlds because he's big and dumb like a barbarian but hilarious as all get-out."

Trip eyed them doubtfully. "Maybe I didn't give it a chance. I didn't know anyone actually watched that."

"Mostly they didn't. Fox kinda railroaded them." Ben shared some regret with Silas, who shrugged in kind.

"Fools!" Silas raised a defiant arm. "I recorded the episodes. I bought the DVDs. Living rooms of America, do you catch my drift? Do you dig?"

"It got canceled?" Trip looked at Ben.

"Too smart. Too mean." Ben shrugged and pointed at the ceiling. "I will spread my buttery justice over their every nook and cranny."

"Egad!" Silas pitched his voice into a heroic rumble. "I started with the comic book."

"Cartoon and sitcom." Ben sighed with satisfaction. He gave Silas a jocky *thwap* on the back. "Really great to meet you, man."

Silas grinned at Trip. "I still want to be Patrick Warburton when I grow up. Actually, if we both got blue suits, you could be Nightcrawler—"

"Shut up!" Trip laughed warmly. "Ben's the best."

"You kidding? He watches *The Tick*. That's pretty obscure."

Just as the aisles cleared, the ladies arrived and began to *scuse-me-sorry* their way into the row. Silas perused the audience; the theater had filled up, and for a matinee the audience seemed exceptionally young and funky. A lot of laughter. *Hallelujah*. Nothing was worse than bringing strangers to a limp performance.

After Jillian sat, she presented her guys with T-shirts that said "I Survived the Splatter Zone." She pointed at the stage. "We can roll around in the gunk after the curtain call."

"I opted to support the arts instead." Rina had sprung for a copy of the CD. She flashed a shy smile at Silas. "Let the butchery commence."

With the rest distracted, Trip leaned over to him and whispered, "You good?"

Silas muttered back, "I like them a lot."

"I think it's mutual. You were nervous."

"No, you were nervous." Silas tried not to grin.

Trip bumped their shoulders companionably. "See? Piece of cake."

The lights dimmed, and a voice told them to kill their devices before the slaughter began. Trip took his hand, which made Silas's heart do a baby chimpanzee somersault.

Cake.

"SHE'S prob'ly not trying to *kill* you." Trip countered.

"Selene sucks. She watches cooking shows." Max gagged at the thought of his regular sitter, a straight-A junior at Chelsea prep. "Ugh."

They had stopped to drop Max off at kid jail back in Murray Hill. The ladies dragged Silas upstairs. Trip flopped down in Ben's armchair in the living room. Ben jogged upstairs to rinse off some of the gore and change his shirt. Silas assured him nothing would stain, which seemed to disappoint the Stones greatly.

Trip still felt smiley and buzzy from the show. *Evil Dead* had kicked every kind of ass, and of course, Silas had charmed the hell out of everyone. "Good show, huh?"

"Yeah." Max made no bones about his irritation at being abandoned.

Because he spent so much time with Ben and Jillian's insane friends, Max got impatient with mere mortals. The downside of being a cool kid... they got tired of being kids. The idea of a babysitter must have seemed like the final insult. "I keep having to fix her phone."

Trip checked his watch. He didn't want Silas stuck up there for ages on goblin detail. They had dinner reservations at a tapas bar on Irving Place. "School night." Trip didn't try to explain the concept of drinks and NC-17 gossip. He felt guilty for leaving Max behind, but Ben and Jillian needed a little grown-up time.

Normally Trip drew while Max played, but he couldn't exactly draw a sex demon with a nine-year-old underfoot. *Hero High* was kid-safe, at least. He could work on it in Starbucks, if need be. But *Scratch* had to stay secret.

"C'mon, buddy. We won't be long. Whatcha gonna do?"

Max shrugged.

"Movie, then? You could have an *Evil Dead* marathon."

"I guess." Max scooped up a muscular black-and-white action figure: Venom, it looked like, Spider-Man's slobbering shark-toothed twin with an exaggerated tongue and wads of sinew. A far cry from the kinds of goofy Silver Age boogeymen Trip had grown up with. DC still took shit for creating the Condiment King, who fought heroes with relish. *Yes, really.*

"Can I see?"

Max handed Venom over to him somberly.

Slouching on the edge of the chair, Trip considered the little bad guy and tried to imagine the fortune he'd earned for his creators. *The greater the evil, the greater the bill.*

"Neat, huh?" Max knelt, watching his inspection of Venom.

The jealousy made him feel like an ass. What did it feel like to have your characters out in the world like this? Trip knew how lucky he was to work in the industry at all. And *Hero High* had been a gravy train. *Still...*

"Venom's an epic character." Trip stood Venom up on the coffee table between them.

"You ever wish you'd made him up? First." Max put his chin on the glass.

Trip laughed. "Well, it took more than one person."

Duh, said the invisible thought-bubble over Max. Little-boy logic. "Someone thought of him. I mean, he's not real."

"The idea, yeah, but he has a whole team. You got writers and artists and editors all working for Marvel comics, and they all stirred things into the pot. A fanboy called Schueller had the costume idea, and Michelinie wrote him as a character. And then this famous artist named Todd McFarlane drew him in a way fans loved. So Venom ended up in toys and video games and trading cards. Twenty years and he got famous enough that Topher what's-his-name could play him in a big tacky blockbuster."

"Which sucked." Max nodded solemnly.

"Given." Trip spread his hands wide, not sure how far to go. Was Max interested or only hoping to worm his way out to dinner?

"So… Venom's more famous than the guy who thought him up."

"Oh yeah. Easy. Venom is bigger than all of them together 'cause he got loose." Trip nodded. "But alla those artists put Venom *together*-together over a long time. Like twenty-five years. And then, other people built things out of him that add to his story. Like games and lunch boxes and more books, and those stories become part of the character, so he stays alive and keeps changing out in the world. So he isn't actually alive-alive, but he's inside a whole bunch of heads, which only makes him stronger."

"Like the flu." Max walked the little doll a couple of steps, then weighed it. "'Cause they shared him."

Trip snorted. "Yeah. Sorta. A really tough germ you can't get rid of, except with being famous instead of fevers and snot."

Max giggled. Snot was always funny in this house. "And that's what you do."

Trip grinned. "And that's what I do."

"Cool."

Yeah. Not so much. How did parents know what to say at these moments? For all he knew, Max's questions might change the course of his entire life. Then again, maybe he was just curious about a favorite toy. Trip ran his hand over Max's messy head, his hair straight and glossy as Jillian's but the same dull brown as Ben's.

"Y'know, Silas has a friend who makes action figures."

Max looked up at that. "Like in a factory?"

That image forced a laugh out of Trip. *Logical.* "No. No, I mean he designs the molds they use to make them. He sculpts the figure first and then works out how the pieces fit. Takes 'em apart. Puts 'em together. Y'know, where they bend and what they wear and the face… then he sends it to the factory."

"*Awe*some." Max hefted the molded resin in his hand. His eyebrows marked a stark line as he considered the possibilities. "So he coulda made this Venom?"

"Well, *he* didn't, but someone did. Venom didn't come out of thin air." Silas was right, or Picasso. *No artist is a bastard.*

Max blinked, and in that blink Trip imagined his godson could see the connected dots that linked the little doll he held to a store and a factory and a mold and a sculptor and a drawing and a story that somebody wrote on a blank piece of paper after a couple of brain cells sparked inside their skull.

Trip still remembered the exact Wednesday he realized that *Vampirella* and *Dr. Strange* were just lines on paper that some shnook squeezed out of their dreams and fingers. Which was the day he decided he wanted to make his own lines on paper—not a bullshit "I'm gonna be an astronaut" wish, but an "art classes every Saturday morning" plan—even when his father scoffed.

"Your friend gets paid to play with action figures?" Max's eyes shone wide and expectant. He looked like his mom when she sang.

Trip laughed. "Not hardly. I mean, you play, but it's an awful lot of work."

Like a match to a wick, the idea lit Max's face. "You'd have to study a lot, I bet."

"A whole lot." Silently, Trip begged Ben and Jillian's forgiveness. He felt guilty for making an infuriating profession seem glamorous. They wanted Max to be a drummer or a game show host, something outrageous and dazzling. "It's probably not as cool as it sounds."

Actually, it was even cooler for a hardcore nerd. Modeling for toy companies was one of the holy grails for sculptors in the industry. But Trip was trying to be an adult and keep the enthusiasm out of his voice.

Max stayed on the rug, percolating. "How'd he do it?"

"He took a whole lotta art classes and anatomy, and after a long time, a company came and asked him to design their toys." Trip glanced at his watch. Surely Jillian had to be finished exploiting his boyfriend's depilatory know-how.

After standing the figure back on the table, for a long moment, Max sat peering at Venom as if he could see something beneath the acrylic and resin. "I wanna do *that.*"

Trip grinned. "Your mom said you wanted to be a heart surgeon."

"Mom says all kinds of stuff. But I'd be better at bad guys."

"Like a surgeon for superheroes."

"And supervillains. Trip?" Max sounded serious again. "Did you ever make up a character from scratch?"

Trip smiled at that. Scratch had this way of sneaking into every conversation. "Lots. But you probably never heard of them. I been drawing *Hero High* for a long time."

Max looked down, old enough to hold his tongue. He thought *Hero High* sucked but loved Trip too much to say so. "I mean one famous character, like Venom. An *epic* one."

Trip squinted. "I've made up lots of characters. Who knows?"

"You'd know. A really cool snotty one that needs a lotta stories." Max knocked Venom onto his back. "That other people share and wanna catch."

Yeah: Scratch.

"One. But nobody's heard of him yet."

Max gave him a weird look. "Why?"

"He's...." Trip shrugged. "A secret." *My secret.*

"That seems dumb."

Ouch. Maybe it was dumb, but one day he'd have to let Scratch loose, and then a whole lot of other people would wade in with their own agendas and ideas. Trip's ownership would evaporate the minute he brought anyone else on board.

Max wasn't buying it. "How can he ever have stories if he just sits on his butt in his secret hideout forever?"

"Well, He's needs to be a secret for now. He's not for little people. So... probably not the flu after all. More like sniffles." Trip felt guilty just imagining Scratch's sexy everything while sitting on the Stones' old couch. Max could never know about that comic and could never see any of his work on it. *Eesh.* The mix of shame and pride sucked.

"You don't know. I mean, if you don't share him, and keep him a secret, how can anyone catch him?"

Trip tried to imagine turning up in Chicago with a crate of naked demon toys. Signing Scratch's dick for fans. *Hard call.*

Trip stood Venom back up on his two little feet. "Why are you thinking about jobs?"

"I'm almost in middle school." Max looked at him.

Trip jabbed a finger at him. "Old man."

"I like a girl. In my homeroom. Julie." Max smiled, as if that explained everything. "She has curly red hair."

"Cool." Trip didn't know what he was supposed to say to a kid in these moments. Nine was closer to a teenager than he'd realized. *Gah.* He felt prehistoric.

"Does that seem weird?"

"Why?"

"'Cause you don't like girls." Max cocked his head and quirked his mouth. "*Like*-like, I mean."

Trip chuckled. "Well, I don't dislike 'em. I just like guys in a different way. Y'see?"

"I guess." Max fetched the *Evil Dead* box set off the shelf and plonked it on the coffee table.

"I think the liking part is more important than the boy or girl part. There are lots of girls and lots of guys, but there are only a very few people you can really and for-truly like."

"Oh brother." Max crossed his arms. "Well, I don't wanna kiss her or anything. I just like talking to her a lot. She's funny."

Trip nodded. "That's key."

"And she has the best laugh ever. Her eyes make little moons." Max smiled to himself.

"Is she nice?"

Max shrugged.

"Nice is more important than people think, and harder to find than they say."

Max popped out the first DVD. "I mean, she's not my girlfriend. She's a friend who's a girl."

"That seems like a good place to start." Trip grinned. "Nobody has to like anyone they don't. That's one of the greatest things about love. You can't make it do things even if you wanna. And if you can, it probably isn't love."

Max held up Venom with a grave expression. "Do you love Silas?"

Trip glanced at the stairs. "Sometimes."

The little boy looked baffled.

"Listen, buddy: it's not a car. Your heart doesn't go in one direction at a time. I mean, sometimes you love your dad even though you're annoyed with him. Or your Julie. She may have the best laugh, but sometimes she's laughing at you."

"I guess." Max smiled at some memory and dipped his head. "That's different."

"Grown-up secret. You ready?" Trip muttered out of the side of his mouth. "Everything's different. No two people are alike. No two feelings. You have to look close." He prayed Silas didn't overhear any of this.

"So when you do love him, what's it feel like?"

"Hmmph." Trip squinted. "Tough."

"Tough?"

"No, it's good. Crazy. I feel like I'm the Incredible Hulk, only instead of angry making me grow, it makes me happy, and every time I see him, I get bigger and bigger till I can't even scare myself anymore."

"Yeah. Maybe. I think he's pretty cool."

Silas built monsters, which made him an instant demigod to a fourth grader. "Me too." Trip had a flash of what Max would be like as a grown-up: no-nonsense but funny as hell. Married to a bossy girl who laughed at his jokes. A loving dad, a loyal friend. Jillian and Ben knew their shit. He wanted them to have another kid. The world needed saving.

Trip raised Venom's bulging arms so the little slobbery villain seemed to be asking for a hug.

Max favored them with a side-eye. "*He* doesn't sit on his butt."

Did he mean Venom or Silas? *Or both.*

The doorbell rang and Max sprang to his feet. "Got it!" His sneakers thumped into the hall.

A young female voice. "Hey, Max." Selene called out as she entered the hall, running late as usual: "Mrs. Stone, I'm here. Fog screwed up the trains." The babysitter clocked Max's movie selection with no small amount of skepticism.

Creaks from the staircase. Trip emerged into the hall as Silas came down, a little dazed but none the worse for wear. He rolled his shoulders, smiling.

Rina poked his back, descending behind him. "Wait till you see those goblin costumes." Max's class was doing a play for the end of the school year. "Your boyfriend is a genius, *pa.*"

"Which means I'm gonna seem like Supermom." Jillian's eye makeup had also changed, though Trip couldn't say exactly how. Her eyes looked luminous and predatory.

"You don't need a cape to be a hero." Silas clomped down the stairs. He reached Trip and slid a strong arm around his waist.

Trip stayed put and tried to enjoy the warm muscle beside him. Who cared whether some high school putz thought gay people were gross?

The grown-ups gathered in the hall under Max's baleful glare.

Jillian hugged him. "Night, kiddo. Don't drink all the scotch."

"You wish." The nine-year-old snorted and shuffled into exile. A DVD menu roared and slobbered.

"Car service is here." Silas headed out the front door, but the ladies hung back a moment.

"*Bellaco,*" Rina mock-whispered. "That is some sweet meathead you snagged."

"I like him. Ben likes him. What's not to like?" Jillian shrugged, a community theater yenta to her marrow.

"He's not a meathead. He's meat-*y.*" The words came out defensive. "He goes to the gym, is all. He's just as dorky as I am."

They laughed at him. *Laughed!* "Bitches," Trip grumbled and crossed his arms. "Will you please tell Mr. Stone we're gonna be late?"

Jillian brayed up the stairs. "Benjy!"

"Yes, woman!" Her husband clomped down wearing a fresh shirt and an apologetic aura. He tugged his lower lip down. Blue-black letters showed stark on the wet pink flesh, "JILLIAN." For their tenth wedding anniversary, Ben and Jillian had gone to a tattoo parlor to write each other's names inside their lower lips in block capitals that pressed against their teeth. Every time they kissed deeply their names slid together, which seemed simultaneously gross, crazy, and sexy as hell. Trip thought about the "BENJAMIN" inside her mouth where no one could see it. *No one needs to.* Showing her the tattoo was one of his Neanderthal straight-boy signals for saying "love" to Jillian.

Selene shrugged in the doorway of the living room, obviously unimpressed by signs of love you couldn't wash off. "Eleven?"

"Or earlier. Call if there's anything." Ben pecked his wife and picked up his keys from the hall table.

Rina peered out the door after Silas. "Whaddayathink?"

"Silas? High score. Tick-sational." Ben tucked his wallet into his jeans. A proud papa smile. His caterpillar eyebrows levitated as he deployed his Tick voice again. "He has a three-pound brain, and it's all smarts. Where'd he go?"

"Outside with the car."

"I'm telling you." Jillian fluttered her lashes. "Hot mensch. All the way from whistlin' Dixie." Knowing side-eye to Trip. "Jeepers Creepers."

"Gate of Horn, man. He's a keeper." Ben thumped Trip on the shoulder.

Silas stuck his head back in the front door. "Ready?" He smiled sweetly at Trip.

Rina looped her arm through his, and Jillian took the other one. "Losers weepers."

17

FUCK the red carpet. No way was Silas willing to share Trip looking like *this.*

Tonight was the affiliate party for *Undercover Lovers.* About six, Silas buzzed his boyfriend in so Trip wouldn't have to dig out the key he'd never used. They always slept at Trip's, either because it was nicer or because certain people had a not-so-secret phobia about unfamiliar spaces. Down the hall, the elevator cranked to life, and even that made Silas smile. A week since *Evil Dead;* they hadn't seen each other in three days, and for the first time in his life that felt like a major fucking deal.

He waited for the elevator's cheerful *ping.* Seeing the suit was gravy.

Now, Silas was used to seeing Mr. Spector in cargo pants and stretched T-shirts. When he opened the door, the suave figure in charcoal wool seemed like a stranger. Trip faced away from the door, his hair freshly cropped. The jacket draped easily on his lean frame. He looked like a dapper rogue from the pulps: a playboy detective with a sword cane and a secret identity.

"Oh!" Trip turned and ended the call on his phone. "Sorry. That was rude. I was calling you. Hi."

"Don't apologize to me. Dressed like that?" Silas bugged his eyes and pulled Trip close. "*Unph.* You needta suit up way more often."

Trip tried to back away and grimaced. "Yeah. No."

"Just saying."

"I feel like such a tool."

Silas brushed his shoulders and lapels. "*Rrrsh.* Sheesh." He squeezed his junk. "I'm wooding up, Mr. Spector. Have a feel." He nudged forward, and his stiffening cockwad brushed Trip's knuckles.

"Hey!" Trip laughed nervously and twisted away to head back toward the elevator. "We're gonna be late."

Who cares?

To follow Trip in the suit proved almost as good as the full frontal. Silas kept his hands to himself, but as soon as the elevator came, he pushed Trip against one wall for a kiss.

"You look handsome." Trip pushed him away gently but definitely. "Thanks. For inviting me. I promise to not be a freak."

"Hey. I don't give a goddamn about any of that."

"Quit." Trip ran a finger under his collar. "You're making me self-conscious. I'm already nervous about all these showbiz types."

"Tonight? Don't sweat any of it. These parties are purely for promo. A lot of people in T-shirts."

"Wait." Trip's wary eyes widened again. "Am I overdressed like this?"

"Not for me."

Scowl. "Goolsby. Should I have worn a T-shirt?"

"The PAs, I meant. I'm doing a bad job of telling you that you look gorgeous." He smiled and kissed Trip's frown. "We're fine. The talent and the suits glam out for the cameras."

"Cameras?" Trip blanched.

Shit. Wrong turn.

"Red carpet BS. We can skip all that noise. Besides, the paparazzi only want the actors for E! and the tabloids. The party is really for the affiliates." He sensed that nothing he was saying was helping. "I only want tonight to be fun. We leave whenever."

"I'm gonna stick close, if that's okay."

"You better. I just wanna show you off. Jee-sus."

Trip wagged his head. "Sorry. I'm being a mutant. I don't do great in crowds. As long as you don't drag me in front of any cameras, I'm good."

"Scout's honor. I want you all to myself." When they got downstairs, they were alone in the lobby, and Silas took Trip's hand and squeezed it, careful to let go before they got outside onto Seventeenth. "We're gonna have a blast. Showtime picked them up for season four, so it'll be super-relaxed."

Overhead a storm was brewing, and the air crackled with electricity.

They took a cab to the Fifth Avenue party space, only to get stuck in the event traffic. They opted to hop out on Twenty-Fourth Street and walk east, past a line of dark sedans that disgorged folks in expensive party clothes. A searchlight humming out front stabbed the curdled clouds.

Trip checked him out and nodded. "This feels very grown-up."

"Well, I promise to be very immature to make up for it."

A clump of star-watching civilians stood outside the lobby. *How do they know?* Only zealous PR firms could explain the public's psychic ability to track down these events anytime, anywhere, faster than the speed of tweet.

They passed security and then took an elevator to the top floor.

Silas jogged his keys in his pocket. "You good?"

Trip flashed a petrified smile. "*So* not my world."

"Not mine, either. I just slap makeup on these yahoos." He winked. He suspected the situation scared Trip more than the crowd. Once Trip got his bearings they'd have a kick-ass time.

As Silas had predicted, the "velvet rope" was a staged area off to one side with cameras aimed at the overlit strip of symbolic red carpet.

"Jeez." Trip walked so close their arms bumped.

Silas scanned the entrance. "We don't even have to run the gauntlet. That's for the actors." *Fuck.* He'd forgotten about Lance and Barney and all the others. He didn't need shit from any of his past conquests, real or imaginary. Well, he'd stay close to Trip. "Thank you for doing this. It means a lot."

The door whores claimed their invite, then waved them through. Trip relaxed the moment they stepped into the dim hallway. With a cautious arm at his back, Silas steered him… not quite embracing him, but making it clear they were a couple.

Silas didn't want to exacerbate Trip's unease, so he didn't take his hand again. Trip still got hinky about public affection when there were too many witnesses; private meant private.

"A lotta people," Trip whispered. "Just don't take off."

"Cross my hard-on, Mr. Spector." Silas navigated a path through the buzz of conversation and the soundtrack for *Undercover Lovers* seasons one and two throbbing through the speakers.

Silas waved at Paul and Tiffany, eating at a table on the mezzanine with a couple of the set dressers. He avoided the food at these things anyways, but with Trip, he'd much rather take him somewhere they could actually eat real food. Hard enough to get him to ingest actual nutrients.

"Shit." Trip bent his head and sniffed at his pit with thinly veiled panic. "I think I stink."

"You're fine."

"I shoulda showered again, but I lost track of time."

Silas leaned in and inhaled. "You smell fucking delicious, Mr. Spector."

Trip blushed. "C'mon."

The party clocked in on the inexpensive side, a large wedding space scattered with gold bamboo chairs and cocktail rounds lit by spots. Neither Showtime nor the producers wanted to waste money to impress a bunch of suits from the burbs. Still, the music was solid, and the affiliates seemed younger and hipper than usual.

On one side, they'd set up a sound booth, next to a small dance floor filled with a lot of straight people who danced like they were afraid their asses might fall off. On the other end stood a small stage with a podium and ten-tops, where older people ate and yakked.

Silas had a hunch they wouldn't stay long. "See anybody you recognize?"

Trip gritted his teeth and peered around before he shook his head. "No. Should I?"

Silas laughed. "Hardly. Hell, I work on the show, and I don't know some of these people. I'm always in the trailer. All I see is actors, and at this kinda deal, they're busy trying to score points with the buyers for these local channels. Next season, next show."

"I guess I don't watch much TV." Trip waved a hand at the room. "I mean, I've watched some of the superhero shows outta loyalty, but I get bored too quick."

Silas signaled to a waiter. "Mostly, television is like bubblegum. I mean, there's flavor and you're chewing, but there's no nutritional value."

Trip didn't disagree.

"And it blows. Perfect for when you wanna turn your brain off."

"What about *The Tick?*"

"That is art, my man." Silas gasped in fake offense. "Timeless genius. That show was so great, television couldn't contain it!" He snickered.

Trip laughed with him. *There's my guy.* "I can never keep track of when things are on, so I always miss episodes. Reruns, sure, but it's kinda noise. I'd rather watch movies."

"I'm telling you, *The Tick* can fix anything." Then Silas spoke under his breath. "You doing better?"

"Much. Thanks." Trip eyed the lethargic dance floor warily. "I'm not really a big party person. Shocking, I know."

"'S'okay." Silas rubbed his back in a small circle, secretly pleased to be able to touch him in public. Tonight felt important on a lot of levels. Sharing his work, braiding their lives. Once Trip had met some of his friends, everything would feel less unnerving to him. *Baby steps.*

"Any parties, really. My family made such a production out of everything. Dinner—always—special. Vacations—a production. Every shirt I owned, every gift I got, gave my mom a reason to cry and perform her generosity and sacrifice for an audience. So I learned to keep my yap shut." Trip shuddered.

"Well, shy I ain't." Silas tugged his arm. "Stick with me, Mr. Spector." Silas spotted Leigh Ann, Francesca, and Benita getting frisky on the dance floor. *Saved.*

His ladies had loved Trip on his brief Silvercup tour; they'd carve out a safe space. "There we go."

Following his line of sight, Trip tightened up again, gnawing on his lip. "Friends?"

"The best, I promise. You'll love 'em." Silas put a hand on the sweet curve of Trip's lower back to help pilot him through the crush. *So far, so ghoulish.* They'd only stay an hour, long enough for Trip to meet and mingle.

"At a party, I thought there would be more... I dunno, partying." Trip grinned.

"Just my crafty plan to get you into a beautiful suit so I can blow you in the john."

Trip blanched and gauged their surroundings, but no one had heard.

"'S'okay." Silas needed to walk on lightbulbs for the rest of the night. *No joking.*

"Gools-bee!" A high voice echoed in the lobby, and Silas turned to spot an expensive-looking waif wending his way.

Oh shit.

Gabriel was a lighting designer who'd ended up in television after he graduated: cute as a button but very possessive. Nowadays he worked as Best Boy on smaller shoots because he was tactful and sharp as mustard.

Silas had picked him up at a charity bash, a dance for some disease. Their similar coloring—golden skin, dirty blond hair—made people mistake them for brothers, which Gabriel had encouraged shamelessly. *That* kinky roleplay had been hot for about two weeks—behind closed doors—and then had gotten weird fast when Gabriel introduced Silas as his actual biological brother and then invented fake parents for them. Silas lost his number after that.

Trip vibrated with barely concealed agitation.

"I thought that was you. Hi, guy." Gabriel slowed to a saunter as he got closer. His eyes flicked over Trip's hands on Silas. Instantly his hard charm snapped on. "Great to see you, bro. You must be...."

"My boyfriend." Silas exhaled. Why the hell had they come to this thing? *Oh yeah.* 'Cause he wanted to show off to— "Trip Spector, this is Gabriel Irwin, who lets there be light." Silas put a possessive arm over Trip's shoulders.

Gabriel stared at Trip as if dissecting his shoes, his suit, his deodorant, and his buzz cut. No doubt he could price the entire outfit, head to toe.

"Nice to meet you." Trip shook the offered hand but didn't seem to notice Gabriel's scrutiny. Maybe he ignored it.

"Gabriel?" A skinny marketing wonk snapped her fingers in their direction. She wore a gold dress with Dolman sleeves that made her look like a Wiccan at a cotillion. "One of the packs is dead."

Silas pushed his chin in her direction and jogged Gabriel's elbow. "You're being summoned."

"Fuck a duck." Gabriel semismiled at them before he answered the summons.

"Gabriel's the production's Best Boy. Lighting admin, sort of."

Two spots of color bloomed high on Trip's cheeks, but maybe that was the heat of the room. "Best Boy?"

"He wishes."

Silas skirted table six, occupied by most of the show's writing staff—already drunk and ornery. All of them wanted to be executive producers, and all of them had projects of their own waiting in the wings.

Art is a hard dollar.

Silas prayed the guilt and panic had faded from his face. He searched for the ladies again. *There*: Francesca and Benita in deep conversation by one of the speakers and Leigh Ann playing the meat in a sandwich with two flexible gentlemen. Silas gently herded Trip in their direction.

They would be fun compatriots, and they'd put Trip at ease. Plus they'd help fend off all the assholes. Come to think of it, the idea of these bozos hitting on Trip gave him a shaky, hollow feeling. Silas didn't want any more awkward ex sightings. Fat chance.

Oh shit, Barney. He didn't need a drunk Barney making a sloppy play in his direction, or Trip's. Benita would scare him off. In less than a month, she'd gotten a reputation for calling stooges on their crap.

Was it dumb to drag Trip so far out of his comfort zone just to show him off? Stupid. They needed to be a part of each other's lives, right? To calm himself, Silas admired the lines of Trip's suit and imagined taking it off him when they got home. Outside the windows, a spectacular view of the Flatiron District. The sullen sky refused to spill its cargo.

The cheesy sax of the *Undercover Lovers* titles blared from the speakers, and most of the room turned to find the source.

"This is the new premiere." Silas stopped and pointed across the dance floor, where the first episode of Season Three appeared on the twenty-foot screen stretched high above the milling crowd.

Trip blinked and watched. "All those criminals are so good-looking."

Silas knew he was making an effort. "We do our best."

Trip contemplated the audience, ignoring the screens. "This isn't as scary as I thought it'd be. That sounds bad. Not as fancy, I mean." They had skipped the screening at the Director's Guild.

"Good." Silas exhaled. Trip just kept fitting into the pieces of his world that mattered. "My glamorous life is not very glamorous."

"I dunno about that."

"Wait till it's your show." Silas bumped him playfully.

Trip laughed. "Mine?"

"*Scratch* on Showtime."

"Bullshit."

"Mr. Spector, don't you ever say never."

"I don't even know if it's gonna get published. Hell, I don't know if I can risk it." Trip swallowed. It hurt to hear the chagrin in his voice.

"I know." He'd seen the work Trip had poured into the idea. He couldn't imagine investing that much energy and then hiding the results. "Hey. You draw this and the right folks see it. Isn't that the idea?"

Trip looked apprehensive.

No sign of Barney or the other bozos at least. Silas relaxed a little and moved toward the ladies again. Then again, maybe Barney would play it cool with all the cameras on him.

Kurt was fun, but it felt so different to come to one of these things with a real partner, not just a partner in crime. "Have you noticed...." Silas brushed the slope of Trip's back absently. "You don't sneeze at my place anymore?"

"Well, apparently I'm allergic to everything but you."

Silas pointed at the bar. "Drink?" Maybe if he went alone, he could avoid uncomfortable pop-ups.

Trip bit the inside of his cheek. "Beer?"

"You be okay here? I'll be right back."

"Sure. Sure, yeah." He straightened his back.

"Two seconds." Silas threaded quickly through the clumps of people to the bar, joked and flirted his way to the head of the line, and claimed two bottles.

Fun to see this nonsense through Trip's eyes, but he didn't really enjoy these things anymore. The affiliates flew in from all these cable outfits to get their marketing materials and get pictures with the stars. The paps used the red carpet area to stage fake candids with the ambitious talent, while the assistants gorged on the free hors d'oeuvres and hooch. Which is why Kurt started coming. They'd get trashed and make fun of muggles while Kurt humped some stud for the TMZ cameras. Silas was about thirty feet from Trip when—

Ska-reetch!

The big DJ in the sky had skipped a track. Lance Tibby had moved in for the thrill. Somehow, in the short time it took Silas to reach the bar and claim two open Heinekens, his ex had scented Trip's blood in the water.

Silas muttered, "What the fuck-en-heimer?"

As he closed the distance between them, jealousy sprouted and wrapped itself around his ribs. Since when did he feel jealous of anyone?

Sneaky fucker. He watched Lance drizzle charm as if Trip were a waffle.

Not knowing any better, Trip would act civil, nod, and smile shyly while Lance ladled snake oil over him. Whatever Lance babbled about would give Trip the wrong impression. Silas needed to get Lance away before he started to spill.

Lie. Just lie.

Silas cleared his throat from a couple of yards away, but it must have gotten lost in the hubbub.

Finally Lance saw him. He simpered and kneaded Trip's shoulder. Trip blushed but held his ground. So much for drawing him out of his shell.

Protective rage rose in Silas, and he turned sideways to slither between a cluster of suits. A drunk director grabbed at his arm and one of the beers sloshed over his wrist. When a couple of yards still stretched between them, Lance glanced his way.

"*Sigh.*" Lance turned to smile with every fake tooth in his head. "I know you."

Silas handed Trip a bottle and tried to sound casual. "You made a friend."

"There you are." Trip smiled fitfully and turned to him. "I just—"

"Oh." The blond actor dropped his hand off Trip's shoulder. "Are you two—?"

Silas jerked a thumb toward the front door and flat-out lied. "Lance, the *Condé Nast* photogs are up front."

Lance pivoted like a starved cheetah spotting a gazelle. As supporting cast, he missed most promo unless he remained vigilant. "Thanks." Without a word to Trip, Lance abandoned them for the imaginary photo call. Silas relaxed his hands.

By the time Trip turned back, Lance was twenty feet away. "We—yeah." He stared at the space where the actor stood four seconds ago. "Where'd he go?"

Silas rolled his eyes, whistling through the graveyard. "Tabloids. Never get between an actor and publicity."

"I guess not." Trip regarded a table of assistants stuffing themselves with limp shrimp cocktail. He leaned close to mutter. "'S'like a comic con with better clothes. See what you mean about gladiatorial combat." The blood had drained from his face.

"Sorta. I mean, a lot of craziness goes down."

Trip swigged his beer. "But I guess it's not the end of the world."

Silas laughed. "Well, nothing is the end of the world, right?" He held up his beer.

"Not so far. Give it time." Trip toasted him.

"That was the first great lesson I learned from comics. Nothing is the end of the world." Silas ran a finger under his collar. "Everyone can come back from the dead. They can fix anything, no matter how awful. Nuclear holocaust, decapitation, the fucking Scarlet Spider." *Worst plot-twist clone ever.* "Writers come in and retcon the fabric of time and space, kiss the boo-boo better."

"Guilty."

"That may be what got me hooked on comics in the first place. Even the end of the world isn't the end of the world."

Leigh Ann and Benita now mugged for a video crew shooting footage for broadcast. Silas waved a hand but couldn't catch their attention. He told himself that once Trip met them, everything would be okay.

"In comics everyone has secrets: secret powers, secret lairs, secret identities, secret weaknesses." Trip paused to mull over something. "Which taught me to fucking pay attention."

Silas raised a wry brow. "Portrait of the comic book writer as a young stud."

The room broke into applause, and a couple of people pointed at the screens. *Blooper reel.* Someone had loaded the outtakes, and in a series this racy, there were doozies. Probably no danglies, but definitely embarrassing moments. Trip set his half-empty beer down to clap. Table eight hooted and thumped the actor who played the mayor.

Silas laced their fingers and kissed Trip's knobby knuckles, risking the affection. Trip tightened his grip but didn't pull free.

Silas eyed him directly. "Does that make you uncomfortable?"

"No. Yes. I dunno." Trip turned Silas's fist over and stroked the chewed fingernails and calluses. "Thanks." He traced the pale scars that wrapped around Silas's meaty palm to the base of his index finger. Trip turned Silas's hand over and traced the broad joints. "I'm working on it. I swear. I can't live in my secret hideout forever, right?"

In Silas's search for the ladies, they had ended up around the tables by the dance floor. Silas almost collided with Barney, nursing a triple glass of something pungent, stopping before he clocked him.

"Hey, Goolsby." Barney sat with his "girlfriend," and both seemed bored out of their skulls.

No thanks.

Trip smiled hello to the closeted actor. Silas saluted but kept walking.

Karma rule. Silas waited until they were several tables away before he studied Barney again. Trip followed his gaze back to the uncomfortable couple.

Maybe to Trip, an actor in the closet might not seem as creepy.

"He okay?"

Silas stepped close and muttered into Trip's ear. "Kind of a bummer. They have the same manager. She's supposed to be his date."

"Eesh." Trip examined his hands, scrubbed and pink. It must have taken sandpaper to get all the stains off, but he had for tonight. That scoured skin peeking out of the cuffs pierced Silas to the core. He grasped exactly how hard Trip was fighting his worst habits. He might be pissing his pants, but he'd put on a damn suit and braved this shit because he cared.

"Must suck." Trip looked at Barney again, blinking. "Secret identity. Be an actor and have to fake your whole life. And for the girlfriend."

"Mmh." Barney had made his choices.

"What do you do...?" Trip turned back to Silas. "When you're stuck like that? When you're at the bottom of the barrel?"

Silas shrugged. "Find another barrel."

"Spoken like a barrel maker." Trip said nothing for a minute, but he sure chewed on the sight of Barney and his date.

The stricken expression made Silas push one last time, against his better judgment, to get Trip out of his own way. "Y'know, Nerd Herd is hosting an LGBT panel in Chicago this year."

Trip blinked before his face fogged with justifications. "There's a lot of weird old-school prejudice in comic publishing. Specially in capes and scrapes. Superhero books, I mean. Most the time, Marvel and DC act like it's still 1963."

"So you'd be part of breaking that down. That's good, right?" Silas waved at the second AD.

"I don't want to break anything. These are guys who gave Bruce Wayne a teenage ward in tights and never thought 'creepy chicken hawk.' They think Wonder Woman is feminist because she isn't married."

"Not *now*. I mean, maybe for a couple old buzzards, but there are lotsa gay characters. Hell, digital is burying all these old setups. The whole entertainment industry is the Wild West right now."

"*Scratch* is the best thing I've ever done."

"And all that time and talent you invested counts. You've spent months laying tracks for this thing. There's no harm in seeing if they lead somewhere."

"Yes? No? It's not like anything I've ever done. No one to answer to." Trip tugged at his cuffs. "Otherwise, come July I might as well sit next to a fake girlfriend in San Diego with my head buried in Cliff's *Hero Heinie* like a fucking ostrich!" He was almost shouting.

Silas made light of it. "Naw. You're being cautious is all. Smarter than me, that's for damn sure. You can't hide in plain sight."

"I don't wanna— You'd never puss around like that." Silent alarm bells jangled silently behind Trip's solemn face.

Eep. Silas frowned. "Hey. Hey, what's the matter?"

"I'm sorta like him. That actor." Trip looked desolate.

"Barney?"

"Heroes don't sit on their butts." He intoned the words like a maxim.

"Says who? What's going on?" Silas glanced at the partiers around them. Trip should be having this conversation somewhere quiet and safe.

Trip cracked his joints so hard that Silas winced. "This is why you think I should announce *Scratch.* Everyone does. I'm hiding out at Big Dog with my Unboyfriend." He glanced back at Barney.

"No." *Actually, yeah, sorta.* Guilt. "You're drawing your book and it'll find its way one day."

Trip nodded as if he didn't believe any such thing. "Out and proud."

"You're plenty proud, Mr. Spector. And when it's ready, you'll let Scratch out to find his audience."

Trip's mouth buckled as he wrestled with a bunch of shit that had no place at a red carpet event. Maybe it was time to cut their losses.

Gabriel and his shimmery Wiccan had begun to hustle on the dance floor. Across the party, Barney tapped his patent leather shoes, too afraid to stand, let alone shake a tail feather. He caught Silas watching and hoisted his glass in a woozy toast.

Trip dropped his chin to his chest and inhaled deeply. "I'm doing it."

"Doing what?" Silas asked, even though he knew full well. *Why the total 180?* The suddenness of it made him nervous.

A light shone in Trip's face, clear and bright. His hands were shaking when he retrieved his beer, but he nodded adamantly. "Scratch."

Silas stared at Trip hard for a moment. "You sure?"

"Pretty much. How sure can you be?"

"Naw. It's just… you can't unslice the bread, man. Once Scratch is out, he's out."

Trip mock-glared. "Can you please not question me when I'm being incredible?"

Silas beamed. He resisted the urge to lick his long neck right then and there. *Baby steps.* "Yeah?"

"No reason not to launch him, hot outta the oven." He rubbed his forehead hard. "I know a good thing. And you know the Nerd Herd people."

"They already love you. Mary and Randy? You kidding? They'd add you in a heartbeat."

Francesca and Leigh Ann waved at Silas from the dance floor. Benita pointed at Trip and shouted something happy. Silas pretended not to see them. Trip might not want to get sweaty or feel crowded on the floor. Besides, if he was serious, they had a lot of planning to do, stat.

Silas squeezed his arm. "You 'bout ready to head home?"

The words seemed to take Trip by surprise. "No. Why? Am I being a buzzkill?" Apparently, making his decision had put his nerves to flight. "I still have to meet your friends, right? Turnabout." He laughed high and bright, chugging the dregs of his beer and ditching the bottle.

Trip looked around them as if he wanted to stand on a table and announce his comic now, in his beautiful suit. He had missed a little patch of stubble on the side of his face, maybe a millimeter at the outside of his cheekbone. Scarcely noticeable, but there all the same. *He was in a hurry.*

For some reason the sight of the tiny comma pierced Silas in a way he couldn't name or describe. No one else would notice or care if they did, but knowing that Trip had shaved so he'd look nice, and rushed to meet him, made Silas feel simultaneously potent and grateful.

He leaned over and kissed the faint comma.

Trip smiled shyly. "What was that for?"

"For tonight. For being so handsome. Talented. Brave." Silas grinned. "For coming to see my bullshit work."

"I thought for sure I was gonna end up faceplanting out front where the cameras are."

"Nope."

"Or y'know… asthma attack, limb loss, chestburst alien." Trip flapped his hands. One side of his mouth pulled down like a goofy practice frown. "Something so humiliating that you'd realize what a complete geek I am and trade me in for a cooler model."

"No such thing." Silas squeezed his hand. "Your secret's safe with me. And you already know all my secrets."

"Bull!" Trip snorted and shoved him. "The only way to know every secret about someone is to invent them. Write them, I mean." He took a swig of Silas's beer. "I know every molecule of the Mighty Mites, right? They can't hide anything from me. Comforting in a way, because I can trust them to do what they need to."

Silas got quiet. "And also a little boring. It's all you, talking to yourself. Best thing about sex is curveballs, anyways. I mean, jackin' off isn't exactly a surprise. Unless you're a schizo."

Trip grinned at that. "You're gross."

Silas shrugged and grinned back, tracing his canine with his tongue. "You're gorgeous."

Trip dropped his warm whiskey gaze. "So, Mr. Goolsby... you wanna come to C2E2 with me week after next? It's gonna be—"

"Duh. Obviously."

Without warning, Trip waved back at the three girls he had barely seen before and swerved their way. Francesca had joined Leigh Ann's sandwich, and things were getting a little NC-17. Hell, someone was actually having fun in this waxworks.

"Where do you think you're going, Mr. Spector?"

He took Silas by the hand. "I dunno, but it was worth the walk."

18

SO FAR, Silas thought the comic con seemed like a half-ass film festival staffed by outpatients and shut-ins.

While Trip picked up some kind of paperwork, Silas went down to the bar in search of Kurt and the Unbored posse.

Thursday night. C2E2 officially opened tomorrow, but this "swanky" Marriott bar resembled every other lame corporate watering hole in America. Even the freakiest and shyest among them might be the reporter who put *Scratch* on the map. The ragtag crowd laughed and squawked at each other as if they stood in Shangri-La and sipped the spooge of the gods out of the skulls of their enemies, but all Silas could see was nine-dollar beers and a lot of stale corn chips. These lumpy lunatics held all the strings.

Kurt beckoned from a high circular booth across the room, way overdressed in a Hugo Boss blazer and a fat tie. This weekend's escort seemed bored beside him: a shortish fitness model with black skin and skintight shirt. In the booth next to Kurt's, Sarah Michelle Gellar looked irritated and tiny in a pack of shouty hipsters.

From Kurt's reserved perch, he surveyed the crowd and held court without the geek stampede. *Typical*. Oddly enough, the crowd treated Silas and Kurt like ghosts. Anything noncomic became invisible as they scrambled to chat up the sodden artists huddled at the bar.

Silas picked his way through the prattling flock. Jolly, for the most part, but a little smellier than your average convention. So different from film festivals. At Sundance, people took two, three showers a day, if they could. Hell, some of the executives got a haircut and a shave every morning, but here, they wore vintage T-shirts and iffy skin conditions.

Stop. Silas had come for Trip and for *Scratch*. Karma rule.

When Silas first graduated from Tom Savini's FX program, he'd gone to a screening of a no-budget film out in Williamsburg: a murky, grandiose heist comedy with rape jokes and makeup like birthday-cake icing. He'd gone in an attempt to hook up with the hot assistant director.

Two hours trapped watching garbage and groping each other in the back row had made them horny, giddy, and cruel. Afterward, they burst out of the rented theater. His AD crush had launched into a top-of-his-lungs tirade all the way across the lobby: the director's tantrums, the cut-rate crafty, the cantankerous leads. Silas had cracked wise about the spaghetti-sauce gore.

As he'd popped the door open—*tap-tap*—fingers on his shoulder. He'd turned to see a complete stranger, all of nineteen, with huge eyes and a scruffy goatee. "I did that shitty makeup for about fifty of my own dollars. Thanks."

Silas never forgot the weary, tortured expression on that poor kid's face. He knew exactly what it felt like to have no budget or time, to pull rabbits out of your ass for a director who funded a film on his Visa.

Movies are a small world. That makeup artist might go on to become a Hollywood powerhouse, and Silas had taken a pointless dump on him at his lowest moment, just to impress some trick whose name he'd forgotten a month later. But he remembered hurting that kid.

From that night on, Silas adhered to a strict three-block karma rule. Talk shit all you want, but put three blocks between you and the subject of your scorn.

So yeah... maybe some of these comic people sucked, but his big mouth could only hurt Trip and hurt *Scratch* if he acted anything but friendly and enthusiastic. The wisdom of the staircase could wait till he and Trip were alone.

The thought put a smile on his face as he navigated the crowded bar. He and Trip, on their first vacation together. He'd never done that, either. *Yeah, buddy*. This boyfriend stuff had started to grow on him, big time.

Now Silas wished he had waited for Trip. Hell, in this room, Trip might be as much of a celebrity as Buffy the Vampire Slayer. If he could just get Trip to fraternize with the enemy, temper his tantrums, who knows what might happen for *Scratch* and for them. He loved that idea: being a power couple with a sexy project and money to burn. In the end, it shouldn't and didn't matter, but the possibility hovered just above his eye line.

Kurt raised his voice as Silas approached. "Smile and the world sleeps with you."

He slid into the booth. "Gentlemen."

Kurt fist-bumped him. The glass in front of him stood empty. He gestured at his companion. "Silas, Todd. Todd, this is my *bitter* half."

Silas snorted. "I'm not bitter."

"Well, mofo, you're certainly not better," Kurt scoffed. "Say hello."

"Todd." The escort sighed and offered his hand to Silas. "Hey."

"But Silas and I are not boyfriends. We are *man* friends." Kurt narrowed his eyes at them. "Miss Goolsby is one of the only people who tells me the truth. Reformed sex addict." He turned. "And Todd collects comics and gym memberships. That's why I invited him. Well, the other reason."

Silas tried to redirect the conversation. "Comics?"

"*Green Lantern.*" The stark planes of Todd's face were exactly the color of Brazilian teak. His pecs and lats were so overdeveloped, they actually made him look shorter, as if his torso was as wide as he was tall.

"We've spent all day getting buffed and plucked at the spa." Kurt draped a casual arm over the bulging shoulders.

To his credit, Todd didn't react.

Silas smiled. He always felt a little sorry for these guys Kurt rented. "He giving you hell?"

"Nah. 'S'good. He's a pretty cool customer."

Kurt chuckled. "Smart boy. Always go after the big tip."

"Medical school." Todd drummed the table with his palms.

Kurt turned back to Silas. "D'ya ever notice that every hustler in the world is planning on medical school or an MBA?"

Todd cleaned his nails with a business card. "That many wheezy geezers up close, you learn CPR." This kid definitely had Kurt's number. "You're just a dirty old man before your time, Bogusz."

"Touché." A faint smile floated over Kurt's face.

"Mostly we end up personal trainers and life coaches."

"Indeed." Kurt held his hands up in mock surrender. He turned to Silas. "Where's the Drip? Hiding in the room?"

"God *damn* it, Kurt!" Silas stared daggers.

"Sorry." He buttoned his lips. "Young Todd's impertinence has got me horny and flustered, and I'm taking it out on your absent boyfriend."

Silas scanned the drink-ringed table. "Because you're a class-A prick."

Todd lifted his glass to that and took the last mouthful of his red wine.

Kurt shrugged. "I am. But it's a world of assholes, so things work out. Cocktail?" He flagged the waitress, who'd climbed the little rise of steps. He lassoed a little circle with his finger. "Another for us, Suzette. And a Jack-'n'-Diet for my friend?"

As she left, he patted the table in front of Silas and for five seconds stopped his performance. "Sorry, Goolsby. I'm sorry."

"Right." Silas turned back toward the exit to keep a lookout for Trip. Surely the LGBT panel paperwork wasn't taking this long. Now he wished he'd gone along rather than tried to snag a drink. *What if he's getting cold feet again?*

"Incoming. Five o'clock." Kurt nudged Todd, who appeared to be watching some side of beef who'd caught his attention. "College baseball. Blew out his knee and now he works in advertising in the burbs. Married to a former model, but they never fuck 'cause it's messy." He frowned. "Some kind of humiliating kink. Furries. Shaving. Diapers?"

Silas didn't turn to examine the object of scorn.

"Hot, though." Todd's gaze took dispassionate measure. "Gym and all. Spray tanner."

"He's headed this way. Expensive fucking hair too." Kurt sat up. "Silas, you gotta see this douche."

"I know you!" A frat-row boom. *Dude.*

Silas stiffened. *Oh shit.* One of his exes. Here? Last thing he needed.

Kurt laughed. "Who is this joystick?"

At first Silas couldn't place the square-jawed gym-rat barreling toward their booth like they'd saved a seat for him. Either he was dressed as John Constantine or he expected a dust storm to whisk through the Marriott bar at any moment, followed by a pack of hellhounds. Floppy light brown hair. Quarterback shoulders and ass. Cock-o-the-walk strut.

Fucking hell. He'd seen that face on photos all over Trip's shelves. "It's Staplegun."

"The who?"

Cliff's rumpled jock routine played well in a room full of freaky orthodonture and love handles. He looked like the guy half the room wanted to hump and the other half doodled in their margins.

"We haven't met, yet." All Silas could see was the sneering plastic calculation, like every entitled MVP Homecoming King asshole who'd kept his life miserable in Alabama.

Kurt muttered, "Hello, three-way."

Silas scolded him. "He's not a hustler. Well, no. Yeah, he kinda is, but not like you think. He's—"

Cliff jogged up the four steps in two bounds and stopped almost on top of Silas. "Hey, bro, I thought that was you." He wheezed, out of breath, his wavy mane mussed perfectly. He wiped his mouth, pulled the dark salmon of his lip open.

Everything he does, he knows he does.

Todd and Kurt seemed hypnotized by the caramel skin, hair, eyes. They browsed the jocky burnt-sugar perfection of him: class president of *Hero High*.

Cliff favored the table with a thirty-two-tooth grin and gripped Silas manfully. "Trip sure knows how to pick 'em."

Where the fuck was Trip?

Finally, Todd turned to ask Silas, "*This* is your boyfriend?"

Kurt jeered. "Chiropractor."

"Hardly!" Silas tried to keep the discomfort off his face. "This is my boyfriend's boss. Well, editor. Staplegun." He said the nickname casually, as if it wasn't an insult.

"Stapleton. Cliff." Cliff shook Todd's hand. Then Kurt's for an extra beat. "Cliff Stapleton. Big Dog Comics."

Kurt ogled openly. "Big doggy-style."

"Nice to see ya." Silas waited for Cliff to leave, expected him to leave, couldn't imagine why he didn't leave. "Trip's their star penciller." Did he expect an invite to join them?

Kurt tipped his head as he assessed the assets on offer. "Maybe he's in the market."

"Ohhh.... Cliff doesn't fuck guys." Silas wiped his hand on his pants before he finally accepted Cliff's manly clasp. *Grah*. Even the handshake felt phony. "He just fucks *with* 'em." He pretended to laugh.

Cliff pretended to laugh back.

They both hated each other and knew it.

"Bi now, gay later." A faint smile played on Kurt's face as he appraised Cliff's appeal.

Silas scowled at them both. "So you came to work the party."

"No rest for the wicked, dude." An awkward blip passed as no one invited Cliff to sit, and then he decided to invite himself.

Cliff plonked into the booth beside him, rested the full press of his body against Silas like they were buddies.

Silas inched away. "I figured you'd set up the Big Dog pavilion, peeing on your hydrants."

"Bigger fish in here." Cliff made it sound like a come-on. "I got interns for that crap. Give 'em a backrub and a couple pizzas and they'll go till midnight." He draped an arm along the back of the booth. "They start to flag, I trot by and flash my junk. Keep 'em on the hook."

"Abracadabra." Kurt clapped and scolded Silas. "Where have you been hiding this shyster?" He flashed his caps and licked them.

Where is Trip?

"Nowhere." Silas stiffened, keenly aware of Cliff's arm behind him on the booth. "I swear."

Todd looked confused. Even Kurt seemed a little weirded out. He caught Silas's gaze and widened his eyes as if to ask, "What the fuck?"

Silas shook his head in answer. *No clue.* Why was his boyfriend's pricktastic boss sleazing on him?

"Man, you are jacked." Cliff rubbed Silas's shoulders roughly. "How much do you squat?"

People fall for this shit? "Uh. I dunno. Three twenty?" Silas blinked.

"I hate the gym." Kurt exhaled noisily. "When we were all little faggots, we did anything we could to skip gym, and now we spend our lives trapped in 'em."

Silas dug out his phone. Still no message.

"I played lacrosse in school and just got into the habit." Cliff flexed without shame or irony. "I only like what it does for my artillery." *Thwap.* He smacked his hard belly with his hand.

No doubt, he'd planned his yeasty straight-boy scent too.

Silas scooted away. "Did you just come from lifting?"

Todd cracked the knuckles of one hand, and then the other.

"Meetings. Hey, bro." Cliff snapped his perfect fingers. "You're a gaming guy, aren't you?" He craned his exaggerated chin to point at Kurt. "Unbored?"

"Yes! Wowza." Kurt pointed at him and leered like a game show host. "Head of the *class*-less."

"I read an article about you. *Variety*, I think." For the first time, Cliff's physique shifted slightly to include the entire table, as if Kurt now existed in his universe because of his star power. "Great booth." Cliff stretched; his shirt rucked up to reveal a strip of sun-kissed abdomen.

Todd laughed. "Wow. Okay." He and Kurt eyed each other. Todd gave a subtle nod, silently agreeing to whatever Kurt had asked.

Silas's smile buckled. "Kurt…. This is not the place."

Kurt ignored him and addressed Cliff directly. "We're scouting for adaptations. Work, work, work."

"Big Dog has a load of family-friendly—"

Kurt snored loudly and flapped a hand. "We like NC-17 meat on our grill." He did something to Todd under the table that made him snort. "M for mature."

"Right?" Cliff winked and took a breath. "Well, we're hoping *Campus*—"

Silas's phone buzzed. *Trip*. Fingers crossed he hadn't created too much of a mess, but Cliff deserved it, and the cat was almost out of the bag. Tomorrow Scratch would get loose and nothing Cliff could do or say would tie Trip down.

Pushing Cliff out of his way, Silas slid free of the booth and smiled as he accepted the call. "Good evening, Mr. Spector."

"Hey." Trip sounded breathless and wind muffled his voice. "Sorry.... Not you, I bumped into a couple guys from DC. Sorry."

"Are you outside?"

"Change of plans. I got invited to dinner with some of the folks from the Eisner Awards. Kind of a huge deal, but they sorta kidnapped me from the lobby."

"Well, you need to eat something."

Trip grunted or sniffled. "Yeah. The paperwork got screwed up, and I just got finished over there." He covered the mouthpiece and whispered to someone. "One sec."

"Probably good to breathe actual oxygen. Why don't I come meet you? I've eaten, but—"

"No. It's gonna be talking shop with a bunch of old guys. I'm just gonna buy a couple rounds, and then I'll meet you back in the room." Trip's voice was tight.

Riiight. Silas swallowed his disappointment. Fair enough. Trip needed to get the Barney out of his system before the panel tomorrow.

He nodded and then remembered he had to say something. "Uh. Okay. Yeah. We're just having drinks. Kurt wanted to meet you."

Kurt stifled a low giggle. Silas glared at him until Kurt went back to watching Todd and Cliff flex their biceps and pretend to like each other.

Just to be safe, Silas stepped farther away from the table and masked his voice. "Your... editor is here. Staplegun himself."

"Cliff?"

"Thatsa fella." Silas exhaled. "He recognized Kurt from an Asskissers Anonymous meeting. You shoulda seen."

Trip laughed. "They'll probably circle and sniff each other's butts all weekend." His voice dropped. "I'm sorry about tonight. I changed the sheets for us."

"Nice. I guess we'll... hang out. Kurt rented some gymnast guy for the weekend. Cliff will have to do more than naked backflips to get hi—"

Trip huffed. "Well... stay out of trouble if you can. I'll be done in an hour, hour and a half." Crowd sounds smothered his words. He must've arrived wherever. "I'll meet Kurt at the panel tomorrow. Okay? Rain check on drinks. You're okay there, though?"

I came to Chicago and he's blowing me off. Silas fought to keep his disappointment out of his voice. "Yeah. I'm a veteran of hotel bars."

"I gotta go." Trip sounded muffled, and then he was back. "Sorry. They picked a restaurant. I'll see you in a bit. Sorry! Sorry!"

The phone cut off.

Silas studied his phone a moment. Trip's habitual secrecy still irked him in ways he'd never expected. He'd never been closeted, and Trip's anxiety about including him on this dinner was fear of being judged by his colleagues. Closets come in lotsa shapes and sizes.

Baby steps.

Trip had gotten braver, and they'd learned to open up to each other. Once he announced Scratch at the panel and put Big Dog on a longer leash, they'd have to do these events as a twosome.

Silas slid back into the booth next to Kurt and leaving Cliff to work his wiles on Todd, who seemed singularly unthrilled.

Kurt patted Cliff's hand. "Big Dog is gonna come bark at our next OutRun event."

Todd tipped his head speculatively, as if trying to see the possibilities. He asked Silas, "Bromance zombie? Closet-case zombie?"

"Sure...." Cliff looked unconvinced. "I mean, it's for a good cause."

"So where *is* the boy wonder?" Kurt ignored him and peered at Silas. "Trip."

"In here, I thought." Cliff examined the gamy crush below them.

"He got stuck filing paperwork, and then he had to meet award people for dinner."

Todd leaned forward. "He's up for an award?"

Silas shook his head.

"Paperwork," Cliff cut in, drumming the table. *Thap-a-dap.* "We filed all that for him."

"Not the Artist Alley table. This was last minute. Nerd Herd."

"Nah." Cliff's sour grimace said plenty more.

"Yup." Silas tried not to smile. "He's speaking on their LGBT panel tomorrow."

"Groovy!" Kurt drained his glass and hoisted it high. "Achievement unlocked!"

Silence.

Cliff opened his mouth and shut it.

Silas sighed with lazy, overblown pleasure. "He's announcing a new project." He manclapped Kurt's shoulder.

"What project?" So Cliff hadn't believed him after all. *Jackass*. Trip had predicted as much.

Kurt smiled very slowly. Even Todd seemed to sense something.

"Well, after you yanked his *Campus Champions* idea, he had all this extra time and energy." Shrug. "He's really excited, and he's got meetings with buyers all this weekend. Three different places, I think." A lie, but it felt good twisting the knife as Kurt grinned back at him. Silas felt like Superboyfriend, able to leap tall prick-teases in a single bound.

"The porno comic." Cliff gaped. "That fucking queer-bait cock book?"

Malevolent glee blazed in Kurt's eyes. "Two scoops!"

Silas mocked the thought. "Not porno. It's graphic and there's sex, but it's not just pee-pees and woo-woos. Or wee-wees and poo-poos."

"Impossible." Cliff's handsome mug had gone greasy and gray.

Todd took a swig. "This book I gotta see."

Kurt mock-sighed and confided to Todd. "Silas has corrupted the poor lad with combo attacks. Rubbing-rubbing-rubbing away at his superscruples."

Cliff's hands twitched and shredded one napkin, then another.

"He's announcing it. Tomorrow." Silas knocked back his whiskey and Coke and signaled for another. "Done deal. Uh-yup. Why do you give a shit? You stole his idea and crapped all over him. You don't own him."

"Well, not legally." Kurt shrugged at Todd.

"You have to stop it." The Big Dog editor's oily charm had evaporated. "Indie comics are a crapshoot, y'know."

Silas cocked his brow and did his best Tick impression, moronic manly superhero. "Mandingo, how I grok your mouth music."

"What does that mean?" Cliff goggled at him. "Why are you talking like that?" he sputtered. "I gotta— There's a deal. I mean, we have an offer on the table."

"Congrats!" Kurt raised a fake toast. "To tables!"

Todd clinked his glass and slapped the wet surface.

Thank you, Kurt. His best friend's prickishness did come in handy in such moments.

Silas thumped Cliff's shoulder, ladling on some more Tick-wisdom. "Mister, I'm about to write you a reality check. Or would you prefer the cold, hard cash of truth?"

A chubby guy walking by chortled in fanboy solidarity, and Silas returned it; it felt like the whole Marriott wanted to help him dismantle this prefab dick-lick.

Cliff wadded the napkin shreds and cast the grayish lump at the floor. "Dude, we're talking a fortune." He seemed to be begging, but he was begging the wrong people. "Seriously. Trip could blow the whole gig. Hollywood."

"Holly would if she could." Kurt grinned, getting with the program.

For the first time, Silas was glad Cliff had joined them. To watch this sumbitch squirm and wheedle felt like ugly justice, like the Joker leering at his victims: *Why so serious?* "Luckily, you got him under contract. Oh… wait."

"He can't." Cliff bent forward on one elbow. "He's my bud."

"Ah, but bud-ness is bidness." Silas grunted across the table. "What is best in life?"

In the middle of a comic convention, he expected the whole room to holler along. "What is best in life?" And they did.

A couple of dorky men in the vicinity pounded their tables. Who didn't love *Ah-nold* when he was still a cartoon?

Kurt leaned over. "We need a bonus round." Todd pushed up from his seat and waved a bulging arm at a waitress. A tipsy girl in a Sailor Moon costume waved back at him. *Tee hee hee.*

"What? I'm not joking here." Cliff sputtered. "The best offer he'll ever get."

Silas grinned with all his teeth and at least one dimple in full force. "C'mon, chum. Don't be an Adolf Quitler!"

"I'm serious. Millions of fucking dollars!" An unattractive squiggle of vein throbbed across Cliff's temple.

"Conan!" Silas bellowed and puffed out his chest, although this time, the line was half Conan and half Tick, a demented man-tastic rumble. "What is best in life?"

Kurt and Todd and about fifteen other comic dorks affected thick Germanic accents and roared. "To crush your enemies, see them driven before you, and to hear the lamentation of their women."

Silas shrugged and turned back to his prey.

Cliff squirmed like he wanted to get up and then did exactly that.

The sozzled comic conners applauded and hooted. One skinny kid in a *Locke & Key* T-shirt poured a beer over his own head. A barful of faux-barbarians grinned at each other like piranha.

Cliff's tan face was plum-dark. "You're all fucking nuts." He turned so fast he almost floored the perky waitress who'd come back with a tray of refills.

For the first time in months, Silas wanted to get well and truly hammered. Trip had left him to party, and so that's what he would do. Kurt seemed to be in a rowdy mood, and two young things from Sarah Michele Gellar's table looked about ready to float in their direction. *Fuck it*. He'd have some drinks, gloat a while, and then head back to his room in time to bump into Trip.

Silas had done right by himself and the man he loved. Things had worked out as they ought; he'd faced down Staplegun as Trip scored points with the old-timers.

Todd muttered something about dogs and drained his glass.

"Well, good gravy. We are a well-oiled machine!" Silas whispered to his glass, a little buzzed and a little better. "Destiny is a funny thing."

"So...." Kurt leaned over to murmur conspiratorially. "What the hell is this sex comic?"

SOMETIME in the middle of the night, Trip woke with his nose buried in the vanilla silk of Silas's neck. His thickening joint had nestled in against that round ass, and he wondered if he'd ground against Silas in his sleep. Trip's dick had woken before he had.

Not home. Chicago.

He had brought sheets and changed the bedding so he could sleep during the con. Between the satiny cotton and Silas purring against him, they might have been at home. His anxieties about *Scratch* had driven C2E2 and Silas out of his head for a few moments. He felt guilty that he'd ditched his boyfriend to hang out with the Eisner judges, but work came first. Silas understood.

Their first trip together. *Holy horny downtime, Batman!*

When had Silas come to bed? Had to have been after one when he crawled in for a hushed quickie, then conked out. Dark outside now, and the navy blue sheets from home whispered under his limbs. He needed to ask Silas what had happened in the bar, but it could wait till morning.

As his horniness bloomed, Trip bit down on the salty muscle that swept from Silas's throat to the swell of his shoulder.

Stirring slowly, Silas arched his back, pushing Trip's pelvis against his ass. His answer was a barely audible growl: "Yessir."

Trip gripped harder, and the nipples under his fingers tightened.

"I love that." *Thaaat*. Silas's guttural pleasure made him shiver. "When you take ahold of me and make me do things."

Outside the hotel windows, the night was an indigo curtain hung on crooked rods.

Silas didn't turn or meet his eyes, but after a moment, he managed to nod. His right hand squeezed a loop of sheets in a relentless grip. "C'mon, man."

Trip whispered. "What do you want?"

"You know what I want." Silas reached for the nightstand. Plastic crackled, and then he tossed the condom.

Trip stretched the latex down his joint and tapped the warm hole with his thumb. "I don't think you even need—" He slid his thumb inside and Silas groaned in permission. "You can take it. You're so open already." Trip slid his thumb free and kneed Silas's legs apart, notching his knob against the greasy iris.

"What time…?" Silas laughed low and dirty as he dropped his chin to his chest. "These damn sheets. I thought we were home in New York."

"Huh-uh." Trip kissed his shoulder blade. "'S'just me."

Silas pushed back his hips and devoured him to the hilt. "Make me. Make me." A horny jock needing his itch scratched hard.

Trip looped one arm around his broad trunk and hammered at him. His boner stung from too much sex, but he lost control. He ran his hand down to where Silas's stout erection jabbed the air.

"I don't wanna come too quick. Just fuck me." Silas grunted, guttural. "Fuck me good."

Trip tried to do exactly that. Some part of him wanted to wring another wad out of Silas, to prove his complete command of the rugged body pressed against him. *Possession.*

"*Tssss.* You're so—" Trip squeezed his ribcage and hunched slowly against the meaty swell of those perfect, plump glutes and enjoyed the wet scratch of his treasure trail against Silas's spine. Every time he touched bottom, Silas quaked and groaned.

"Jesus. *Fuh*-hucking. Chri-hist." Silas's muscles shook with the thrusts.

For two guilty seconds, Trip thought of those bound action figures from childhood. Not that Silas was an action figure, but his manly captivity and his hunger to have Trip hold him down and ravage him made Trip feel like he could do anything, that Silas needed him to take total control, for both their sakes.

"Hungh. Hunhh-*ungh.*" Grunts, delayed and rhythmic and seemingly involuntary. Cradled against the tangled sheets, Silas's face had gone slack, loose with panting. "*Huh*-ungh."

"Good?"

"Go slow. Go slow," Silas begged in a choked rumble, his wet lips smashed against a dark spot on the sheets where he'd drooled. His powerful body sprawled boneless and begging, eyes low-lidded.

The Judge and the scary coach Silas had feared and his high school locker room. All that lust and pain had burned away his imperfections so they fit together like this.

Cosmic rays. A secret serum. A radioactive spider bite.

Trip squeezed Silas hard from behind, forced the air out of his lungs. He turned the handsome face roughly toward his and brought their panting mouths together.

Silas flinched and hung on. "You're making—"

"Yeah?" Trip pressed his hips close to the round glutes and ground for a moment.

A bead of sweat ran down Silas's temple into his hairline and he smiled.

"Beautiful. Beautiful." Trip's hips drilled in short hooking thrusts that ticked the spot just under his ridge. "My Silas."

Out of control. Out of control.

"Give it to me." Silas crooked his head hard and his eyes rolled to white.

Blam. Trip surrendered to the lightning and pushed his hips forward so hard he almost crushed Silas facedown into the pillows as his seed raced out of him. His heart swung in his chest, lazy surging thumps that shook his vision. He squeezed Silas hard enough to mark him.

No straight lines, no solid ground. Terrified and hopeful, Trip imagined a shared life without rails or walls. He'd come this far. Whatever the odds, he wanted it. His heart knocked hard. It wanted in or out.

Silas trembled against him. His erection still prodded the twisted sheets, untouched.

Trip reached down, but Silas slid free of his cock and stretched.

"Nuh-uh. I'm just about perfect. *Nnngh.*" He sighed. "My whole body is—"

"I wanna...."

"No sir. Fucking doesn't always have to be my load." Silas shuddered.

Trip sucked on the fingers of one hand and then the other to get them slippery before reaching across to where they could do the most damage.

Silas flexed his chest and tried to hold still. "Too sensitive. Oh gah."

Trip pinched the tight nubbins and let them slip through his fingertips over and over, tugging gently but firmly.

Silas juddered and squirmed, as if chilled, and his pole jerked stiffly: once, twice, three times. The crown glossy and dark. Crystal ribbons of precum leaking from him. For a moment, Trip thought he could force Silas to squirt just like that. As he bucked and struggled, his club pressed hard into Trip's flank and his eyes danced.

"Wait! Wait." A shiver chased down Silas and he ground his teeth together. "Just one second. Oh my—Jesus fuck. Hold on." His hands held Trip's forearms squarely. He gasped and trembled again, his nipples stiff as erasers. His eyes floated closed and he sighed, shakily. "*Pffew.*"

"Okay. Shhh. C'mere." Trip stroked the blocky pecs one last time and then spread his arms. "C'mon."

Silas shuddered again and folded against his side, breathing raggedly.

"You sure you don't need to come?" Trip squinted wickedly.

"You ever seen me shy?" He laugh-coughed. "I'd tell you if I did. My pecker's fixing to fall off."

Trip snickered.

Silas twisted to face him. He still had a boner and pillow lines on the side of his face, which made him look even more adorable.

"That monster gets so far up inside me." For a few moments, Silas admired the thick greasy erection and milked its weight. "*Ungh.* Gooder than grits." He flipped Trip fully onto his back and skinned the condom off.

"You don't have—"

"Hush." Silas tied the latex off and dropped it beside the bed. "You smell so fucking good. Your jazz." Without warning, he swiveled and sucked the sore, softening length into his mouth. The tickling pressure of his tongue was so delicate, it almost hurt.

Trip bucked and hissed in surprise.

With gentle thoroughness, Silas slurped the last of the spunk off. Finally, he let the shaft slide free and kissed Trip's belly. He took a deep breath before he fell back into the pillows and let Trip gather him close.

"I think that is what is known as a midnight snack."

Silas rested his weight carefully on Trip and smeared all his worries about Scratch and Cliff and Artist Alley between them.

"I swear." Trip kissed the thick shoulder and his eyes stung. "You are not like… anyone." He scooted up against the headboard.

Silas followed him, resting his cheek on Trip's chest. "That was just about…. That was perfect, Mr. Spector. Sometimes I want it sweet, but sometimes I want you to just pin me down rough and take whatever the hell you want."

"No comment." Trip loved to smell the semen on Silas's sweet skin, to feel that primal ownership as he squeezed Silas closer.

Silas chuckled and snuffled. The pillows had smashed his gleaming hair flat on one side. "Mr. Spector, you can wake me up like that any time. I mean it."

"Mr. Goolsby, I think that can be arranged." For several long seconds, he imagined what it would be like to go farther, to fuck Silas bare, to pump a load into him and eat it out of his stretched hole… then he blinked the thought away for fear he'd jinx it.

Silas had unlocked something in him he'd never let loose before. Maybe they released it in each other. No Judge, just them.

The clock said three something, but Trip didn't want to fall asleep. Wired, not wiped.

"I love your sheets." Silas slid his arm under his neck and smiled.

"You do?"

"Duh." Silas petted the bed and smiled at him.

"You know...." Trip squirmed an inch closer. "My sheets are completely strategic."

"Howzat?" Silas scrunched up his face.

"From when I first moved into Manhattan. My family sucked, so I developed this theory: wherever you live, you have to want to come home." Trip drew his knees up and smiled. "Everyone should live in a place that makes them happy when they open the door. Except... when I first moved to the city, I couldn't afford a nice place to live. Money was tight. F'real. I went through like nine sublets in a year. Real dumps, but my sheets were at least six hundred threads per inch, always."

Trip smiled to himself. He'd bought his first set of "fancy" linens on clearance at Century 21 without telling his parents or anyone. Sixty-one dollars for a mismatched navy-blue set. It had emptied his checking account. He never regretted the purchase. He'd washed those sheets to tatters.

"A foldable palace." Silas stretched, rigid for a moment, and relaxed. "That's genius."

"Well... you know how allergic I used to get. Thread count helps there too. Almost all those apartments belonged to friends doing me a favor, so I couldn't make a fuss. So I bought one really expensive set, and when I'd move in, first thing, I stripped the bed and my sheets were clean and beautiful come the night. Slept like an angel. Since then, I'm *always* happy to get home at the end of a rotten day." He couldn't keep the smile off his face.

They grinned at each other as if they'd gotten away with something. Happy bandits on the lam.

"Mmmmmh." Silas stretched; his legs whispered as he slid them against the lustrous cotton. "Camp out and snuggle with yourself." His eyes sparkled in the dark. "Except, how do you make yourself get out of bed?"

"Exactly!" Trip giggled low. "My whole fucking problem. Don't you wanna just stay here?" The impact of what he'd said hit him, but he didn't try to unsay it as he normally would've. "Like spooning with yourself." He squirmed against the bedding and scrubbed his face against Silas's gilded chest. "I feel like I've kidnapped the captain of the football team."

"Naw." Silas petted him distractedly. "Center." A flash of sharp teeth.

"Sorry about dinner."

"'S'fine. I defended your honor in the bar, Mr. Spector. Shoulda been there."

"You did, huh?" Trip cupped Silas's semisoft cock protectively.

Silas coughed. "Best I could. Kurt even helped out."

Trip didn't ask what that might mean, but he should've been there, so he had no right to complain. He shifted Silas over and pulled the covers up over them.

Outside, a faraway siren approached and receded.

"I swear." Silas rubbed one thick arm in circles on the dark blue cotton. "You know when you pet a horse and your hand just slides over the grain of the hairs? Slicker than oil. But if you go against the nap, that shit feels like burlap." His Southern accent had deepened. *Burr-laaap.* "Your damn sheets feel like a horse you can only rub the right way. Only you pet it with your whole body." He squirmed and smiled again. "I keep trying to find the wrong way to rub, and I can't."

As he watched in the shadowed dark, Trip started to get hard, even though his dick was spongy and sore from overuse. "Yes, please." He growled and clambered over, half on top of Silas. "Well, you have an open invitation to rub my sheets anytime you like."

"Oh really." Silas gave a sloe-eyed blink. His erection still hadn't relented.

"That's what the man said." Trip scootched a little closer. His thickening cock pressed against Silas's hip. He dug his chin into the beefy shoulder.

Silas grunted in pleasure and whispered, "You ready for tomorrow?"

"Mmh. We should get some rest."

"Mr. Spector, I'm afraid I may have to come and camp out in your bed pretty regular."

A squint. A kiss. A question.

"Mr. Goolsby, I'm afraid that will be no problem at all."

A nuzzle. A smile. A promise.

19

THE best thing about comic conventions is also the worst thing about them: they are a thermonuclear fusion of geek enthusiasm.

Trip had spent enough hours in artist alleys over the past four years that he considered himself a professional fanthropologist. The operation for the Chicago Comic & Entertainment Expo was pretty slick. Not as overwhelming as San Diego but not a rinky-dink Wizard con. Registered as an artist, he picked up his badge and scooted off to find out where they'd located his table.

On their flight from JFK, Silas had insisted he planned to work and he meant it. Trip had already scored him a C2E2 professional badge; Silas took that seriously. Despite Trip's protests, Silas insisted on waking up early to help set up on Friday before the hall opened to the public. Truth be told, Trip liked coming to the convention center at sunup with someone rumpled and handsome who cheerfully downed bad coffee and a breakfast burrito.

With Silas helping, he got his table set and dressed in record time. When they set up next to Anne Cain, the process had gone about five times faster with an extra set of hands. Silas intuited what he needed and double-piled the boxes he hauled around with startling ease.

Trip gave him a wry grin. "Are you showing off?"

"No, sir. Too lazy for two trips." Silas smiled back and flexed arms pumped from rushing. "Good, right?"

Trip loved seeing Silas turn into a big Alabama kid the minute they walked through the door. Unlike Trip, he had no reservations about walking right up to the Top Cow and Marvel teams and introducing himself. He'd never worn a professionals badge before, so getting to see the booths coming together and honest-to-God pop culture rock stars wandering around had turned him into a puddle of dorky glee. And when they asked what he did and he said, "yes-ma'am-*movies*," the reciprocal ass-kissing had gotten Olympic.

Across the room, Geoff Johns and Joe Quesada wandered the floor like civilians. Every comic convention existed in a kind of bubble outside space and time, an alternate reality built out of folding tables and carpet squares. Exhibitors spent the entire con season on the road trying to cop face time with the fanboys.

Artists could make a solid income by appearing on the con circuit. Most sold original artwork, pencils of paneled pages, cover inks, or old Bristol boards. Any artist could do a brisk business in sketches. Even nontalents cleared a couple of bucks. The heavyweight stars had waiting lists that filled up in the first fifteen minutes of a con. George Perez was so sought-after that he raffled his sketches off for Heroes Initiative, which provided health insurance to pros in need.

Trip didn't have a huge following, but *Hero High* had enough of a devoted fanbase that he'd gotten to know a couple of the regulars.

The Mighty Mites' squeaky-clean image attracted a very odd stew of homeschoolers and nostalgia addicts. And mostly Trip ended up drawing custom sketches of the *Hero High* cast: Princess Quantum sexy at the prom or bulging close-ups of Alphalad. He knew their specs so fully that his hands moved on autopilot. Still, in a con as ginormous as C2E2, he'd clear a few grand easily... triple the cost of the table and his airfare.

Of course, his *Scratch* announcement would change everything. For the first time, he couldn't hunker down on a folding chair and chat with aficionados. Announcing a comic was a risky proposition in the best of circumstances. This book would ruffle feathers: gay, occult, erotic, demon? Any one of those was bait for several types of bigot.

Maybe that's the point. Bravery usually looked stupid from the outside.

His inner Scratch crowed at the idea of pissing that many people off. Silas had given him pep talks on the plane and as they unpacked. Still, Trip had enjoyed dinner with the old-timers last night, and who knew if he'd ever get the invite again?

Trip planned to announce *Scratch* at the Nerd Herd's LGBT Comics panel. Even the fact he'd agreed to attend the annual homo event made Trip queasy, but these groupies would tweet the fuck out of the new title, and they had the power to build a little anticipation that could help get the series financed and distributed.

Now, with the panel in four hours, Trip had calmed enough that the idea of announcing *Scratch* at the LGBT panel didn't make him want to vomit. After today, Scratch would belong to the fans.

Nothing on display till this afternoon. Once Scratch debuted, that toothpaste would never go back in the tube. Silas had pulled out all the *Scratch* swag they'd ordered and stashed it under the table: posters, T-shirts, and even a couple of cover flats. If all went well, they'd set the ball rolling with the announcement and have a rush this afternoon.

His book. Their book.

Wisely, Silas had left all the strategy to him, which helped Trip's nerves when it came to the possible backlash. Trip still had doubts about how Cliff would react. Most of *Hero High*'s diehard fanbase might flip, and with Hollywood circling Big Dog and talking about acquisition, the stakes were brutal.

If nothing else, Cliff had taught him about the pitfalls of niche markets and careful spin. He hadn't seen Big Dog yet, but that was one of the hurdles. Cliff managed to stay out of sight. Trip expected a metric fuck-ton of grief.

With Silas there beside him on the ground, Trip had a cohort and conspirator to help him get shit done. Little things.

Hands down the best part. Trip had never gone to a con with an actual bona fide boyfriend. In the past, no one he'd dated even tolerated comics, let alone had an interest.

The minute the doors opened to civilians at ten in the morning, Silas used his phone to take pics of a laughing group of forty-two Slave Leias: every shape, color, size, and gender you could imagine.

Slave Leias weirded Trip out. For one thing, he'd always thought the *Star Wars* movies sucked: all of them. Maybe because he'd grown up at a time when they were things his elders called hip, or maybe because he'd never been a sci-fi buff. Capes, okay. Mutants and monsters, absolutely. But space opera left him cold. *Star Trek* and Wookies just didn't have a place in his geeky heart.

So the idea of hundreds of fans sporting a metallic bikini and a leash just seemed slightly off-putting. Like accidentally finding a greasy thumbprint on someone else's porn collection.

Trip didn't like manga or *Maus*, but he got them, and they *were* comics. But the slow inexorable encroachment of Hollywood on the comic conventions felt like a betrayal by his own kind. *Star Wars* and *Star Trek* haunted the comic cons disproportionately. He simply ignored them. It was San Diego's fault, all those ecstatic consumers corralled into one space for E-Z advertising. Comic fandom had built this empire for twenty years and sold out in twenty minutes.

As if to prove his point, a Jedi appeared. On the landing above the convention floor, a tubby man in his forties, dressed elaborately as Darth Hemorrhoid, leapt and sliced the air with a two-bladed lightsaber, doing some kind of frenzied exhibition. His audience? Three cynical ten-year-olds. *May the Farce be with you.*

Once upon a while ago, Trip had been one of them, all of them, really. He snuck into the city from Westchester, happy to stand on line for hours and share mythology with his fellow fanatics… the valiant dweebs who hunted Easter eggs and *hatched* them. He totally understood the power of a borrowed hero. He remembered a time when a single picture or line of dialogue could save his life. He looked back often, so he'd never look down on them.

Trip thumbed through his binders of research—costumes, designs, and logos for about thirty of the major superheroes—that had saved his ass on any number of custom sketches.

Silas stooped to eyeball the boxes under their table. "You sure you don't want *Scratch* up? Even the teaser?"

"Not till we announce. A cover is one of the fastest ways to create buzz, and I only got the panel spot because I promised them the exclusive. We'll have enough pushback that we need to get Diamond and Wizard behind us if we can. They run an article or even a couple blog posts, and we can take that to the pubs."

"Sure. I just want to see him."

The *Scratch* banner had turned out even better than expected. Six by nine feet, the big incubus at his most seductive and destructive, beckoning from the Horn Gate. *Got an itch?*

They'd done this the right way: a smaller con, friendly crowd, an LGBT panel, Silas here to make showbiz noises and charm the suits. There were about six publishers that might have real interest. Hedged bets. Once Scratch and the fans found each other, they would sweep away any lingering anxiety Trip harbored.

The Artist Alley sketches would make him money, and the *Scratch* promo and the media kit had cost him a couple grand at most. Silas had balked at the price tag, but Trip had money in the bank and he understood the importance of giving the collectors something to remember, a fantasy they could hold in their hands. He'd stopped short of paying to color the *Scratch* interiors: that was several grand a publisher would front as a show of good faith.

"Folks are gonna piss their pants." Silas looked as antsy as a kid in front of a pile of presents. "How does it work?"

"The collectors sign up for sketches first thing. *Hero High* crazies, mostly. But at a con this size, they'll keep me drawing most of the day. They go to panels while I do my thing. For my sanity, I try not to take the sketchbooks back to the hotel unless it's a real commission. They just want custom art. Usually a little racy."

"Why have I never come to a con before? This is bananas." Silas tapped Trip's table.

Trip followed his gaze and sniffed. "Fanthropology in the wild."

Silas glanced around at the other folks setting up. Big name artists surrounded them, good for Trip. Mike McKone and Phil Jimenez shared one of the corner tables, spread with massive portfolios that showed their pages for Marvel and DC.

Silas flicked his eyes at several chipper, over-tanned figures who unpacked stacks of headshots onto their tables. He mumbled, "Are those actors?"

Trip muttered back. "Yes... and no. At larger cons, Gil Gerard still shows to sign *Buck Rogers* stills. Burt Ward brags about the double-jock he wore on TV to rein in Robin's huge dong. Smaller cons, fake celebrities turn up. Y'get stormtrooper six from *Empire Strikes Back* or demons from *Angel*. One-show wonders. Extras from cult movies."

A lot of regulars made their living pushing autographed headshots to hardcore devotees who might remember them.

"Ah." Silas blinked. "Eep."

Trip shrugged and scratched his leg. "Yeah. They used to freak me out, but I think it's a good reminder. They're one of the morals. Whenever someone gets big for their britches, I remember Adam West hungover and arguing to the point of fisticuffs with a fifty-year-old fan over an episode title. True story."

The sketch line formed quickly. Silas wrangled people into some kind of order and even produced a clipboard for sign-ups out of thin air. Trip felt like a celebrity, but more than that, like what he did mattered to someone who mattered to him. Heady shit.

By 11:00 a.m., Trip's list had filled up, and for the most part, the fans had scattered to their various panels while he drew commissions.

Rather than going back to the room to catch a couple more hours' sleep, Silas stood behind him and rubbed his shoulders firmly, as if Trip were a boxer in the ring.

The tender kneading melted him, though he couldn't dismiss the awkward self-consciousness at the attention. "You don't have to do that."

"I wanna. Am I hurting you?"

"No." He dropped his head forward. *Head rush.* "Fantastic."

"Guys." Rey Arzeno walked past lugging a portfolio and a wheeled suitcase. He raised an arm in weary greeting. They'd been on the same flight. He wheeled toward a corner table and unfurled an ARZENO banner.

Silas leaned closer and murmured, "Are you embarrassed 'cause I'm groping you in public?"

"Nuh-no." *Not much.*

"Well, I can stop, but listening to you groan and whimper has given me a huge, rude stonker and I forgot to wear briefs, so it could get indecent if I step away." He bumped the ridge against Trip's backbone.

Trip wheezed in mortification. "Silas!"

"So you, sir, are my human curtain for the next five minutes," Silas muttered. "Or I could sit down before I bust my nut in my jeans."

Trip sat very straight.

Silas sat down. "Nobody saw anything." He pressed against his tented zipper.

Trip gave a grim stare up the concrete aisle toward the entrance. "No sign of Staplegun."

"Neither hide nor hairball. Last time I checked the Big Dog booth, the interns were setting up the display."

"You should go check out the rest of the con." Trip realized it sounded like he wanted to be alone. "If you want, I mean."

"Okay. Scope the competition." Silas rocked on his feet. "I won't have any trouble finding my way back."

Behind the entire table and across its front, vinyl banners showcased *Hero High* splash pages with Alphalad and the Mighty Mites in oversaturated magenta, aqua, and orange. Cliff had designed the setup to be visible from fifty yards away; inspecting it at close range gave Trip vertigo.

"Yeah. No." He chuckled.

Silas started to walk away and then paused and turned back. "You doing okay?"

"I am." Trip peeked up from his sketch and smiled. "I'm jumpy, but I'm better than I thought I'd be."

"You're being really goddamn brave."

"I guess." Trip plucked at his collar. His eyes itched and felt swollen for the first time in months. Probably moldy in this place. "Nothing brave is ever a smart idea."

"Listen, billionaire vigilantes, sending your baby to Earth in a comet, blocking bullets with bracelets... all that shit is a fuck-awful way to deal with evil. It's courageous and stupid and beautiful, but completely bananas. We like to watch that stuff and read about it because we want to stay excited, but we *need* to stay alive."

Trip coughed and blinked. Out of habit, he rooted around in his bag for a Benadryl and took it with a swig of Diet Dr Pepper.

"Gah." Silas stared at the soda in horror. "Do you want breakfast or anything? Something biodegradable?"

Trip's stomach had tied itself into a noose. "I've got a couple Slim Jims and a bag of Combos in my kit. I'm fine."

"I meant food, Mr. Spector. You gotta long day and I'm just a tourist. Can I get you something?"

"Nah. Go check out the booths." Trip dredged up the two strips of processed meat. They felt like fishing lures in his hand, greasy inside their vacuum-sealed sleeves. He just needed to settle down and get into a groove with his regulars, drawing the old familiar Mighty Mites by rote, and he'd be fine. "Me and Slim Jim go way back."

"Jesus." Silas wouldn't leave it alone. "C'mon, you can't eat that crap. How about I get you a sandwich and some water?" He rocked on his feet. "Humor me." He planted his heels.

"I'm fine," Trip snapped back. He needed time to get his head together. "Don't worry about it."

Silas scowled, but he stood his ground, kept his voice low and level. "You're gonna be trapped back here for hours, and that way—"

"I'm plenty skinny and I'm already freaking out. Why do you even give a shit?"

Silas barked back, "Because I love you, idiot!"

Silence. *Oops.*

Silas went crimson. He'd stopped breathing, and he'd dropped his eyes to the table between them.

Crickets.

Artist Alley got very quiet. Comic pros Trip had known for five years gauged the two of them with high brows and ears like elephants. Anne Cain gave him a big shmoopy smile, bless her.

Trip should have said something back, something real, but a whole crowd had trained their eyes on him now, so instead, he gave a nervous smile. "Thanks."

"Sorry."

"No, I mean it." *He said he loves me. Say something back.*

"I'll just—" And then Silas was gone, wiping his sweet, stubbly face.

Trip had fucked that right up. A wave of weakness crashed over him and tugged him under. Helpless, hopeless, heartless. What was he supposed to do? Thousands of people watching. Declarations weren't his style, and Silas had blindsided him.

He'd make it up to Silas later. He'd panicked because of his dread of the *Scratch* rollout. They'd go out tonight and celebrate, just the two of them. Silas knew how Trip felt anyway, even if he'd never spoken the words. Things would work out. He just needed to get through this crazy day, and then he'd figure out a sexy apology that would make clear how much Silas meant to him.

He glanced at his list of sketch sign-ups and decided to tackle them from the top: a four-character sketch of Princess Quantum fighting three Vulgarians.

What had Picasso said? *If I don't have red, I use blue.*

This gentleman wanted the poses on the sexy side. Not for the first time, he wished he could afford to fly Dolores from Uruguay so they could share a booth.

Trip dove back into the drawing, uncapped his pen, and hit the edge on the jawline. One of his teachers had beaten that lesson into him: the secret to depicting a beautiful woman was the line of the throat. *True.*

"Triple X!"

Cliff waved at him from the entrance to the main convention hall. He wore a Big Dog sweatshirt with the sleeves ripped off to show his tan guns. The hand he waved looked dirty, so he'd probably just come from finishing their booth with whatever interns he'd charmed into servitude.

Cliff appeared jittery and bright-eyed as he approached the table, nodding and glad-handing at Trip's neighbors like a cokehead. He didn't seem pissed about anything. No sign of grouchy Staplegun. *Good.*

Trip let out a breath. Maybe Cliff wasn't gonna make trouble after all. One less thing to worry about before the Nerd Herd panel.

Cliff rapped on the table. "'S'up, hot stuff."

Trip capped his pen and slid the drawing to the side. "Paying the rent."

"I figured you'd have a crazy-ass line."

"Up the alley. Silas got them all onto a list, and I'm booked for sketches through Sunday."

When Trip had first started drawing the Mighty Mites, he'd signed at the company booth, but wrestling for space with the other artists and the spread of Big Dog titles made for a hellish con all round. At least in Artist Alley, the folks who came wanted *his* work, and Trip had a little room to breathe.

"I mean for autographs." Cliff crossed his arms and his pecs bunched.

Trip clicked his teeth together. "Yeah. Not really. A couple, I guess, now and then. Mostly fans want original art." His fans didn't really want *Hero High* nearly as much as he'd thought or as Cliff wanted to think. They wanted pictures.

Cliff took that opportunity to step behind Trip's table and sit down in the empty chair beside him. His feet brushed the boxes of *Scratch* posters and shirts, though he couldn't know that. "But Issue 51 has done crazy business. You should see the numbers."

He peeped back over his shoulder toward the main floor, then at his watch. "Big Dog's been mobbed all morning."

Maybe it had been, and maybe the crowd wasn't something Cliff whipped up for the photo ops. He often gave shit away and used booth babes to keep the space jammed. He'd even taken his own shirt off a time or two, though he denied it.

Cliff rolled his hand making the tendons bunch. "Those new *Hero High* pages have gotten a lot of attention in Century City."

Trip crosshatched shading down one side of the characters. He'd darken it with markers. "Where's that?"

"Hollywood. Sorry. Feature executives are always hunting for product." Cliff kneaded Trip's shoulder slowly. "Apparently some D-girl caught your act at Forbidden Planet last month. Came by us first thing, she's bringing her bosses over to meet you." He ran a hand over Trip's stubbled scalp.

"Who?" Trip had no idea what he meant.

"Development, dude." Cliff clucked. "They know that indie's where it's at. DC and Marvel have already gone conglomerate. The smart folks are sniffing around us because small fry mean big deals."

Trip wiped his nose and sniffed in frustration. What did he know from movies? He just wished Cliff didn't sound so eager and desperate. Silas talked a lot about film people, but he never gushed or gawped. He treated it like a business, pro and con.

"Actually, Silas knows people too. He does creatures." Trip placed a wax pencil on the table in front of him. "Maybe you should talk to him."

A look of interest and gratitude completely failed to make its way to Cliff's face. A frown did. "He's below the line. I mean suits. We just gotta get into the right parties, and *Hero High* will go global." He seemed pissed.

Trip sighed. He'd tried. In the end he didn't care, and if Big Dog sold the property, he'd be free anyways. "So that's the master plan. The one that's great. Right? That's what you wanted to see if I liked?"

Cliff's jaw tensed. "Obviously." He spread his arms at the convention center. "Why the fuck do we come here if we're not gonna do battle?"

Trip peered up and down the aisle. "Well, I sketch. The fans come by, and I draw things."

For a split second, something skittered across Cliff's face.

Does he know something I don't?

"Sure. And that's cool. Gotta feed the freaks." Cliff wiped his hands as if he'd decided something. "Great. So you'll do your thing, and I'll see what I can line up for us."

He squeezed Trip's neck.

Trip had never noticed how much Cliff rubbed and groped him. Maybe he misconstrued it, but now that he had Silas in his life, the constant pawing weirded him out a little.

A ruckus drew their attention. The line at Rey Arzeno's table clapped and hooted at some kind of giveaway. Arms waved in the air. Cliff leaned back and scanned the alley for something.

Trip felt completely unqualified and ignorant. For a split second, he wished Silas was here so they could face each other man to man, so he'd know what the fuck was real and what wasn't. Everything they said was so diametrically opposed. They couldn't both be right, and they couldn't both be smart.

Cliff spread his shaking hands wide. "Dude! Look at *Walking Dead*. Look at *Scott Pilgrim*. *Hellboy*? Some dork in a cubicle picked that shit up at Golden Apple and *wham*... the creators are living in Maui and bathing in the blood of virgins."

"Well, yeah, but all those titles have sex appeal. I mean. They're not exactly family- friendly."

"Which makes me a genius. Well, us." Cliff glanced at him. "We'd be the first."

"Right. Sounds great." Bent over the page, Trip laid in the uniform logos in pencil.

Cliff snapped his fingers and pointed. *Without irony.* "Great."

Had they agreed on something? "What's great?"

"You agree. With the plan."

"What plan, Cliff? You just told me that some comics become movies and that some movies make money sometimes. We're in a building with a hundred thousand fanatics who all love the same thing."

Trip looked back at the line that had built while Cliff flapped his arms. Preteens with mothers wearing appliqued sweaters and too much makeup, and fathers in polyester pants. They watched Cliff uneasily. *Our fans are repressed.*

He grew embarrassed for both of them. Still, Cliff could hop around the convention center trying to part execs from millions of dollars.

Scratch would have its launch and earn its own fans.

"I'd like to talk to Silas about this." Trip had no interest in a fight, but Cliff had to understand, right?

"Dude. Why?" Apparently, he did not.

"Well… he's in film. And he's my…." He frowned. "With me."

The Unboyfriend made an inscrutable face. "You sure?" Cliff opened and closed his mouth.

"Never mind." Trip didn't bother to hide his exasperation. "The point is: I'm happy and healthy, and Silas Goolsby is the best thing that ever happened to me. This crazy little comic I've done showcases my work and has a lot of buzz around it. One of my friends has pushed it to *her* fans. Romance writer."

"Romance." Cliff spoke as if the word was a long hair he'd fished out of vanilla ice cream.

"And so it's sexy. Who cares? Even you said my *Hero High* pages are the best you've ever seen. Silas is really good for me."

Cliff chuckled nervously. "That's good."

"I'd like you to give him a chance." This wasn't going to happen easily. "I mean, it's pretty serious. Three months. For gay guys that's like ten years."

"Dude, no offense. I don't give a fuck about your love life." Cliff scowled. "I'm here doing business. I am fighting to put you on a bigger map. I'm trying to score publicity that could move fifty thousand copies of a book you create, bro." Cliff glared. "Feel me?"

Trip tried to swallow. Mouth dry. Chest tight. He hated confrontation.

"This dipstick boyfriend of yours is filling your head with fairy-tale bullshit. He's got you drawing porn. He has you coming out of the fucking closet. I'm trying to get you nominated for an Eisner Award." He stepped back and sighed. "Grow the fuck up, Trip."

"This is about *Scratch*."

"Obviously!" Cliff raised his voice once and then glanced around them to make sure no one heard. "I have spent four years grooming and fattening a prestige property, and now I've brought it to the slaughterhouse. And he wants you to piss it away. I got an earful in the bar."

Trip squeezed his fists and let them go. Why did Cliff hate Silas so much? *What happened last night?* Invisible ants marched across his shins and forearms. He refused to scratch the maddening itch because he couldn't go to the Nerd Herd panel looking like a burn patient.

"I've got a movie lined up." Cliff dropped his voice again. "No one's supposed to know. We blow it if there's a leak. I've got a six-figure offer that will get *Hero High* on screen in two years. With republication and full rebranding. TV." He pursed his mouth. His eyes slashed back and forth at the folks in their vicinity. "Bullshit now."

No one seemed to be watching. *Small mercies.*

"Movie." Trip licked his dry lips. "And you've known this how long?"

"A week. I got confirmation yesterday, and I came to find you in the fucking bar last night."

Fuck. Now Trip understood. Silas had defended the new book. Trip hadn't been there to keep the peace. And Cliff couldn't fight back or he'd have blown his movie.

"Panel. Porno." Cliff stood and clapped him on the shoulders. *Like old times.* Cliff spoke out of the side of his mouth. "*Fffth.* You do whatever the fuck you think is right." He chuffed in resignation and started to walk away.

Rey Arzeno cruised Cliff's ass and whistled silently.

"Come by Big Dog later so you can sign copies for the movie peeps. They might still want 'em. Never know."

"Hold up." Trip stood. And came out from behind his table. "Are you serious?"

"Hollywood, bro."

Mike McKone kept his head down. Anne glanced at him, and her expression seemed guarded. Had she heard anything? Had everyone?

At that moment, Trip realized they stood in a building with tens of thousands of people and in a matter of moments, he might march up on a stage and set himself and his career on fire for their amusement.

"Cliff." Trip stopped short, and his editor turned, handsome and doomed. "Why didn't you say anything?"

Cliff scratched his head and gave a surly laugh. He started to walk away, answering over his shoulder. "I just did."

As TRIP scurried across the main hall, a yaoi flash mob exploded around him like a summer squall. He barely escaped with his pants.

A roar of laughter. Was he late? Trip picked up the pace, jogged a little. Hoots and applause. *Shit.* He'd lost track of time talking to Cliff, and now he looked like a dick walking into the LGBT panel late. If he'd known about the movie earlier, he could have canceled.

In the hall, two twinks in Ozymandias jerseys gave him a high five, and one older Mystique clapped for him with a wacky grin on her face. Why was everyone so fucking happy that he was late?

Hall B, Hall B. The door was jam-packed. *Great.* Now he'd have to *scuse me-pardon me* his way through a standing-room crowd so he could stand up and make no announcement at all.

As he approached the knot of fans wedged into the doublewide doorway, a chubby Asian grandpa turned and spotted him. "There he is!" Then they all turned, and miracle of miracles, the knot untied itself, and the people created a narrow passage that let him slip inside.

More applause and a lot of raucous laughter. Had the Nerd Herd started without him? He finally stepped into the room and picked his way to the stage up front.

Scratch stood there in the center of the aisle, gleaming and naked in a spotlight.

Ropy muscle and wicked points glimmered at his brow and fingertips. No navel, and every inch of his exposed skin painted a creamy pearl that blazed under the lights.

Silas.

His bohunk boyfriend had dressed himself as the incubus, from the tousled lavender hair to glossy cloven hooves that let him stand and walk like a beast on hellish tiptoe. Beautiful, yes, but *naked* in front of several hundred people.

Correction: there was no spotlight, but the iridescent body paint was so pale, he seemed to be lit from all directions, luminous even in a bright room. The entire crowd took pictures and video of Scratch in the flesh with phones, tablets, and cameras.

A fucking spectacle.

Silas wasn't completely bare-assed, but he might as well have been: he'd covered his cock and crack with some kind of translucent skin that flexed over his unmentionables, painted the same lustrous ivory as the rest of him. When he moved, the millimeter of creamy silicone was thin enough to show veins.

The lenses clicked overtime, and Silas ate the attention like sirloin. The fans pawed at him and snickered. He hadn't noticed Trip yet.

Trip had never wanted to hit anyone in his life, but right then, if he'd been closer he would have belted Silas, so when he spoke, it came out too loudly.

"What the fuck are you doing?" His stomach turned over.

Silas turned, and the smile on the Scratch face died. The hubbub around him abated as the room watched him walk on his hooves to Trip... so sexy but *so* naked.

"It was a surprise."

More flashes as cameras captured Scratch from every angle. Twitter had to be going nuts.

"You're fucking nude. In front of a gigantic crowd of people."

The demon eyes twinkled, still optimistic, as if he thought he could cajole Trip into a good mood. *Ha ha, your boyfriend's getting fingerfucked by strangers in public.*

"I'm your booth babe." Silas wore some kind of contacts that made his irises opalescent.

"I don't need a booth babe. I don't want a booth babe."

Up at the tables, a lady with a buzz cut under an Apocalypse helmet held up two fingers for two minutes.

Silas spoke softly. His accent got thicker as he got closer. "I just came to help out. I didn't announce anything."

Not me.

"Goddammit, Silas."

"Okay. Okay. Too much. I didn't know—"

Trip watched the people staring. His heart jerked rhythmically in his ribs.

"Hey. Hey. My mistake. I tried to add a little razzle-dazzle to take the pressure off. I thought you'd dig it."

Trip glared. "No you didn't."

The buzz cut woman squinted, then spun her hand in a "move it along" signal. The people on the LGBT panel looked alternately charmed by the nude demon in their midst and annoyed that he'd stolen focus. Everybody had projects to pimp.

The demon face scowled at him for the first time. "I called to give you a heads-up, but you didn't answer your phone."

"Left it in the room. And I was stuck in Artist Alley with Cliff."

Silas's confusion was obvious.

"About *Hero High*. We got a movie."

Silas smiled then, open and sweet as summer. "Congrats! Oh babe, that's wonderful." The demon took a step forward to embrace him, but Trip stepped back. The smile flickered. "Whatsamatter?"

Upfront, Ms. Apocalypse spoke into the mike a little too closely. "Ladies and gents, we're gonna get rolling here in a minute, if Mr. Spector will join us—"

The heads in the room turned to stare at him like bullies in an anxiety nightmare.

"We are experiencing"—Trip spoke quietly—"technical difficulties."

Silas stepped aside, uncertainly. "C'mon, you're gonna do great." He stretched his Scratch claws.

"Technically." Standing next to his ass-naked, demon-seed boyfriend, Trip steadied his voice and addressed the room. "There's been a...." He couldn't think of the word. Someone took a picture of him chewing the air like an old dog as he groped for whatever the goddamn word had been.

The buzz cut hissed into the mike. "Change."

"Change." Trip tilted his head.

"Change?" Scratch muttered.

Trip held up a finger. "Please stand by." Keeping his eyes on the industrial carpet, he took Scratch's muscular pale arm and dragged him into the hallway. The door swung shut with a crack.

The pulse thumped visibly in Silas's throat. His smile turned into a dead stretch of lip muscle. "Trip, what is going on?"

Hubbub-what-the-hubbub. The crowd took to the Internet with typical conferocity. Conventions thrived on gossip, and bloggers lived for this shit. The tweeting and Facebooking and Tumblring had already whizzed past them into the ether. *Hero High gets Horny. Alphalad assraped by Asmodeus. Trip Spector an Ig-bay Ag-fay.* He remembered his mother sneering the words "that way" the day she tossed his first sketchbook.

Trip pinched the bridge of his nose as he tried to stop his brain from slithering out of his nostrils. Too mad to let himself see Silas, he searched for the right words for a good thirty seconds. He stared at the tiled floor and one cloven hoof as people walked past them.

"Spector, will you fucking talk to me?"

Trip looked up, and Scratch, in the flesh, stared back at him out of fire-opal eyes. To his credit, Silas had done full Hollywood makeup, suitable for shooting a few inches away. His entire body had a shimmer that invited the hand and eye.

"You're standing in the hall." Silas crossed his arms over his bare chest. "What happened in there?"

Trip shook his head. "Why did you do it?" He gestured at the flawless makeup and the near-nudity.

"You were announcing the comic. That's an LGBT panel. Friendly crowd, eager to get the word out."

Trip snorted, an ugly short chuff of judgment. "I didn't know you were going to get your pork out for the whole fucking con."

"C'mon. It's a painted suit. Like a latex speedo." Silas frowned at his crotch, his knob and balls clearly visible. "It looks ruder than it is."

People took pictures as they walked past. Trip pushed Silas against the wall and stood close, trying to block the view by using his too-skinny body. "Cliff gave me a piece of good news while you were trying to unleash fucking *Arma-gaydar* in the middle of a comic convention."

Stop talking.

"Staplegun." Silas said the name with clear distaste. "Perfect. Just in time to fuck with your head before the panel."

"Doesn't fucking matter, though. Because I'm not announcing *Scratch* on the LGBT panel. All I had to do is say 'secret project,' and I'd have covered my ass. Hell, if Cliff hadn't kept me so long, I could have pulled myself from the panel completely."

"I didn't know that, did I? You didn't tell me."

"Hot costume, man!" The fat Jedi from earlier gave Silas a thumbs-up.

Trip glowered at the retreating figure before turning back. "I noticed Kurt trailing around after you with his meat on a stick."

"He's a game producer hunting for licenses. He goes to every con he can stomach because he can scoop the major outlets. And he brought a bodybuilder to tap his sap, so it's not like you have worries on that score."

"I can't compete."

"It's not a fucking game, Trip. It's not a race."

"Of course not. Not with Kurt, I meant *you*. I wasn't—"

"We're a team. At least one of us is a grown-up having a grown-up relationship with grown-up history and grown-up expectations."

Trip wanted to slow everything down. He wished he'd said "I love you" back to Silas this morning. How much of Silas freaking out was because Trip had ignored his accidental declaration? *Had* Silas freaked out, or was Trip misreading shit again? "This doesn't have anything to do with us. I'm talking with a naked demon, in a Marriott, about what's left of my career."

Silas frowned. "Right."

"What does that mean?"

"You're telling me that Cliff sleazed over you and whispered cyanide in your ears and that has nothing to do with you scurrying back into your cage with your tail tucked?"

"We got a serious offer. Hollywood."

Silas turned. "Actually, Cliff said as much last night when he stuck his hand down my pants." Trip flinched. *That can't be true.* "And what a coincidence that he told you ten minutes before you announced this book that leaves him out in the cold."

Chilly doubt froze Trip's bowels. Would Cliff lie? Had he? If Trip could just slow everything down and get a grip. "Silas, I don't want him."

Silas blinked at him.

"I used to, when I was an idiot and lonely, but I know what he's about. I'm not that naïve." *Anymore.* Trip wiped his nose. "I don't want anyone but you."

"So act like it."

Trip hugged himself. Embarrassed by the jealousy but unable to throttle it. He rubbed his sweaty arms. The hall was baking hot. Was there no A/C in this barn? "If you can be jealous, so can I."

"Okay. And I'm allowed to tell the truth." The frown on Silas's face seemed patronizing. "You don't even know if you have a deal. But that asshole said 'boo,' so you got scared."

"I didn't get scared. I *am* scared. I'm—" Trip gulped. "I'm just holding off on doing anything with *Scratch* until I know the facts."

"Trip. I didn't do all this just to score some book. I don't even work in comics. I helped you because I love you." No pity.

Trip flicked his gaze to see who might be eavesdropping on their spat.

Silas noticed. "Never mind. My mistake. You're too afraid to let anyone love you."

"That's not true."

A roar of laughter from inside the LGBT panel. Pray God, they weren't talking about the lover's tiff happening out here in the hallway or sharing pics of Scratch arguing with his creator on Instagram.

Silas stared, making Trip even more self-conscious.

"Before I got all made up, I bought you something today. Promethea action figure: mint-on-card." Silas waited for some kind of response.

Involuntarily, a smile dug at the edges of Trip's mouth. *Good present*. But then he looked at Silas stripped to his skin in a hallway and the smile died.

"You know why fans pay more for mint-on-card? Certainty. You know what you're getting. Thing is, you don't want to share. And then you assume everything is gonna be dipsy-doodle, but it isn't. Right? Life turns out complicated and compromising."

Trip breathed fast. He felt like a lunatic fighting with Scratch. Then again, maybe Scratch felt pissed too. Maybe that was why Trip felt so shitty. He'd fucked over his boyfriend and his creation.

Silas didn't waver. "Children love toys because they get to play at destroying the world and making it do whatever they wish it would. They want miniature animals and people and cars and houses so they can pull out the eyes and crush them to rubble. Hell, video games let little monsters dominate and devastate entire countries and galaxies and ecosystems because that is the natural impulse of all humans. We are a race of *powerless* control freaks. That's how mythology happens."

Silas bared his fake fangs. "Who buys comics? Who lines up for ten hours to get into Comic-Con and spends a fortune dressing up as a pop-culture delusion? Who makes superhero blockbusters happen? All those little lost megalomaniacs wishing they could go back to believing the world could fit under the dining room table. Cliff manipulates your fear and lust so he gets what he wants."

"He got me a movie deal. You know what that means!" Lightheaded.

"Where's the deal?"

"A movie is a movie. Maybe this is my break."

"There's no such thing, babe. You know there's not. Breaks are a bullshit headline the tabloids make up to sell papers."

Trip glanced around as fans passed in the hallway. No one met his eye.

Except Silas. "I have never lied to you, Trip Spector. And Staplegun lies to you all the time, but you take his word out of habit, like I'm invisible."

"I'm sorry."

"No. You're not." Silas backed away. He studied the walls and the floor. "You're not." His composure broke. "This is who you are. Maybe this is who you wanna be. Oh my God, what have I done?" Beneath the Scratch makeup, Silas cried.

"Put my whole career in danger."

Silas closed his eyes and huffed a deep breath before opening them. "Life can never be mint-on-card... everything dry and clean and perfect. Boxed forever. No dings, no dents."

"I know that."

"But you want to keep me under wraps. That isn't a relationship! That's a psychological problem. You wanna live like a *ghost*, haunting the shit you care about."

"Then why do you want me at all?"

"Because I know you. The real you. Only that bullshit superstud editor has you wrapped around his meat so he can pay you starvation wages and keep you—"

Trip spoke over him, feeling an irrational need to defend Cliff. "Cliff doesn't keep"—he was shouting—"me...." His voice trailed away.

"Yeah. I was just gonna say 'on a leash.'" Silas closed and opened his mouth, as if more words wanted to slip out.

A slice of afternoon sun cut the air between them and gilded Silas's forearms but left the rest of him in shadow.

"Maybe you've decided I'm a made-up character." Silas shrugged. "Like I didn't exist till I found you in Central Park and ate your brain. But I did. I do. I'm not a fucking action figure, mint-on-card." He scowled.

"And I'm not a meal ticket."

Kerblam. If Trip had swung an atomic sledgehammer, it would have done less damage.

Silas turned with horrible slowness to regard him with distaste. "And who the fuck said you were?" He spoke so low that his lips hardly moved, and he gathered his hands into fists. "When have I ever asked you for anything?"

"That's not what I meant." Trip backpedaled. He'd used Cliff's insult for effect without thinking. Their words lay scattered around them like shrapnel, little poisonous piles that should never have seen daylight.

Silas took a step closer, his voice raw with anguish. "You used my face and my body to build an entire comic, and I thanked you. My whole life and career is on hold because I believe in you. Here I am. I have done nothing but support you and help you and protect you." A thick vein thumped in his forehead.

Now Trip cried, too, hard enough to blur his vision. He couldn't look away, and Silas kept pushing and pushing. *All of this is my fault.* "You're right."

"Well, you're fucking wrong, Trip." Silas poked at him, gave him no space, no room to turn. "If you knew me, why would you waste two seconds worrying about Kurt? Why would you take Cliff's word over mine? Hey, if it's just you alone, you can grease up and I dunno... *disasturbate* for the rest of your life. Panicking about shit that's never gonna happen and getting off on risks you'll never take. But you aren't alone. Cliff's there helping you do it so he can use you."

"Like you used me so you could do this." Trip waved a hand at the Scratch before him. "Show up at my panel like an anatomically correct doll that anyone can play with so long as they hose you down after."

Undo!

His eyes widened because he wished the words back.

Some things can't be unsaid. Silas's mouth clamped into a grim fence with no horizon.

Trip had gone too far, but he couldn't stop his stupid mouth from spitting out whatever paranoid delusions his brain had cooked up at midnight: when the phone rang and rang, when Silas hadn't returned from the bar. *You have been judged.*

The wide eyes darkened. Silas looked grayer and more ripped open than he had as a walking corpse. "Fuck you." He opened and closed his fingers spasmodically. "I thought—" He glowered. "I thought you knew me better than they did."

"I thought a lot of things." Trip gritted his teeth. "I was wrong."

"No, Trip."

"I was. And you were too. And this... all this is exactly why *Scratch* is over."

Silas stopped moving. All the fight seemed to whoosh out of him as if he'd pulled a cork that left him limp and boneless.

A stocky man covered with Brillo Pad hair approached them carefully, his arms held away from his torso as if hauling buckets of paint across a slippery floor. "Is there a problem here, gentlemen?"

"No, sir. None at all." At first Trip thought Silas had spoken, but then he realized his mouth had moved and that the sounds had come out of his throat.

The guard grunted but didn't leave.

After one shaky breath and another, Silas seemed to stop waiting for whatever. He peered down at his talons as if they belonged to someone else, as if Trip had drawn him in pencil and threatened him with an eraser. "Okay."

Trip stared back, semiaware that people walked past them, volunteers unstacked chairs, and fans shuffled into the room, but he only saw Silas staring out of Scratch's eyes.

"I loved you." Silas shrugged and wiped his cheeks, smearing the paint. "My bad."

"Wait—"

But Silas had vanished. Long gone. *Retcon.* Trip covered his eyes and sagged against the wall.

"Jeez. That was a fucking spectacle."

Cliff.

One big lacrosse hand patted him and squeezed. Trip stepped away. "Don't touch me."

"'S'allright. You're good."

Trip scowled. No, he wasn't. Why did everyone keep telling him how he felt? "Piss off."

Cliff took him by the arm and steered him into the john. Nine steps up the hall and to the left. Cliff ignored the lines and pushed Trip into the handicap stall. "You're fine, Tripwire. Pull it together. This is your job."

It is? Then I need a raise. But he nodded back, as if Cliff's words made sense. He couldn't catch his breath, it wheezed and whistled through his ribs as if he were a skeleton.

"C'mon. Get yourself cleaned up. I want you to meet some people."

Suits, he meant. The beige tiles vibrated under Trip's blurry eyes. The bathroom wasn't empty. He grimaced and braced his hands on his legs. "Gonna barf."

"No, you're not. You're a pro." Cliff opened the stall door and stepped out.

Costumed passers-by rubbernecked unsubtly as they headed for the urinals. Was he still crying? Trip wiped at his face with numb hands. They came away wet.

"I shouldn't have said that stuff to him."

"Whatever." Cliff's caramel eyes flashed. "You got your monster, didn't you? Once we hit the multiplexes, you got hot cock on tap." He winked. "Splash some water on your face. You look like a used tampon."

Like a zombie, Trip cupped his hands to sip water and splash his raw face. He swished the water around his teeth and spat it out. He didn't bother to dry, and the water ran down his throat into his collar. Who cared? He'd zigged when he should have zagged, and time refused to roll backward.

Where oh where were the retcon fairies when he needed them?

At the door, Cliff clapped his hands to hurry him. "Chop-chop, man."

Trip's stomach churned, and he examined the fluorescents as if the undo button might appear overhead. If only he could retcon this whole horrible day, unwreck Silas and unfuck himself. But where would he go back to? This morning before he'd crapped all over Silas? Or the day he'd started drawing *Scratch*? Maybe the zombie run in the park?

Chop-chop.

If only God would lean over the page with His big eraser.

"We've got an entire feature film division waiting on us in the bar."

The hall filled with happy con-victs. The fans scuttled to the urinals to piss before the next panel.

What the hell had he done? Trip swallowed and tried not to choke.

Cliff squeezed his shoulder. "You're not gonna regret this."

He already did.

20

FOR best results, never give a makeover when you look and smell like a goat's nutsack.

At least Silas had showered and brushed his teeth before his apartment buzzer went. He ran a hand over his face. "Saturday. It's Saturday." *Good to know.*

For the sixteen days since he'd flown home from Chicago, he'd expected Trip: a call, a visit, an e-mail. Anything, really, that would rebuild the bridge burned between them. Silas had passed through angry and sad into queasy anxiety. He'd gotten so jumpy, he heard the phones ring in his neighbors' apartments, even lying in bed. He hadn't slept more than a couple of hours since the end of April.

His cramped living room scarcely had space for his futon and the makeup chair, but at least he felt at home.

When Rina called night before last and asked for a favor, he'd spent the entire two-minute conversation thinking she was speaking in code, that she had a message for him, that Trip was listening in to check on him. He'd said yes out of desperation.

Ka-bing. His stupid doorbell sputtered and tinkled because the landlord kept forgetting to replace it. He squared his shoulders before he opened the door, and the hallway's stifling air smacked him in the face like a giant waffle.

"Silas! Thank you so much." Rina appeared nervous and washed out before she hugged him hello in his hallway. As he'd asked, she had washed her face and pushed her hair back with a bandeau. "Hot as balls out there. You're sure this is okay."

He shook his head in confusion. *I'm not okay.* Not even a little. Then he realized she meant getting made up.

For a moment, Silas held his front door open and wished he hadn't taken the call, wished he didn't like her, wished he could undo a whole buncha shit that couldn't be helped. *Retcon.*

"I like the beard." Rina rubbed her own jaw and batted her lashes. "Very dashing."

Again, Silas almost had to translate what she said and then remembered that after coming back from the con, he'd stopped shaving. He hadn't gone to the gym, either, or gone out. Out at Silvercup, Tiffany had pouted and forced him to sit in the chair while she trimmed his fuzz and shaved his neck just so he didn't look like an undead hobo.

He still held the door. "Come in." He kept forgetting where he was.

Awkward.

Rina gave a minnow-quick smile. "Blonder than I expected. Your beard. You really are a *rubio.*"

He closed the door and plunged his hands into his pockets. "You want something to drink?"

She shook her head and let out a breath. *Relieved?* So maybe this drop-in really was innocent. She just needed some event makeup.

She walked back toward his living room carrying a small satchel while a thin vinyl garment bag swung on one raised hand. The rattling window unit made the space feel smaller.

He flapped a hand at his digs. "Please pardon my wreckage, Miss Apostara."

Rina eyed the fanboy clutter a little skeptically: a *Nightwing* mask on a *Swamp Thing* head, action figures peppering shelves higgledy-piggle with paperbacks and hardcover comic archives, a framed *Spider-Man 3* poster signed by Toby and Topher because he'd worked on the second unit right out of school. No embarrassing porn, but only because he'd always slept around too much to need it.

She fidgeted for a moment before she hugged him. "He"—Trip, she must've meant, whose name must not be spoken—"woulda died if I told him, but I figured you'd understand."

Or not innocent. Maybe she was doing a little fact-finding with her face. *Fine by me.* That tiny treasonous part of his heart that held out hope suddenly went on alert.

She dissected him head to toe. "*Querido*, you doing okay?"

Truth? Lie?

"No! Yeah. Great. I've *Tick*-binging." Silas faked a broad smile and shrugged.

"Tick?"

"Superhero sitcom. Patrick Warburton?" Silas dialed his voice down to manly-man and bent his smile into a smirk. "I sure would like a slice of your righteous combat pie...."

"*Wonder Woman*—" She held up two hands and closed her eyes as if guilty. "—is my crazy campy crack. Lynda Carter? I swear. Half-Mexican, that dame, and 100 percent perfection. I love *SVU*, *Walking Dead*, but *Wonder Woman* has gotten me through apocalyptic shit." A girlish side shrug.

The conversation teetered, right on the verge of embarrassing talk-show confessional. If Silas had breathed the word "Trip" aloud, he'd have lost his shit and all kinds of horrible truth would have spilled out, lubricated by tears and chocolate. Rina watched him, obviously waiting for the yea-or-nay signal.

Silas throttled the impulse and clubbed it back into its bony cage.

Rina looked away and put her purse down. "Well, this morning, I got a paranormal book signing out at the Union Square Barnes & Noble, and at least two news crews will be there because we got bestsellers who are flying in for the dog-'n'-pony. I aim to piggyback like there's no *mañana*."

He could do this, just pretend she was just a funny client, not Trip's friend. "Wardrobe?"

She held up three hangers inside a vinyl garment bag and hooked them sideways on the coatrack to unzip. "Raw silk. Vintage. Sort of a purple-black."

"Aubergine," he declared and cracked the opening wider.

"I love a man who can make colors sound dirty." She grinned.

"Cross-dyed." He wondered if Trip had helped pick this out, if he'd seen her model it and convinced her to splurge. "Great suit."

"I gotta stand next to J.R. Ward. Feel me?" She fluttered her short nails at him. "Baby, I went and bought a pair of Givenchy boots I cannot *even* afford because the Warden is gonna be there in full effect, and you know what that means!"

He didn't really, but he got the gist. "So you want nighttime for daytime."

"Extra vampy, hold the trampy. Like, more *Lust for Dracula* than *Breaking Dawn*." Rina squeezed her shoulders together to amp her cleavage. "If I'm hauling the girls out, no way can I do sparkly anorexia."

"Got it." Silas gestured at the bathroom. "Clothes first. I've got a smock."

Rina plucked the garment bag and swooped into the bathroom. She nudged the door so it swung partially closed. "The authors are all supposed to show up natural. So naturally, everyone pays like a thousand dollars to get their face did." A zip and rustling from the bathroom. "With the Warden? Bullshit, says me."

Silas pulled his swiveling office chair in front of the full-length mirror in his little work alcove. He exhumed a clean smock from his duffel. It felt good to move and do and talk to someone sassy. After zombieville for the past couple of weeks, Rina's energy left him little room for a pity party.

"Jilly was gonna help, but she wanted to draw shit on my face with a puffy marker." Her voice echoed against the bathroom tile.

On a whim, Silas unearthed a pair of dental acrylic fangs he'd cast for the Scratch makeup. At least they'd get some use. Trip would never know.

The bathroom door swung open. "I knew you did, like, creatures, but I figured you hadta do glamour too." Rina came out in the black-purple pencil skirt and a gunmetal-gray corset.

Instead of sitting, she chewed on her hair and continued to flutter. She studied the chair as though analyzing an alien life form. The silk suit paled her skin, and the sun brightened her hair.

"News cameras shooting with overhead lighting? Okay. Okay." Silas did some quick cosmetic calculation and pulled out a Kryolan palette.

She let him snap the whispery smock over her. "But mainly I need you to turn me into a paranormal *goddess* for the face to face with the fans. Photos." She spat the hair out in irritation. "That zombie bridal video? Seventy thousand views. It sold so many books, my publisher contracted two more in my series."

"Your throne awaits."

She plopped into the seat and closed her eyes. "My need is great, Mr. Goolsby."

Silas didn't react to that. She must have heard Trip say it a thousand times and didn't understand.

As Silas smoothed translucent foundation onto her skin, part of him quailed. *Please don't let her talk about Trip.* And the stubborn weakness in him countered, *Please let me know he's okay... if he is.*

"Publicity is life and death." She speared him with her eyes.

For starters, he needed to get her calmed down, STAT. *First rule of makeup: Never underestimate the power of vanity.* He'd just get her talking about herself. Fastest way to calm actors down—writers couldn't be that different. "I knew you were a writer, but I never knew which books."

"Romance. But urban fantasy, so fangs and spells and all." She squinted at him as if she expected him to scoff or scorn. "What does that look mean?"

"What look?" His face hadn't changed, but obviously this was a sore spot with her.

"You don't read romance." She closed her eyes to let him paint. "I'm like a romance evangelist."

"Nuh-no." He brushed the heavy weight of her dark hair and straightened the bandeau that held it off her forehead. "Well, no... I guess I haven't."

"But you seen *Underworld*. You like comics."

"Duh." He sniffed.

"Romance is not all corsets and gangbangs." Her eyes met his in the mirror. "Anybody who's over like... thirty thinks romance novels are just rape-porn with mood lighting." She quirked her mouth in irritation. "*Fifty Shades of Fingered by Fabio's Fuckery.*"

"I'm only twenty-nine. Jeez," he joked back. "I figured romances meant fancy talk and lotsa copulating in moonlight." He shrugged. "With Fabio." A laugh. "Okay, yeah. Sorry."

"Y'don't have to be a chick. Y'got a heart. Y'jerk off. Y'get bored with TV. You obviously grok imagination." She perused the framed *Hellraiser* poster and the

Nightcrawler statues and the piles of Spider-Man comics on the table. "Happy endings."

Was she talking about her own books or the comic or Trip? She stared into his eyes as if she expected him to read her mind. *Paging Jean Grey!*

Silas ran the sable brush over his palm, pretending he understood.

"But you steered clear of romance for no good reason." Rina shook her head. "Dumb. You'd love 'em, I bet."

He feathered dusty rose onto her cheeks. As she turned back front, she touched her temple gingerly. And finally, she settled enough for him to keep painting.

"So I had a crazy thought...." He held up the fake fangs as a silent question. "No presh."

"Yay! Yes, please." She opened her mouth.

"They won't fit exactly, but they'll last the afternoon."

She squealed. "See? My series heroine is a vampire archaeologist. Diana Prince meets Lara Croft. A little dusty, a little busty...." She sat back again. "Jillian thought you might try to give me a split skull or a bullet hole or something."

"You sound disappointed."

She laughed. "No, hun. I just didn't know you did glammypants too. Where'd you learn to put on lipstick?"

Silas used cotton wadding to hold her lip back and dried her incisors. "I gotta be able to doll folks up too. When I moved into the city, I took classes at the Designory, MAC, pretty much anywhere they slapped paint that'd have me."

He leaned in to daub denture adhesive onto one canine and then pressed the acrylic fang down gently. "When I got out of high school, I blew off college for the FX course with Savini out in Pennsylvania. He did *Friday the 13th.... Dawn of the Dead.*"

"Ungh." Rina gave a tiny nod and kept her eyes closed.

He pressed the other canine into place.

"You're good now." After the adhesive set up, he removed the wadding.

"Feels so freaky." She closed her lips carefully and scrubbed them over the fangs. "Sharp!"

"Just go easy with them for a bit. Head back."

He drabbled the wet maroon over her full lower lip, then tipped his head to gauge the result before smoothing it with a pinky.

"That feels bizarre. Are you painting a clown mouth?" She smiled, and he had to wait until she stopped to continue.

"A wet brush will give a better line. Always use a brush for your lips. Tube lipstick is for soaps and hookers." He darkened the middle for effect. "There we go."

"Good to know." Rina licked her white teeth, pausing on a pointed canine. "Pays to go to a professional. These days, I gotta lotta men reading me."

"I dunno. I'm not much of a reader. Comics, yeah, but I like movies."

"You might be surprised. Some stories don't make movies. I mean superheroes, spies, serial killers… sure. But there's some feelings you can't put on a screen." She balked and laughed. "Not *that* kinda movie."

He hadn't watched porn since high school, but he liked her candor. "I know what you mean. Movies are never romance."

"Not unless it's fancy costumes and olden times to snag an Oscar. Or comedies, where everyone acts like a jerk right up until they hook up."

He sponged some contouring along her cheekbones and under her jawline, exaggerating the perfect oval of her face and luminous eyes.

"You'd think Hollywood might notice. They got all these millions of people lining up to see one type of movie, so they don't bother with all the other people who got no interest in that. It's like every flick has to be something that can be a game… until they just seem like video games, and the only people who go are the ones who wanna play 'em."

Silas tipped his head. A sift of powder to finish, a little more pencil on the lash line. "So what should I read? Of yours."

Rina evaluated him in the mirror. "Romance just means a relationship and a happily ever after. *Scratch* is a romance."

He held the sponge midstroke, and they did not look at each other. He breathed while she breathed, and the unspoken name wove the air around them.

Silas lowered his hand and broke the spell. "*Scratch* is about sex demons. I mean, the human sidekick has a crush on…. Oh."

"Obviously." Rina watched his fingers twisting her hair into a coil as if they were solving something. "Sexy hero. Big complications. Makeover. And then he meets… his match."

"I see what you mean." Maybe she had come here on a fact-finding mission for Trip after all? Maybe this was all a ploy to see what Silas wanted. "*Scratch* is a phenomenal book." Maybe he could get her to spill a few coins in kind.

"It is." Rina's new fangs peeked out from behind her lips.

"Shame to just give up on it."

"Yeah." Was she doing this on purpose? Why wouldn't she bite? She probably thought he and Trip were a bad match as well? For all he knew, Rina had nothing but scorn for him and had warned Trip to cut bait.

Her gaze rested on him for a long moment. "Never make a permanent mistake to solve a temporary problem."

He sensed she was waiting for him to confess something, anything. As much as he wanted to know what had happened, so did she.

Home stretch.

He took a moment to dab a dull taupe onto her temples. "We're almost done." Just for polish, he daubed a charcoal dot under each eye and smudged it up into the lashes, making her appear hungry and haunted.

"You got quiet." She'd closed her eyes, but she tipped her head toward him.

Again, Silas had the sense she was trying to open a conversational door best left bolted shut. Again, he went for the vanity dodge. "Yeah. Your skin is unbelievable. I mean, you barely need foundation. You can wear almost any fabric, d'you know? Orange, even."

"No sir!"

"Well, maybe. But I'm saying, if you wanted to get a little hipper on your *maquillage* for different events." Silas shrugged.

She blinked and opened her eyes. "You got nice skin too. One of the first things I noticed about you."

"I wish!" Silas chuckled. "Hardly. High school, I broke out constantly and nothing worked. Accutane, tetracycline, mudpacks. I used to pray for Halloween so I could cover my face up. Pockmarks and pudge."

"C'mon!"

"Wasn't till I graduated from college that I realized I wasn't freakishly fat and ugly."

"Oh hun." Rina clucked and shook her head. "Well, look at you now."

"Yeah. Beating 'em off with a two-by-four."

"The way you shine, people can't get enough of you." Her forehead creased. "My brother says ..." She cautiously tasted the tip of each fang before talking up at the ceiling. "'If you love life, life will love you back.'"

He pressed his lips shut and nodded, but he didn't reply. He couldn't.

"You beat yourself up before they get a chance." Her mouth turned down.

"Naw." Silas shrugged. "Life still beats me up plenty."

Her eyes opened and caught his. They both waited, not saying Trip's name but surely thinking it.

Rina whispered up at him, "He loves you." She held his gaze gently.

Head shake. He didn't want to rehash it. He'd only just managed to sleep an hour here and there in his empty bed. "Trip was wrong for me. I'm wrong for him. Completely."

"'S'none of my business. I mean, what the hell do I know except what he says and you say, but respectfully? I say you're both wrong." She exhaled. "Trip knows he fucked up."

"Great. Swell." Silas put the brush down a little too hard.

"He's being stupid, Silas. Childish. Cowardly. You name it. But it's just a bunch of old baggage he's dragged around with him. The Unboyfriend and worse." Rina shrugged. "You shouldn't take it personally."

Silas turned to glare. "I am a person! How should I take it?" He wished he'd taken ninety seconds to shave and put on real clothes. How stupid would he feel if he melted down in a *True Blood* T-shirt and sweats, like they were old friends? She was Trip's Girl Friday, and he was an asshole for forgetting that.

Rina took a deep inhale. "He just hasn't had all that much practice being a grown-up."

"And I have?" Silas pretended to put his kit back together.

"You're not hearing me."

"I am, though." Silas leaned his butt against the edge of the table. "Honesty is a great place to start a relationship, but it doesn't entitle you to one. Saying a bunch of mean shit that makes you feel superior doesn't produce soul mates out of thin air."

"Trip has a bad habit of writing lines for people. He's an...." She groped for the word. "Imperfectionist."

He snorted.

"Seriously. For whatever sicko reason, he can't stand things going too well, or he starts to panic and freezes up. He's so used to shit going bad that he sometimes gives it a nudge to get it there quicker."

"Nothing personal. I'm sure."

Rina frowned, ready to make some case or other. "Well, like you say, you're a person. But no."

To shut her up, Silas spun the chair so Rina saw herself in the mirror.

"*Cabron*!"

She looked like a silent movie vamp gone feral. Petal-pale color on her cheeks, contour softening the jawline, and her lower eye smudgy to the point of bruised.

He crossed his arms proudly. "That'll sell a book or two."

"With the suit?" Rina touched her face gingerly. "It's... wow. Those bitches are gonna have a litter of pit bulls." She licked her lower lip, and her mouth shone like a poison plum.

"Good." Silas laughed out loud, first time in over a week. "I could show you how to do most of it. 'S'not too complicated."

"Are you *insane*? Now I wanna come over here every morning."

"You bring coffee, I'm down." Silas wiped his hands on his towel. "If you wanted, I could build retractable fangs that actually fit."

"Retractable?" She scowled comically from under the vampy makeup and then got distracted by her reflection again. "And like, could you do this for an author photo? Mine sucks platypus dick."

"Well…." Much as he admired her, he had to remind himself that this woman wasn't his friend. In the parlance of Manhattan breakups, Trip got custody. Apparently she hadn't gotten the memo.

She crossed her arms over her ribs. "Purely professional, yo. I won't make it weird for you. I like you and I want to hire you."

"Lemme think about it." Silas pretended to put brushes away. "Things are hard."

Rina stared at him with the doe eyes. "I know, *querido*." She tucked her feet into the black leather boots and zipped.

"And seriously, the airbrush and the rigmarole just gilds the lily. Ninety percent of this you could've done in a moving taxi in ten minutes if I showed you how." He wiped his hands on his sweats and plucked his cell phone off the table. "Scorcher out there. You want me to call a car service?"

"Who am I, Charlaine Harris? Subway for me!" She took out her wallet and raised her impeccable eyebrows.

He waved the notion of payment away. "No chance."

Rina quirked her bee-stung mouth. "Well, then, let me take you out sometime? Just for kicks." She crammed her leggings and the empty garment bag into the little satchel.

"Uh, sure." He'd never let that happen in a million years.

"Hell, if you wanted, you could wait an hour and come to the signing, and we could grab lunch after."

"I don't think—"

She floated the possibility with a hopeful vampire smile. "Trip'll be there."

"Yeah." It wasn't a question. A wisp of regret tickled inside him. No way he'd say what she wanted him to say.

"If… you wanted to come with me now, you'd see him." She stood up, then stomped and shuffled in the black boots.

"I would." His regret lapped between them like water in a tub.

"Ugh!" Rina shook her head. "Men are so fucking stubborn."

"Only when they're right…." He shrugged. "Or wrong."

"Okay." She stopped swirling for a moment and took his hand. "You're okay, baby."

"Okay." He nodded, but the nod was a lie.

Rina held the satchel of street clothes in one hand. The aubergine suit looked like some kind of slippery orchid. She glanced sideways at him. "Goddess?"

"Amen." He appraised and approved with a nod.

"Wish me luck."

In a few minutes, on the other side of town, Trip would see her and kiss her and know who'd painted her face. Silas wished he'd thought this through. Or maybe not. Maybe Trip would see it and think Silas had coped while he'd made the worst mistake of both their lives.

Silas picked a thread off her lapel. "You're gonna kill 'em."

"Great." A naughty smile. "As long as I get the photos first."

"Spoken like a best seller." As she clicked to the door in her Givenchy boots, he double-checked to make sure she had everything. When he got there to unlock it, she was waiting for him. "I wish I knew your secret, Miss Apostara."

"*Pfft.* That's nothing." Rina inspected herself in the hall mirror and smoothed the jacket over her trim waist. "You just find something you would die for and live for it instead. Okay?"

He unbolted the door for her and inclined his head as he stood aside. "I promise."

Without warning, she bussed his cheek and was gone, clacking toward the elevator and the blazing daylight outside.

He threw the bolt and caught sight of his dim, swollen reflection. Scruffy and bedheaded, but on one rough cheek, a perfect kiss like a bruise.

21

TRIP was hiding in the Stones' basement, losing a staring contest with a poster.

Right now, on this particular sultry Saturday two and a half weeks after his nuclear implosion in Chicago, Rina had roped him into attending a signing at Barnes & Noble, but he couldn't get his shit together. Jillian was waiting, ready to leave for ten minutes, but he'd made up some bullshit excuse that he needed something from downstairs. He came down to visit the boxes of swag he had stored down here in the cool, gritty dark.

Trip shut the door. Beyond it, a decrepit hallway led back to the garden and narrow, uneven stairs climbed up to the world of the living. *No thanks.*

For God knows how long, he sat studying the life-sized Scratch in the corner. Jilly must've swiped one before the con. Across the top, a smoldering logo: "SCRATCH"—and at the bottom, the comic's tagline: "Got an itch?" The pale, gleaming muscle of Scratch himself filled the rest of the vertical rectangle. The wicked eyes, the marble-hard skin of his torso where the smoky wings fell back, and the hand reaching toward the viewer... just provocative enough without being pornographic.

An ad campaign for an audience of one. A poster no one would ever see. A story he'd never share. Thrill and guilt at the same time. *Not a bang, but a whimper.*

At the very least, it could hang over his bed. He'd still created it. And Scratch's book could wait; there was no reason why he couldn't wait for Silas to cool off, then buy him out and come back to *Scratch* in a couple of years when he'd had some mainstream success. This was a door opening. Right?

Yeah.

With luck, it didn't lead into a trap or a brick wall.

Outside, the scalding streets shimmered like a griddle, the air choked with pollen. Today was a huge deal for Rina, but she and Jillian had given some ominous hints that Silas might show. *Potentially ugly scene.* So instead Trip sat in the basement and stared at the bones of his dead project and tried to work up the nerve to tell Jillian he was too chicken to go.

He just wanted to look at Scratch in peace. *In pieces.*

Even with the lavender-gray hair and little goat horns that sprouted from his brow, Trip's painting and the character there so completely personified his superhero fantasy of Silas that for one bleak moment, Trip wanted to lean against him and beg for help. Like a child, he secretly wished the photoshopped demon would tug himself free of the vinyl and stride across the studio to tell Trip what he secretly wanted, as if he didn't know himself.

"I just about peed myself first time I saw him." Jillian's voice startled him from the doorway. "I mean, who wouldn't sell their soul?"

She held up two tumblers that smelled like bourbon.

Shit. If Jillian had poured daytime booze, he must look worse than he realized.

"Can you tell?" Trip jutted his chin toward the poster. "That it's him."

Jillian snorted and bulged her eyes at him as though they'd both escaped from a mental hospital. "Kiddo, there's so much Silas in that thing I can taste his precum." She handed the drink to him.

Why do I feel guilty? "He said I could use it." He shrugged, chest painfully tight. "Silas. I mean. He signed a release and… everything." He stopped talking.

"Duh. He's not stupid. If anybody ever painted me that gorgeous, I'd handcuff 'em to my bed so they kept on doing it."

"Snazzy though, right?"

"Better than. Like you mighta loved him a little." She perched on the edge of the table and studied the display, squinted at it critically. "Or more than a little." She bent. "Rina called."

"I can't go."

"I figured. Big crowd, anyhow. She'll get it."

"I don't—" He wiped his nose and frowned at the alcohol. "Everything feels too loud and too bright. Sharp edges and screaming. I can hardly stand up." He pursed his lips waspishly. Some selfish part of him wished she'd go back upstairs, and yet he didn't think he could be down here alone. He tapped a taped box. "Why do you have a case of candles?"

Jillian blew a raspberry. "Two years ago I forgot to grab the right ones at the store, and we had to use birthday candles. Max didn't care, but I felt like such a failure. I wanted him to have an authentic experience and… birthday candles?"

"Good thinking."

She patted the package. "Hanukkah in a box. My son gets the Jewish experience, and I'm not using sizzling birthday candles that snuff themselves out."

He picked up something pale from the top of a large plastic storage drum: a half mask with horns. This was one of the silicone forehead pieces designed for the theoretical booth babes he'd never hired. "Prosthetic."

"There were about eight of them in with the cases. Max helped unpack them, so he musta been play...." She rubbed her palms on her legs.

"'S'fine. I'm glad someone's using it. I feel guilty storing it in your basement, but I just—"

"We have room, booger." She smiled with her mouth, but not her eyes. "There's no rush. God made time, but man made haste."

"Thanks." Trip scowled at his own stupidity and impatience. He'd never told Silas how beautiful he looked as Scratch. With all the other bullshit at the con, he'd forgotten to confess how eerie it had felt to see a character he'd created walking among mortals.

The Scratch pictures taken by fans had gone viral within minutes, and they didn't even know the character's name. In the past few weeks, thousands of people had written to Trip and the other panelists to ask about the gorgeous pale demon in their midst. Facebook and the comic forums had gone berserk with speculation. Of course, only he and Silas knew the truth, and they weren't telling. Trip glanced up.

Jillian was still watching him.

A car horn blared outside, and a screech of tires drew her eyes to the tiny window high in the basement wall. She patted his thigh, and for once it didn't make him uncomfortable. "You ever play chess?"

"Whaddayamean, chess?" He wiped his nose.

She shrugged. "Benefits of a liberal arts education."

"*You* don't play chess. Who the hell plays chess?"

"Listen, during the Cold War, all Soviets taught their kids to play chess."

"Okay...." His eyes still felt raw, but nothing in the air hassled his allergies. *In my head*. He hadn't used an inhaler in ages. He'd breathed for months like a normal person, so long as Silas lay beside him.

Jillian spoke in the singsongy voice of a children's-theater milkmaid. "When the Russkis were still being all Soviet and rushing around trying to win gold medals and get to the moon so they could do ballet and gymnastics in peace, they wanted all their kids to learn how to play chess."

"The Communists, we're talking about. What does that have to do with comics? I don't get it."

"The thing with playing chess is that you have to make a decision, see? Always."

Trip grimaced in exasperation and shook his head. "So?"

"No skipping. No coping mechanism. Each turn you have to choose, no matter what. You can't *not* move. Your only choice is to choose." She snapped her fingers. "The USSR liked kids learning that they couldn't sit on their asses and wait for anything, that they always had to take a step, even if it was painful. Workers of the world and whatever Karl Marx Brothers shit you can imagine."

He exhaled with almost-laughter and fell silent. "That sucks."

"Um, yeah. And it's true." She nodded as if she'd shown her math to him. "I mean, it's harsh and all, but the Communists won a whole bunch of gold medals for eighty years because those poor little bastards learned to make fucking choices every time it was their turn. Brutal, but real. And even though they're Russian again and broke, and nobody is forcing them to play chess, it's a different way of getting through a life."

Trip turned his back on Silas's hungry eyes peering out of his demon's face. "Kurt would agree with you."

Jillian raised her hands in frustration. "Who the hell is Kurt?"

"We never met." Trip pointed at Scratch and therefore Silas. "Friend of his. Game designer. Kind of a prick, but a smart, successful prick." It dawned on him again that he had built a wall between their lives. *Another point for Mr. Goolsby.* "He produces the OutRun zombie events. Fan of Rina's, actually."

"Well, then obviously he's a genius." Jillian rolled her eyes and got back to the point. "No matter what, you're gonna pay, so you better fucking play, Trip. The trick with mistakes is that you should run *to* them, not away from them." She shrugged. "You have to do something with them, make them something. I mean, everything in life is fun or educational."

"Silas..." Again, he felt stupid and rude. Had he really said all that passive-aggressive shit to the best man he'd ever dated... hell, ever known? "...discombobulates me."

"Okay." Jillian squatted next to him in front of Scratch and hugged her knees. "Know something? Every goddamn night, I run from the bathroom and jump into bed because I still think Freddy Krueger is hiding underneath with his finger knives. Poor Benjy. Seriously. If I'm first under the covers, it's no big, but if it's the middle of the night and I have to pee, I will run and jump and scare the ever-loving crap out of my husband."

"Why?"

"Because a grown woman lands on top of him in the pitch dark. That's scary."

"No... why do you jump on him?"

"Because in my head, it's the 1980s and I live on Elm Street and some deep-fried pervo janitor wants to kill me for kicks."

Somehow, Trip couldn't imagine Ben's facial expression at the moment she pounced. As if he planned to draw it, he tried and failed to see the shout or shock or grimace or whatever. Ben must keep that part of himself hidden from his family, even from friends. He was usually so stoic about his wife's high spirits. He loved the tornado because it took him to Oz.

She pointed a pale finger at him. "But here's the deal: Benjy's a *mensch*. We been married for eleven years because that man prefers being woken up to me dissolving into a puddle of panic in a dark bedroom."

A couple of months ago, he would've mocked her, but now he knew all about shared insanity. He'd found someone who caught him when he jumped.

"Ben has gotten good at *Nightmare on Elm Street* detail. He knows why I jump and almost looks forward to it now. Every time he just grunts and scootches over and kisses my neck and pulls me close." Her eyes were damp.

Trip regarded her serious angular face. "And sometimes *he* jumps into bed, right?"

"Well, not Freddy, per se, but he has his phobias. Spiders and breakdancing. Same diff. That's being married. Jumping into bed onto him and he still nuzzles you."

He took a small sip of the bourbon, moistened his lips, really.

"Trip." She shrugged. "You can't lose what you never had, you can't keep what's not yours, and you can't hold on to something that doesn't want to stay."

She squeezed his hand. *Marco!* He squeezed back. *Polo!*

"I have to meet with Fox on Wednesday…. All set, y'know. Big Dog deal."

She raised her glass, but her expression did not toast the idea.

"And then everything might be different."

"If you say so." Jillian narrowed her eyes. "That's a pretty big might."

"The Mightiest." He wiped his face and snorted unhappily.

Scratch stared at them from the poster, which made him feel shitty. Reason number six hundred and sixty-seven why he'd stuffed this shit in the Stones' basement.

"Just don't close up."

"No. I know. I'm all messed up in my head." And Fox wasn't even what he meant. As much as Trip needed order, Silas had this way of unleashing chaos with a smile. "You can't plan a hurricane. Silas changed…" He squeezed the *Scratch* horns in his hand. "…me, I think."

"I have to go to Rina's signing. You can stay."

Trip dropped the silicone piece back on the tub and pushed it back against the wall. The bottom scraped the gritty concrete floor with a satisfying finality.

Jillian glanced over his head, as if an untamed thought-balloon might spill his beans. "What are you thinking?"

"I can't stand the idea that he's somewhere in the city, just a mile away, thinking I suck."

"I thought you didn't care about him."

"I never said that."

"Then you do suck. 'Cause that's how you acted. Like his feelings didn't mean shit and you had other fish to fritter away."

Trip admired the painting of Scratch reaching toward them with slick, scaled arms.

"Chess, kiddo." Jillian followed his line of sight to the banner. "He's not dead. You're not dead. Make a move."

"How? I made every move I can!" He rubbed his eyes.

"Have you called him? Have you confronted Cliff about his bullshit? Have you found a way to salvage all the work you did on your demon?" She tucked her black hair over one seashell ear. "You mighty-might."

"Now? After… everything. Well, that seems like a fuck-awful plan."

She reached out and petted his scalp. "Sometimes the worst idea in the world is the best option you've got."

He nodded.

"Whatever you think you're supposed to be doing, whatever plans the universe has got for you… you're not finished. It's not done. You're not in a box. You have not completed your mission in life, *comrade*." That last word came out in a Soviet accent as she stood.

"How the hell do *you* know?"

"Oh, honey." Jillian and her frown looked at him for a long moment, but she didn't touch him. "You're alive."

She hugged her ribs and left. Trip heard her scuff up the stairs after she closed the basement door. He sat staring at it in the cool concrete silence while he worked up the nerve to climb.

EVEN with three pornstars flying in from Budapest, Kurt didn't bother to answer the door. *Typical.*

When Silas arrived for Mr. Bogusz's birthday blowout, portfolio in hand, he had to let himself into the apartment and follow the sound of his best friend's voice.

His watch said seven, which made him an hour early for the "festivities" Kurt had thrown on his own behalf: cocktails, dinner, and some kind of late night jock pile Silas inevitably skipped. Usually he came to have a drink before things kicked off, but tonight he wanted to discuss something serious without witnesses. Under one arm, he had something he planned to show Kurt, if he could steal five real minutes.

A chef and two cater waiters *clinked* and *swooshed* in the kitchen, and the dining table gleamed with the good setting. Kurt had put on the swank for someone, and Silas did not want it to be him.

Annoyingly, Kurt gestured and nattered at high speed on the phone in his office. He waved when he noticed Silas and gestured toward the living room.

Silas glanced at his watch. No guests for another twenty minutes at least, so he had time.

Once there, he took off his jacket. He'd worn a suit because Kurt told him to look sharp. No doubt Kurt wanted to pimp him out to some corporate yahoo. His version of good friendship: tossing a big wiener on the grill.

"Grah!" A tortured moan.

Silas jumped at the low shout. *Scared the bejesus outta me.*

In one of the leather armchairs sat Ziggy, dapper in wool slacks and an open-necked dress shirt, but his mouth buckled with managed pain.

Silas's heart gave a happy jerk. Had Kurt started seeing him?

"Aighh!" Ziggy took another rattling breath, eyes opened wide as if he'd been scalded and just as quickly relaxed. He pounded his right thigh a couple of times.

Silas reached toward him to help, second-guessed it, and let the hand drop. "Y'okay?"

Ziggy panted with his mouth open and winced. "I'm—" He closed his eyes hard and rolled his head before opening them again. He gulped painfully. "Bad too-day. Bad day-ay. Shouldn'ta come."

"Likewise. I'm Silas."

"R'member." The programmer closed his eyes and rubbed the leg. "I was a *dick.*" His voice sounded as though someone had held it down and broken all its bones. "Zigg-gy."

Silas tried to interpret the signs. Kurt had invited his handsome programmer to dinner. *That's new.* Maybe Ziggy had managed to get through a few defenses. Maybe the fancy table was meant to impress him.

Ziggy turned toward the window with the noble profile of a Florentine etching. His long hair was brushed into burnished waves that curled at his shoulders. The chalky blue of the dress shirt turned it auburn as an antique penny. He'd obviously made a concerted effort to spiff up for the evening. Was this his first invitation to the boss's bachelor pad?

They sat awkwardly together as they listened to Kurt wheedle and bark in another language from across the apartment.

After a few minutes, Silas attempted conversation, because he didn't know how not to. Like holding a door or saying sir and ma'am. "Glad you made it. I mean, I'm glad I'll have someone to talk to tonight."

Ziggy let out a heavy breath. "I'll try." He blushed, and half of his mouth pulled down. "My legs were do-iing better, theh-hen they were not." He crossed them awkwardly. His dress shoes were so new that the soles were still glossy. Actually, all of his clothes looked new.

Silas battled a pang of sympathy and guilt. *Please don't let Kurt shit on him.*

Kurt often included a couple of escorts for dinner parties. He loved to watch his real friends try to interface with juiced-up rent boys and the epic faux pas that arose as both sides attempted to play nice.

Silas grinned uncomfortably. "I got roped into the party last minute."

"Join the cluh-ub." Ziggy's hand cramped, but he jerked an impatient thumb in the direction of Kurt's yapping. "He's a bull who carries his owwwn fuckin' china sh-shhop around with him."

"How many people did he invite? Any idea?"

In the office, Kurt laughed loudly, a fake guffaw that was supposed to sound hearty and encouraging.

They glanced at each other.

"Guests haven't been deliv-rrred yet, he only ora-orderrred the sausage platter this afternoon."

"Great." Silas held up a warning hand. "Kurt's parties can get a little nuts." For Ziggy's sake, he prayed a new leaf was on offer tonight.

"Yah." Ziggy licked his lip. "Normal. Normal-ly I skip 'em. But he had news that couldn't way-yait. So now, I'm holding-ng my dick out here while Mr. Jackass yells into the phone like a walking spleen." He frowned at his feet. "Like being ouuut-side of a prinnn-cipal's office."

"On his birthday? Who's he bitching at?"

"Dun-no. Planning that zom-*mom*bie run shit." He shrugged. "He's all-ways tryin' to tell me about 'em. *Fpphhtt*." Ziggy flipped Kurt off crookedly with a hand that wouldn't quite obey him.

How embarrassing for Kurt. He had to know Ziggy had no interest in a running event.

Silas'd probably end up doing makeup for the next OutRun, scheduled around Pride in June, a little over a month away. They'd have wrapped *Undercover Lovers* by then.

Ziggy winced again, his eyes unfocused.

For a trickle of seconds, Silas considered inviting Ziggy to come hang out in the makeup tent, just to give him a place and a way to participate, but he worried it might seem patronizing or invasive, and he had no idea what Ziggy and Kurt had going on between them.

An awkward silence fell. Silas knew the programmer was in pain, and he seemed embarrassed by it. Kurt's muffled blather floated around them, and the waiting did feel like detention.

Silas wondered, idly, if any of the guests tonight actually wanted to be here with Mr. Bogusz. Odds were good that everyone, other than him, was on one payroll or another. He wouldn't trade places with Kurt for anything.

"Where's-a man? Yours." Ziggy flapped a hand at Silas impatiently. "I want'd to meet-im."

His heart seized a little. "You mean Trip?"

Ziggy blinked. "Comic guy."

"Yeah. Uh." Silas bit his lip. "We split. Broke up."

"M'sorry." Ziggy bounced his leg jerkily. He looked embarrassed. "Tha's not good."

"Wasn't my idea." He shrugged. "Never had a serious boyfriend, not like… that."

Ziggy studied him, long enough to prompt an explanation.

"He decided that I didn't fit the life he's pretending to live." Silas frowned, not caring if he sounded as bitter as he was. *No more masks.* That was something at least.

Kurt's voice rose in the office. "'Xactly my point."

Ziggy nodded and scratched his tangled head. "Men are retarded." He snorted, peered at something tucked behind his feet against the chair: his battered crutches. "They're so fucking handi-cah-capped, I can't believe they aren't born with these bolted to their hands." He kicked at them.

Silas hadn't noticed them there. Why wasn't Ziggy using them tonight, when it obviously hurt to sit?

"Nuh-thing's perfect." Ziggy's chin jerked defiantly, and the clean planes of his matinee-idol profile angled hard toward the light. The tendons in his neck knotted and released. "No-body."

In the other room, Kurt barked something negative into the phone.

Silas looked up into Ziggy's hooded gaze. They didn't nod at each other, but they might have. Ziggy grunted and wiped his chin with jerky imprecision. How long had he and Kurt circled each other? Silas had no idea.

"Trip kept wanting to change me." Silas leaned the portfolio against his chair and wished he hadn't brought it. "He kept asking advice and showing me shit and dragging me along while he dreamed up this whole crazy scheme that was bullshit anyways."

Ziggy tucked his hair behind his ear.

"I shouldn't have come here tonight."

"You talk to h-him?" Ziggy spoke softly.

"No."

"Came out wrong." Ziggy shook his head and then asked deliberately, "I meant, *can* you stil-ll talk to him?"

"He wouldn't. We didn't have the same feelings for each other."

"Ah." Ziggy gripped the chair. "Sucks."

In the other room, Kurt said something about lawyers and currency while he leaned and gazed out the window at his three-million-dollar view.

Ziggy watched him for a moment, face like marble. He blinked hard and jogged his head as if it stung.

Silas nodded at nothing. "Anyways, it doesn't matter."

"*Ppff.* You retarded? Everything matters." With a wince, Ziggy scooted forward in his chair. "How did he feel?"

"I have no idea. He had other plans he wouldn't share."

Ziggy's brow bunched. "Then how-ow do you know it's dif'rent?"

"He set me up. We had gotten so wrapped up in this project of his that I helped too much. His comic book. I'm a grown-up. I didn't think it was a job, but then he… fired me, is what it felt like."

"So he try-ied to tell you." Ziggy's left arm flexed uncontrollably and they both ignored it. "Communic-ation."

Silas examined Kurt's blind back. "He didn't, though. He didn't need me or want me or… anything. No idea how to communicate. Possession. No one else allowed."

"Y'mean." Ziggy blinked. "The ff-fans or you?"

"It was fucking art. His. And he wouldn't turn the thing loose, let it go. Or couldn't."

"Which is why he was allll-ways asking advice and showing you pages and try-ying to drag you into it even though the comic is his deal. Thaaah-at's called sharing." Ziggy's wrist bent hard, folding his fist toward the rigid forearm. "Or as some stupid assss-holes put it…" He opened his mouth. His tongue struggled to shape the word. It came out as a gasp. "…love."

Silas froze. Blinked. Swallowed.

Was that true? Maybe he'd forgotten what it was like to invent something from scratch. *So quick to judge.* Years of working for chump change on indie flicks had left Silas wary of working for nothing, except Trip's project wasn't work and was certainly not for nothing.

And then he remembered the night he'd unveiled the Judge, and Trip's open, grateful face. Silas had paid attention to something that mattered to them both, and that had meant everything to Trip. Life had changed for them that night, but he'd never stopped to ask *why.*

Ziggy fiddled with the cuff of his shirt. The skin on his forearms was still pink, like he'd deliberately hidden the crutches when he arrived. He glanced back toward Kurt's stern voice and then at his watch. His right foot twitched until he pressed it against the floor. He stuck out his chin.

No. Trip hadn't shut him out at any point. For all his neuroses, he *had* shared Scratch. Sure, he'd been demanding and sullen, but that went both ways. Even jealous and petty at the end, but he'd always included Silas in the stuff that mattered.

He'd showed up, been *present*. Until Silas and Cliff had pushed him at the con and he'd panicked.

Shit.

Silas had judged him when they both knew better. He'd swung a huge scary gavel and Trip had jumped back, toward the fake safety Cliff represented. The devil he knew.

"What…." Silas wiped his nose, not caring that he probably looked as ugly as he felt. "The fuck have I done?"

"Mmph." Ziggy's head wobbled, a gentle, painful palsy. "Been a deh-dick." He mashed his lips together and smiled, but his eyes were wet. "Bee-een a guy." Another hard blink that made him seem about fourteen. "Been ah-uff—" He scowled and shook his head in frustration as he strained to get a word out. "Fraid!" He punched his thigh hard in irritation. "Fraid."

Frayed? Like fabric?

For a beat, Silas started to ask what "frayed" meant, and then he knew. *Afraid.* Yeah, fucking terrified… and frayed too: worn around the edges by mistakes and rough handling. Even if Ziggy had said the other word by accident, he was dead right twice over.

Silas's mouth buckled, and he shook his head as Ziggy had, without the same excuse. A stupid tear slipped free. He ran the back of his knuckles over it to smear it into submission, but Ziggy hadn't seen. He'd trained his cold wolf eyes on the handsome salt-and-pepper head across the apartment. He looked tender and angry as an orphan.

Frayed.

Right then, Silas finally knew what he should have said in Chicago. *Wisdom of the staircase.* If he hadn't worked so hard on that goddamn incubus makeup and gotten his ass handed to him in front of a thousand crazy fans. If Trip hadn't shocked and hurt him so casually.

Behind his desk, Kurt held up four fingers and scowled at them, whatever that meant. Four minutes? Four grand? Four hustlers?

Ziggy exhaled painfully and his eyes shut. He blinked at the window and the sky with terrible patience, a wingless creature pondering flight.

He was frayed and afraid, too, and Kurt. Rina and Leigh Ann. His producers at Showtime. His parents in Alabama. Hell, every goofy ex he'd ever dated and discarded, every human being he'd ever met. Even that asshole Cliff. They all scrabbled around to hold threads together while their world unraveled.

The secret seed of all superheroes: falling apart. Everyone who had survived childhood ended up tattered and terrified. Locked in a kryptonite dungeon, bound with their own magic lassos, mutated and mutilated. Trip more than anyone else. And yet he'd walked away, because the sharing felt like theft. *Sick.*

Silas turned. A flash of his drawing of the Judge wielding his ugly gavel. "He's *my* villain," Trip had said.

No shit.

Maybe that's what being a couple meant: not that you were brave for each other, but that you could let someone be scared or damaged without judging them. Sharing monsters. Knowing theirs, giving them yours.

With this thing, I thee wed.

Ziggy glanced toward the office again and scrutinized his nail-bitten hands, scarcely able to sit but too proud to stand with his crutches. *Frayed.*

In the office space, Kurt's voice ebbed and flowed as he paced back and forth in the office, wheedling and crooning. The words seemed indistinct and chipper.

Silas thought he understood: Ziggy wished Kurt would see him clearly, but he hid everything that mattered. Kurt hosted his charity zombies because he forgot Ziggy could never run.

Kurt spent himself on hookers, and Ziggy kept him honest. Most likely, they'd never inch any closer because they knew all too well how frayed and afraid they were.

They love each other. Silas tried to laugh and frown at the same time. "You're like his spirit animal."

Ziggy snarled, "The fuck?" He shook his head slowly at the sight of Kurt on the phone not seeing them.

Silas grimaced awkwardly. For all Ziggy's bitching, he knew Kurt's monsters and kept track of them. The pissedness was protective.

"Nothing. Spirit animal. Inside joke." He should have kept his mouth shut. "With... nobody, really. Never mind."

Ziggy picked up his crutches and swung onto his legs without using them. "I think you have to have a fucking spirit for that."

In the kitchen, clinks of silverware on china.

"Fuck thii-is." Ziggy teetered, his pale eyes wide, perfect nostrils flared. "Fuck Captain Ass-tastic in there and fu-uhhk his checkbook of steel." He put the unused crutches over his shoulders like a fishing pole. "I'm gonna go-oh to the gym. I need a blowjob. Go *hoh*-home, smoke a joint after." Even in his button-down shirt, he resembled a Medici prince tasting vinegar, disappointed by the grubby, gruesome world he was forced to rule.

Before Silas got a chance to respond, Ziggy moved with startling, jerky speed as he stomped to the front door on his brand new shoes and yanked it open to exit.

Across the office, Kurt raised his voice and stepped in their direction, holding up fingers. "Two secs. Two secs, Zig."

Silas sat uneasily in the slick leather. He'd trespassed on a private moment between them, even though they weren't together and this wasn't private.

Wham. The front door slammed shut, and the grouchy programmer was gone.

"No! It's a go." Kurt strode toward the shut door. "We did it. I gotta tell him. "Achievement unlocked!" He brandished a fist.

"Did what?"

Kurt tugged the door open. "Zig!"

"You're such a schmuck." Silas covered his mouth and blinked at his best friend.

"He knew what I was doing." Kurt let the door drift shut.

Silas cocked his head, measuring his friend. "Lucky him."

"I bought his controller." Kurt looked hurt. "They agreed."

"Kurt, he was waiting when I showed up. He sat out here waiting forty minutes. You can't treat people like that. He's not a hustler."

"Nah! He doesn't care. He bitches for effect."

"How do you figure?"

"Because he'd say something. Tough as a boot. And Ziggy's not exactly shy."

Silas stood, slowly. "The only guy you give two shits about just sat out here waiting for you like a stray dog while you tried to drive him away. Because you're fucking afraid."

Frayed.

"Of what? Of what?"

Silas put his jacket on.

Kurt held up a hand. "You're leaving?"

Silas pressed the heel of his hand against his eye. Why in hell had he agreed to come to this bullshit circus? *Dinner with strangers.* If Kurt wanted to rent a room full of fake friends, Silas certainly didn't need to sit around and corrode the illusion.

"You need to meet this stud I got lined up. Spanish banker. Ten-inch dork." Kurt craned his neck to see into the dining room. "Bitch, at least have a conversation. Men like him do not grow on trees."

"No. Men don't. We're not fruits or nuts or anything else." Silas sounded like his dad, and the thought made him proud. For a moment, he missed his dad so much he could hardly breathe, wished he could call home and ask for advice. He shook the thought away. "We barely grow at all."

Kurt hissed. "You cannot walk out before she serves the soup."

"I don't give a fuck about the soup." Silas hefted the portfolio he'd brought as an afterthought.

"C'mon, man. I can't eat dinner with the caterer. I got a ton of guys coming."

Silas knew full well that retcon was impossible... but maybe he could make amends from a distance. He walked back to the foyer with Kurt trailing. The portfolio handle almost scalded his hand. He had never asked Kurt for anything.

Kurt stepped closer and lowered his voice. "This is embarrassing. You're embarrassing me."

"Well, then, I'm a rotten person and I'll never go to heaven."

"Silas, I'm trying to be your friend."

"Same here." Silas pushed the heavy portfolio into his hands. "Happy birthday, dickhead."

"You already gave me a present last week."

"I know." Silas had bought him a vintage Coleco game system he'd found at a stoop sale in Queens. Kurt loved retro gear, and none of the guests would know that or bother if they did. Kurt would never admit that shit to people he wanted to impress. *Too frayed.*

Kurt's forehead wrinkled and he scowled at the black leatherette in his hands. "So… what the fuck?"

Silas heaved a ragged sigh, as if the world was a candle he could blow out. He looked at the portfolio and made a wish. "That's for someone else."

22

"I'M SORRY. Who are you supposed to be?"

Late on a Wednesday, Trip arrived at the Fox offices in midtown, not sure what to expect. At a minimum, he had expected to be expected.

"Speck?" A college-age receptionist wearing a vest and a beige tie examined him like a slug.

Trip faltered, scratching his forearms. "Uhh. Trip Spector. I'm here for the *Hero High* meeting." *Wrong building?* He fished his phone out of his pocket and paddled through to the appointment to confirm: May 29. Had he gone to the wrong floor? Was he early? The clock said five p.m. Cliff had said they might head to drinks and dinner with their new producers.

The fuck?

Trip peered past reception into a vast cubicled cavern hemmed in by fishbowl offices. Privacy came at a premium in here. A lot of young professionals in hispter casual sat computing and muttering into telephones. No one smiled or even looked in his direction. *Suit-itis.* So much for showbiz.

"Trip Van Winkle!"

Cliff waved from a doorway about thirty feet down the line of enclosed offices.

The receptionist half smiled and waved him back without a word.

Trip dropped his jacket over his itchy arm and picked up his portfolio. He walked slowly toward his beaming editor. Cliff's tie was askew, and he seemed a little tipsy. *Good sign.* Obviously some kind of sleazebag accord had been reached.

Cliff waved him into a curtained conference room and gave the thumbs-up to someone outside. The sour receptionist, maybe. The room had a cherry laminate table polished to a blinding glare. About forty-five Aeron chairs ringed it, all angled just-so by the corporate maintenance fairies. Sixty grand in furniture. Staplegun had dragged out two seats at the near end, and there were two bottles of water.

Where is everyone?

Trip hung his jacket on one chair as he entered. One wall was solid glass gazing over the east side of midtown to a bruised sky. *Almost dark.* "I thought we were going to get a tour of the facility."

"Nah, fuck the tour. 'S'bullshit, bro. You can do it later."

Trip slid the portfolio onto the table without opening it. He'd brought it in case one of the suits couldn't visualize for shit. Silas had warned him repeatedly about the power of pictures as leverage with these drones.

Cliff seemed weirdly triumphant and definitely boozed up. "I wanna talk before they come back."

"Back from where? Did you go out for drinks already?"

"Teleconference. Hollywood's three hours behind. I told the guys we needed a few minutes." Cliff took the chairman's seat at the head. *Dad's seat.* He spun a little as he threw himself into the chair like a triumphant brat.

"You already met with everyone?" Trip sat catty-corner and peered around them in confusion. "Do we need to sign?"

"I already signed for us." Cliff flapped a hand. "For Big Dog, I mean. But we're signed, sealed, deliberated."

Trip let that sink in for a moment. "That so."

Cliff stared at him as if waiting for Trip to give permission. "Really proud of us. I did good."

"And what about meeting with Fox Features?" Trip turned the chair so he wasn't facing his tipsy editor.

"Family. The all-new Fox Family wants our book, man!"

"Fox Family Comics?" Trip hushed his voice. *Are these rooms bugged?*

"They're pretty edgy, dude."

"Fox Family is gonna be edgy?"

"With *Hero High* on their relaunch lineup.... Yeah?" Cliff gulped air and smirked. "We got 'em but good."

Trip hissed and glanced at the door. "Cliff, are you insane? I mean, I'm not exactly marching in my underwear, but I like to think I have a shred of integrity." A pellet of doubt plopped into Trip's stomach and fizzed viciously. "So what about the movie?"

"Well, it's a TV movie for prime time, but that's major. Even bigger. I mean, millions of—"

"Cliff? You sold them the option to produce *Hero High* as a TV movie for...?"

Cliff stroked the air with his hands carefully, petting an imaginary sabertooth. "Millions of dollars in advertising. Exposure. And they launch the book as cross-promo."

"You don't even listen. You say these words like 'prime time' and 'millions' and you think it means something." Trip blanched. Silas had predicted exactly this, and he'd been too weak and stupid to see it. "You're telling me I should be excited because they're gonna make *Hero High* for twenty bucks with Kirk Cameron playing Alphalad in a tinfoil suit?"

"A package deal. Fox Family has a whole new lineup in process. They publish it and then they do the movie." Cliff regarded the king-of-the-world view beyond the sheet glass: Manhattan as a toy. *Assembly required.* "First they relaunch the comic, then they'd have an option—"

"*Option.*" Trip held up a finger. Thanks to Silas he knew what that word meant to movie people. "Not an actual movie deal, just the possibility of producing a movie if they choose, for which they paid us...."

Silence. Trip's stomach growled, and not from hunger.

Cliff swiveled and spoke in undertone. "Trip, I promise the Fox guys are not trying to shaft us."

"Wait." Trip gripped the chair arm. "You promise or you believe?"

Cliff eyed the door. "What the fuck difference does it make? I've got a contract, a guarantee. We are standing outside the castle." His face looked greasy and anxious.

"No." Trip studied the bones under the skin: handsome, certain, and cunning. Just shapes and angles humans were hardwired to trust and lust after. "You're just singing words because maybe I won't notice. Fucking lollipops and rainbows."

"They set up the *Hero High* movie, and all we gotta do is give them twelve issues of the All-New Mighty Mites."

"We?" Trip crossed his arms. "Wait-wait-wait. *We* redraw twelve issues of twenty-four pages each. How much are *we* getting paid to do that complete reboot?"

Cliff's mouth opened and closed. Obviously his sexy fratboy programming didn't allow for people to question his version of reality. "As a... favor to them."

"A 288-page favor?" Trip's voice rang sharp and clear. Now he prayed the suits were eavesdropping. "Dude, if I'm gonna be a whore, I'd like to make a couple bucks."

Pause. Maybe the Unboyfriend was sobering up. "You'd be a consultant...."

"On a theoretical TV movie. For a Fox division that went belly-up a while back. After I redo a year's work for no pay on a book I hate."

Cliff started the pep rally. "We have a huge devoted fanbase. Your fans will flip."

Trip flashed on *Undercover Lovers* affiliates party, all those "stars" jockeying to keep their jobs. "Do you know how many titles get optioned and killed? Hell, these days *channels* don't last a year."

"*Hero High* has sold a hundred thousand copies. Fox is superhot for us. As a transmedia package." He hooked quote-y fingers in the air and nodded. *Captain of the bullshit team.*

"They're paid to be excited, Cliff. That's their job." Trip crossed his arms warily. "See... a suit always thinks he needs to keep his idea and guard it from other people because someone might take it. Then he holds the idea down and lets everyone come fuck it until it's dead. Because suits don't have ideas; they only have gists and impressions."

Cliff froze in place as if trying to catch an invisible rat and glanced at the open conference room door. Then he stood and went to it and pushed it closed. *Thwick.*

Trip scowled. "I'm not a fucking soft serve, Cliff. You can't just pull a handle so high-fructose mush squirts out."

"That's not—I'm not pulling your handle." He eased back into the chair; his winter-gin breath made Trip want to gag.

"No, you're not. But you're trying to." Trip's breath wheezed and rattled in his lungs. "We took a shitty idea and tarted it up with other shitty ideas, and now you want me to celebrate because a whole group of talentless idiots who only *rent* shitty ideas are offering us the chance to come sit on their toilet."

Cliff stared at him like he'd grown another head.

"Stop hustling me like you're good at it. If you could pull your skull out of your rectum for ten minutes, you'd know better." Trip was just talking to himself. He kept seeing Silas in Chicago dressed as his demon, wounded and wonderful. "But you won't. You don't. Fucking Christmas, Silas was right." Trip's eyes got hot, and then his cheeks were wet. He swabbed them ungently.

"I understand cold feet, and I know you're not comfortable with this kind of compromise—"

"Comfortable!" Trip started to stand, but his legs felt squashy as pipe cleaners. "You lied." He stayed put, unwilling to look away. "You killed my whole book for smoke. You stood there in Chicago and looked me in the fucking face and lied about what they offered."

"Bullshit! That's bullshit."

"This isn't a movie. There's no deal here. You just pimped me out to a Fox gangbang. Fox Family! I ask you. So you can sit at lunch with some other spray-tan tapeworm who chews with his ass and lies when he breathes." He fought his dry mouth to swallow, audibly. "Oh my God."

"Triple-cream, chill out." Cliff laughed then, a loud wide-open jock laugh like they were just joshing around on the bus. *No big.* He used his MVP voice. "These guys have access to money. And no, they aren't offering us the moon. What about it? Sure, sex sells. Barbecue sauce. Rock stars. The Doors had great music, but do you think anyone would have listened if Morrison hadn't had the jumbo tube steak in leather pants and that face?"

Trip pushed himself out of his chair with shaking hands and put air between them.

"Dude—" Apparently, the greasy gears behind Cliff's handsome skull had cranked forward. "Jim Morrison found out his band had licensed 'Light My Fire' to sell Buicks, and he flipped out. Threw this lame pussy tantrum about making a couple million dollars. Now, we're supposed to feel like that's awful and rock is great, but that princess choked on his own puke in his twenties. And Buick is still going strong."

Trip circled the conference table and paced on the opposite side. "Idiot." He questioned which of them he meant. *Idiots.* "What have I done?"

Cliff leaned in. "But you know what? Now Jim Morrison is a genius, even though he died a fat junkie. Every fucking memory we have of him is from one photo session because he had the decency to go to Paris to snuff it."

"Wow."

"I know, right?" A smug smile on Cliff's chops.

"Not 'wow, you're so smart.' That was more of a 'wow, you're more pathetic than they said, Staplegun.'" Trip shuddered and spat. "Silas warned me, repeatedly, and I fucking ignored it because I thought he was jealous. Silas, jealous of anyone."

"We'll be able to write our ticket."

Trip nodded. "I'm just the gas that gets you there."

"This is a once in a lifetime opportunity, and it'll give you all the things you ever wanted." Cliff's wheedling charm felt like an insult. They both knew it was bullshit.

Trip swiveled. "I want to write and draw my own book. Will it give me that?"

"I promise."

"Great. Then let's give them *Scratch* instead and see what they say. Man up!"

Cliff held up a stop-sign hand. "Not that. Well, not that right now, at least."

"Some promise." Trip shook his head. "That lasted, what, like four seconds?"

"But later, sure. Alan Moore wrote eco comics and philosophical comics and fucking porno comics too. Full-on jizz-books."

Trip watched while the lies fell out of that mouth like rotting teeth. "After he *left* DC." Trip narrowed his eyes at Cliff. "Do you think I'm stupid? He ran for the hills and dug a tunnel when he got there. Moore hates DC so much that he's given up credit on entire hundred-million-dollar movies just to get away from these putzes you envy."

"Maybe Moore's a bad example. My point is that even if he hates 'em, they gave him market share. You get the gist—"

"The fucking gist is what's ruined the entire world." Trip sniffled and shrugged. "You think like a suit. You have their fucking disease. Suit-itis." Without thinking, he used Silas's word. It just slipped from his mouth like he owned it. "You don't have any ideas of your own, so you borrow one or steal one and sit on it like a stubborn chicken trying to hatch a grenade. Afraid to stand up and too namby-pamby to sit down."

"Dude, I'm not afraid of anything." Staplegun sounded like he'd pissed his panties.

"But artists always have another idea. 'S'the thing that suits and whores don't understand, because they find one dumb idea and hang on tight. You assholes think if we sing about lollipops and rainbows that kids are fooled because they get the gist." He shrugged. "They know."

Cliff's confusion filled the space between them.

"Forget it." Trip understood, and that was plenty. "You want this so bad, you'd stab *yourself* in the back to get it. Lollipops and rainbows. Lollipops and rainbows. Oh my God."

"What does that mean?" Cliff fumed.

"Just a reminder. They all warned me and I wouldn't see. You're only a suit with better packaging." He laughed at his own stupidity, without any pleasure. "Mighty Mites may be something you can whore out as heroes to someone, but not to me."

Cliff huffed and sneered. "They're fictional!"

Trip waved his arms, and his face heated as he roared, "Of course they're fictional. Everyone is fictional! We all invent ourselves, shitwit. That's what being alive is. Dad's big pen squirts us into Mom's open pages, and then we have to fill in the blanks, make our lives up, color things in so we're worth reading." He sounded like Silas, and for an irrational moment, he wished Silas could see him doing the right thing for once in his pathetic life.

Chop-chop.

Cliff stood unsteadily at the head of the table, arms swinging: *Dad carves up bullshit for Unthanksgiving.* "It's a transmedia property. Manufacturing heroes is a fucking business."

"They aren't heroes because you wave your big veiny wand. They're heroes when they save the world from itself."

Outside the wall of windows, muddy dusk had fallen.

Trip paused and rubbed his sore eyes. "Are these thieving *schvuntzes* ever coming back?"

Cliff glanced at his watch and at the door again. "Maybe they got stuck in the conference call."

Dusk?

"Ah." The last pieces clicked into place. "I'm not supposed to meet anyone." Trip pivoted to face the Unboyfriend in slow motion. "There was never a movie. Or a deal. A complete lie."

"Huh?" Cliff's mouth worked. "We're sitting in the Fox conference room." At his collar, his pulse juddered visibly. Troubled waters there.

"Alone. They let you come take a fake tour. They didn't want to meet us." Unblinking, Trip crept back around the table. "This was a buncha kabuki bullshit to convince me you're a wheeler-dealer." He smiled unhappily. "'Cause you only open your cock-holster to tell more whoppers."

The Joker unmasked. Green Goblin revealed. Magneto in a plastic prison.

"That's not true, bro." Cliff's gaze rested cobra-still on Trip. "I promise." He shifted in his borrowed big-shot seat.

"More promises. Gosh." Trip sat back down in his chair slowly. "If I held my ear to your chest, I'd hear the ocean."

"Foot in the door, is all. We know these guys, and once *Hero High* fits their specs, we're golden." Cliff swallowed whatever was in his mouth. His face was pink.

Trip frowned. "You believe that."

"Maybe. There's no way to know the future. It might." Cliff shrugged and tried to make his eyes sparkle.

"Might! Might is *right*." Trip sniffed. "Might is your whole problem. You might be gay. I might be lonely enough. Kids might like our bullshit. Fox might make a movie." Trip slapped crap off the lacquered surface. "Might, right?" A pen hit the window. "Might, maybe." A water bottle hit the wall. "Mite, bug." He swept pages onto the floor. "And you"—he howled at his lamebrain editor—"are the mightiest mite of all. A big fucking maybe bug, who bullies everyone into shoveling your shit."

My fault. Trip rubbed at his mouth haphazardly. Cliff didn't know any better, but Trip did, and he had still looked Silas Goolsby in the face and done the wrong thing. Eyes wide and pants around his ankles so these monsters could fuck him over, faster with less fuss. *I'm a monster.*

Trip whispered, "I'm so sorry."

As soon as he did, he realized he was talking to Silas a couple of weeks too late. Those words belonged in Chicago. For one misplaced moment, they were at the con panel starting from *Scratch*. An alternate universe where Silas made miracles out of nothing and Trip had screwed up and apologized instantly and everything was a joke and he took his demon's hand and walked into the future.

Cliff peered at him anxiously and leaned forward. His large palm drew circles on Trip's back, as if rubbing a tummy from the wrong side. "There's no need to apologize."

Trip jerked away. "To you?" His voice came out louder than he'd intended. "Why would I apologize to you?"

"You said—"

"I'm a sorry motherfucker for wasting so much of my life carrying you up a wet shit hill."

Cliff clasped the arm of Trip's chair. Something flickered behind his eyes. "Wait... wait.... Before you trip out. What if you used a pseudonym for the other book?"

The rickety resignation Trip had cobbled together in the past few weeks crumpled inside him: a house of cards built of nothing but Jokers.

"Stay in the closet, you mean." Trip crossed his arms, and mimed patience he didn't feel.

"I don't mean like that."

Trip lifted his brows slowly, his eyes tight. He could almost hear Cliff's brain scrabbling inside his skull like a rat frantic for a way out.

Cliff dabbed at his mouth. "I mean... maybe *Scratch* gets published under a different name." He reached across the corner of the table toward Trip again.

Trip swatted his hand away. "Hey, maybe *Hero High* should be under a pen name. That's the dreck I'm ashamed of." He cleared his throat and bit his tongue. "I don't need a secret identity to live my life. I'm not a caped crusader. I'm just a guy with a pencil."

"Dude, I get that you're nervous, and I get that you're giving shit up. Do you think I'm not? I've seen you pour yourself into this. You've been there for me every step of the way, and I'm there for you." Cliff scooted to the edge of his chair so their bent legs interlaced like cogs. "I've always liked you, man."

Chop-chop. Who's there?

His plump basket nudged Trip's knee.

Right then, Trip understood perfectly: the deal being offered and the devil in its details. Right then, any guttering attraction he'd ever felt for Cliff Stapleton the Third winked out like a candle flame. Without shifting a millimeter or saying a word, the Unboyfriend had taken off his mask, and what remained of his groomed, calculated fratboy studliness had all the appeal of a sticky linoleum bedspread.

"I...." Trip kept the sarcasm out of his voice. "After all this time, you'd actually, finally fuck the faggot for real, to convince me. Go ahead, big guy! Drop your drawers."

Cliff's hand hesitated and slowed.

"Like radioactive jock itch. Unreal." Head shake. "After flirting and stringing the dumb queer along for four years, to milk the pages out of me, you'd let me stick my big bone in you to close the sale."

The Unboyfriend appeared genuinely bewildered. "No!"

"Oh!" Trip did the sexual arithmetic and realized his mistake. "Oh wait. Even better. You don't even know me well enough to make the right offer. You think I'm a frail pussy-Jew, so I need *you* to put me down on all fours and do the honors." He cackled in disgust. "Some honor."

Cliff's mouth worked the air, stupidly. Apparently, he had to work to rewire his assfuck assumptions.

"We're not all imbeciles. Trouble is, you're sexy, so we all pretend we don't, but heads-up... we notice. Everyone." Trip's hands, of their own volition, gathered his crap: bag, hat, portfolio, phone, all the scattered pieces he needed to take with him when he made his escape. "For the record: you're not bisexual, you're a *sociopath*."

"Swear to God, bro. If you bail now, I will never look back and you will never get another opportunity like this."

"Promise?" Trip's face felt hot and his smile manic, his teeth bared like a rabid dog as he spat, "Lucky fucking me."

"You're making the worst mistake of your life."

"Which one, Staplegun? The part where I betrayed the person I care about most, or maybe torching the best work I've done in my life, or the part where I tell you to fuck yourself with a rusty grandfather clock. I'm up to my eyeballs in rotten ideas and god-awful decisions." Trip realized he was shouting. "Chop-chop!"

"Trip. Think!" A rim of sweat stained the edge of his collar. "You can only pull the trigger once."

Trip affected a Jimmy Olsen blankness as he stood up. "Golly, Captain Cocktease! Are you sure?"

Cliff didn't like that very much. "You are not gonna wreck a multimillion-dollar deal for some horned superdildo with a pointy tail."

"No, moron. I'm gonna wreck it for me."

His former editor sat stock-still, apparently straining every cell of his body to appear sincere and casual even though the telltale pulse jumped under his jaw. "Goddamn Goolsby. And that stupid demon dick book. Some buttfuck bubba wanted you to himself and turned you against—"

"You and your noble intentions? Zzzzt. Wrong tactic, *bro*." Trip stared into the golden retriever eyes without smiling. He wiped his damp hands on his pants. He wanted to take a shower, to scrub himself. He spoke in a near-whisper. "What in my life was so bad that"—scowl—"*you* might be the better choice?"

If Silas could see me now....

Trip grabbed his portfolio so quickly it swung wide and narrowly missed clipping Cliff. "*Scratch* is better than anything you'll ever look at. Silas Goolsby is more of a man than you'll ever *blow* to get ahead." Trip might as well have spoken Assyrian. "I've been a moron."

Cliff held out the pen. "So be smart." He slid the contract over the desk.

"I think that's a superb idea." Trip stood and yanked his jacket off the back of the chair so hard it flipped and fell. "You know the best way to predict the future? Invent it."

"Spector." The Unboyfriend begged, naked in his panic. He'd pulled his tie loose and his mouth broke. "Please don't do this to me." He glanced at the door that led to the bowels of Fox.

"You—" Trip slung his backpack over his shoulder, absurdly gratified when it slammed against his back a little too hard. "—can shove *Hero High*—" If only a hundred Mighty Mite backpacks could fall from the sky and crush the bullshit out of him. "—up your uptight Unboyfriend ass!"

He let the lethal smile die, turned, and walked away. He threw the door open so hard it shook the sheetrock. All the cubicle drones watched him go, twitchy as schizophrenic rabbits.

Too claustrophobic for the elevator, he went to the staircase, wished the alarm would scream so he could sing along. No such luck. All the way from the twenty-eighth floor, he took the stairs two at a time, almost wishing he could throw himself down them and end up in a mangled pile so his outsides would match his insides.

He emerged through titanic glass doors onto Avenue of the Americas. "*A nation of bullshitters.*"

He'd misread everything, misjudged everyone, most of all himself.

At least the midtown sidewalk was semiempty, even if the streets weren't. Night had fallen, thank fuck.

Rina was at some huge romance conference in Kansas City. Ben and Jillian had taken Max to a wedding. He tried to think of anyone to call he hadn't treated like feces. For one whole block, he considered going to Midtown Comics to cool off but didn't think he could keep his shit together if the staff recognized him. There was only one person he needed to tell, but Trip had sent him straight to hell.

Walking against the traffic, Trip let himself cry; the slow tears felt hot on his stupid, stubborn face and smeared the headlights into crosses. He bowed his head and trudged downtown into the graveyard glare rolling past him.

23

FUCK Queens. Fuck Showtime. Fuck me.

"Second skin!"

Silas plucked at the heavy mold, roughly tearing chunks out with his hands and cursing under his breath. Air pockets had formed under the surface on this shoulder plate. Either he hadn't cleaned the molds properly or he'd rushed the fill yesterday in the muggy air. *Amateur hour bullshit.* But they'd shoot the actor in close-up, and the damage was past salvaging.

Third one today. Never so off his game. Better to pack it in and start tomorrow. Hell, maybe it'd rain and the humidity would finally break. He'd cross his fingers for a June storm and run a new appliance in polyfoam in the morning. The producers would never know, but he hated procrastinating till the day of. Besides, painting at last-looks made for crapass footage.

Nothing like being sweaty and pissed off at nothing in particular.

Undercover Lovers wrapped in six days, so he'd stressed and sweated all week at Silvercup. Suits started dropping in to watch dailies, and the whole writing staff churned out last-minute pages to clean up continuity glitches.

He took a swig of lukewarm water out of a bottle and wished he was back in Manhattan, on the air-conditioned couch, watching cartoons in his boxers. He didn't even want to go out. A year ago, he'd have dragged his ass to some bar with Kurt and fucked someone in the john just to clear his head, but somehow he couldn't work up the interest.

Pathetic.

Now, at least, he had definitive proof that he sucked at this relationship shit. He'd lived like a zombie for the past month, lurched between home and work, and he hadn't seen much at either. Nothing from Trip since Chicago, and he hadn't risked reaching out for fear of another beatdown.

A sharp knock on the outside of the makeup trailer.

"Goolsby, I am done, son." Francesca leaned in the little doorframe. "Over and out the catflap."

"Already?"

She stepped inside and pulled the door shut. "Listen…." She leaned to see if they were alone in the trailer. "You gotta sec?"

"Paul and Tiffany are doing the prison fight." Normally, Silas would have done it so he could sneak in a little extra detail, but somehow, he hadn't worked up the mojo. "I'm cleaning up. Long-ass day. I'll see you in the morning." He scratched at a dollop of Cine-Wax on the counter.

She closed the distance between them. "Nah, man. I mean I'm done-done. "Today's my last." She smiled and blinked.

"What the fuck-owitz?" Silas sat down in the makeup chair and swiveled to face her. On a long season, people came and went, but not a rock like Francesca. *Hugs and shrugs.* Weariness chewed at his joints. "It's the sixth of June, show wraps on the fifteenth! They're fucking idiots."

"No. It's good." She sat in the makeup chair opposite him. "I got offered a show of my own. It's a low-budget pilot, and who fucking knows if it'll go anywhere, but I'm getting paid and I love the ladies doing it."

"Congratulations." Silas carefully balanced the grin on his face and didn't elaborate. TV production was like sticking your arm in a garbage disposal and daring your enemies to flip the switch.

She laughed. "You don't have to soft soap me, man. It's a terrible fucking idea, I know. Makes no sense, but my gut tells me it's the right thing. Y'know?"

"Okay. Lord, but we're gonna miss you. I figured they'd give you a producing credit, at least, next season."

"That's as may be. But I'm a chick at a table fulla dicks, and you know how that goes." Francesca shrugged. "I don't wanna write, anyways. This is a good shot."

Silas sighed. He almost remembered being that brave back at the beginning. When had he gotten so damn old? "You like your team?"

"Sh'yeah. I handpicked 'em. That's the thing. Dawn wrote this kinky script she wants to direct and scrounged up about a mil-two in funding and a commitment from Netflix for distribution." She seemed so sharp and full of optimism.

Silas tried to hide the rush of pity. Hundreds of off-network pilots got made every year, and a handful got distribution. Homegrown TV pilots were for crazies only.

"Kind of a ladies-night-out thing. I mean, not like Lena Dunham, but no-budge sexy thriller."

"I'm really happy for you." He swallowed around the lump of sympathy in this throat.

"Leigh Ann and Benita are gonna do the pilot for scale. Benita's starting to get a name. Plus Leigh Ann started dating that Joe Manganiello guy, and he's agreed to play the hustler in a three-way if we can work around his *True Blood* schedule. With ass even, because well, *because*."

That was better. A thick, hick, werewolf dick would give them leverage, at least. Silas could see the logic. "By any means necessary."

"Shooting in Louisiana this summer." She spoke with the singsongy optimism of a travel agent who's never left home. "Would you ever....?"

Oh shit.

"I mean...." She paused at the door again. "I'd love a chance to work with you again. If you'd ever be willing to, y'know, come play in the mud."

"Duh!" He'd help out if he could, but no way was he gonna move to Louisiana for the summer for some crazy shoot on a shoestring. Part of him hated the thought of leaving New York, because then he knew that would shut the door on Trip forever. And the rational side thought he'd be crazy not to cut bait. *Fuck it.* "Actually, I'd love to help y'all out."

Francesca's double take almost made him laugh. "F'real? Wow. Okay."

"Pinky swear." Silas held his up and she took it. "You cover my meals and my travel, and I can sleep on whatever floor you find."

She laughed. "Bitch, I've leased a whole plantation for about a buck, with one wing for housing. It was a hotel in the sixties. Air-conditioned, no less, and a honky-tonk on the property. I scored tax breaks out the pooter." She gave him a side-eye. "Shoot's twenty-four days. I'm bringing a caterer in from New Orleans for meals and crafty. Plus y'got a budget for a crew of four."

"Jeez." He sighed in relief. "Easy favor."

"You thought I was gonna drag your ass down there to sleep in some tent?" She puckered skeptically. "Goolsby, you got self-esteem issues."

"I got worse than that." He crossed his arms, slimy in the tepid air. "But, my daddy used to say, 'Kill all your demons and your angels might fly off.'"

"And bring your boyfriend if he wants to come. Hell, call him your assistant. We'll find something for him to do." A big fresh-baked grinning invitation. "Betcha."

"We...." He swallowed, though his mouth was gummy. "He called it quits."

"Oh shit." The smile mildewed into grimace. Her eyes shifted right to left on his, unsettled as a housefly.

"So...." He shrugged. "Yeah. Naw."

Francesca blinked in sympathy. "Sorry. Agh. My bad. I shoulda known that."

Silas shrugged. "How could you? I didn't exactly hang a neon sign out front."

"Well, maybe it'll be good to get away. I hear Cajun boys are mighty friendly. Gator baiters."

"I know all about 'em. I grew up down that way. Gravy is a beverage and butter is a condiment." He giggled with her. "All I need's a lip fulla tobacco and a spoon of Crisco to get things going."

"Gross!" She cackled and shoved him. "You could show us the back roads."

"Yes, ma'am. I could, at that." A real smile snuck onto his face. *See?* Not so bad. He'd sublet his apartment and hide in the bayou for a spell, pigging out on gumbo and fried bread. Maybe a vacation hookup with a hot redneck who thought six-packs were something you drank. Just what the doctor ordered. He'd spend a month boasting and coasting, come back tough as nails and twice as sharp.

Excellent plan. Repeat it enough, maybe he'd start to believe it.

"Well, I gotta turn in my receipts. I just wanted to—" She hugged him impulsively. "Thank you, Silas. I didn't... expect that. We're gonna have a blast."

Fingers crossed.

She knocked on the doorframe, and then she dropped down to the concrete outside, thumped the door shut behind her, and was gone.

He should feel relieved. He hadn't bothered to line up a gig, and his savings looked patchy. He'd spent too much of the spring worrying about Trip and not enough hustling for work. Nearly June, and the only lead he had was a haunted house gig that wouldn't start until August at the earliest and wouldn't pay reasonable money until September.

A rush of gratitude coursed through his veins. Without knowing it, these ladies might get him back on the rails with none the wiser.

His stomach growled and he foraged for a granola bar in his kit. *Nope.* He'd skipped lunch too. He'd have to run down to crafty to snag whatever scraps the extras had left in their wake.

He paused to wash his hands and splash his face with water, and ignored the circles under his eyes. He needed a break, was all. Some time outside and real food cooked by humans. Maybe one weekend, he'd rent a car and go visit his mama's family. Alabama was only a couple of hours away, and he hadn't swung down in a long-ass time.

Silas sauntered to the craft services tent they'd set up next to the parking lot that stood in for the prison lot. The B-unit was shooting coverage and inserts off to one side. A couple of bored PAs paced outside the active jailhouse set.

The tent was open, and though the food had been whittled down, he spotted a lone banana tucked under a pile of sandwich bread.

"Fuck a duck, you stealing my banana?"

Silas spun and found a lanky college kid considering him with a loose, soft mouth: cute, dreads, all of twenty years old and a hundred and forty pounds. This twink was one of the stunt doubles. Larry? Harry? *Who fucking knew?*

"Gary," the kid offered and pointed at himself, his limbs smeared with perspiration. He wore a pair of Lycra bicycle shorts, his veiny snake stuffed down the right leg almost to the hem. When he lowered his hand again, he stroked the bulge lightly.

Silas gulped. Involuntarily, his pecker woke up and rolled in its cotton cradle. Even now, when he felt uglier than a lard bucket fulla armpits.

Gary's bulge shifted. He ambled toward Silas, all the time in the world. The snout of his salami was trapped right behind the seam, firming up as he petted it. "Need a snack?"

How long was that thing?

The tent was hot, and though the table shielded them from two sides, they were visible from most directions. The stuntman's cockiness left him powerless, and his appetite sloshed over the edges of his common sense.

Silas trembled a little, and his mouth got wet at the risk and rudeness of it. *Everything he loved, on a plate.* Normally he'd have crooked his head and taken this kid to the honeywagon for a quick BJ. What did it matter? His nuts ached, snugged tight by celibacy. He hadn't had sex, even jerked off, in a month-plus.

Gary's tool had gotten fully rigid, stretching the blue Lycra away from his body as he advanced. A wet blotch marked the fabric over the swollen mushroom cap. He kneaded his schlong in invitation. "C'mon, guy."

Silas's brow clouded in confusion. What was wrong with him? Friendly, no-strings hookup, and he couldn't even muster a smile. Some internal switch had been thrown. Hell, five years ago, this coulda been him on location, flogging his hog in a pair of bike shorts and lobbing come-ons to get attention. Ten minutes from now and it'd be a fun memory... a goofy escapade he'd confess to Kurt over a beer.

Here, this gangly punk waggled relief in his face: lean, hard, and horned up. At the end of the day, it'd just be a blowjob or butt rutting or whatever they ended up doing. And who would know or care or remember anyways?

I would.

As if scalded, Silas dropped the banana on the table. It tottered onto the floor, but he didn't bend to pick it up.

The leggy stuntman's smile faltered, as if he knew he'd misread the pinball but hoped to tilt the machine. He tucked his fingers in his waistband and tipped his hips. His branch of meat was a fat J from crotch to inner thigh. "You need some help?"

"Naw." Silas stared him in the eye and nodded firmly. "I'm good." Whatever he needed did not involve hanging around on a film set trying to bag sweaty strangers out of boredom.

That was it: all of this strutting and prowling... bored him.

I know better.

He nodded again. Nothing was the same. He'd get through the next four days, put *Undercover Lovers* to bed, and then haul his ass to Louisiana if he had to ride a raft all the way there. *Fuckleberry Finn.*

The easy smile lingered on Gary's pleasant face. This one wasn't used to rejection. He shrugged but didn't drop his shoulders fully. "You sure?"

Silas frowned. "I'm not good at being sure of anything."

Except he *was* sure, sure of one thing, and that was gone for good.

TRIP finally left his pigsty because he was too embarrassed to face the maid while she scaled the grim Himalayas of wrappers and cans.

He spent the afternoon sitting at the Westside piers, drawing and arguing with himself. The wind churning off the Hudson whipped the trees hard. Finally, hunger and a lingering sense of his own insanity drove him home for lunch and sunblock.

"Trip Spector? I'm Kurt." A small dapper man with salt and pepper hair stood on the bar's stoop right in front of Trip's front door. "Silas's friend."

"Bogusz?" Trip shifted his weight on the sidewalk. What was he doing here? *My archnemesis.*

"You're taller than I expected." Kurt sported a herringbone suit, but no tie.

"I don't have time for any bullshit." Everything had burned down and this cocky schtoonk came by to kick the ashes? "We already broke up. You win."

Kurt raised a cup of Starbucks. "He said you were obtuse, but fuck's sake."

"I'm not interested."

He raised one dark eyebrow. "Duh. I'm not here for kicks."

"Yeah." Trip didn't need any more proof he'd fucked up. "I'm saying no thanks."

"I'm not here about your pitiful sex life. Or Silas, even. That's between you two and your big diddler." Kurt scowled, but he didn't move out of the way. The strong gusts made his jacket flap around him.

Trip snatched his keys out with a *blang-jangle*. "I think that will do for my thankless crap ration today. Thanks."

"Right." Kurt took a guzzle of coffee and made a sour face. "Gotta get upstairs and sit on your scrawny ass some more? Better yet: why don't you head to Port Authority and watch a junkie pick a fight with the wind?"

Trip jerked his head to the side. "Excuse me?"

"You don't have a job. You blew the Fox deal. You don't even have a project to piddle around with. You've sent a single résumé out since you shit-canned yourself—to the *New York Times* art department. I checked. You won't return calls. Or e-mail."

For two blinks, Trip weighed the wisdom of scuttling back to the piers or hiding out at Ben and Jillian's. The uncanny wind scoured the street, pushing at both of them and pasting his clothes against his body. Tattered newspaper flags flapped around a streetlight.

"This morning is the first fucking time you've left your house in nine days." Kurt wiped his face.

"Are you spying on me?"

"Jesus H. Christmas." A Gucci briefcase sat propped against the door behind his leg. "I'm trying to have a conversation with you. I've been trying to talk—"

Trip ignored the little bastard. For once, being taller than someone let him feel confident. Kurt might be in better shape and make a fuck of a lot more money, but he came up to Trip's shoulder. The primitive pleasure of shouldering an adversary out of the way surged in Trip's chest. His keys clinked in his hand and he opted to just climb the stairs.

Kurt scuffed out of the way and bent to pick up his sleek briefcase.

"Piss off, Bogusz. I don't need any grief. Silas and I are done, anyways." He jammed his key in the lock.

"I don't need to stalk people, Drip. You do understand that, yes?" He sipped the coffee again. "Mind-boggling. Gimme five minutes. I'll pay for your time." Kurt rooted in his pockets.

Trip turned. "What?" He couldn't believe the arrogance.

"I'll pay you to listen for five minutes." He scraped bills out of his wallet. A couple of hundreds that fluttered in the wind, eager to blow away.

"What are you, Lex Luthor?" Trip stood on the threshold and stared down at the Kurt's stubborn face and the folded cash in his hand.

"I'm serious."

Trip didn't answer, but he didn't close the door. Out of the swirling air, the foyer seemed unnaturally quiet. He trudged up the crooked red stairs to his front door one flight up. Kurt climbed the steps behind him. He unlocked and entered his apartment but didn't bother to invite Kurt in.

Trip dropped his backpack before he turned.

"I see why he digs you." Kurt scanned the space with a vague smile on his face. He tossed the money on the kitchen counter. "You have a real gift for being a pain in the ass." A snicker. "Evil twin."

Trip tried to suss the angle. *Ugh.* Kurt probably needed some shitty concept art or a poster drawn. "Five minutes." Nothing he could say would matter, and much as Trip hated to admit it, he could use that cash on the counter. He'd forgotten what it was like to be an out-of-work illustrator. "How did you know about the *New York Times*?"

"A little bird." Kurt took another mouthful of coffee. "Rey Arzeno paints for us. He clocked your name."

Trip didn't nod, or smile, or whatever it was he'd normally do with a person he didn't loathe. "Tick tock."

"May I sit down?"

"Are you tired?"

Kurt drained the coffee and set the cup on the table. "I had a gander at your graphic novel. *Scratch*."

"That's impossible."

He sighed. "You mean you didn't draw the book? Or you mean that I don't have eyes?" *Blink blink*. He picked up a Guy Fawkes mask from the shelves and pursed his lips at it.

"It's dead."

"As in, you tried to *kill* it." Kurt held the mask up a moment, next to his face. "A masked man once said that ideas are bulletproof."

Trip's eyes bulged in irritation. "It's not published. Never will be. It was a shitty idea anyways."

Kurt replaced the mask on the shelf. "For someone who keeps fucking up so spectacularly, you sure are certain about everything." He rummaged for something in his briefcase.

Thwap.

A new black ITOYA portfolio, eleven by seventeen, slapped onto the drafting table in front of Trip.

Kurt creased his forehead dispassionately. "Helluva hallucination." His face stayed neutral as a balance sheet.

Confused, Trip spun the portfolio to face him before he flipped open the leatherette.

Scratch.

Puckish eyes teased him from inside a clear plastic sleeve, now lovingly colored in ripe jewel tones. Silas stared back at him and reached out. Well, not *Silas*-Silas, but the orchid-silver demon-Silas he'd penciled and inked for the cover of issue one... beautiful as a prisoner's dream.

"Fucking ferocious," Kurt said, and Trip didn't bother to agree.

Every muscle, every hair, every glint in the cover urged the reader to take his hand, to surrender and slip inside.

Got an Itch?

Trip shook his head. Somehow, the double-size page had been printed in full musky color. Someone had painted his pencils and inks till they blazed and flexed under his scrutiny.

Dolores!

He knew her work so well, and she surely knew his. Without any guidance from him, Dolores had breathed life into his inked panels: the burnished skin and the forsythia glitter of the feral glare. The pale violet of the exposed nipple and the downy sweep of forearm and the faint blue of blood thrumming under the sinful skin: seductive and savage.

"Who wouldn't pay to fuck that?" Kurt frowned appreciatively.

"I haven't"—a garbage-strewn alley in olive-grays and browns. The slutty curse-thugs. The subterranean passage lit by pitchforks. Extreme close-up of the Judge's knotty knuckles as he held his massive gavel—"seen these...." Dolores had painted the crepe-y translucency of the scarred skin so faithfully he could taste the brimstone.

You have been judged!

"Yet." A page of narrow panels showing the library and zooming in on the cursed book. "How did... you...?" In Chicago, he'd sacrificed all this to slave in the Fox mines, drawing sexless dolls for Cliff. Now he didn't even have that excuse. "I haven't... seen these colored."

"Artists." Kurt snorted. "Ridiculous."

Next painting, Scratch's muscular frame perched on a ledge like a bird of prey, guarding his lover, licked by moonlight. He could hear the husky voice calling him into the dark: *Dreamer.*

All of *Scratch 1: Horn Gate* was here, carefully assembled in the protective sleeves.

Trip pressed the heels of his hands against his eyes as if they might pop out of his skull. "Bullshit. This project is dead and buried. You should know; you watched me dig the fucking grave in Chicago."

"Ah-ah-ahh." Kurt wagged his finger. "Ideas are bulletproof."

"I don't understand." Trip flicked through the later pages: the rescue, the seduction, the abduction. He wanted to linger but needed answers too.

Kurt ran his finger along the edge of a bookshelf.

"You've had this and didn't show me." Trip frowned. "Took your fucking time. What do you want?"

"The early bird may get the worm, but the second rat gets the cheese."

Trip flipped the polyglass page, knowing what came next.

Kurt tapped the table as if hypnotized. "Ah. This one."

There it was, as he'd imagined it: Scratch opening the Horn Gate. His double-page splash showed an enormous ring woven out of antlers and cinders. Inside the spiky, spiraling portal, Scratch cradled his bruised mortal lover as they escaped into their hellish happily ever after.

Fool.

"Mmph." *Plip.* A drop fell from his chin and hit the plastic. He smeared it away surreptitiously.

"Exactly." Kurt nodded once. "Everyone I've shown it to has had the same reaction. To your artwork. The concept. Even the title."

"*Scratch.*" Trip touched Silas's face and discovered Kurt scowling at him.

"Off the charts." Kurt drummed his fingers next to the portfolio. "I have two manga companies in a bidding war before I've even licensed the damn thing."

He wiped his eye. "You have no right."

"And did I claim otherwise, Mr. Spector?" Eye roll. "Lucky that you're so goddamn talented, because you can be unbelievably dim."

Trip pawed through the protective vinyl sleeves, drunk on Dolores's careful painting, and then returned to the Horn Gate and the two men standing before it. Without meaning to, he'd given Scratch's transformed lover his own body. He wished Silas was here to savor these with him. His guilt strangled his pleasure in the pages. "Why would you waste money paying for colors?" These pages would have cost upward of two or three grand.

"I wouldn't."

"Then—"

"Our mutual acquaintance." Kurt squinted in brittle impatience. "Obviously."

"No." Trip shut his mouth. "Why would Silas do that?"

"May I speak frankly?" Kurt braced his hands on the table. "You're a totally unworthy opponent. By some undead miracle, you managed to find my best friend in a bush and rug-pull his entire life. You made him happy. He made you smart. But somehow you fucked that up so spectacularly that you have no job, no book, no man, and no options." For all the bile in his words, Kurt's face remained dispassionate. "Every fucking door slammed and locked in your own face, by your own hand. And a stomach full of swallowed keys."

Trip laughed without pleasure. "Right. You're right." He coughed and wagged his head.

"This isn't charity. I can't *stand* your ass, but—" Kurt shrugged one shoulder. "—I respect your work." He waved a casual hand at the gigantic handmade comic on the table. "Silas paid for that dame in South America to sprinkle her Photoshop pussy-pudding over these. He brought me the book because he had a hunch that we might be able to do some business."

"What business? You make video games."

"Obviously. Games need stories and heroes. Entire franchises have grown up around a single hook or playstyle. *T-Wrecks* started as a children's book. *Chopping Mall* happened when I predicted linear shooters had run dry and binge players wanted gore in their sandboxes. We evolve."

Trip hesitated in confusion. "You want to buy *Scratch* for a game?" He remembered Rina laughing at him on this holy floor. "It's a romance. It's an erotic paranormal romance."

Kurt grinned at that, steepling his fingers under his bearded chin. "Mmh."

Trip scoffed, "No killing or shooting. There's not even much combat. Hero's almost naked most of the time and seduces anything on two legs."

"I give you...." Kurt reached into the glossy briefcase and tossed a small black claw on the table between them: three spindly plastic fingers rounded into bulbous tips. "The Talon."

"Scratch doesn't have chicken claws." Trip shrugged.

"Not costume." Kurt held up a scolding finger. "No. No. It's a prototype. An accessory for all major platforms."

"I don't get it."

"Surprise." Kurt sighed, impatient. "It's a wireless game controller unlike anything currently in development or production."

Trip picked up the little gizmo, which weighed more than he'd expected. The surface felt slightly squishy, and the fanned prongs could be bent into position. "A joystick?"

"For your heart." Kurt tapped his temple. "Short arm is an ear piece, second's a microphone and photodetector, and the longest rests against the carotid artery." He tapped his throat under his jawline. "Measures pulse, temperature, humidity, position, conductivity, and biometrics and a bunch of other stuff you don't need to understand and probably couldn't."

Trip held it up to his right ear but didn't actually attach it. "For games."

"Think of it as an *emotional* joystick. It uses a player's hormonal and mental state to direct actions on-screen. Coolest tech ever." Kurt's grin took ten years off him.

"That's... unreal." Trip turned it over. The longest claw sported a flat angled pad a little wider at the tip, almost like a tongue.

"Only a prototype at this point. My team needs to recode the driver, playtest, and we got a shitload of research coming in from Cambridge. My lead programmer wants to take point, and I mean to let him. Which means I need a unique game, pronto."

"And your game needs a hero." Trip looked at Scratch, who looked back with pitiless eyes from the oversized *Horn Gate* cover.

"A hero that seduces his audience. A story that isn't slaughtermatic. Love and death. An emotional rollercoaster without rails. Maybe some diabolical puzzles and some gothic horror. Think about it: we ditch violence, what do we need?"

"Fucking…"

"Ding-ding." Kurt tapped his nose. "Sex."

"…hell." Trip covered his open mouth with his hand. The idea seemed crazy and possible at the same time, as if he'd pivoted and walked through a brick wall.

Like chess: you have to move.

"Listen, 80 percent of gamers are male because 95 percent of games depend on primeval fight-or-flight code hardwired into XY primates." Kurt cracked his knuckles. "*The Sims* shook the snow globe, epic best seller with ladies. Get me? There's this whole audience itching for a new type of game. Something subtler and more cooperative. Complex characters. A provocative journey."

"A romance."

"Gold star, Spector." Kurt sniffed. "My craziest programmer brings me this wacky-ass technology, but we got no game to drive it. I've spent four months combing through pitches. Rut city. Rehashes and retreads."

"You wanna use *Scratch* to launch this… Talon." Trip held it up and spun the little claw. "For a video game." Trip felt like he was trying to have a conversation underwater… at night… in Korean.

"Gah. Yes! You really *aren't* bright. Well, eventually we can pitch it as a movie, too, but Hollywood is in the shitter at the moment. A title like this will be a fucking rainmaker for us. Build a massive audience way faster. I mean, duh? C'mon: Scratch, the interactive incubus?" Kurt crossed his arms so tightly his elbows almost met. "It's like *Scooby-Doo* with boners."

Trip stared at the hypnotic colors of his filthiest fantasies smeared on Bristol boards by Dolores. Maybe they'd hire her as well. He regarded his shoes, feeling like a nine-year-old. He thought of Max. *More like a four-year-old.* "You can't show that."

"Fuck can't." Kurt jerked a thumb at the superhero posters on Trip's wall. "Unbored Games already shows people getting blown up and butchered at strip malls. Nudity even! *Miss Demeanor* takes place in a leper colony bordello." He took a breath.

Trip wished he could ask someone. *Silas.* "What's your nefarious plan?"

"You let me ride you, and I'll do the same, Speck." Kurt sat back. "'S'not Hollywood, but you give us a shot, and that horny son of a bitch will be in millions of living rooms within three years. We'd license the graphic novel, the character, the name. Granted, you'd lose out on a movie deal… for a while."

What movie deal? "The comic doesn't exist." Silas had done this for him, and for the book. Maybe there was still a chance.

"Yeah, you screwed that pooch, but a printed comic only costs, what, eighty grand? A hundred? I spend that on three TV spots. Truth is, the cost of your graphic novel would be absorbed by the marketing budget. How long is each issue?"

"I'd only finished the first—"

Kurt studied the cracked ceiling as if it were an abacus. "Fine. So we'd commission a, say... twelve-issue arc to start? Maybe through Image or IDW, so we keep control. Build up interest in your li'l devil while Ziggy debugs that bendy bastard." He thrust his chin at the Talon. "That's *my* blockbuster."

Trip's entire body hung breathless as if waiting for a sneeze that wouldn't come. "And Silas has discussed all this with you."

"No. He leaps first, then looks. He has hunches. Instincts. Faith." Kurt rocked back, and his face hardened. "You're like me, aren't you. You want proof. You want to be paid every time. Silas makes his monsters for joy. 'Cause it's fun." He sneered jokingly. "Dolt. But it's why I love him."

What?

"Probably why *you* love him." Kurt frowned.

Trip looked down at the portfolio, but he saw Silas beaming at him while they drew each other. Silas sketching the Judge, then holding him after. Silas made up as Scratch in Chicago. Silas crushed when Trip had rained poison down on all his best intentions.

"No one's making you walk through the door, Spector. No one's taking this damn project away from you or selling you up the river. He's not your shitty parents or exes or whoever the hell has left you so gun-shy and fun phobic." Kurt pushed a box of tissues across the table at him.

Trip realized what Silas had tried to give him. He realized how much his betrayal at C2E2 must have cost. What had he done? Unable to stop himself, he gasped and sat down before his knees turned to noodles.

Kurt pondered him, tipped his head to the side as if he was contemplating a roach crawling across bone china. "For the record, you treated him like complete shit."

Trip nodded.

"Thing is, Goolsby's gotten so good at reading between the lines that he stopped *reading* the lines. He trusted you."

"I didn't know." Trip's heart jerked back and forth in his chest like a trapped squirrel. "Any of it."

"No kidding, jackass! Even after that, he just handed a brave new world to you. That's the master plan. You wanna ditch, just pay him back the three grand for the colors. No harm, no foul. And fuck *you* for being an idiot. Fuck *you* for hurting my friend."

"That's not what—"

"I think he's retarded to want anyone, let alone you, but he does."

Trip opened his mouth to protest and realized he could not. He stared toward the window at the blustery daylight, wishing he could thank Silas for saving his life before he'd set about destroying it. "He always wants to play with his toys."

"And you want to protect them."

Trip shrugged, feeling stupid.

"Me? I'd rather pay for what I get. I think all this monogamy shit is for suckers." Kurt shook his gray-flecked head, looking older than he could possibly be. "But if you want to play in his sandbox, you can't handle your heart like a packaged action figure and never use it."

Trip sniffed. "Mint-on-card."

"Whatever. They're called action figures for a fucking reason."

Trip rose. "Have...." He closed the portfolio under Kurt's ruthless scrutiny. "Have you ever said something you couldn't unsay?"

"*Pfft.* Every time I open my fucking mouth, Speck. We're more alike than you think."

"This project isn't just mine. I mean, he's everywhere in it. Silas."

"I noticed." Kurt closed the briefcase deliberately. "Maybe you can convince him that Team Scratch needs a good creature designer. We're gonna need models, composites... hell, makeup for the street teams."

No. Trip started to object and thought better of it. *Pressure.* "What am I s'posedta do?"

"You're an artist. Get creative."

Trip blinked. "There's not exactly a straight line between point A and point B, here."

"He's a guy. If you can't appeal to his heart, appeal to his vanity."

"Y'know...." Trip glanced at Kurt. Much as it pained him, he could see their similarities. And just as quickly, he fought the urge to judge himself and Kurt and everyone else, swinging the fucking gavel down just 'cause it felt good in his hand. "I may have to stop hating the idea of you. I could use a good enemy."

"Suit yourself. You'll always be Drip to me." But somehow the way he said it wasn't an insult.

A tickling wisp of anticipation made Trip shiver. *Why not?* Maybe he could tear the package open and get on with his goddamned life.

"So... wanna come out and play?" Kurt steepled his fingers under his beard. "Unless you got a better idea."

"I need to think about it." Trip petted the portfolio as if he expected it to wake up and maul him. "Can I keep this?"

"It's already yours. He just let me deliver it. I'll have contracts drawn up."

"Fat chance." Trip choke-chuckled in resignation.

"Well, you won't know until you talk to him." Kurt flicked the Unbored card onto the table and picked up the now-empty Gucci briefcase. "Horrible. I don't know which of you is worse."

Reaching for the little rectangle of cardboard, Trip shrugged and took it. "I do."

24

AFTER three days of binging on *Teen Wolf* and Little Debbies, Trip ended up in the Monster Hospital supervising amputations and transplants at *Chez* Stone.

At the absolute last minute, Jillian agreed to brunch with a few actor chums who'd flown in for a wedding to which she wasn't invited. She called Trip in a panic because they could only meet this particular Saturday, and Selene, the dyspeptic babysitter, had gone to Guatemala to build latrines... leaving Trip in the shit.

As it happened, on this particular Saturday, June 15, Trip had sworn he was not going to leave his apartment for fear of doing something idiotic. Today was the *Undercover Lovers* wrap out at Silvercup, and a squishy, treacherous corner of him wanted to give in to his worst stalking impulses.

He was already enough of a schmuck. He'd spent seventy-two hours mulling Kurt's offer but hadn't worked up the cojones to call Silas. Having ingested every molecule of hydrogenated, freezer-burned, shrink-wrapped carbo yum-yums in his apartment, he agreed to babysit so he wouldn't jump any guns.

Trip rang the bell again. On the other side of the door, feet thumped down the stairs.

"Mom. Jeez." Max's high whine said plenty about the morning they'd had, and when he opened the door, he broadcast his annoyance through a pair of safety goggles.

Jillian lay across the hall with her tongue stuck out.

"Hey, kiddo." Trip waved hello to Max and winked at Jillian. "I see your mom died again."

Max shrugged, stepped over her legs, and led the way back to the kitchen.

Behind him, Trip heard Jillian clamber to her feet and curse.

The Stones' kitchen was painted a chocolatey brown and lined with stainless cabinets and appliances. As much as Jillian loved cooking, Ben hated it, but he knew exactly where his bread was buttered. After hosting that many *shabbos* dinners, Ben had gone all out with the upgrades, and rumor had it Jillian had fucked him almost senseless out of gratitude.

Max adjusted his goggles and seated himself at the round table in the breakfast nook. Pieces of action figures lay out on newspaper. Apparently, he had some kind of terrifying craft project underway.

Trip went to the fridge and poured himself a tall glass of seltzer with a splash of cranberry. He took a cold swig and then went to check on the boy wonder. He almost choked.

Max had needle-nose pliers, a selection of files and awls, and several X-Acto blades arranged in careful rows. He'd plugged in a soldering iron and a hot glue gun, and they rested on an old plate that showed scorches from previous operations.

"Oy!" Trip gestured at the hardware. "This looks like Build-a-Bear for mental patients."

Max tapped the table. "I'm doing surgery." And he was, transplanting appendages with ruthless efficiency. "What?"

"I'm gonna mutilate myself."

"So don't touch anything. It's fine." He bent to plug in a small grinder.

Trip ventured closer. "See, you are a doctor."

As he watched, Max stuck the Alien head and parts of a plastic octopus onto a gargoyle's body, which resembled the many-limbed lovechild of Conan and Cthulhu.

"Yeesh." Max hissed and shook his hand. He blew on his fingers.

Trip forehead furrowed. "Is that safe?"

"Duh. That's why you're here." Max analyzed an orange leg that wouldn't do what he wanted. "I cut anything off, you bring it to the ER."

"Hurrah." Trip sat down at the table with his glass. "Although, I can promise that I'm more likely to get hurt than you are, cutting up dolls."

Max gave an incredulous smirk. "They're action figures."

"Yeah, 'action figure' was what Hasbro called them because they figured boys wouldn't play with dolls."

Max eyed him. "Duh."

Trip leaned against the chair arms. "How is it not a doll?"

"I dunno." Max inspected the little sinewy body. "Doll means a buncha other stuff." A hot blob glooped onto the torso, and Max prodded it with a nail. "Why's it matter?"

"It…." Trip shut his mouth and opened it. "Doesn't. I guess. It's just a word."

A wet towel lay folded on the table, already streaked with dust and smears of melted plastic.

"I'm learning how. 'S'way better than coloring." Max hissed at something and scooped up the soldering iron and a long clamp. "My mom likes it 'cause there aren't lines for me to follow." Bitter black smoke sizzled up from the little body. "Almost got him."

"Huh." Trip sipped his seltzer. Seeing all the pieces on the table made him anxious in a way he couldn't rationalize. What did it matter? Max was having fun. Hell, he was making something. Trip reached out to examine a couple of the dismembered figures. "Y'know? Some of these are worth real money. Or were."

"H'yeah. We bought them on eBay."

"Digging up the graveyard. Dr. Frankenstein discovers the Internet."

Max held up a headless torso. "I paid almost twelve bucks for Hawkman."

There had to be at least four action figures torn apart on the table for their parts. *Transplants 'R Us*. The collector in Trip cringed. He'd always taken such obsessive care of his toys. He had kept a couple mint-on-card that were worth hundreds now. "I guess those aren't mint anymore."

"I don't collect 'em."

"I could never do that." Trip fiddled with a tiny leg.

"Whaddayamean?"

"Put pieces together like that."

"But you draw things." Max used some kind of tiny screwdriver and a pair of tweezers to pluck vigorously at part of the head. "Didn't you ever fix your toys?"

"I was too nervous I'd cut off my arm or poke out my eye."

"That's why there are parents and teachers." Max chipped at a foot. "Prob'ly a good idea someone looks out for us until we finish growing up."

"I don't think that happens. Ever." Trip fiddled with the little arm. "I think you grow up as long as you'll let yourself."

"Growing-ups!" Max laughed and put the soldering iron down on the plate and shifted his goggles to the top of his head. "See? He's mutated now." Max wiggled the wings about a centimeter.

"They move! How'd you—? They're not supposed to move."

Max gave a lopsided little-boy shrug. "Dad helped me add two extra joints for the wings." He leaned over the little body, his tongue trapped between his teeth as he sculpted with his tiny fingers. "I usually start out with a plan, but then it doesn't always go that way."

"Happy accidents." Trip tried to remember who had said that. *Silas*. He shook his head. *Move the fuck on*. At some point he'd have to give himself permission to stop hoping. He thought of Kurt's Talon and the *Scratch* game that might have been. *Mighty-might*.

"What?"

Trip exhaled. "What-what?"

"You made a face."

"No. Nothing." He shifted his attention back to Max's experiment. "Happy accidents are a good thing. Best things I've ever drawn came out of screwing up, even though it scares me."

Max studied the mutant figure and then Trip. "Why are you scared of a drawing?"

"Not *scared*-scared. Just nervous." Trip covered his embarrassment with a fizzy sip.

"Dad says being scared is good for your heart."

"He's probably right." Trip smiled. "I knew I was making a mistake, but made it anyways."

Max got very quiet. He fidgeted with the little figure again. He frowned at the toy and then laid it down carefully, making sure he didn't injure any of his modifications.

"Is that what happened with your boyfriend?" He didn't look up. "Silas?"

Trip lowered his hands and let out a breath. Jillian must have talked to Ben, and walls had little ears. The Stones worried about him. "What do you know about that?"

"Nothing. My mom said you were happy with him. You seemed pretty happy."

"I was." Trip picked up someone's little green PVC arm. *Hulk? Martian Manhunter?* What would his dad have done if he'd pulled his toys apart? "For a while there." He felt selfish. For a moment, he envied Max his cool parents, everything ahead. For a split second, he wished he could go back and undo everything, retcon and get it right this time. *From Scratch.* He shrugged.

"But now you're all depressed."

"When I was growing up, kids didn't usually talk about this stuff."

Max scowled at him dubiously. "You mean 'cause you like guys." He shrugged. "Whatsa big deal?"

"Good question." *Just a word.*

"Silas seemed nice. At the show. He sure likes you."

Trip dropped the green arm. "Not anymore. I did something stupid and mean."

Max wrinkled his nose and paused to wipe his sculpting nail on the wet towel. "Dad says people mostly act dumb when they're scared."

"Maybe so. You think I get scared?"

"Everybody gets scared sometimes." Max shrugged. "Mom is scared of Freddy Krueger and he's a joke."

"I probably get *too* scared sometimes. Too much imagination."

"Prob'ly. That's prob'ly why you draw monsters and bad guys so good."

"'Cause I'm not done growing up?"

Max unplugged the glue gun. "Prob'ly why they don't suck. Y'know?"

Trip snorted in agreement. *No shit.* "Well, you're right. But we still get scared. Grown-ups."

"Duh." Max wrapped the cord around his hand. "Like this one time I stepped on a nail at the lake, and Mom had to take it out and she was crying and trying to goof around, but she was more scared than I was. I knew. Her heart went crazy on my ear."

"She imagined the worst thing."

"But it wasn't the worst. I didn't even cry. Well, not much. It just felt weird 'cause I didn't expect it. My feet were cold."

"Your mom loves you more than anything." Trip remembered the nail incident. Max had been six, maybe? He could imagine how panicked Jillian had been in the moment. He remembered Ben's gray face when Trip had taken muffins and juice to the hospital. "More than *Friday the 13th* even."

Max laughed at that. "I dunno. That's a lot." He put the smoking glue gun to one side.

"She wanted to rescue you. And you wanted to rescue her."

"We were both scared, but we didn't run away." He gave a little boy nod that summed up the logic. He poked at his shoe. "I still have a mark. It was so gross." He grinned proudly. "It, like, *gooped* out. Not like on shows."

Trip nodded.

Max scraped his shreds of plastic and glue together into a small heap of olive and tan, all the leftover muscle and tentacles. "But if she stepped on a nail I'd run to her, not away."

Trip brushed the scraps of plastic into his ink-stained hand. "'Cause you're brave."

Max snorted. "No, dummy. 'Cause she loves me." He shrugged. "And I love her."

"I do too. Your mom and dad don't mess around."

Trip had a flash of infant Max in his crib with hands the size and color of erasers. He shut his yap and nodded before he said anything mushy. He couldn't wait to know Max as an adult, to watch him wisecracking with kids of his own. At least that was something to look forward to.

"So...." Max squinted one eye and pursed his lip. "Why don't you invite Silas for *shabbos* next Friday?"

"Not a good idea."

Max rolled his eyes. "And since that's dumb, I'm betting you're scared, which is even dumber because Silas is nice. Scary doesn't mean *bad*."

And every idea is scary at first. Trip stopped breathing for a moment.

Max pulled off his goggles.

"Sh-eesh." Trip sat back and crossed his arms loosely. "When did you get to be such a player?"

"I dunno." Max seemed confused by the word.

"It's a compliment. 'Player' just means you're good at the game. Life. I been trying to figure this out for a month, and you did it in about ten seconds."

Max's gap-toothed grin lit up his face. "Oh. Cool."

"While you were mutilating dolls, even."

"Action figures." Max brandished his plastic chimera.

"'S'just a word, though." Trip held up the handful of chips and slivers. "Y'know, you're pretty sneaky for a superhero. No one's gonna see through your secret disguise."

"What disguise?"

Trip crossed his eyes. "A snaggletoothed, cowlicked dwarf."

"Shut up!"

"With a booger ranch and a soap allergy."

"You suck." Max shoved him.

Trip looked down at the plastic shrapnel. "You want me to throw these in the garbage?"

Max groaned. "No way. They're not garbage."

"Sorry! Sheesh."

"I'm doing Poison Ivy next." Max opened a coffee can so Trip could scrape the plastic flotsam inside.

"If you say so."

"These are my..." Max rattled the can with his pudgy hands. "...happy accidents."

Trip stopped moving. A bitter bubble of laughter burst out of him. "That's good."

Max held up his little melted-together monster. "I think he looks better like this."

Trip considered the messy creation in Max's palm. *No such thing as a grown-up.* "I agree." He grinned. "What happens to him now?"

Max snorted in exaggerated patience. "I play with him."

"Oh." Trip felt like a dolt. No packaging to worry about, was there? He laughed out loud, startling himself. "Lollipops and rainbows."

"That's what my mom says all the time. She's nuts."

"She seems that way, but only if you don't know her. And that... would be a mistake."

"Yeah."

"You just reminded me of a joke." Trip drained his glass and held it up. "Who discovered water?"

"What?"

"Old Jewish riddle." Trip crossed his arms. "'Who discovered water?' You know that one?"

"Gimme a sec." Max scowled at the floor, plucking at his lip. "I dunno."

"That's the answer." Trip winked. He opened his arms and did a great impression of Max's mom in *Fiddler on the Roof.* "Who discovered water? I dunno, but it wasn't a fish."

Max didn't react. He waved his little boy hand at the tools on the table. "So when you have Silas back—"

"I don't have anyone. Silas may only wanna be a friend. Or not even."

The tiny homunculus stood on the table between them, ugly and serene.

"Sure." Max sighed melodramatically. "So... *now* will you draw me with a chunk of my head missing?" Blink, blink.

"Deal." The kid had probably calculated his charm assault, but Trip didn't mind.

"Something really gross I can take to school." Max folded his crumpled, crusty newspapers and threw them away.

"Duh!"

"And don't tell Dad." He punched Trip's knuckles with a goblin's smile. "I want it to be a surprise." He scurried out the door into the hallway.

Trip wondered if Silas would go early to the OutRun on Pride Sunday, if it was an awful idea to crash, and just as quickly decided he didn't care if it was awful because it was the growing-up thing to do.

"Max?" Trip paused at the table. "Thanks for being smart enough for both of us." He wanted to make sure Max had heard him, but by the time he reached the hall, his godson had already scrambled upstairs to his room to save the galaxy with the glued-together hero he'd built out of monsters.

"CAN you fix my skull?"

A muscle-bound drag-waitress held out a fuzzy wet piece of brain to Trip.

"Makeup's right there." Trip pointed toward the long tent he'd watched for an hour from his chilly predawn perch in Central Park. The butch waitress mumbled thankfully and clacked in that direction.

After 5:00 a.m. on Gay Pride Sunday, the lightening sky showed a giant bowed banner that read "OUTRUN: WALKIN' CLOSET." The tents and temporary buildings rose suddenly around him and spat out zombies in a steady stream, the apocalypse in reverse.

Trip stood on a little knoll and surveyed Kurt's army of groggy volunteers: half in festering makeup and half in T-shirts with a hungry, angry Closet Monster on the back. He switched his portfolio from one sweaty palm to the other. The parade kicked off at noon, so the charity run would shamble ahead at eight.

Inside that makeup tent, Silas and his crew had to be whipping all their baddies into fighting shape. Every time Trip heard his voice or his laugh, he felt simultaneously elated and more than a little ill.

For two weeks Trip had weighed Kurt's offer. On Tuesday, he'd schlepped out to Silvercup only to find the *Undercover Lovers* set demolished and Silas long gone. Never in all their months together had Trip paid real attention to the shoot or Silas's work. Another bungle in what seemed a *leopard* of blind spots. The dark rectangle where the makeup trailer had sat told him nothing. Silas had left and the show was done. "TV shoot down near New Orleans," they said. They wouldn't even let him leave a note.

In some strange way, seeing the empty studio made Trip feel like he had managed to catch a glimpse of Silas after all.

He didn't have much time, so he'd called Kurt in a panic. Yes, Silas was heading South. No, Kurt refused to get in the middle. "Your fucking fallout," he'd said.

Out of pity, or calculation, Kurt had put him on the Unbored volunteer list for Pride… and here he was in Central Park, here and queer and not even a little proud. Horrible longing and guilt kept him frozen in place under the lemon-chiffon sky, still waiting for the sun to paint the horizon.

Better to catch Silas in private, but the crowd kept multiplying like maggots. Cheerful OutRun volunteers herded runners toward the starting line and their straggling monsters toward makeup. Trip peeked at his phone again. With the volunteer badge, all he had to do was walk in there. Tomorrow Silas would be shooting a thousand miles away with shitty reception and hot actors like low-hanging fruit.

For the past hour, Trip stood in the dark as he worked up his nerve and watched a club being built. A good fifty yards or so from the makeup tent, a crew of burly carpenters had erected a temporary disco. Trip had never seen a dance floor being hammered into place with mallets, but he saw where the speakers and the bars would hang. Drills whined nearby, and he heard the dry *squa-crack* of a crowbar splitting wood. Someone's iPod pumped Pink remixes.

Between the tent and the emerging party space, chairs and tables had been set up, about which some forty zombies ate doughnuts, chatted, or texted while they hung around waiting for their cue. *Surreal.* Pallets of lumber and lights lined one path that stretched past them and the trees between the makeup tents and the disco.

Weirdest thing, the unfinished party space looked a lot like the wrecked sex lounge from the climax of *Scratch*'s first issue: shattered bar, jagged stage, rubble crunching underfoot. The only thing missing was the Horn Gate, chewing the air around the heroes. Watching the construction, Trip felt like he was flipping through *Scratch #1* backward.

A hollow *clang* behind him drew Trip's attention back to the lumber-lined path that bent toward the dance floor.

Twenty feet away, a brawny man in a pair of overalls and a white tank top squatted, using his square hands to balance a three-foot box on one shoulder. As he strode past the building materials, the fur of his thick forearm shone dark gold in the gloaming, and the denim stretched over his round haunch. Raw maleness on the hoof.

Jeepers.

The easy confidence of that massive body took Trip's breath away as it crunched across the construction like a... barbarian. The man paused briefly to answer some kind of inaudible question from someone hidden behind the lumber. Even before the square face turned, Trip anticipated the molasses drawl, felt it in his bones the way dogs smell an oncoming storm.

Heart in his throat, feet disobedient, he found himself taking jerky steps into the undead mob breaking their fast. Trip's head pounded, and he fought the impulse to duck out of sight and disappear among the trees and corpses.

"I'll be right...." Silas stopped when their eyes met. "Back."

Trip held up a hand in greeting. Relief swamped him and his legs wobbled. He grabbed the back of one of the folding chairs for a moment to steady himself.

Silas didn't smile or speak, just shifted his weight. He looked so wholesome and handsome in his overalls and soaked undershirt that Trip's mouth went dry.

"I didn't wanna bug you working." Trip pointed toward the stage. "You a carpenter now too?"

Silas held up a hand. "Fuck off, Spector." His hazel eyes were dead and cold.

"I will." Trip counted to three. *Easier said than done.* "If you want."

Silas shifted his weight. "Left some cowls curing in their lockup. I'm working." His bicep flexed to keep the box balanced. "My team is executing. I did the designs."

"Looks great." Trip gestured at the bar. He tried to laugh casually. "Actually, this looks like—"

Silas nodded back, giving no ground. He glanced away and trudged past Trip toward the makeup tent. He said nothing, which said plenty. Just outside the entrance, he dropped the box with an ugly crash. Whatever was inside sounded heavy and broken now.

"Everybody...." A woman Trip recognized from New Year's poked her head out of the flaps. "Oh—?"

Eyes on Trip, Silas muttered. "In a minute, Tiffany."

"Kurt needs you to check in for press, and we got thirteen no-shows." She looked from Silas to Trip and back. "And we're still waiting on that flocked compound."

"A *minute*." A growl at the ground.

She blanched and vanished.

Where's a Horn Gate when you need one?

Trip approached the big man tentatively, wishing the crew across the way were building the club from his comic book and that Scratch would swoop in to help him before anyone walked away. "Silas."

Silas stopped. He wiped his hands on his chest.

"You want a hand?"

Silas huffed negatively and crossed the zombie holding area in the direction of the dance floor.

Undaunted, Trip followed. Apparently, he was gonna have to earn every millimeter on this one.

Who's counting?

Tension arced between them as they walked. A couple of volunteers and zombies waved or called to Silas and got no reply.

Trip put his free hand in his pocket. "Silvercup said you were headed south."

"H'yuh. I got offered a job by a haunted house outfit from Texas. Creature design for a chain of houses all over the US in the fall."

"Congratulations." Trip couldn't tell if he was supposed to be pleased. "What are you gonna do?"

"Well, it's health insurance, at least. Six weeks of work, and I don't have to fly down till we do castings. Feels very grown-up. But Kurt did this OutRun for Pride."

Trip exhaled. "Walkin' Closet."

"Yup." Silas stopped walking at the edge of the skeletal DJ platform.

On the ground, a pair of battered ten-gallon buckets sat tucked against a pallet. Trip reached for one.

Silas muttered, "Don't help." He squatted to lift a heavy drum in each hand. The damp swell of his shoulders bulged with the wobbly weight. The first feathery glimmers of sun traced his straining overalls and the bright fuzz on his chest.

Trip ran his eye over the temporary club's sheetrock and scaffolding like scattered panels from his comic. "How'd Kurt get permits for all this?"

"Money." Silas mock-sneered. "MTV is doing a special. Benefit for suicide hotline."

So Kurt hadn't said anything about the Talon. "Good. That sounds really good. Are you gonna—"

Silas bobbed his head cheerlessly and lugged the huge buckets across the patchwork dance floor and back toward the makeup tent. "No. I'm gonna go shoot a pilot with some friends of mine. Believe it or not, they're even paying my quote."

"That's great." Trip squeezed the slippery portfolio handle. "You make it sound like I'm judging you."

Silas arched a skeptical eyebrow. "You aren't? You didn't?"

Trip chewed on that. *Had he?*

A hairy roadie in cutoffs stepped out of their way, coiling cable from palm to elbow. He mumbled a greeting.

"I'm happy for you, Silas. I'm not jealous." Trip drifted closer to Silas, didn't touch, though close enough that he could.

"*Pfft.* All packaging, anyways."

Trip put a hand to his forehead. "And you gotta tear the packaging off anything great. Mint-on-card toys must suck."

Silas cleared his throat. "I figured you'd be waist deep in *Hero High*-jinx by now. Cliff poking your coals t'keep the heat on."

"No! Big Dog is done. Bridge burned, no do-over. I quit. Like axes and poison quit. Seriously." Trip held up a *bitch-please* hand. "I attacked Cliff in the middle of Fox. I did what you said. Everything you told me. You were right and I'm sorry."

"Great." Silas looked as grim as the Judge. "Congrats. Now I gotta job to do."

Back at the ragtag breakfast buffet, another swarm of freshly made-up ghouls had emerged and beelined toward the doughnuts and folding chairs. Silas watched them walk with a stern expression on his face.

"Tiff: silicone!" He dropped the bulky drums outside the tent and kicked them, but he didn't retreat into his tent.

Good sign?

Trip kept his tone casual. "You look great. I mean, you always look great, but it's really great to see you." He winced. "Looking great."

"You too. You haven't been eating." Silas crossed his arms.

"No. Yeah. I know." Trip thumbed the loose waistband of his cargo pants. "I've been working. I—"

"Forgot." They spoke the word in unison, same pitch even. For the first time, a reluctant smile flickered across Silas's face, until he wagged his head to shake it loose.

Silas heaved a deep breath. "Trip, why didn't you call me? Ever. Not once."

Trip opened and closed his mouth like a trout.

"Which told me a fuck of a lot about what was important."

"No."

"So you did call me?" Silas glared at him. "You called the wrong number for sixty-four days?"

"*No.*"

Silas wagged his head in disgust. "I'm so stupid! Somehow… you fuck off to parts unknown, and I'm suddenly thirteen years old and the fat loser again." He rubbed his eyes. "One more sign I need a therapist or a fucking drug addiction I can afford. Know what? I'm checking out crafty last week, hottest fucking stud tries to gobble my knob in broad daylight. Do I care?"

"Do you?" Trip wouldn't look away.

Silas seemed confused.

Trip pressed. "I don't. I don't think any of that shit matters. I think life is complicated and messy."

"I can't." Silas turned to consider the tent, his back a wide wall.

Finally, Trip said aloud what he'd thought for over a month and wished Silas would look at him when he said it. "I missed you."

For several moments, Silas didn't react. His back remained still as he faced the trees. Then his shoulders shook, and at first Trip thought he was crying, but the nonsound coming out of him was uglier than tears. Silas began to laugh without making any sound or sign of happiness. Finally, he glanced back at Trip and laughed so hard he trembled, his mouth turned down.

"What?"

"Not a thing." Silas punched his thigh hard, then shook his head and spat.

"I'm sorry."

"You hurt me," he said. His hoarse voice made the truth sound final.

"I know. I know I did."

Silas wheezed and wiped his nose. "Trip, everything can't come from one person. It's a two-way deal. But there are certain things you can never undo or unsay."

"I know." Trip peered at the brightening sky. "You blow shit up, it changes. I know that." The impromptu dance floor had come a long way. The putrid horde had swollen to nearly a hundred and fifty cheerful ghouls happily slurping caffeine and munching fried dough as the Godzilla sun finally rose, radioactive over the trees. Trip exhaled. "I can't just rearrange wreckage and unwrite history. Sweeping up the broken glass and replacing it doesn't mean that broken things unbreak themselves. No retcons for the shit that matters."

Standing under these lush trees, he remembered the gray day they'd met, with Trip terrified about running in a circle in broad daylight and Silas in his zombie costume, all his insides on the outside, the raw heart oozing behind shattered ribs.

Somewhere in the past six months, he'd done some growing up.

"So…." Trip shifted on his feet. "Kurt made me an offer."

Silas frowned a little. "He has a weakness for whores."

Ouch.

Trip unzipped his portfolio and balanced it on his right arm.

"I don't need to see anything, Trip. Don't wanna." Silas closed his eyes. "Please."

Trip opened it and revealed the finished cover for the first issue of the comic: Scratch slick and smoldering, so completely and obviously Silas he felt sleazy admiring it. "I can't even draw him as someone else."

"This fucker doesn't exist anymore. He's dead."

"No. Scratch's a survivor. We're gonna publish it first of the year. Long buildup. Full marketing campaign in advance."

"We?" Silas looked wary.

Trip took a breath. *Here goes nothing.* "Kurt bought it for Unbored Games. He's publishing the graphic novel."

"Kurt-Kurt?" Silas's mouth moved uncertainly for a moment. "My Kurt."

"You set it up. You gave him the book."

"Yeah, uhh…. Not for that. He's not a publisher."

"He's an opportunist." Trip snuffled and planted his feet solid. "*Scratch* is gonna become a video game. Some kinda rainmaker, he says. The comic book is like… parsley."

Silas shook his head. "The *what*?"

Someone blew a whistle, three short blasts, and the crowd of zombies stood at attention. A pretty Black Widow with a clipboard climbed onto the table to read off a list of locations. Long pale rays warmed the hazy air as the sun crept higher.

"They're branching out or something. I dunno. With some tech thing, and you brought *Scratch* to him." Trip rocked. "Gonna make us very rich."

Silas looked at him sharply.

"You and me." Trip let his arms drop, not hiding behind them or hugging himself. They hung loose at his sides, and he took a deep breath. "He wants you to come do creature design for it. And makeup for the promo. You'd have your own team under you. Full control."

Silas snapped his mouth shut and rubbed his face roughly. "A sex-demon video game." He chuckled in the back of his throat. "Crazy fucker."

"He gave us a publicist. We're going to leak it during Pride this afternoon. Big float with some kind of teaser. We get to ride on the damn float." Trip pointed southeast-ish. "*Shirtless*, if you wanna."

The zombies, several hundred strong now, cleaned up the breakfast area and shuffled to the starting line.

"Bullshit."

"For real." Trip opened his arms. *Bring it on.* "We may even become a political statement."

Silas stared at him openmouthed. "Who will?"

"Us. *Scratch.*" Trip leaned forward and hugged himself. "Kurt has this batshit notion Scratch will piss all the right people off. Major press coverage and some kind of new gaming hoo-hah needs the right story."

Silas blinked, as if he remembered something. "Fucking Ziggy."

Trip tapped the *Scratch* card. "Our little devil got the gig."

Silas nodded with his hand over his mouth. "No."

"Silas...."

He stepped closer and poked Trip to punctuate. "No. No, we don't license it. No, you can't make me into a game. No, I won't work with you. No, I can't believe Kurt would stick his nose into our shit unless you told him some stupid empty lie. No, I don't think any of this is a good idea."

Trip held his gaze and whispered, "There's no such thing."

Finally, Silas stared steadily at Trip like the effort killed him. "I missed you." A humorless laugh closed his eyes. When he opened them, the redness had turned them deep mossy green.

"Sorry." Trip's own eyes welled up.

"Not like, gosh-I-wonder-what-Trip-is-doing missed you. I mean I actually started to feel like I'd survived some horrible amputation and part of me had been hacked off and lost in a haunted warzone being gnawed by the walking dead. I missed you because you were *missing.* I actually spent weeks trying to imagine what you were doing at any given moment... obsessing, really." He didn't wipe his wet cheeks. "Trip must be seeing the new *Superman* this weekend. I wonder if Trip's asleep. I wish I could swallow Trip's load right this second. Trip needs to stop and eat now, something not dyed or in plastic. I even went to watch the Big Dog office doors a couple of times, like the Little Match Queer, when I knew you had pages due, just to make sure you were okay, but then you... I dunno: vanished."

"I quit. I fucking quit." Trip pressed his eyes with the heels of his hands.

"Are you crazy?"

"I guess so. I think so."

Silas shrugged. "I loved you." His mouth broke. He looked away.

Trip didn't blink, but he closed his mouth before he said anything. *Shut up and listen.*

"For a stretch there, I thought I was gonna end up in the hospital. I didn't eat for four days and then threw up for a week. Lost twelve pounds fast. I had to buy new pants. First time in my life losing weight didn't make me feel better, I can tell you that." He glowered at the trees. "Asshole."

"I am an asshole." Trip nodded. "I didn't do anything I said I would. I couldn't do any of it. Everything was bad. Sleeping, living, working."

"Good." Silas didn't sound happy at the thought at all. "Good. I hope it was fucking awful." He wiped his face.

The sun had fully risen from its grave, and the air was shot with gold and green. Volunteers in the Closet shirts scurried in pairs and trios on their ways to whatever. A steady stream of bodies poured from makeup toward the rest of the walking dead.

Trip thrust the portfolio at him, wishing the light was better. A blush rose over his cheekbones. His stomach twisted and tied itself into a sloppy bow. "Best work I've ever done. I mean it. You make me a better artist, Mr. Goolsby."

"Well, you made me a basket case, so I think maybe that's not such a great deal for me, huh?" Silas scowled.

"No, Mr. Goolsby." *Happy accidents*. For a second, Trip remembered holding the plastic handful of Max's artistic shrapnel. Shared pieces. He smiled. "You are my demon and you possessed me. Body and soul."

Silas glared and opened his mouth as if to spit out a response, but Trip cut him off.

"I wanted to deserve you. My damn hero is—" Trip flipped open his portfolio to extract a drawing of Silas's face. "—*you*. I spent all this time, weeks and weeks and weeks, drawing you and drawing you, before and after, but when you went and I couldn't see you in the flesh, I just put you on the page."

Trip rifled through the folder and a few pieces fell, too small to stay in place. "I couldn't miss you or I would have lost my mind. I think if I'd had to miss seeing you, I'd have just given up. So I didn't let myself." Another sketch fell and another, until Trip squatted and laid the portfolio on the ground, trying to gather them.

Silas bent his knees slowly and looked. And saw.

Trip fanned through the drawings: Silas flipping the bird, Silas cutting okra with his rough hands, Silas leaning back with one leg crooked, the plump jut of his nuts just visible. His mouth eating a peach. His legs climbing a ladder, cock bobbing. Sometimes his face peeked out of the paper, but even faceless all of them were undeniably him.

Not Scratch.

Finally Silas reached out to paw through them: his eyes, his ankles, his treasure trail, the back of his knees... hundreds and hundreds of doodles and sketches and studies... matchbook covers and folded posters... some in pencil, some in charcoal, some fully inked and painted in throbbing acrylic. "Wow."

A portrait of Silas's powerful back, the insistent curve of his buttocks doodled around the margins. A full naked torso, the manly jawline to the fat jut of his penis.

"These are...."

"You, Mr. Goolsby. They're you. They're every inch of you that I could still find in here"—Trip tapped his noggin and flashed his eyes like a lunatic—"and catch on paper. I'd saved up, apparently. And then you were gone, and I just kept looking and looking until I saw you everywhere. I almost died, I looked so hard. Until I was so full of you that it ran out of my hands onto the pages. I know every line and arch. I know you, Silas. I know you." Tears starred his lashes.

Silas gulped and pulled out a loose sheet of vellum with a pencil study of his hands, the scars reproduced precisely in ruthless, affectionate detail. Behind it, a double-page watercolor showed Silas on all fours straining and wet as if being pounded from behind, his mouth open and drooling, his hair matted.

Trip shrugged and bent his lips into a tired frown. "I'm not even ashamed. It kept me from losing my mind. Meditation. You don't know. After the first week, I worried that I would forget moments, and so I drew them. Everything I could think of, every angle. I dreamed about you. And I tried to capture you so I wouldn't lose a single second of a single moment, because what if I never got to have them again?"

Sketch after sketch of his ears and chin, Silas's blunt fingers and wide shoulders.

On the footpath, three passing goons in Unbored hoodies spotted Silas and stopped but didn't come closer. Trip knew he was running out of time. He held up a hand, hoping for five more minutes.

Silas pawed further, and loose pages slipped out too... a ballpoint sketch on an ATM receipt, a drawing of his abdomen on one page of lined loose-leaf paper, his broad nose on the back of a postcard. Carefully, he gathered them all back into the portfolio.

"If you were gone, and I was gonna stay alive, I needed everything I could manage to capture while it was bright and right in front of me. It was just easier to let my hands learn you by heart."

"No."

"Please, Silas. Let me love you. We already did the hard stuff. Please." Trip zipped the portfolio shut before handing it over. "The rest is easy."

"I don't think I can take it."

"You're gonna come build the Horn Gate for Unbored, just the two of us with the time and money to do it right. Conjure up Scratch and that goddamn Judge and we're gonna tell a story, you and me. A long one, and it has a happy ending." Trip took another step. "Color outside the lines, and the only lines are ones we draw. It's a romance, I'll have you know. Rina promised."

Silas leaned into the sunlight. A glistening diamond fell from his chin and hit the cover silently in a wet dot. "You broke me."

Trip watched him carefully. "And I'm sorry. I got scared. I'm afraid now. Know what I mean?"

"Can't. Can't." Silas shook his head but wouldn't look at Trip. "I don't think I can."

"Please look at me. I'm standing here loving you, and I want you to at least look me in the eye and say no."

"I don't think I can." But Silas did open his glinting eyes.

"You make me braver than I've ever been in my life. Please don't give up on me." He ran his hands over the stubble on his head. "'Cause I'm not afraid of anything but that."

Silas studied the ground, but the corner of his mouth tipped up into a little goofy smile that lasted all of a heartbeat.

A squawk on one goon's walkie-talkie, and he held up two fingers. At the makeup tent, a cluster of volunteers fidgeted impatiently, eyeing them. Silas ignored it, but Trip couldn't and didn't give a damn who saw him telling the truth.

He pressed closer. "I hate to say it, but I'm simply not gonna take no for an answer. It's a trick I learned from an Alabama boy I fell in love with so hard...."

Silas looked up, riving pain and raw hope carved across his face. The trees overhead and behind him glowed green, and scalding daffodils dotted the ground. Somewhere nearby the runners had started to show up, a laughing, chatting crowd ready for Pride.

Trip nodded. "Oh, once upon a while ago. Studly sumbitch with raw hands and a thing for big dicks. You know what he said to me? 'Don't postpone joy.'"

"He did?"

"And I don't mean to."

Silas squinted. "And you loved him, huh?"

"Present tense." Trip rested their brows together and took a slow lungful of the ink and vanilla scent he'd gone crazy trying to imagine for the past month. "You make me feel like I could right wrongs and leap tall buildings." He wiped his nose and prayed it wasn't as swollen as it felt. "You pushed me to take all these impossible risks and it kept working. You would say all these nice things that I couldn't believe, and I forgot to pay attention."

"No shit." Silas glanced over Trip's shoulder and fired a finger-gun. With that, the volunteers scampered up the trail toward the starting line. The goon trio lumbered after them.

Work to do.

Trip covered his mouth and laugh-hiccupped, wishing he knew how to explain. "I get...." He ran his hands over his face in frustration. "Dunno."

Silas stroked his jawline. "Get?"

"Torn open, buttons everywhere." Trip sighed and closed his eyes. "Like Clark Kent pulling his shirt open to reveal that big red S. Except it feels like I pull my shirt open to reveal my chest, and then I pull my chest open to reveal my heart, and I pull my heart open—"

"Why?"

"—and there's the whole world waiting to be built from scratch."

They grinned shyly at each other.

"And Scratch. He came out of that terrible pulled-open place. *You* make me wanna live in there, but I'm gonna need help, because every other part of me wants to close it and cover it up." Trip stood and offered a hand.

Silas took it and rose. "Clark Kent." He let go.

"You're like Superman, and I'm stuck in disguise with the glasses welded to my face and my cape at the cleaners. Every time you duck into a phone booth to save the world, I vanish. And that doesn't mean you should stop saving the world. I'm still in there."

"Bullshit." Silas crossed his arms over his faded overalls. "I can barely save myself."

"I love being rescued. It's fucking addictive. 'Kay? But every once in a while I'd like to return the favor." Trip took a step closer. Somewhere close, a car honked on one of the hidden roads that threaded through the park.

Silas glanced at the makeup tent and at his watch. "You're right." His dimple appeared. "I know you're right."

Trip pressed his palm against the firm slope of Silas's chest... touched him right out in public. His heart thumped and he ignored it. "Sometimes I gotta crawl back to my lair and put myself back together. Being alone isn't the same thing as being selfish."

"That's awfully adult for someone who lives on Ring Dings and jalapeño potato chips." Silas poked him to move, and they veered along a curving path past the prep area where a group of runners clambered into costumes.

"Hey, we don't stop growing up, right? I mean, it's not like one day you throw a switch and you're an adult just 'cause you're taller and you have pubes."

Silas nodded. "Fair enough." A soft flame burned at the back of his brindle eyes.

"So we both open our shirts and chests and whatever and smush the big red mess together. Big mistakes. Beautiful disasters. The worst ideas. Deal?" Trip inhaled deeply, tried to take his time and give time back.

Silas swayed on his feet, watching Trip as if waiting for some kind of proof or guarantee.

Trip held up a hand, scout's honor. "Goolsby and Spector. We'll make it formal. Legal. Contracts and everything."

"I gotta go do the pilot next month down Louisiana, but they're flying you out as my *very* personal assistant, bubba."

"Uh-yup. I do believe I feel sexual harassment coming on."

Near the starting line, a news crew filmed four giant coffin-shaped boxes that stood to one side, their doors swung open so the trio inside each could breathe: monster closets.

Silas started walking, very slowly, toward the gigantic OutRun banners and the stands where zombies had gathered in orderly rows. They laughed and listened as a chirpy queen gestured instructions to them. "I think Spector and Goolsby sounds better." He ran a hand over Trip's shoulders, squeezed his bare neck, not letting go. *A test.*

Trip leaned into the touch. "Fine… then you get majority share so if I act like a paranoid schmuck you can punish me."

"Stop."

"I'm dead serious." Trip favored him with a superhero smirk and pitched his voice to a radio announcer's rumble. "We are not two men… we are ten men!"

"Umm." Silas gawped. "Did you just quote… *The Tick?*"

"I watched every season. Sitcom and the cartoon actually. Great fucking writing going on. For real. Ben Edlund's a genius."

Silas blinked but didn't smile. What was he thinking?

Just ask, idiot. "What are you thinking?"

"You surprised me." Silas stuck out his lip. "Not many people do that, y'know, but you keep pulling rugs and springing traps. Hard to get used to it."

"You willing to try?"

"Don't think I got much choice."

"Just one." Standing in the wan sunlight, smack dab on the starting line with the entire park and cameras and God watching, Trip pulled Silas into his arms and brought their mouths together in front of the whole damned city.

Startled, Silas opened his lips a little and Trip took full advantage. He drove his tongue deep and crushed all that tawny muscle against himself like a raft in a river.

Silas whimpered in the back of his throat when Trip brushed fingers down his tailbone.

The sun rolled over them, and someone yelled in approval and applauded. Trip refused to let go. *Tickety-tock.*

Silas grunted and struggled at first as if he wanted to protest, but Trip wouldn't let him free, just kept their mouths closed together and gripped the back of his skull with one hand and pushed into the side of his overalls so he could take a sweaty handful of that beautiful hard butt.

Silas raised his fingers to their lips and whispered, "Trip."

Only then did Trip lean back and look. Whistles and waves from the bleachers where the walking dead received their final instructions. Their skinny captain tried to shush them with his hands, but the hooting zombie troops in decrepit clothing waved doughnuts and applauded the public display of affection.

"Jay-sus. Warn me next time." Silas shook himself and then braced one hand on Trip's ribcage.

"If I warn you, how can I surprise you?"

Silas rolled his eyes. "You're such an asshole."

"Why?" Trip sputtered. "What did I do?"

"The right thing. The worst thing."

Trip stole another kiss and took Silas's hand, grinning at their ragged, rotting audience, and gave a little stiff bow.

Silas watched and whispered, "You okay?"

"Think so." Trip dropped his head on Silas's shoulder. "Is that your army of *dork*ness?"

"Something like that. They gotta get into position soon."

At the press table, a middle-aged fairy princess sat on a table fanning herself with the *Post*; a dog curled at her feet like a dirty Q-tip. Their eyes met and she offered Trip a grin as wicked as the one he gave back.

A lone ponytailed figure on crutches gave Trip a salute he returned reflexively. The man stared hard for a moment, then gave a jerky bob of his head to Silas as if they knew each other.

"I'll be damned," Silas murmured.

Trip hooked his arms around Silas's back and rubbed his cheek against the stubbled throat. He groaned. "I missed this."

"Serves you right."

"The drawings helped, but they don't have your... stink."

"Fuck off." But Silas squeezed him close and nuzzled his ear. He took a deep breath at the nape of Trip's neck. "Uhh. You're giving me a huge mutant boner."

"Well, that's one of my superpowers."

"But only one of 'em." Silas rocked the ridge behind his zipper against Trip's thigh. Silas's wood flexed. "Public place."

"Private joke." Trip took a breath and pinned him with his eyes so there was no mistake. "I love you, Silas Goolsby... and until I can get that through your thick skull, you're gonna have to deal with embarrassing displays of affection."

"Well." Silas blinked. "I'm fixin' to love you back, so I'll have to cope." He squeezed Trip's fingers but didn't let go. "Spector and Goolsby."

"Duh." Trip stayed there a moment, wearing a lopsided grin. "But sometimes I get to leap tall buildings too."

Head shake. Silas studied their linked hands. "I think Kurt's run is starting."

And how. A honking, rhythmic horn ripped into life twenty feet away.

Silas looked and whispered, "Zombie extras, go."

"We're in the way." Trip tugged at his boyfriend.

"Naw." He didn't move. "Wait."

Sure enough, though they stood their ground, hundreds of putrid, tattered ghouls surged around their little bubble on the starting line in search of their places. Trip held his breath, but as it happened, they were perfectly safe. Several of the monsters thumped Silas as they passed and gave him a thumbs-up, for the makeup probably, but to Trip it felt like a hundred hard-won blessings. Silas held up his hand to accept high fives as they trotted past, and then Trip did too, smiling back at them.

And then the pavement was clear. Silas shrugged and his eyes were wet. "'S'my favorite moment in the run."

Mine too.

A wall of wailing sirens made them raise their heads. The rainbow-colored crowd bellowed its approval, ready to run hard.

Silas squeezed him. "Where we going? Wanna sneak out and head home?"

"Nah. You need an assistant this morning. Then the parade." Trip clasped the rough fingers. "And I'm feeling awful proud, Mr. Goolsby."

"Later, then, Mr. Spector." Silas scratched his messy bronze hair.

"So... whatsay we go sign the paperwork with Kurt."

Silas smiled at that. "Deal."

Shouting. Applause. A chorus of gym whistles. The first group of laughing joggers lined up outside a gigantic tent that leaked chemical fog, ready to run for their lives.

"I should check on Kurt and the crew." Silas pushed his hands into the pockets of his overalls and rocked on his feet. "Thanks for saving me."

"Thanks for teaching me how. I was... afraid."

Silas turned with the question on his face.

"Let's get to work." About fifty yards away, the rising sun beat the Reservoir into hot brass. Trip started to walk back toward the tents. "Coming?"

A beautiful, open, little-boy smile bloomed on Silas's face. He looked about three inches taller and five years younger. He shook his head and whispered something inaudible.

"I didn't hear you."

Silas winked. "Y'didn't need to." A deep inhale.

"That okay?" Trip knew the answer but asked anyway.

Silas didn't even nod, he just beamed with his eyes closed and his head tipped back in the sun for a few seconds before he responded. Then the wide eyes sparkled. "Feel like walking?"

"Fuck that." Trip winked. "I feel like flying."

Don't miss Scratch in

DAMON SUEDE grew up out-'n'-proud deep in the anus of right-wing America and escaped as soon as it was legal. Having lived all over, he's earned his crust as a model, a messenger, a promoter, a programmer, a sculptor, a singer, a stripper, a bookkeeper, a bartender, a techie, a teacher, a director... but writing has ever been his bread and butter. He has been happily partnered for over a decade with the most loving, handsome, shrewd, hilarious, noble man to walk this planet.

Damon is a proud member of the Romance Writers of America and currently the president of its LGBT romance chapter, the Rainbow Romance Writers. Though new to gay romance fiction, Damon has been writing for print, stage, and screen for two decades, which is both more and less glamorous than you might imagine. He's won some awards but counts his blessings more often: his amazing friends, his demented family, his beautiful husband, his loyal fans, and his silly, stern, seductive Muse who keeps whispering in his ear, year after year.

Damon would love to hear from you. You can get in touch with him at:

http://www.DamonSuede.com
http://www.goodreads.com/damonsuede
https://www.facebook.com/damon.suede.author
https://twitter.com/DamonSuede

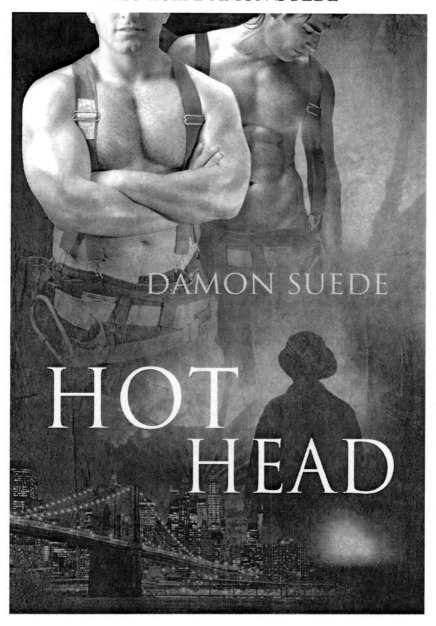

Also available in Spanish, German, and Italian

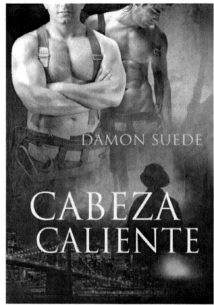
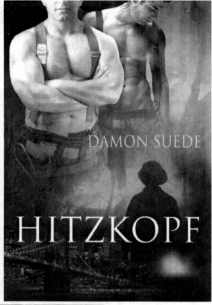
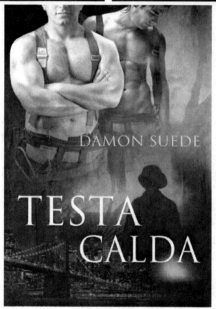

http://www.dreamspinnerpress.com

Also available from DREAMSPINNER PRESS

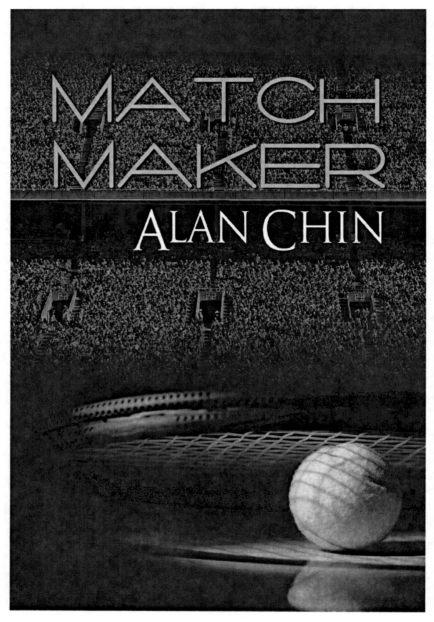